D'ARTAGNAN. THE KING MAKER

D'ARTAGNAN

THE KING MAKER

AN HISTORICAL NOVEL

BY

ALEXANDRE DUMAS

AUTHOR OF

"The King's Gallant," "All For a Crown," "The Count of
Monte Cristo," "The Three Musketeers," etc.

TRANSLATED BY

HENRY L. WILLIAMS

Fredonia Books
Amsterdam, The Netherlands

D'artagnan:
The King Maker

by
Alexandre Dumas

Translated by Henry L. Williams

ISBN 1-58963-256-7

Copyright © 2001 by Fredonia Books

Reprinted from the 1901 edition

Fredonia Books
Amsterdam, The Netherlands
http://www.fredoniabooks.com

PREFACE.

Dumas and "D'Artagnan!"

The Inseparables!

This banner-knight carried "the Extraordinary Author's" fame all over the reading world, and won homage through his favorite—everybody's—and the most characteristic hero in noveldom.

It was by the Gascon Free-captain, inextinguishable and ever-living in his native wit, that Dumas' talent was displayed at the first flight. Bold, sustained and vigorous, all could trace to what heretofore inaccessible height and on what delectable ground it would lead us.

As there is no historian more popular and more credited, and no novelist more historic, so his type and model of the Noble Adventurer, brave as his sword, steady as his aim, faithful to virtue as to his King, remains the chief admired and endeared to students as to his own chronicler.

In Louis D'Artagnan, "the Illustrious Dumas" (to use the King of England's epithet) did what was accounted impossible: created a character. It was thought that times, pressure of men, compact with society, pinches of crises, these formed a man. But our originator was always modest—strange this in him termed plagiarist, monopolist, vainglorious! But let Dumas protest in his own words:

"I am a humanizing and vulgarizing story-teller. Naturally, and without pains, I am dramatic. My stories are first composed as plays, the opening clear, the end short and all interesting. Action ejects, shapes and animates my conceptions. A statuary and not a painter, I embody sooner than I sketch, model rather than paint. Disciple of the Realistic School, Shakespeare's, Sheridan's or Schiller's, my characters are in fast dyes, not evanescent tints; they do deeds and do not maunder over them, prosing, poetizing or philosophizing. Hence, any actor can slip into my casts—Melingue was my D'Artagnan, the body to my phantasm."

Well, Dumas was unjust; for the more he is read—nay, the more intimately he is studied, the more consummate and imposing he becomes as a prodigy; clearness of the alabaster lamp, whose body lets the rays diffuse; taste true, because yours and mine, a woman's or a girl's, the idler's or the toiler's; what verve and fluency! the purling spring becoming rivulet, river, delta, ocean! a mind that produces wholesome fruit, tart yet sweet enough, plentiful as the wild crab.

As Raphael exclusively loved one model; as one fond head appears on all the marbles a sculptor carves, so D'Artagnan, cherished by his own literary father as by his own friends, reappears throughout the Dumas Gallery.

In one he is chivalric, in another he may be modern; here, a play-actor; there, Coconnas marching gallantly to his doom; in peasant garb, our simple, honest Ange Pitou; in the age of plumes and starch, a beau; as "Yacoub," Jealousy itself; as Dantes, the Avenger! but it is Dumas' D'Artagnan, by a trait if not complete. Such a Proteus might well flag—but as Dumas was indefatigable, so is D'Artagnan revived on touching new ground.

Such ground! The scene of "D'Artagnan, the Kingmaker," is unknown land—even at our later day! Portugal! the Peninsular! the great rival of Old Spain in conquering the New World. The European Hermit-Kingdom! It was a flash of genius which shot itself into this dark, mysterious corner, brimming with surprises, and revealed how much passion, courage, humor, and sterling virtues struggled from the tempestuous coast to the debated capital.

But on this crude stone D'Artagnan sharpens his sword and his wit; he meets unaccustomed foes, but defeats them as if familiar with their attacks; he inspirits the dullards, he enchants the sluggards, he thrills the masses, and bears off the crown—to give it to the heir with that loyalty and self-sacrifice peculiar to the lion-hearted gentleman-of-fortune.

Alone, his Quixotic Restoration of the Braganzas would be satiety of mental feasting, but allied with him in his exploits is the choicest spirit of the "Four Musketeers"! Porthos! "Our *good* Porthos!" whose rich humor, smooth patience, unfaltering friendship, and mighty fist make him so cheery that many a reader, divided in admiration and affection, cries, enraptured: "If I were not D'Artagnan, I would I were Porthos!"

In the same way that Dumas' devotees journey to Marseilles and scratch their names on the wall of "Monte Christo's" cell (that prisoner only existing in Dumas' mind), so may we expect the readers of this engaging and instructive story to travel—in the spirit—along the course of its pages where the "Kingmaker" brings the true monarch to the audaciously recovered throne.

Portugal, in this work, becomes another memorial to the vernal writer, a stranger now to no land, an idol to every appreciative reader.

H. L. W.

"I am the long-looked-for guest of the Petrel." See page 17.

D'ARTAGNAN, THE KINGMAKER.

CHAPTER I.

AVOID A NEW INN.

In the middle of the seventeenth century, to the west of San Sebastian, on the Bay of Biscay, then a fortified port (and not a watering-place) of northern Spain, was a hamlet known ephemerally as Las Salinas.

It was salty in every respect, but salt had failed to preserve it; on the contrary, salt had been its ruin.

It was a cove beneath a highland, where the sea incursions had made a delta—the point inland—and smoothed the finely-grounded granite sands into flats, furrowed by ditches as regular as if traced by human hands; these were salt pans for which Nature consulted no engineer.

A fisher, perceiving this advantage, had begun salt making on a fair scale, augmenting his plant by the assistance of his family, and finally his fellows in the craft, of which the Apostles were the patrons.

Soon the growth of the little saltern was strengthened by disabled seamen, discharged soldiers, since the great wars were presumed over between Holland, France, Spain, Italy, Austria—aggressors, allies and combatants by turns. At the end came rovers, sea gypsies, not averse to a few days' work where the *alguazils* and constables would not suspect them to be honest toilers.

In time, Salinas gained a name. As the cove, though exposed to the very focus of storms, was deep in its channel, and the highlands partly shielded it, small craft dropped in. Petty fishers, sardineers, tunny catchers, and even the cod fishers, stopping to cure a catch, instead of going home, so that they could continue with the "buckalow" to vend on the African coast. They eschewed Las Salinas on the return, but that was because they carried gold dust, ivory, spices and merchandise, on the whole above the Salinaists.

Unhappily, fortune, in this world, attracts envy and covetousness.

Little by little, more slowly on the land than on the seas, Las Salinas' reputation spread until it had reached San Sebastian.

San Sebastian, for the most part, was swayed by the class of which Virgil rhymed—they profit by others' laborious accumulations.

The governor of the fort and town at the time was Don Nuestradamus Palliro, who, as pro-ruler for King Philip IV., then reigning, had a coast right to anything "cast up" by the waves, and, on the face of it, salt seems to be comprised in this elastic scope. At least, without consulting the Spanish Grotiuses, he meant to exact his toll. Hearing this, the champion knight of the good Sisters of Maria, Star of the Sea, remembered its claim on all sea produce; and what is salt but a production of the sea—a sort of skimming of that great open kettle of the Atlantic? And, being asked to lend his armed marchers on a visit of inquiry to Salinas, the noble Don Esteban de Sagres, Lord of the Salt Marshes, considered that he had a special grievance, under the Crown, against any one manufacturing salt without each bag being stamped and sealed.

In the last instance, while these gentlemen conferred, the Bishop of Catalona considered tithe was due him on this industry, since the fulness of the earth—and the sea —are the Church's.

In short, what with soldiers, javelin men, constables, *gendarmes,* all about their several captains and chief clerks, a formidable force dropped off the cliffs, as from the clouds, upon unwitting Salinas.

Being gentry accustomed to spend their earnings as received, at the inn in their midst, which was mart, exchange and refreshment hall, they were perfectly unable to pay any tolls and taxes, rightfully or otherwise demanded.

Whereupon the disappointed cohort seized the stoutest

of the penniless saltmakers and talked of lugging them
off as hostages for the cess required.

Upon seeing their chiefs arrested, like so many
brothers, the fishers, sailors, soldiers out of uniform, and
the women of the hamlet, fell upon the strangers with
uncouth cries of war in sea lingo and rural dialect, and
beat them off with oars, boat hooks, rudder staves and the
like. The Spanish, in order to preserve their lives, were
glad to leave the captives with their friends, consoling
themselves with the last word: "They would come
again and give the victors rue to mix with their salt
cakes!"

It is a fact that a true nomad "marches lightly."

Being men of the ocean firstly, and saltmakers sec-
ondly, they made a pyramid of the tools of their temporary trade and set fire to it, after a preliminary bathing
with tar; then they embarked all their families, household goods and gods—if these pagans worshiped any one
and on any day but that of the Good Thief!—and, when
the locusts returned with an army at their back, Salinas
the Hale was Salinas the Wasted.

To the devourers—burnt meat!

The inn ought to have remained, a large structure in
oak and stone; that was counted on, but you must not
count on your host or his inn. As by witchcraft, that
only real building of the town had disappeared. One
could discern the site, for the foundation stones and tree
were there; but the wood had been sawed off at every
post, and the iron securing the stones against storms
which would have made children's building blocks of
Trajan's Column, had been wrenched out of the leaden
sockets. As for the wine casks, said to be in its cellars,
since your saltmaker is fabulously thirsty, there was not
even a cellar; all the contents had been hoisted out and
the breeze had steadily played at filling it to the brim with
a quicksand which almost swallowed up the explorers
under the eyes of their companions.

We say that this solitary shelter had been depended
upon.

The soldiers had been promised it as a guardhouse,
and the civilians reckoned on having a portion as a custom house.

Arabs would have asked if this work was for the glory of Mahommed, and, if the answer were in the negative, would have burned the place; these Christians meant to conserve the building, but to store away their levies in it.

But it was gone, past preying on, or praying for—we quote a clerk who was facetious, but whose merry mood did not long continue. Indeed, there came on, while the soldiers were searching the district, one of those north-west blows, which sailors afterward describe as a "fresh wind," but which landsmen remember as the worst tempest of the age. Such make the Bay of Biscay no pretender to the title of "Cemetery of the Atlantic." Such depth have the waves that one expects to see the lost Atlantis' inhabitants looking up at poor drowned man, and such force have the breakers that the spray covers the land for half a mile inward.

This particular nor'wester was accompanied, or rather stripped from time to time by gusts out of the north, probably all the way from the North Sea, which brought sleet to mingle with the rain. The knights, captains, monks, soldiers, mariners and clerks suffered a night of anguish in the desolation, so that, in the dawn, sneezing, coughing, wet to the skin, their armor rusty and their swords congealed in the scabbard, they straggled back to the port, disconsolate as if they had passed the time in purgatory without the time being allowed off their score.

Thereafter, Las Salinas was accursed like the Dead City of the Plains, where Lot's wife, incrusted with salt, stands at the gates.

The fishers and smugglers procured their salt elsewhere, being far-roving persons, and only a very few poor 'long-shore roamers, with fishers who contented themselves with near-at-hand game, ventured to return to the deserted village. They scooped out burrows in the shifting sands between detached rocks, for their wives and children to thatch them with seaweed, while they sailed out where toll gatherers were scarce.

It was, therefore, with surprise that a man, who must have expected to see this little Tyre in her majesty, reined in his horse after coming down upon the plain, once covered with snowy, glistening salt pans. He reined in his steed to that steed's satisfaction, however, though it was one of those slab-sided, raw-boned, long-legged brutes, called, in France, *"clamponniers,"* from "clamp," that is, a heaviness of tread. In fact, this one's big hoofs opened like a camel's in the soft sand and enabled him to get a foothold which had the one defect that he went in so deeply that he could barely draw it out, and when it came, it made a sound of suction like reports of a mortar.

The man looked around and sighed, like one thoroughly disenchanted—his illusion dispelled.

He must have been furnished with a description of the spot before the beast descended and the people destroyed the village, as the Jews destroyed the Holy City to spite the Emperor Titus.

It had been a hot day, and while he might be of cast bronze, having that complexion of southrons, baked from birth, and did not show fatigue, it was not so with his ugly mount. It did not care to move a step farther in the trying and fickle sands, so different a footing to the turf on the mountains.

The sea was tolerably calm for this part, but it tremulously refreshed the long streakings of purple across the whitish golden glare; by the tint, one could understand the Spanish discoverers calling platinum white gold.

The illimitable swell softly rolled in with slow grandeur, the deep just heaving as though Neptune, slumbering in the wave-hollowed caverns, troubled the mass with his ponderous breathing.

Only a few tiny sails dotted the enormous green expanse, like daisies on a well-tended pasture.

All the fishers were out at sea. Their families were in their kennels, enjoying the sole luxury of the poor—idleness.

The traveler had come over the inland, not the coast, high along the shore, sloping down to it or rising abruptly, all the scene visible from below.

With the melancholy of a stricken pine, a tall mast rose mockingly of trees like a gallows, for it had a crosspiece, the signboard of the vanished tavern dangling by a corner, one bent spike refusing to let go its hold. It was the sternboard of a rowboat anciently, which, perhaps, had been in civilized parts, for it was lettered in Latin characters, "The Black Petrel," but the hanger of it at the inn front had probably judged the literacy of his neighbors justly in surmounting the line with a daub of asphaltum, representing a flying blackbird.

"The Black Petrel," read the stranger, if he could not recognize the delineation, "assuredly, I see the creature, but where is its nest?"

He must have had excellent sight for, presently, he spied an all but invisible column of smoke, spirally rising out of a hole in the overhanging cliff. This was one of those holes made by pressure of the sea in a mistral, when these outlets became "spouting horns."

It oozed out like a dying whale's "blow," fine as spundrift.

The air was dry, and the smoke almost instantly was dissipated.

But the traveler could distinguish spray from smoke by another good faculty of his—smell.

"Cooking!" he muttered, beginning to champ his mustache, as his horse had been champing his bit, "and on a generous system, I take it. There is conger, olives, onions, pork and I know not what in that mess. If it be but for one diner, then I have to meet a Titan in his cave. Certainly, the inn has withdrawn its kitchen into the solid earth. But why? I was not so badly misinformed, after all! There was a village, and there is an inn, though cramped up in the mountain."

He seemed to be one of those spirits, common to an earlier period, who went to discover and did not wait until another had preceded them and made a chart for guidance.

He alighted nimbly in spite of the extremely heavy boots worn by riders, which would turn a musket ball, and unbitted his grateful horse. He was sure that it would not stray far, where nothing alluring presented, and that no one, a judge of horseflesh, would attempt to decoy it afar. So he walked, disembarrassed, toward the hollow of the bluff, with a firm and graceful tread, although the boots, with their other disadvantages, were a new purchase.

Such seasoned leather, soft as silk though thick, and good workmanship could only have come out of the workshop of a cordwainer of Cordovan training, where the tradition was maintained.

His Moorish saddle was probably of the same origin.

As he mounted the ascent, he perceived some signs of a path. Bare feet and bark-soled sandals had traced it. It led him in under the beetling barrier to the sea's continual encroachment, the sides of spar fretted intricately and fantastically to equal the finest efforts of the artificers of the Alhambra.

"'Sdeath!" exclaimed he, with Spanish accent fortified with Gascon, "this is the inn. Faith of a gentleman! have we the Northmen scourers of the sea again upon the rocky coast of his majesty of United Spain and Portugal, that even that hallowed institution, the tavern, respected by German riders and Italian bandits, should shrink with terror into the granite?"

As if to prove how wrong or right was his surmise, there darted a man out of the opening and shadow beyond, who blocked his way, but hospitably. For he opened his arms and his hands in that gesture which signifies in that latitude that all that the house contains is at the order of the person motioned to.

It was a host, whether the opening was an inn door or not.

Accustomed to the dusk, the traveler looked over the man's head, the more easy as he was short, and distinguished a rough inner portal of ship oak, fit to resist a battering-ram; and, beyond, the beginning of a corridor, wide, or a room, narrow, prolonged by the obscurity, into indefiniteness.

For a fitting description of this cavernous hostel, one would have to search "Ossian."

There was an attempt to light up this vast interior: a ship lantern swung on high under a stretch of canvas, supplied with oil, and that less strongly smelling. Several candles, certainly such as are made for churches, were stuck in cracks on the rocky wall. All these rays fell on a table, evidently from a great West Indiaman, since it was of mahogany, not well known to European cabinetmakers; it had benches around it, carved by seamen's knives; on it were miscellaneous articles, silver and pewter drinking vessels, some ecclesiastical in aspect, others adorned with arms of high families, whose representatives probably never honored the Petrel; Bohemian glasses, curiously delicate in such a rough place; Dutch and Flemish mugs, German cups and pitchers, English jugs.

A capacious brazier in the Moresque style held glowing charcoal, but the chief culinary shrine was a wood fire on an enormous flat stone, from which, up the natural chimney, floated that column betraying the modest nook of the Petrel.

This steady light showed also a terra-cotta image of a saint in Sevillan pottery, highly glazed, probably female, as there had been attached to its base a strip of parchment in Gothic type, appealing to one.

It was the stock curative cure of this marshy ground, no doubt, for its lines might be thus translated:

> *"Charm of St Agnes to dispel the shaking fever.*
> Tremble and go!
> (First day, shiver and burn!)
> Tremble and quake!
> (Second day, shiver and burn!)
> Tremble and die!
> (Third day, never return!)"

A similarly saintly image, but in rougher work, and dyed instead of being glazed, had these words incised on it, and filled up with burnt rosin to make the old English text apparent:

> "This be Sint (sic) Dennis, to me dear,
> For love of drink and, eke, good cheer!"

Doubtlessly these objects were precious and had been transferred from the original inn when its removal was decided upon.

Over the hearth fire, by an old anchor chain, swung by a pulley hook, as used to hoist a whale up for cutting off the blubber, such an immense iron pot as slave ships had in order to cook as much porridge as possible at one heat.

If it had been full, it would have contented a regiment. As it was, more than the bottom was covered with a fish stew, mingled with vegetables such as seaside heights supply, but not in variety or delicacy.

"So, this is the Petrel's Nest?" said the traveler, half-whimsically after surveying the picture, delightful to a Teniers or a Zurbaran, for its appeals to the gross senses and its light and shade.

He might be testing his host, for he spoke in Portuguese.

The landlord replied, after the same furtive manner, in Cantabrian, that ancient tongue of which it has been said none but the natives can speak it, and they with difficulty.

To redouble the astonishment at having a gentleman guest, the speaker was startled to hear the reply in this same mode, and more fluently than in Portuguese.

"Then, I come to an anchor!" He sat astride of a bench, easily enough, and demanded:

"Your name?"

"Pedro. Sailors from the north, as I am not tall, call me Bitts, likening me to the two Samson-posts which secure the anchor cable, or the hawser is snubbed at——"

"Then, Master Pedro Bitts, see that I have a bit for my teeth!" showing perfect ones under the black mustache. "I am the long-looked-for guest of the Petrel."

As if he fully understood these tyrants of the roadside, even when there was no worn road to their abodes, he slapped his side where, from the chink, he carried a pouch well lined with coin.

As if this sound were almost unknown, the host waited to hear the echo before hurrying, with a broad smile, into the depths, but beckoning the other to follow.

First, the traveler looked back, not from any apprehension—Heaven forbid such a jolly fellow excited that emotion—but to see how his ungainly steed was faring.

The inestimable *clamponnier* had stumbled along the ledge with a sea-footing, stuck a hoof into a fishskin and, thus slippered, reached the first hovel. Here, after a sniff, and concluding, with the fine epicurean taste of his species, that the maritime thatching was edible, he began to strip it off. A couple of brown children at once jumped out and stared with spellbound eyes at this creature, which bid fair to eat them out of house.

"I see that Plegon has made himself at home in Salinas." observed his master. "So be it with the rider!"

CHAPTER II.

THE PETREL CHANGES HANDS.

The fearless wayfarer plunged into the passage of the obscure den, fit for serpents, hermits, bandits and those ogres whom the common people believed to occupy subterranean refuges.

On reaching the middle of the cavity, he saw that it was roomier than suspected from the exterior. Indeed, it was a hall of which the stretched canvas, an old mainsail, was the velarium, cutting it into two stories. It was so blackened with smoke that he had not reckoned the extent. At one corner a ship's wooden companionway was used to ascend to this upper floor.

In another corner, the two tops of a clumsy ladder come up through a hole, suggesting the wine vaults, since a vinous aroma permeated the stagnant air.

Odd bales and casks encumbered the sides, being used as seats and lounges when the company was numerous —evidently a rarity! but there was nothing for the timorous to take alarm at.

The host and he stood before the only other tenant. This was a very strong and stout negress, to whom Pedro, sturdy as he was, looked boyish and slight. She was of Nubian blackness, not the warm brown of other negroes, but unshiny jet. She had a ladle with which a pond could be baled out or a bull be stunned. With this, as if proud of her mess, she began to stir the kettle swiftly to set the newcomer's mouth watering.

"It is the 'slow-boiling fish stew' of Marseilles," explained the host. "It is fish, fish and fish to us here every day! I wish I could take a week off and go into the country, where there would be nothing but meat and fowl, for a change!"

"Well, I came from there, and I shall enjoy this very much."

Convinced by this that he had an easily-contented patron, the man waved his hand in encouragement to his

cordon-bleu, and busied himself with the other preparations of the meal. He set one of those loaves on the
table, common where bread is baked at one time for a
fortnight, flanking it with a knife so broad as to lead it
to be supposed a portion of a scimeter; salt in a silver
reliquary, chased with sacred emblems and a dedication to
a saint; two kinds of pepper in a calabash, divided by a
pearl shell, and silver plates, massive and sculptured as
works of art.

The table had no cloth, but the scarce and beautiful
wood, defying the sailors' whittles, was smoothed and
polished by grease and bare arms, so that it was bright
as a mirror.

Taking down one of those high flagons which have
gone from vogue since toping went out, he dived into
the hole down the ladder like a powder-monkey into the
magazine. In the hollow, he could be heard singing in
a mellow voice:

> "And some are wrecked on th' Indian coast,
>   Thither by gain invited;
> Some are in smoke of battle lost,
>   Whom a dance and lute delighted!"

Although the flagon held a runlet's eighteen gallons,
he lugged it, frothing over, up the ladder like a puff of
eider-down; that he had broached a cask the guest had
heard, with ravishment, it gurgled so rapturously.

The negress had braced herself by tightening a yellow
zoner, or belt, which Christians are compelled to wear in
a Mohammedan country; she put forth a strength which
she might not be suspected of, and tilted the great kettle
over so as to spill some of its delicious medley into a
ewer of gold, and carried this to the table as if it were an
egg on a plate.

"The sky bless you all!" This seemed to be her con-
ception of a grace.

Instantly the air was transformed. What one had inhaled of a balm superior to Gilead's was but a mean fore-
taste of the perfume overwhelming the space. The guest
clapped his hand, like those voyagers, who, sick of the
bilge, tar and wet sailcloth odor, rejoice at the off-shore
breeze from the spice islands. To be so enlivening, and
at the same time so soothing, was a triumph of culinary

harmony; each contribuent component to this programme
was distinct; pork fried before it was associated with the
other ingredients, fish of all sorts, sweet and bitter herbs,
onions and their fierce brother, garlic; these blended into
the supernal hodge-podge.

The guest stretched his rather long arms as though,
metaphorically, to embrace the delicious dish, seized the
loaf like his dearest foe, and with the shortened scimeter,
sliced off one piece for a sop, another to eat and a third to
wipe his spoon on. He was supplied by precaution with
one of those comprehensive instruments, embracing, in
one handle, knife, spoon and fork, which the Italians invented and which other nations were slow in adopting.

The negress knew what a fork, a spoon and a knife
were, but never had she seen persons eat with them or
hold them in combination. She followed their move-
ments, which were not slow, with the eyes of one watch-
ing a conjurer's wand.

The traveler used the spoon so quickly that the host
felt enforced to apologize for him, while secretly admiring such prowess and compliment to his *chef's* abilities.

"He comes from afar, and from the island where they
open oysters with pitchforks! Again, these tall blades,
they are hollow to their boots!"

Twice only in ten minutes did the amateur of fish stew
stop ladling it up, which was to cool his peppered tongue
with a copious draft of the wine, not homemade and
keenly sour; also he partitioned off these drafts with
gobbets of the bread, made of Indian corn from Africa,
since the natives, indolent about tillage, preferred to import such breadstuff rather than grow wheat.

At last appeased, and only spearing a bit of fish here
and there in the tureen, he leaned back, with his shoulders
against the wall, and assumed the attitude of one who—
the main piece of life's business over, next to sleeping—
thought of less carnal matters.

The host, who had been admiring his prowess as a
trencher-man, changed his expression to a judging one.

He scanned a man in the first prime of life, that is,
about thirty years of age. He was dark brown, with
golden-bronze reflections on the cheekbones and other
sharp proturbances. He had not a wrinkle, but he was

weatherbeaten from snow as well as sun. His sable hair and beard were trimmed close, as if to wear the morion, still used by some prudent warriors. His mustache was also cropped to prevent its being entangled with the steel-cap chin strap, on occasion, or a bedrabbled plume.

He was compactly built, rather muscular than bony; rather sinewy than nervous, but a bunch of vitality slept under the hardened skin, prompt to be called into action. His cheek was tanned, and his hands blackened, as became a traveler out of the south.

Sober was his dress, unidentifiable when nearly everybody wore habiliments denoting a profession, a craft or a class. The cotton velvet was cut for him, full where movement was wanted untrammeled, and the embroidery was real threads of gold, though delicately done. His trunk-strings were leather, for wear; his hat, feathers of a rare African bird, but short. Although an excellent rider, his boots were not too elegant on straight legs, not yet bent by the horse's barrel.

Gold spurs and the fine rapier denoted the gentleman—although all except merchant, muleteer, shepherd, miner or peasant, put on spurs and carried a sword. But it was one thing to carry a sword, another to wield it; by the wrists, somewhat enlarged, and the biceps of the right arm, one might conclude that this was a long-exercised swordsman.

His nose was sharp and eaglelike; such are predestined men of war; his mouth was firm, but he could smile, and winningly. His eyes were black diamonds, almost insupportable in their piercing glance, when fired by great feeling.

Withal, that strange commingling which made what we call an all-round gentleman of action; captain on the land and on the sea; indifferently presiding, by order of his king, or that of his whim, on poopdeck or charger's saddle.

In vain did this human gamecock assume, as now, a peaceful position—even a civilian less expert in judging men than a landlord, knew it was a leader.

Equal to any fortune, these men wore ascetic garb, or court insignia, steel in the camp or counselor's robes, drank the rinsings of the buffeted ship's water cask, or the finest wine in the court favorite's boudoir. No one offended them, for such might rise on the morrow far above their highest flights.

Surfeited, the guest ceased to play with the tidbits. This seeing, the host, who had not for a moment thought of sitting unasked, leaned half familiarly on the table edge, under pretense of refilling the cup.

In his turn, the gentleman scrutinized his boniface.

He saw a man of the typical Portuguese, rather than the Spanish race; neither Catalan, Celtiberian nor Hispaniolian—just Portuguese.

Short to ungainliness, thickset to clumsiness, but agile; tigerish in spring, when aroused; brave to rashness, firm as a rock in opinions or duty; honest, to his fellows, at any rate; a good neighbor, if you were his kin; prone to form sudden friendship and as sudden enmities, not to be blunted this side of the grave.

More intelligent than he wanted known, Pedro had a deep wit, sharpened like the carver on steel by frequent frictions. The foes of the lower grade were innumerable—tax collectors, beggars of all kinds, begging priests, petty lords, extortioners who were like those mites that bleed fowls to death by their numbers, if insignificant individually.

He was one of the past century, who followed circumnavigators to the confines—cool under the tropics, merry in the Arctic Circle—combating, as if everyday dangers, though perfectly novel, the cannibals, monsters of sea and woods, savages like those of the ancient chroniclers; never flagging, never awed and never driven back.

Returning home, these "demons of the ocean" tranquilized their conscience by making peace with the church, at cost of half their hard-won treasure, and with the remainder settled down in their vineyard, or shop, or fishing boat.

The more enterprising, like Pedro, occupied wayside inns, wanting but little life after so much activity.

Strange—illiterate, dull, slow—such men made at a pinch good governors, like Sancho, at Barrataria.

"Host Pedro," began the guest, swallowing half the fresh draught of wine, "now that you, under Heaven, have given the journeyer a good supper, though the chief dish was without name——"

"The English seamen, judges of eatables," returned the host, with vanity, "reckon that Quaqua, there, makes the best 'chowter' this side of the line!"

"Chowder?"

"It's the noise a pampered child makes over the pap, and so does a man, surfeited with that fish stew, over the viscid, stringy, appetizing mess!"

" 'Chowter' is a good name," responded the feaster, nodding. "The sherry is as sound as if squeezed from the grape, and your Edam cheese is a treat, after the goat's-milk curd I have been using. Now, as the capsheaf to a good meal is a chat, what say you to some of that while your servant——"

"Please your honor, it is my slave. I rescued her from the Morocco pirates, and glad I did, as she is a cook of the first quality, Chop One, as they say in Macao, thrown away upon eschewers of that succulent 'bird,' the pig. Eh, Quaqua, Pedro master?"

The blackamoor bowed submissively and grinned.

"We talk, then, while your good servant prepares my bed—I should say, shakedown," trying to conform his order with the ostensible resources of the Petrel.

"We have a bed meet for a lord," corrected Pedro.

"So much the better, as I have been sleeping on my horse's back, a bony one! or on straw in the inns of the south. All is one to a sleeper in the van-foss or the ground dried by the bivouac, as you may guess."

Before leaving the fire. the negress replenished it, and it blazed attractively, with ship wood saturated with tar and grease and spitting out variegated flames, the traveler turned round to it and stretched out his boots toward its curling serpents.

"How goes trade, Pedro?"

"It cometh not in this direction," said the man, bitterly.

Then, as though the question had driven the spigot into a full-to-bursting cask, Bitts poured out the story of the rise and fall of Salinas, with the diffusiveness of those old-time historians who could not pass a battle

without giving the speeches in detail of the command-
ers on both sides.

He gave with rude eloquence the addresses of the
captains, the monks, the goose-pluckers (tax-gatherers),
and other enemies of the blotted-out community, and
the replies of the injured settlers.

"It seems to me," said the captain of fortune; "that
your last reply, though unspoken, was the most effec-
tive; you removed the bone of contention from the
hungry curs—that was pleasurable! Down with those
worriers!" and he tossed off the heel of liquor. "This
is what causes you innkeepers and salt makers to adore
authority!"

"And the Portuguese to adore the Spanish!"

"Portuguese or Catalan, we all hate the oppressor,
from the hireling who snatches the reals, to him on high
who battens on the same."

"You have mistaken your calling. You are an im-
prudent fellow, and no true host, who should be of no
nation and censure none. It is all very well for your
namesake on high to sift out those who would pass
through his gate, but Pedro, the earthly, should not
challenge his guests. It is time," pursued he, with emphasis, "that a man undestined to a landlord's apron,
should retire to study a better course! What do you
say, since I am one who rides straight at the Turk's
head, to taking the vacation you lusted for? Let to me
your inn for a month—say, for ten philips of gold; or,
since you do not dote on the king's head on a coin, let
it be gold moidores of the ancient Portuguese monarchs."

"Let my house? Accept ten philips?"

"Unclipped, unsweated!"

Pedro plucked at his bristly chin, considering. But
his slave, with the well-treated slave's familiarity, and
perhaps because she was consulted by her master, had
no such hesitation or incredulity. She flopped down on
her knees between the fire and the offerer of this magnificent hire, and proceeded to pull off the traveler's
boots, saying, without looking up:

"Agree to the lord and master, Pedro."

"Of course, I agree! The house is a dead horse!"

"What, do you not own it?"

"I own this cave as much as any one, for the earth is the taker's, I take it! But as for the title of the inn and its appurtenances, they come from the inn that we carted into this hole. I think that he who furnished the means to build out here has a claim on the property and good name!"

The traveler did not argue. He knew what obstinate heads the Portuguese and Spanish peasants wear.

"When we began the salt-making in a large way, the Brothers of the Coast, seeing its importance, asked the aid of their banker."

"The Brothers of the Coast! Their banker! Ho! Ho!"

The exclamation might be caused by the pain of the wrench the woman gave on attacking the second boot. It sounded like satisfaction, however.

"The Brothers of the Coast; oh, we poor fishers, shipmen, shore-scramblers, from Cape de Verde to the English Foreland, we have to be united to make a good breast against the elements and the land-teasers."

"It is a copybook motto that 'Small things grow by union!' Approved, friend Pedro!"

"When you see two hands clasped, on a flag at the fore, it is the Brothers; and if you hear, 'All for each, and each for all!' it is the Brothers who utter it."

"A profound Christian invented all that!" said the guest, sighing beatifically, for the other boot was off.

"On the contrary," corrected the landlord, "it was the West Indian pirates invented it. Like them, we have a fund: Everybody pays in so much per head, and at stated times. We pension off a sick or wounded member, even as a king does his pensioners, only we use our own money! And we care for the dame and the kids. And——" here he hesitated, but the slave, who had picked up a pair of Morocco *babouches* and was warming them at the embers, nodded for him to go on fearlessly.

"And we spend the money as we would our blood, look you!—to save our brothers from the navy——"

"Of any nation?"

"Oh, a seaman is an Ishmael, like him in Scriptures; every hand is against poor Jack!"

"This is a harmless doctrine when you preach it on your deck; but on land, since the land belongs to one majesty or another—sometimes two or more claim it!—it sounds like treason!"

Pedro flipped a flake of fish off his sleeve as if he cared but slightly for kings.

"Well, since this union is no secret to those whom it concerns, the naval officers do not often call the muster of a fisher of good size, our fund swells. And as Jack cannot keep a fat purse long, we decided on putting the pile in safe hands."

"You have been a sailor, eh? Well, in all your voyages, you may have come upon the phœnix, the roc, the vampires, and what not, but verily you have chanced upon the *rara avis desiderata*—the man who can safely be intrusted with money! Pray tell me, since I would like to impart the information to certain friends, what is he—a magician who scorns gold, an alchemist who can make it, a cenobite who does without it, a——"

"To interrupt your lordship, it is a Jew!"

"It is true, they have all the ready money in Europe!"

"Faith, what with killing them off, what they hold, —and they hold it with a limpet's tenacity, by the token —this same money is in fewer and fewer hands. So these few are protected, for who has so many friends as he who can benefit his friends?"

"Pedro, the Innkeeper, you are Pedro, the Philosopher! You could give cards to Alfonso, the Wise, and come out winner!"

"My lord, you cannot have traveled far in these regions without seeing that we have inherited from Moor, Arab and Egyptian, and they have wisdom. Men of pith, to repeat their sayings, is to become a sage! The accumulated cash being in our way, we made a stumbling block of it to the Jew."

"I never tripped over mine in a heap!"

Pedro laughed, and the negress, tenderly slippering the guest, grinned from one gold hoop, in which a parroquet might swing, to the other, in her ears.

"So we sea dogs, like dogs in office, have our banker,

or, rather, bankers, for you know that, spite of the Inquisition, the Jews carry on business in Spain and Portugal. The banker of the Brothers of the Coast is one and yet is legion; he is Soleiman, of Silves, in Algarve; but he is Soleiman, of all over the two kingdoms, for one Jew is an atom, which goes to make up his whole tribe. I can go to any Soleiman, make the sign of recognition, and be paid what I desire."

"Many a king, who would starve before he would partake of your chowter," said the cavalier, "would desire a crop of your gold-bearing Soleimans!"

"Well, falling behindhand in my dues to the Brotherhood, I had to provide them somehow. I mortgaged to Elizor Soleiman my inn, my fish boat, and my share in the salt works. Since I have done no business either as saltmaker or innkeeper, I am forfeit; the property accrues to him. It is fate, as the Mohammedans say; it is fair, say, as a Christian, and an old Christian, too."

"But here you have ten gold pieces!"

Pedro looked at the coins without avidity.

"That is a special godsend. I do not know that I shall turn it over to the fund."

"It is clear! You think that hiring the place is a prejudice to the lender on it? The Jew may come down and interfere with my enjoyment?" Here the cavalier luxuriated in suppling his feet in the slippers.

"Eh, the rich Soleiman, of Silves? Ha, ha! Half Algarve is signed away to him! He trouble himself about this scheme? This inn in the rocks? Besides, this is no season to travel! He may be fond of money, but he would not brave the nor'westers, not for the rent of Lisbon Castle!"

"I suppose not!"

Pedro left him as if there was no more to debate. He went upstairs and the canvas-ceiling roof, though stretched over rafters of spars with seamen's skill in scaffold-lashing, moved and sagged under his heavy tread. Presently he returned, covered with a second suit of clothes, over which was a voluminous sailor's dreadnaught, with a hood like a sentry box, and an oilskin cap over a red nightcap. He was prepared, evidently, for the storms he spoke of. Throwing back the outer covering, he disclosed a broad belt of sharkskin, enriched barbarically with beaten silver, in which he thrust the breadknife, and into a pouch appended he put the gold pieces.

Thus accoutered, he strode to the doorway and looked out on the village and the sea, like a mariner who took no course without being sure of the weather.

While gazing, he hummed a ballad which would have accorded with the buccaneers from whom the Brothers of the Coast derived their financial policy:

> "He that can kill a man,
> Murder and plunder precisely,
> It's he is the man that does wisely!
> And may climb to a chair of the State!"

"Some," said the novice at the helm of the Petrel, "would not prefer a host singing such sentiments! Yet I doubt not, he is a good fellow! Perhaps, by the tail of his canticle, he is ambitious! Well, he may serve!"

CHAPTER III.

THE POWER OF A QUILL.

In acquittance, the guest who had become host put a small gold-piece into the negress' hand, plump and ashy-grey in the palm; she closed it upon it greedily and tucked it away with less reluctance than her master. The ex-landlord looked round too late to see this generous action.

"You may be luckier in this hole than out there," said he. "There is going to be foul weather."

"I will let you a room if you do not like the weather," said the Gascon, humorously.

"Well, if you are weather-bound for a week, you will have Quaqua for company. Upon my fist! I know not a defter hand at a *tabor*, and her thick lips were shaped for the *flageolet*. I fear that you will have no customers for a while.

"You are wrong; I expect one visitor, at any rate. I am not likely to wait for any others."

"Lucky landlord! had I had the promise of even one, I had not had those megrims which hinted that I ought to retire into the cellar and blow myself up with a cognac-cask!"

He seemed to have waited for this announcement.

"If any one comes for me, and I am out, taking the excellent air," went on the other, partly to the man, partly to the woman, whose comprehension he doubted, "he or she is to be housed and nourished with the best."

"You hear, Quaqua?"

But the stranger was a man of precautions. He drew out of one of the boot-tops, provided with a pocket and flap for a pocket-pistol, either of fire or of firewater, not a bottle, but a boiled-leather case containing an ink-horn. a reed pen and some paper, rolled up to occupy little space. Spreading a leaf of this on the table, he wrote a few lines with much study, as if no regular clerk. Rising, he took advantage of the doorpost, from which the fire heat had sweated the tar, and, using this as a paste, pressed the paper on it so that it adhered beyond the possibility of the wind removing it.

Pedro shook his head; as for the negress, she contemplated the writing like a witch's spell.

"May I live to be as fat as that cardinal who was called the Eighth Hill of Rome!" cried he, "but I shall not, then, read the inscription! May your visitor be a better clerk, or it will be thrown away upon him as well!"

Thus indirectly appealed to, the writer read as follows, the same intelligence being conveyed in different languages, but he spoke in Biscayan, which was not there at all in characters:

"Caballero Luis de Gannarta awaits you on the last day of February."

"Oh, I address the honorable Knight of Gannarta," observed the resigned host, apparently taxing his memory without avail.

"Exactly, the finest old house in the Vale of Tempe?"

"Anan?" queried the puzzled sailor.

"The erudite have disputed as to its site. Every patriot thinks it is in his land, as it is the most blessed of spots on the map; but I, who am a Gascon, hold it to be in Gascony, and I will uphold it with my sword!"

"Oh, let it be in Gascony! So your honor is a Gascon?"

"A Black Gascon! But the Black Prince of Darkness is not so heavily tarred as he is painted in church crypts!"

Pedro grinned.

"It is certain that if he were courting an earthly princess, he would not apply to a painter-priest for his miniature!"

"Come, come! you may not be a friend of the priest, but you need not be that to the devil!"

"My lord of Gannarta, that person and his legions have not done me as much harm in forty years as the nobility, the law and the priesthood in forty days! There are living witnesses! Gannarta——I knew a master of the Barcelona Galley of six hundred oars who——"

"A Gannarta never rowed in a galley, or commanded one!"

"Stay! that was a Gurnetta——"

"A fisherman ought not to blunder like that! A Gur-netta is a fish, while a Gannet—see our emblem over our great door arch in the Vale of Tempe—is the Wild Duck! I am *solus* of the Gannartas—numerous flock, but the wildlings meet their quietus early! Well-a-day! wild duck never laid tame eggs!"

"But for so many lines, that says very little!" objected the observer.

"That is true. I have written in several tongues, as you stick several hooks on your cod-line! I want to catch something. You see there few tongues, as they can be written by an unused hand. Spanish, French, Dog-Latin and, best of all, the frank speech——"

"Sea lingo? Good! That is like the multiplying gun at Carthagena, work of a subtile Moor, which fires four or five times at once, or one by one, being so many bar-rels, lashed together——"

Gannarta nodded, as though he had seen, or heard of this advance in artillery.

"Still, why use four tongues to a person with but two ears?"

The man, at his ease, did not seem displeased at this garrulity on the part of one who had not laid down that trait of the landlord with his office.

"Simply because I do not know the nature of my caller, or his nation—whether man or woman, knight or base, seaman or landsman. So I write in French, in case he comes from the north or any court; in Spanish if he dwells near by; in Latin if he is clerk, or from Italia, nurse of colleges; and in frank speech if he is better in mine eyes than knight, courtier, beggar or clerk—in short, a sea-skimmer—a Brother of the Coast!"

The ex-publican grinned.

"I will send you their custom," said he, bowing and turning.

The negress, in whose charge he left the new owner by a sign, executed one of those abject salaams which offer the whole to the master.

Gannarto shuffled to the door in the slippers.

The sky was part clouded, indeed.

Secure as to himself, the good cavalier thought of his steed.

"In passing through the village," said he, "will you order one of the urchins to stable my horse? He is better to carry than to lead, better to be thrown down for a breastwork than for a dinner, for it has come next to eating him in some of our tight corners! By the way, where do you lodge to-night? You are never going off soundings under that threat?"

"In one of those boats drawn up high and dry. I am itching for the open blue. I shall go out there just as soon as one, returned, makes the next venture."

"Oh, if I shall see you again, off and on, this will be a desirable port!"

Pedro doffed his outer cap, and said, half-apologetically, half-coaxingly:

"Master mine, if your honor seeks diversion while waiting for the unknown visitor, why not come out a-fishing? I promise you good sport!"

Gannarta smiled as though the wind were blowing his way.

"I like to catch fish; it was my boyish delight in the Gulf of Gascony! But suppose, being green, I am caught!"

"You, sir?"

"You said that the naval officers—Dutch, French or Spanish—pressed men into their service. Now, I am one of those dogs who snarl at any collar but of their own choosing; and, as I am not, unhappily, a Brother of the Coast——"

Pedro looked the speaker up and down like a recruiting officer for the marine.

"I am not going to dispute that if a man-of-war officer saw your honor on a fisher's deck, through one of those *Gallego* tubes——"

"Galilean tubes—an Italian sage—don't rob a man of his glory——"

"Galilean tubes, by which the distance is brought down, he would order out his cutter and bid his crew row hard to overhaul your honor and carry him under his colors——"

"You see! Better a host of the Petrel, even, than a

gunner or a topman on a fighting ship, particularly as
it might not let me off a day to keep my tryst with the
unknown!"

"Bah!" muttered Pedro, evidently arguing with himself. "A Gascon and a gentleman! Less than that will
recommend you; besides, I may have lost credit with the
money lenders without doing so with the Brothers of the
Coast. Become one of us, and we will laugh at the
press gang!"

"Brother," returned the cavalier, frankly but seriously, "I laugh but rustily when I laugh alone. The
more, the merrier my laugh! I will go fishing with
you!"

Pedro put on his hat, drew the hood over it, and said
gleefully:

"A good sleep! I shall come for you!"

As Gannarta felt his legs cooling without his boots,
he hastily waved adieu, and hurried within the cave to
sit close to the fire.

The negress had waddled about to tidy up the den, and
then sat down to her own meal of the boiled fish; after
which, not forgetting the wine, she went and sat down in
a corner, out of the light, and, clearing a German spinning wheel, she proceeded to reel off a tuft of flax, singing to the whirr an African song not more reassuring,
to judge by the intonation and her gnashing of teeth,
than the sea-rover ballad of Pedro.

But, though the gloom deepened by the untended lamp
going out and the fire burning low, the host was calm.

"Death of my life!" muttered he. "I am consoled for
my long and little fruitful exploration of old Lusitania,
and the disappointment of no tidings from Paris, by this
happy episode. A prospect of fresh fish for breakfast,
which King Louis has not in his palace, and of being
made a Brother of the Coast! In case that imperialist
invasion is no longer to be dreaded, since they assassinate
the generals of it, whom they cannot defeat, and we con-
tend no longer with Spain upon the Pyrenees, who
knows but our fleet, reconstructed by Cardinal Richelieu,
may look for a diversion on the deep? Not always victorious, it may greet the reinforcement commanded by the

Chevalier Louis d'Artagnan, the flying squadron of my Brothers of the Coast!"

Whereupon, the Chevalier d'Artagnan, *alias* the Caballero de Gannarta, its anagram, finished deliberately a cup of wine which he mulled at the dying fire and spiced to his taste, and without wanting any usher, climbed up the steps Pedro had mounted.

He found himself in the loft, with its canvas flooring, alone.

Without probing with his sword the suspicious bales and bags about the room, he kicked several into a layer, reclined and stretched himself until a snug depression was scientifically formed, and was soon as fast asleep as his horse, in another niche in the cliff.

As for the negress, she completed her skein conscientiously, as a diurnal task, raked the coals into a heap under the backlog, drew back the dried rushes so that they could not catch fire, and into another heap. In this she laid herself, with her huge feet to the ashes. Then, taking out of her neck scarf the gold piece where she had rolled it up, she twirled it about between her fat fingers as a child would play with a doll, and went off to sleep, humming to this unwonted windfall.

Verily, the wind had been tempered to the Black Petrel! it had a golden lining to its nest!

CHAPTER IV.

THE ATLAS.

The end of the seventeenth century was distinguished by its quibblers, anagram-makers who played upon words; there was also much playing upon swords; and, sometimes, the two arts were combined in the same individual, as witness M. d'Artagnan, who had converted into *Gannarta* his family name.

But unless the reader, who would have divined this without hint, has an acquaintance with the reigns of the thirteenth and fourteenth Louis, he will not have the same perception of this gentleman's character, employment and aims as that which these pages are intended to furnish.

Louis, Knight of Artagnan, in that Gascony whose lively and boastful people have given the term of "gasconades" to extravagant stories, was, as he boasted, a black, or thorough old Gascon. His father, who inherited knightly spurs, had flashed his sword in the wars of religion, often charging side by side with his prince, Henry, then King of Navarre, another "little cradle of great men."

He retired, broken-spirited, on the assassination of that lamented and popular monarch. With that sword, and paternal recommendation to such brothers-in-arms of his as had thriven at the court of "the Green Gallant's" son, Louis XIII., young D'Artagnan had journeyed to Paris to commence, at the early age of eighteen, that career of officer of fortune, common to penniless springalds.

Distinguished at the outset in the street brawls, only notable because the laws forbade them, while the princes who wanted practised swordsmen encouraged them, the young man earned a reputation for premature coolness, superior handling of the sword, and prudence not often found in the southron. King and cardinal were ever at odds; only, as the king had a younger brother, pet of their mother, who cherished inimical designs against him, he had to lean, at times, on his sole friend—the Cardinal Duke of Richelieu, Armand Duplessis.

This prelate, the greatest of the several Primate-Premiers of France, "envied above and hated below," was the Atlas who bore on his wearying shoulders, in 1640, the known world.

Buckingham and Olivarez in vain tilted at him, and he had fended off the great captains, even a Gustavus Adolphus, in the Thirty Years' War, with consummate diplomacy from that rich prize, France.

It was because Richelieu was a soldier before he was a statesman. At the siege of La Rochelle, he had perceived military ability in D'Artagnan, though merely a subaltern in the Queen's Lifeguards. He had secured his admission into the Royal Musketeers before the defeat of the Huguenots and English was accomplished; and on the victorious return to Paris, he had appointed him captain commanding the Royal Musketeers.

Proving worthy of this post, though it was far from presenting military opportunities, the court being one of intrigues, D'Artagnan was promised, on the creation of a Household Brigade of all arms, horse, foot and wall-guns, a renewal of the office, shelved since Montmorency, of Lord High Constable of France, preceding ever the marshals of the field.

It was a sword of Damocles which did not fall.

Bearing the delay like a courtier used to broken promises, and like a soldier a slave to duty, D'Artagnan continued to guard, not only the king and queen, but the prime minister. For recreation, as he would sarcastically say (sarcasm being the venting of chagrin in the baffled courtier), he was allowed, with a company of Musketeers, to figure in the external warfare of the time. The overrunning of Savoy, repulses of Spain, and stemming the current of the Imperial Invasion, in the French Period of the Long War.

So it was that the man of thirty odd was an experienced soldier and captain, to say nothing of that diplomacy of the alcove and drawing-room marking the soldiers of the rule anterior to the minority of Louis XIV.

But at last, at the close of the year 1639, the cardinal had one of those attacks which denoted a termination of his activity. It was followed by a renewal of his sagacity, foresight and daring, but how long would the recovery hold good?

This time the doctors would not foretell, and he was of the modern school of rulers who did not have recourse to astrologers.

He called the captain of the Royal Musketeers to his private study.

With soldiers, the governor had always frankness, as far as he chose to go.

"M. d'Artagnan," began he, with that tenderness which he entertained, or at least manifested toward contemporaries of his brilliant days when he sought fame as a poet, a dancer and a singer, his model rather a Rizzio than a Strafford, "we have beaten back the Doubleheaded Eagle and the Lion of Castile. Each is preparing for another dash at us, but we must cripple them. France needs suspense from this incessant war—it must recuperate, also! A young king may follow, and we know from the prophets what his reign will be."

"It is plain, my lord, that, for a space, there is nothing at home for soldiers to do."

"Right, not for those of your youth and unsapped activity. You should take the vacation so long merited."

"I thank your lordship, but never have I applied for leave of absence. I am at home in the barrack or by the door of my king. My father, at the paternal fireside, is in good health for his age. My friends, retired from the army, are enjoying their reward. My pay is in arrears, it is true, and the long-projected project of a household brigade is still in abeyance—but I can live on a handful of gleanings, and your highness' esteemed favor. I have not written in for a holiday."

"A servant of the realm must obey orders, to rest as well as to act," returned the cardinal-duke, smoothing down his gray chin-tuft with his rare smile, which covered usually hidden meaning. "I desire you to repose—in anticipation of a busy time to succeed—in which you will succeed! all your wants will be filled—all your wits required."

"In this case, your Eminence, I will most readily obey and repose!" replied the young captain, taking the ball on the bound.

"Rest to you is not reclining on a couch—it is a change of exercise. You will take a jaunt. The route is of your own selection."

"I would rather leave it to your Eminence, as I do not have a world-wide correspondence——"

"Well, as I advise perfect tranquility——"

"The dream in the guardroom, between watches, has been perfect tranquility," observed that plastic D'Artagnan.

Richelieu turnd his stiff neck slowly and directed his gaze on a well-viewed map, almost covering one side of the study, with a humorous expression as if, on second thoughts, it were not so easy to indicate a spot, even one, not perturbed by his protracted efforts to raise his country into the first power.

"But where, your highness, to find perfect tranquility?"

"Ah, that is like answering him who wanted to know—nearly seventeen hundred years agone, what is Truth!"

Rolling his padded easy-chair on its castors to the wall, he laid the feather-end of his pen on a spot.

Unlike the other portions of the chart, it did not bear many or any dent of the thumb nail, or dots of ink, or pricks of pins.

"The Peninsula," said the musketeer, in a surprise. "A Frenchman go into Spain for tranquility? Oh, your Eminence!"

"Farther——"

"And fare worse!"

"No, I point to Portugal."

D'Artagnan shook his head as to one who advised a voyage to the capital of Prester John. The fact is, at that time, Portugal was *terra incognita* to the rest of Europe.

"Ah, I see that the wranglers in the Sorbonne were wrong in not pronouncing Portugal the site for the millenium!"

"Not exactly as Parias preached it," returned Richelieu, smiling like one who relished wit, especially in an unexpected quarter; "but by comparison with the rest of Europe, it will pass, my chevalier."

"After all, it is indifferent to me."

"Portugal," said Richelieu, wheeling his chair back to its place before the table, leaning back into the sumptuous

cushions and closing his eyes, as if, for once, he had no
fear of a dagger being drawn on him, "Portugal is no
longer the fiery forge where were struck out and fash-
ioned those men of iron who set out, like Jason, to conquer the outer world, as passengers start daily for Or-
leans or Lyons. What daring ship-prows, what heroic
swords! they left the unknown seas and smote those gold-
bearing rocks which defended savages unwritten of by
Pliny and Herodotus.

"You will see her churches and palatial monasteries
coated with gold, the mortar that binds the marble costlier
than Parian, cemented with spice water, the images
studded with precious stones, all wrung from tough and
poisonous claws, but brought home with the black and
red kings who contested their disposal, slaves to help in
that building. Her discoverers, adventurers, sea kings,
merchants, traders—you will see nothing but their tombs
—and unless the Portuguese are different in memory
from us, those tombs neglected—unfindable!" This a
passing pang.

"Some fifty years ago, it was absorbed by Spain, and its
independent spirit quenched in blood. Time was when a
conquered vassal gave no trouble for his life; so, his gen-
eration; but the grandsons alone, having time to feel the
old impressions revive, and the dread of the victor decline—these raise their crest! Now, Portugal should
quiver with the throes of producing a native deliverer. I
have questioned those who ought to be well informed.
They all say that Portugal is placid as the carp ponds at
Fontainebleau."

"My lord, the rustics say—and I have learned a great
deal from rustics, who are a store of past wisdom, if not
of new ideas—that a river is still because either very dry
or very deep."

"That is it. My informants may be superficial.
Hence, I would rather rely on a non-prejudiced observer,
who goes fresh to his mission, who is loyal to his king,
and the good of the realm. All the more so as he never
swerved to pick up the crumbs of the table, or served for
them. You may have seen a picture in my gallery, by a
Florentine, named—tut, tut, the name—it escapes me—
but the picture is in my eyes as in his who painted it, 'The

Good Servant,' of the Holy Writ, who served while only waiting——"

"Faith, your grace, it is harder serving when one has the knife and the itching to carve!" said D'Artagnan, significantly, albeit, with his feigned bluntness.

"So, it is understood between us; you take your vacation in Portugal, where you will not be disturbed by acquaintances. As for strangers, I hear that there even the alms-cravers are marked for courtesy."

"My lord, I am the last person to pick a quarrel with."

"At least, those who have done so were the last to do it."

"I shall visit Portugal," said the musketeer, as if the premier had selected the object of his devotions in the Holy Land.

"If in studying her orange groves, vineyards and ancient battlefields where the Saracen was driven back, you find that my *quidnuncs* were not capable *nucios,* why, behold one glad to alter my opinions on recreation parks. I will rule out my ideal Portugal from that map! Alas! I have left but few areas where, when I retire, I can raise my cabbages!"

"My gracious lord, I am ready, for the first time in ten or twelve years, to take a furlough thrust upon me!"

CHAPTER V.

TO PORTUGAL.

"Captain mine, you will therefore proceed to Portugal by your own road," pursued the minister of the King, "in your own disguise, at your own pace. Take time, and do your business well. You have six months' leave. Only, as next year is Leap Year, and should be easily remembered, there will be a messenger call for you at a rendezvous long since jotted down. There is a pretty fishing place on the Bay of Biscay, frequented, if frequented, by smugglers, masterless soldiers and shipless seaman. It is under the weather of San Sebastian, but unseen from its insignificance by its lookouts. It is called by those who know it, the Black Petrel."

"If it please your highness, the Kuril, its local and seafarers' name, is a bird which has some peculiar significance to them. I have known the fishers of Gascony, who would not kill one for the world, carry one, found dead, in their caps as proudly as a knight carries his lady-love's glove."

"I agree that it may cover an occult meaning. Do you know the Biscayan coast?"

"My lord, as a neighbor. I am a Gascon. I have been blown out to sea, when a boy, and have had to bide my time for the return with those who picked us up. I am, as you see me, no strange fish in those waters, from our Gulf to the Gib."

"So much the better," said the statesman, never conferring with a man on affairs without having looked up the notes his secretaries preserved of every one of note. "Since you learnt French so soon and elegantly, I suppose that you have the facility of tongues——"

"I am not like that ancient king who could talk with any of his numerous peoples; but my budget will serve me. The Emperor Charles V. said that a man who spoke five tongues was equal to five men. I am, therefore, a sextuple man, since I can ask for bread, bed and drink in six, namely, French, Gascon and its allied dialects, Spanish, German, Italian and the seaman's odd lingo."

"I see that while others in our outlandish campaigns picked up earnings, you picked up learning," said the statesman, yielding to the punning propensity which great men indulged in, singular to a later breed of critics. "I foresee that you will, from a conversational point, enjoy your turn-out-to-grass!"

"But I am ignorant of Portuguese," concluded D'Artagnan.

"The upper class use Spanish as the court language. The clergy, Latin. The common orders, close and dogged, says my Secretary Crosnier, like the Atlantes in all lands who support the high stories, use but five hundred words as a current vocabulary."

"My lord, in three months, I will hobnob, then, with Goodman José like his oldest boon companion."

"For the last time, good! I know you are the same on hill as in hall. Will such a lazy saunter be costly?"

"Your eminence, when the wheel is well greased, the cart goes farther. Moreover, the ungreased wheel calls attention by its squeaking."

"You shall have no stint. Show this signet of mine to my treasurer or the king's, and draw whatever you deem sufficient. When, on the last day of February next, you are at the Petrel, my messenger will supply you freshly and to any amount for the enterprise for which you, my captain and trusted friend, consider Portugal a favorable field."

Not often had Richelieu called one his friend, less often his trusted one, and rarely shown what was his friendly trust by allowing him to carry out a project of his, practically on his own impulse, with unlimited funds.

D'Artagnan bowed, with moisture about his eyes.

"Oh! I am well aware that gentlemen of the sword despise the purse, which has its potency, believe me. Is there not an olden couplet as the tag for it? Let me see?

" 'It is the sword doth order all!
'It—it—mum-mum-mum——' "

"'Makes peasants rise and——'" here the corrector stopped at a pretendedly hopeless cast.

"'And princes fall!'" continued the prelate, steadily. "That treasonable outlook was—now, the purse may brain a man, if full, and the strings strangle him, if empty. I speak metaphorically."

"The purse," said the musketeer, sadly. "When officers are clamoring for back pay, when the taxes come in by driblets, since the collectors have sticky fingers——"

"Tush, it is a teeming country! We know, D'Artagnan, that a king's cheese goes half away in parings; but, to the glory of France! her nobles are not impoverished. I know a lord whose strong box is open to the faithful servants of the state——"

"My lord, your pensioners are envied above those of the king or the queen, there's no disputing!"

"You soldiers think yourselves dogs in the roasting-wheel, who turn for others to get the meat, but ye shall not always have the rind and the trimmings and the hot splashes! You are ambitious, captain?"

"To take ambition from the soldier is to chop the spurs from the knight!"

"Well, you who come to town in leather, walk in velvet now. We will find gold, not copper lace for the suit, rely on it, on your return."

"My lord, your well-known generosity——"

"Mark you! The latest satire says of me: 'Breasts stones enfold, as blood runs cold!' but I will prove to my adherents that it is good shelter under an old hedge!"

"My lord, when we were enemies, I did never scruple to advance my admiration for your support of your friends. Now that I have the favor to possess your lordship's amity, I have said no prayer but 'Lord love no other until France has a better governor!'"

"As the soldiers' blood is the captain's glory, so is the minister's trust his greatest testimony."

"May I deserve that trust, come martyrdom or marquisdom—that is my only prayer. In sum, your eminence, I am to take your money in my pocket, and my life in my hands, and spy Portugal. It seems to me—merely the captain on scout duty, and not a political intriguer, like the Marquis de Rambouillet, our Ambassador to Spain—that the rose in King Philip's cap is likely to become a thorn to his side!"

Richelieu had leaned well over the table, charmed by the ring of this confident, incisive and manly voice. At this observation from his carefully-chosen confidant, his glance rose, clear and searching, as though he were again of the junior's age. It seemed to both that their spirits communed with nothing earthly between. Thus are two diamonds, brought into contact, declared to be genuine and inappreciable, by their own sparks.

"Memo.," said D'Artagnan, drawing the huge ring on his finger over his gauntlet, which he had put on, "I am to cover all the ground I can of this *Ultima Thule* between this and the end of the coming February. Under the wings of the Petrel, bird of storm, but likewise of sunshine, I am to meet your money-carrier for means to pay the laborers whom I should employ to heap up such a barrier on Spain's frontier as it will take her all her time to remove; or it will crush her."

"Spain is halting. He who will not look before him, shall look behind him."

"A cunning captain may certainly succeed by attacking a foe in the rear!"

"She has forts, and the Spanish soldier is redoubtable behind a rampart!"

"Pooh! gold goes in at any gate——"

"Save the golden ones of Heaven."

"I shall have laid out my burden of that kind before I am ordered through there!"

"That is all. I thank the stars that they sent a capable man."

"Yes, my lord, whose shortest answer is doing a thing!"

Richelieu fell into abstraction. Did he doubt that he had ventured too far; confided an important operation to a Hercules who would beg to be relieved of the burden?

D'Artagnan, who had reached the door curtains, lifted them to make sure that the door was closed. He listened to his soldier breathing on the other side as he leaned on his partisan. Then, returning with a noiseless step, he leaned over the table so that young head and old one almost touched, to say:

"One thing, Eminence! In event of my examination showing that with good changes the people may lift the standard of insurrection against the Lion and the Castles, who is to lead them?"

"There is a ballad which goes about the streets," replied the minister, as if he were expecting the query. "But you do not keep record of all these effusions, as my scretaries do." He sang with his quavering voice, so unlike that which had in its day charmed Anne of Austria:

> "If Fortune exhibit a crown,
> He'd be but the stupidest clown
> Who'd lift it to quick put it down—Oh, gay! Oh, gay!"

"*Certes!*" cried the musketeer, drawing himself erect. "I have ambition. I am not above the flatteries of my star; but it is as a soldier. Great acts encourage greater! But I am not conceited enough to seat me on the throne of Manuel, the Lucky!"

Richelieu smiled. The world was a workshop, where he knew the place of all his tools and drew them out only as wanted.

"They would not tolerate a foreigner!" said he. "Not even Louis the First, of Artagnan. Let us rely on Providence," continued he with that spice of hypocrisy inseparable from the cardinal-minister. "If Providence determines that there shall be a revolt and that revolt is to become a revolution, it will also provide a head for the vacated crown."

D'Artagnan left the room with a nimble step and a loaded heart, but a lighter one than he had entered with.

The old premier took down one of his splendidly-bound books, an old tragedy, of which he loved the sonorous, but not very enlightening lines, saying before he plunged into the pages, like one who had no concern in one quarter at least:

"A good youth! Ah, I have my flaws; but never should Sixty advance by throwing down Thirty!"

CHAPTER VI.

THE PETREL.

After his peregrination, sounding Portugal to its depths with a view of measuring its loyalty for its sister kingdom, D'Artagnan was entitled to his rest. Thanks to the perfect peace of abandoned Salinas, and the savory if primitive cookery of Dame Quaqua, which he varied by handing over to her spit and pans, sea birds shot with a gun he found and furnished up, the chevalier felt ready for the second act of the drama, the cue for which would be presented by the herald promised by Cardinal Richelieu.

Not a soul had entered the hamlet up to a morning when several small fisher boats stood in. They hovered about so long that the lonely hotelkeeper feared that he would never serve his novitiate toward these navigators. Accordingly, having noticed a post of ironbound Catalonian pine stuck in a rock, reached at low tide by a reef, which mast was topped by a basket of metal used as a fireholder, he shot off his gun in the air and went out to stuff a truss of eel grass into this cresset. The sailors very properly understood that firing a gun in the air and showing the green signified peace and, probably not dreading one man, steered in and ran their boats upon shore at his feet.

They preceded Pedro's return with quite a little fleet.

These forerunners were greeted, not only by the musketeer, but the children, with whom D'Artagnan had made friends by the distribution of sweetmeats of Quaqua's confection. Petty gewgaws, gathered in his own travels, won over their mothers.

Hence, in a few minutes, he was drinking with the fishers in the cave as if he had been innkeeper all his life.

After Pedro returned he went out with him. As their catch was rich, the men held him to be a person who carried luck, and he was almost torn to pieces thereafter, as each boat wanted him to sit in the thwarts and utter

those cabalistic words which do, or do not, bring fish to
the hook.

Still, the messenger did not come.

He did not shrink therefore from letting himself be
transferred, under Pedro's wing, into a larger vessel,
making longer trips, and soon increased his knowledge
of the extent of the watery territory overruled by the
Brothers of the Coast.

A little drop or two of his blood and that of Pedro's,
the latter portion transfused in his veins, as the like was
done toward the ancient master of the Petrel, made them
"blood" brothers, while a ceremony, garnished with a
blood-curdling oath, converted the landsman into a full-
fledged Brother of the Coast.

Thenceforth, M. d'Artagnan, whatever the number of
men he commanded on land, might congratulate himself
that he had a little navy at his back, composed of the
lawless and landless, it is true, but not to be condemned.

There was a good amount of Portuguese, or those
who had sailed from Portuguese ports, in the Brotherhood of the Coast.

"I do not say," mused the plotter, "that Cardinal
Richelieu will live to see Portugal free—but I think he
will have invitation to the coronation of a king other
than the present bearer of its sceptre."

He began to believe that the messenger from France
was not hurried—that he would not anticipate the day of
the limit of his arrival.

So he continued his trips, without closely counting the
duration.

It was while he was thus absent from "his" inn that,
one afternoon, a man rode into Salinas on a mule.

He was young and dark; he was bowed by study
rather than years, or as one of a race bred under the
yoke. He was well-advised if he had been directed to take
baths here, for he was unkempt and unwashed, almost
like a hermit who had taken the vow not to care for himself. His clothes were in keeping; old, worn, mended
very badly and with patches not of the original stuff.
His mule and D'Artagnan's horse, which was grazing
on wild asparagus on the cliff together, would not fetch
the price of one pony in a fair market.

This rider had debouched from the southwest upon the salt marshes. He halted, went on again, and halted, like one who did not perceive expected landmarks.

If he pushed on, it was spurred by growing uneasiness and disconcertion.

Indeed, no doubt having seen Las Salinas in its high days, he was pained by the devastation. Where were inn, storehouses, sheds over the drying beds, where the pans, where the crystals glittering like crushed pearls in the merry sun?

After various stoppages, moaning to himself like a bereaved one on a battlefield, strewn with the slain, this broken-spirited traveler reached the group of hovels where children and matrons were splitting newly-caught fish for curing, on a very small scale as compared with the former one—intending to smoke them instead of using salt.

"What are your wishes, sir?" cried the oldest woman, a wave and wind-shaken hag, in whose wrinkles shone grease and brine; she had gray hair, but was strong as a man.

"The inn! The Black Petrel?" he returned, looking about him as if he hoped he was only suffering from sun or sand blindness.

"There is no inn, sir!"

"Please your honor, the Pe-te-rel has flown away!" lisped a bright child, roguishly.

"Hold your tongue, imp! The inn and all our houses have been swept away by the broom of Beelzebub!"

"What, a whirlywind?"

"Of the landsmen's contriving—those landsharks!"

"Landsharks?" looking round as if expecting to see a marine nondescript.

"They left nothing to sole a shoe with, or fill a sea snail's pack."

"You must be mad—or drunk!"

"Drunk! it is drunk on starved mice, then! We had nothing to gnash but driftwood!"

"Pray, make clear. What are the landsharks?"

"Ho, ho, ho!" chorused the urchins, "he does not know what landsharks are!" and then they drew off to a distance, losing all interest in this ignoramus.

"Why, sir, the *quadrilleros* (squad captains) of the Bishop of St. Sebastian, the governor's soldiers, the Holy Brotherhood's *familiars,* and his majesty's fiscal officers——"

Whereupon, curbing her flow of vituperative caustic, after consigning all these "landsharks" under one head to a sea of fire eternal, she related Salina's destruction, calling all the saints, martyrs and holy days to witness her truth. To her, it had been a miniature Tyre.

Her listener was sympathetic, engrossed in her narration of the doleful fate.

"Bad, by the Sacred Writ!" said he; "but, natheless, they must have left something!"

"Go, pry in the sea where the sharks swarm—do they leave you any bones?"

"But they are not heathens to burn an inn! They, who do not spare wine, do not smash the flagon! It is of old written that he who soils the dish he ate of is accursed thrice!"

At this period, when home life was a garrison existence, the family head a dictator, the children slightly superior to the servants, and the menials slaves, to ruin a hostelry was akin to demolishing a sanctuary! Even an A' Becket could not always find an inviolate sanctuary, but everybody found an inn, that temple of equality (provided there was a purse).

"What have they done with the master? Had he no servants?"

"Oh, there was master enough! but Pedro Bitts and the boys were away fishing—or they would have had a word to say, with points between the words, forsooth! And his cook, the blackamoor, Quaqua, she was over the ridge, too—or she would have pretty soon thrust a hot poker into a cask of Schiedam and blown up the myrmidons!"

"They seem to have chosen their time of descent well!"

"Still, they did not get everything! We plucked the Black Petrel, and put everything worth keeping in that hole up there."

Her stock of verbiage exhausted, she, for the first time, perceived that she was addressing a Jew. Convert, or pervert, or revert, or primitive, this matters not—he

was of the race abhorred. She turned the backs of all
the children of her brood toward him, made over them the
sign of the cross, and the gesture against the evil eye on
her own account.

She hurried away, screwing up her rugged lineaments
at having unwittingly condescended so greatly.

Used to such humiliating homage, the son of Abraham
simply shrugged his shoulders as if one straw more or
less did not increase the load, lifted up his eyes in a
questioning way, and rode his mule up to the cave indicated.

He dismounted slowly, having stiffened limbs. Submissively he called out: "House, there! ho, house!" and,
as no reply issued from the uninviting opening, he warily
ventured his nose inside.

The negress must have been aroused from a siesta, as
she arose with a cannibal's gape. She approached lazily,
like a cloud detached from the smoke and gloom.

The fire was nearly out; why cook when the appreciative D'Artagnan was not at home to enjoy her art?

She did not recognize him with any warmth, at all
events.

"I am seeking Senor Pedro Bitts," said he. "You
know me? Elizor Soleiman, of Silves, in Algarve."

A glimpse of brightness did appear in her glassy eyes.
"It is a time since we saw you!" said she.

"Is it the same time as he has owed me for rent, and
other matters?"

"What?" cried she, blazing up so that from dead-
black she became purple. "Do you demand rent when
we have not a house over us?"

Unfortunately, the money lender had recognized the
furniture.

"By the letter of the law," said he, sternly, "the business is still carried on, when the sign is not pulled down!
That has been decided in the High Court of Burgos."

"Burgos? What do we care for your burghers here!
Nobody but a madman or a Jew would assert such a
claim upon the very ruins! And you, to flaunt the law!
I should think you and your tribe had had all the law,
church, state and local, that you wanted! ay, to boot!
But do not you block up the doorway! with all those

fisher folk scoffing at our being indebted to you for rent
and 'other matters!' Oh, come in!"

The tone would have harmonized with the act of emp-
tying a kettle of boiling water over him, but her growl
was oftener forthcoming than her bite! Soleiman obeyed
with trepidation.

"Oh, yes! squint around! Admire what a badger hole
the Spanish cormorants left us to stow the wreckage in!
Nay, these things were not down in your invent-a-story!
Mainly, they have been cast up by our good Father
Neptune, kinder than the Spaniard or usurers! Ah, it
is true, as the master says, 'Where avarice rules, humanity stands off in the offing!' There is not a pot or a
pan here of what you lent Pedro, a miserable sum,
piastre for *piastre!*"

Elizor was so convinced of the ruin that he wrung his
hands while he recovered his breath.

At the opening, the mule looked in curiously, as if to
learn what chance there was of its obtaining food and
drink.

But his master thought only of his own wants; yet a
glance at the fireless gloom dispelled any idea of temptation to transgress his rules, if he deemed any bread un-
hallowed in his distress.

The Petrel seemed picked to the bone.

"Peace!" said he, mildly, to the African, "when one
will not bicker, two cannot. Is not that fish hanging
up over there? I will cook one with my own hands, if
you will blow up that cheerless fire."

"Oh, I will cook it for you! I am not going to let a
man, and a Jew, spoil good sea food at a fire of my
kindling. After all, you are a kind of guest, if unwelcome. There is wine, also washed up from off soundings!"

"I thank you. I will cook the fish. And have you
water?"

She was making a bellows of her mouth at the revived
fire; she pointed with her elbow to a corner; a spring
bubbled out and trickled into a trough to run off the
crystal stream and not flood the cave.

He went there, drank out of his hand as a cup, like a

Stoic, and returned to sit nearer the outer air, saying,
without her heeding:

"Let me think!"

He crossed his legs, hid his face in his hands and reflected deeply. In his close abstraction, he squeezed his
hands until the joints cracked; that might have been
merely a popular exorcism against evil spirits.

Disheartened by this inattention, the mule flapped its
ears, emitted a strangled cry and drew back and out-
wards, finally straggling toward the horse above, by circuitous ways.

The Soleiman of Silves seemed too young a man to
suffer such prostration for what should be a petty loss;
very poor or miserly he must be who broke his heart
over this blow to the salt industry and the future of the
tavern for its employees.

But he was dwelling on it.

"They were thriving so well," muttered he. "I had
orders for them to supply all Brittany with salt, to be
delivered, as Pedro would, in the teeth of the royal tithe-
gatherers. It is much to have a minister wink at things
which despoil the nobles but keep the poor people alive!
And the vanished hostel! It must have done well, for
that Pedro is a superior man who makes every one he
meets his friend. He is no waster, although in the way
of business he sets the lead. 'Gentlemen, fill up! in a full
glass there is no chance for a headache to creep!' I have
heard him! noble sentiments in an innkeeper! But all
gone—cask and spile! By my ancient faith! Nobles of
Spain! you shall bleed for this, and from the heart, too!
King of Spain, you shall lose your best investment! Ah,
if those licensed robbers, after having leveled my village
—for I helped create it—had only perpetrated the irony of
sowing the foundation with salt, the scrapings might return ten or twelve *per centum*. Robbers all, from the
crown to the earthsill!"

Suddenly, the negress rose; the fire had lingered and
she made it blaze by pouring in some terebinthine out of
a jar. With the glare she was transfigured. Instead of
a greasy cook, she looked, to the astonished guest, a
pythoness in her cave of destiny. Brushing by the la-

menting one, which contact farther aroused him from his
brooding, she went into the doorway.

She whistled like a man, through a filed tooth, and
slapped the notice appended by Captain D'Artagnan to
the jamb.

Surmising that this was an authoritative order emanat-
ing from the despoilers of Las Salinas, the Jew rose also
and stood before it. He must have been learned, as he
understood at a flash, reading the Spanish lines:

" 'The Caballera de Gannarta expects' me on the last
day of February, eh? Oh, the emissary from my lord
the duke, eh? There is no further delay, then; that
long-laid-up money will be wanted, and I may not play
shilly-shally with Louis XIII.'s first minister as this
burned-out innkeeper does with me. What does he demand the cash for? and money so dear now! Is another
war in sight? Oh, these great jugglers, for the Richelieu is a great one! They play pitch and toss with the
balls on the sceptre as they do with cannon balls!

"Is it with England this time again? They say that
its king is in a desperate plight. It would not be the
first time on record that a monarch went to war abroad
in order to gain a peace at home with the less daring
commercial spirits, whose bulwarks are the counter and
whose weapons are the pepperbox and the yardstick!
Would the land of grain and that of the grape join to
crush this land of orange groves—vine stake and hop pole
clash? But the hog should not look up while they are
threshing the fruit down! Woe is me! I am so upset
by this calamity that I liken myself to the hog now; mur-
rain breed! Misfortunes come in pairs, like doves;
this loss on the salt marsh and of the inn, and the great
duke demanding his money!"

Staring at the writing on the wall, he continued:

"Coming back on the twenty-ninth, eh! Easy-going,
this cavalier! Methinks that, for a million or more, he
might have stayed here until I arrived; is not the rule:
'The first come about money, waits for the other!' Perhaps the lonesomeness disgusted him! It is the barren-
ness of Gomorrah! Where am I to find decent quarters while awaiting the duke's envoy? San Sebastian?
My brethren never had a good word for its Jewry. It

might not be safe for me, if it were known that I and
the Soleimans shouldered the men who shouldered the
bags of salt! Oh, the lot of Israel is a hard one!"

He shivered at renewed contemplation of this scurvy
retreat, which had been made bearable to the musketeer.
But then, the musketeer had not lost money here; indeed, he expected to receive money. They were at opposite ends of the telescope.

"Well, I shall stay here, and make the best of it. I
do not suppose that black priestess of Satan would hesitate to poison me in some diabolical mess! I must prepare my own food. I shall have to keep close, too,
since I had not the means to scatter a handful of cinq-
reis among those brats, and colored scarves to bestow
on their dams. That virago will set the village about
my ears!

"But whom have we here as the Caballero de Gannarta? I do not know the name, but the astute duke
would not send a nonenity to draw a million! It is
mask for an active spirit of the French court, which
never wanted yet such to cozen a Spaniard, a Levantine;
but not, this time, a Jew!" He smiled with pride, and
the firelight showed him less rigid and pinched of fea-
ture. "Some *nom de guerre*! A lieutenant who is going to be employed in the state engineer's plot to blow
up or build up—what?

"Who does he mean to place on high, or bring low?
Whom replace; whom displace, and in whose favor?
But for these intriguers, and the fighting men whom
they control and gull with pledges of glory, the world
would be heaven; no wars, no enmities; nothing but
trade! These swaggering caballeroes would become
sheriffs, and their bravoes just servers of writs and en-
forcers of judgments, if in such a millenium any one was
delinquent!"

A thought seized him.

"Oh, the Pope! This Urban hangs on to the chair
like a lamprey! A successor might be lenient to us,
and no more should we shudder at the Holy Brotherhood, with its torches extinguished and its cross-handled
sword snapped! Richelieu, the next Pope!

"My father, the only Soleiman in France, in trade

with Bearn and Navarre, equipped his father, simply a captain who lacked for boot and breeches and a war horse, for the wars. What if I shall be equipping the cardinal for his next ecclesiastical promotion? It will be the interest on his millions well invested!

"This Spain is a giant, cruel as the giants are, but he loses his limbs one by one; and France, as the giant-killer, furnishes the pigmies with the hatches to hew them off! And our people supply the handles, and sharpen the blades—and—hem! perhaps buy the fragments for the fleshpots."

"Master," interrupted the negress, who, no doubt, had no religious prejudices, but did not desire his company as a usurer, "since you follow up your house by its pieces, stay with them while I go to sleep at the Dame Usula's. It is a widow of a fisher; I nursed her boy through the marsh fever, for the spell of St. Agnes did no good! I am welcome there."

This announcement traversed his plan, but he nodded with the resignation which branded the contemporaries in his creed, and in no way did he stay her in her flight, leaving him alone.

CHAPTER VII.

A NEW BIDDER.

Before it came on dark, it was necessary to arrange for the long night. As the fire had been lit and was brightly burning, and a supply of fuel was at hand, that trouble was removed. But, wary and suspicious, first of all, he took up a brand, shook off the superfluous sparks for fear of fire, and, with many misgivings, climbed the stairs to explore the loft which had puzzled him. He made a more thorough search than his predecessor, but returned satisfied that mischief would not fall on him, unless the whole cliff gave way under the two horses which he heard over his head.

Returning, he was going down into the cellar; but, at the sight of a profound and unfathomable darkness, to which his light was mockery, he contented himself with a simpleton's test. He called out, "Is there any one there?" and as no answer came, tried to believe that it was untenanted.

The brand scorching his hand, he searched about and found, in a box of priceless cedar wood, a bundle of such large tallow candles as the Catalonian lead miner uses, hanging up by rope-yarn wicks, like so many gallow's birds. He lighted one and put it on the table where his seat commanded a view of the doorhole.

Completely ignoring his mule—the act of one not accustomed to riding, perhaps, rather than inhumanity, although that is a characteristic of the Peninsulars, he began to read and check a handbook of accounts.

Spite of his apparel and general aspect, so mean and sordid, he was at home among these figures, in four or five to a row, and involving startling amounts, even if expressed in francs, pistareens or milreis. His fine features exposed the absorption and relish of a money-spinner, doubled by an arithmetician.

At dark he laid aside the manual to take up the fish, broiled finely on the glowing coals. With bread, hard and dry as old Parmesan cheese, carried by himself in his gabardine, he made his supper, perhaps the first meal he had that day.

He had appeased his appetite when an alarm at the aperture caused him to spring up, regretting that he was not a man of war who could have utilized some of the arms about the cave.

It was only that mule, which, reinforced by the *clamponnier*, thrust its head in.   He tied it up by the outlet, threw it an armful of rushes, of which the horse amicably partook, they pulling out mouthfuls by turns, and hung an old sail across the passageway, as much to keep out the air currents as the animals.

Lighting a third candle, so that the other should not leave him in the dark, it approaching its end, he resumed his calculations. He frowned and smiled by turns. By his gloating look, one might consider that his mind's eye was peering into a strong box full of gold and silver and other valuables.

He was startled by the sound of more than one step without.

The horse neighed and the mule whinnied. Poor outcast, he wished to make friends with even his haughty cousins.

The heavy ones were man's—maybe Pedro's; a lighter one, which neared the doorway, a woman's, hardly Quaqua's, for its ease and alacrity. Thieves would not come, with supporters perfectly careless concerning the noise they made. He was a little reassured as he stood between a desire to flee and a belief that he could not escape, by the light steps stopping at the ingress as if the person were not bold.

At the same moment, a gentle rapping with a small white glove, made the doorpost resound.

"Gloved? Whom have we here?" he asked himself, hiding the memorandum book in his sleeve. "The creditor was an offender against the functionaries and would hardly more seek to set them upon me than the fishers! After all, I have come, as far as he was entangled, simply for my dues. Hark! it is a woman! Oh, let us face the danger! I am not the fool to carry my treasure on my back!" smiling with the superiority of the few educated at that time. "Let the Gentile shrink who knows not the virtue of letters of 'change! Now, may my intimate gods (Teraphim) be good to me! I will open, though the nine worthies stood without——"

So muttering, he drew aside the canvas with a hand that did not tremble.

The mantled figure did not advance. This embold-ened him to challenge loudly:

"What is wanted?"

"I want the way in, in the first place!" It was a sweet voice utterly unlike any he had nerved himself to hear. By an imperative motion, the white-gloved hand waved him aside, with a fan she held, one of those with which a man might have been stunned, so heavily was the handle incrusted with crystal and other second-rate gems.

"A woman—a lady!" stammered he, drawing back in amaze, while still holding up the screen.

What was a siren doing on this sterile shore? Are there nereids to come out of the wondrous deep?

"Are you going to let me pass?" proceeded the voice, as if the speaker were not accustomed to being delayed.

"If there are mermaids," murmured Elizor, running his long, dry hands through his tangled black hair, "this is the queen of them. Why do you ask to come in?"

"Because this is the public house of Las Salinas."

"You are right. It is the only house, if it deserves that name. But there is no accommodation, lady. Why should you want to enter here?"

"Know, eccentric boniface, that I am eccentric also—I want to do good!"

"Truly? to whom? I—I am only the host for the time being—I am a landlord perforce."

"I can put ten moidores in your box, temporary host, for an eternity, for, judging by your promontory, you love and you hoard gold."

"Ten moidores—thirteen gold philips," repeated Elizor, quickly, not resenting the personal remark, and licking his lips so that their color was revived.

"Open straight! There is a flaring torch in the village below. I do not wish to be seen by the clowns."

Judging that he need fear nothing from a person who shunned what shadowy publicity Salinas offered, he drew up the sail-like tapestry still farther and ranged himself beside its stiff folds.

The mantled and hooded woman stepped past him.

Thus he was allowed to see, a little farther out in the obscurity, two or three large and handsome mules, to which his was a caricature, caparisoned richly by the glint of metal adornments; they were held by two or three tall fellows, in gray livery; they held staves, which, in his eyes, resembled spears.

"This is not only a fine, but a great lady," thought the present holder of the title to the Petrel, seeing this guard. "We never know what angels we may entertain; but, assuredly, I did not dream that Pedro had visitors of this quality."

"Good-evening, Senor Pedro Bitts!" began the intruder, walking up to the table and the candle, as if she had no reason to shun the not overpowering lustre.

This ignorance of the person whose name she used wrongly, contradicted her pretense of having been in the cave before.

Elizor saw, as the hood opened, the face of a beautiful girl of scarce twenty, whose fair complexion had no need of the black plaster patches to set it off. But, on second thoughts, it seemed to him, as was not unseldom the case, these patches, cut into formal shapes with fine sciscors, might be emblems of recognition.

In his admiration, he let the error pass.

"Good! you have let down the hangings. It is not necessary that the varlets should guess the nature of our confabulation."

"The fact is——"

"Or see the splendrous interior of your refectory."

By the curl of her tremulous nostrils, it was clear that she had inhaled the smell of the fried fish, and no more approved of it than of the scene she derided.

He did not take up any of these sneers.

As if the air was oppressive, she flung back the opened hood with a toss of the head.

It coiled around her neck, robust and massive, though so juvenile, and broad shoulders, like a Venetian duchess, after Bronsino; knots of rosy ribbon decked each shoulder, perhaps such favors as women give gallants to

signalize them as upholders of the cause they espoused.
Her ears were small, close to the round head, and pink;
her eyes black and lively; her hair abundant and only
brown, not black, as one expected in strict harmony with
her other traits. Seed pearls in long ropes were twined
in and out of its braids and increased the mass which
crowned her, and would have broken the shock of a sabre
cut—if even a Turk could think to strike at this master-
piece of nature, perfected in the court.

"I beg your ladyship's pardon, but I cannot guess at
your title?"

"You are putting the very remark to me which is a
question I cannot answer," returned she, pertly.

Elizor had a doubt. While he certainly was to meet
by appointment Cardinal Richelieu's emissary, there might
be other business than monetary. This court lady was
clearly just the one to carry out a plot on lines very different from those he was fated to travel in. He took up
the candle, snuffed it with tremor, as the snuff was large
and hot, and held it to the writing on the post.

"If you would please to read, my lady?" said he, with
respect from adorable source—her rank and her beauty.

Probably thinking it one of those prints carried by
peddlers from door to door, to be stuck up in inns, barber
shops, farriers' smithies, and public resorts, she gave it a
careless glance. Then remembering that in these times
none were justified in letting even trifles pass, she gave it
a more interested look. Next she read it.

Now the Jew believed that she read the French first,
which convinced him that she was in the scheme; on the
other hand, a Spanish lady might understand the tongue,
although of her foes.

"How now?" cried she, more amused than irritated;
"do you take me, sirrah, for a Duchess de Chevreuse, the
intriguante, who disguised herself so neatly as a cavalier
that she deceived the officers of the port, trying to prevent her escaping out of France? No, I am not intertwined with this plot—for, I warrant ye, sirrah! there is
a plot when the workers involve four or five nations!"

"You may be a duchess without being La Chevreuse,"
replied Soleiman, stoutly, not caring to be considered a

common innkeeper, and convinced that the Petrel was the stage to no petty play, "and you need not be clad as a cavalier to carry things off cavalierly!"

"Hoity-toity! what a fine wit in a coarse tavern!" said she, but with good-humor.

And to show her contempt for this inferior, she deliberately took up a handglass and a comb suspended at her side and rearranged the ringlets on her forehead, as if the Jew were a footman.

"Then you do not come to the Petrel to meet the caballero signing himself there?"

"Then you talked wit—now, you talk nonsense!"

"But are you pursuing any object——"

"Methinks you are questioning me. Never mind, I am probably pursued."

But if she were apprehensive, a second thought about her attendants, who would certainly not let her be surprised, came to her relief.

"Pursued?" echoed Soleiman, not eager to be arrested in even such rare company.

"No; not closely, at any rate! But I am always exposed to pursuit, master of the Petrel; but not of your tongue. I may have been followed from Fontarabia, but not to this remote spot. Do not flatter yourself, chief inhabitant of Las Salinas, not yet is your hamlet a court resort!"

"It is no place—the village has been swept away! And as for the Petrel Inn, the sad walls would mourn the master only that not even are the walls left. All that was useful has been put in this cavern of the winds."

"A tempest?"

"By a commotion stirred up by those fomentors of turbulence, the clergy, the tax-farmers and the lords of the coast."

"I have nothing to do with them—they less with me, I trust. My ride was irksome." She took a seat, using her cloak as a cushion on the bench, without too much repugnance. "Let us pass the time more profitably, boniface of my heart!"

"So we have business together, uninclosed by a plot?" said the Jew, wondering that his racial points had not provoked more raillery than she had freely given. "Senseless widgeon that I am, I was not to imagine that!"

"Business on my side—pure pleasure on yours."

Elizor had the wit to pass a compliment, but he had the sense not to attempt a sally. The remembrance of the staves of the serving men without deterred him. Never would he lose a business gain for a jest, however good.

"Hem! It is late for——" He was going to say "a great lady," but he corrected himself and filled the ellipse with "business."

"I am going to offer——"

"The ten moidores alluded to——"

"Yes, Master Pedro. I put down a question before I do the coin, which are here." She held up a satchel, also attached to that comprehensive chatelaine, the substitute for pockets. "Can you let your house to me for a term?"

"Eh, what?" faltered he.

"Let your inn to me. That will not disturb any customers, as far as I can see."

"I—I—but such a poor place—such a fine patroness——"

"A sorry inn may shelter a great head," said she, gravely, for if she knew him to be a Jew she must have believed him a converted one—for few of the orthodox had the inquisition left in Spain. "Nay, I speak generally——" seeing him bite his lip. "The inn for my use and the ten gold pieces for yours."

"I have no objections, but—this may interfere with ——" he pointed to D'Artagnan's intimation.

"Oh, the expected caller on the Caballero de Gannarta? On the last of February? No, it will not conflict with my arrangements."

"He may come—both may come—it is the only way I know of for two persons to meet!"

"You positively overflow with wit—I know where to send one to the next court wishing a jester! Lord knoweth that the courts are all sad and should not have abolished that officer! If they are gentlemen they will not cross a lady——"

"Well, things go by halves in this world. One may be a gentleman—the other a lout——"

"Then the lord will cudgel the lout if he is impudent to the lady!"

"Oh," muttered Elizor, to whom this phase had not presented itself.

CHAPTER VIII.

THE THIRD TENANT.

"Well," grumbled the money-lender, "I will not answer for the consequences."

"Take your coin."

She put a silk purse on the table, wherein the gold pieces glittered through the fine meshes like fish in a net. For the first time in his life Elizor put money away without counting it. The loftiness of this lady daunted him; he would as soon as have thrown a pebble at her as hinted by an act that he doubted her honesty. Still, he had had princesses come to pawn their jewels with him.

"And I do not require answers, except to my questions."

He waited for those questions, but none came; she was examining the room.

"Is there anything I can do for you, before I leave you the inn, yours from ceiling to sill?" inquired he.

He began to shiver at the doubt that he should find any cover for his head, poor proscript that he was, within easy march that night, and yet the ten pieces so easily gotten would drive away sleep.

"Is there a window—a cranny open to the sea?"

Elizor had noticed a crack in the rock. He pointed to it. A current of air set in through it which shook the blackened cobwebs over their heads.

"There is one—it has given me a crick in the neck."

"Anticipating——" she finished, with a playful gesture, pantomiming a suspension like Jove's candles, which was neither in the sea, in the air, nor on the land.

In a niche, about head high, stood a statuette, in Della Robbia ware, of the particular divinity of the seas, "Our Lady of the Star of the Sea." Between the negress, who was a heathen, and D'Artagnan, who was not often indoors, the lamp had been suffered to go out; a three-ply screen of that Sarreal alabaster scraped thin and used for glass was set before it to enable the light to burn steadily.

"Put that wind guard in that hole, and place the candle in it."

Though the woman was the embodiment of haughtiness and independence, at least toward him, somehow he felt averse to quitting her. Perhaps it preyed upon him to earn the money too easily. He obeyed her with alacrity. He robbed the saint of her translucent screen without any reluctance, and, by mounting on a bench, fixed it in the hole. As she kindly handed him the light he set that under its protection.

"Have you not more candles?—yes, I spy several!"

"All at your ladyship's service."

He had laid them out to have one in burning all the time he should sit up.

"Light two more and range them in a line in that apology for a casement," said this modern Persephone, bringer of light, or offerer of it to the utter darkness.

The three illuminants could not be seen in the village, so it seemed gratuitous.

He carried out the instruction as truly as those servants would have done, who waited with all the patience of the Spanish.

Elizor stepped down, looked at the trio, and, turning his features, showed all his perplexity.

"The friends of the fishers at sea light a taper to the saint they favor when they are homeward bound," explained she.

Soleiman slightly shook his head; this was not one interested in a fisher.

"Therefore, I implore the Trinity for those on the deep."

The Jew made a deprecatory wave of the hand; not that he dared doubt the efficacy of appeal, but he was superstitious in his own way. Even the Gentile may indulge in a little weakness.

"Have you another outlet to this den?" demanded she, suspiciously.

"Not that I know of." In looking round as she did, his head rubbed a swinging pigskin distended with wine and he shuddered.

"They are honest folk out there?"

"They are only fishers now. We had smugglers and

wreckers, for these old Biscayans are as fierce and greedy
as when the Roman found them tough birds to pick.   But
that is not here nor there—or rather," added he, with
the equivocation second nature to his fellows, "they are
not here."

"Go your way, then!   Mark, you are not to inquire
about me or my business at Salinas."

"From the moment I have been paid I trouble myself
and my dealer no farther!   You, too, have proved my
best friend in these worst of times.   It cost me heavily
to travel hither.   You have paid my wayfare back!   May
you be blessed in your undertaking!"

Then he said to himself: "It is undoubtedly a great
dame.   I may need her influence some day!"

Still he sighed.   His glimpse out of that crack had
shown him a leaden sky, fog rising over the shore, and
cold was on the blast.   But this person who had bought
the right to deal out the hospitality of the Petrel was one
to let even her servants battle it out in the open; a dog
she might allow in—a Jew, never!   He bowed with the
submissiveness of those long down-trodden, and crept
out under the sail.

The two lackeys had made their mules comfortable by
tying them under a projecting ledge, where D'Artagnan's
horse had shown them the best corner.   But they stood
there, erect, drawing their short cloaks round them,
propped on their staves, hardy as the Highlander watch-
ing his sheep.   They stood like sculptures.   They paid
no more heed to him than to the flecks of scum which,
sliced off a rising breaker, were hurled over them, hissing
spitefully.

In the north the sky was dyed indigo, with a small,
round, luminous spot, resembling a great brooch on this
mantle.   A seaman would call this a "storm eye."

Elizor shivered and tightened a rope belt around his
one ample outer wrap.

"If Pedro found a cave for the ruins of his inn stock,
why may I not find one for my head?"

Yet the idea of scrambling among those pit holes between rocks with jagged points, and coated with oysters
having razorlike edges, made him shiver again.   He un-

loosed his mule and dragged it out with reluctance on both parts. He sadly mounted.

The men paid so little attention to him that he did not care to speak to them. They probably believed that their mistress had given him a commission to carry out.

"Animal instinct is great," mused he. "This beast may take me to a refuge against the bad weather. Ah, I came in vanity and I depart in darkness, relying on a brute to deliver me from the shadows that walk at dead of night! Well, rather a robbers' cave than this, where that proud and haughty scorner presides at the board!"

For an instant the lady thus apostrophized appeared at the doorway. It was to speak to her footmen, however.

"Scipio! 'Sebio! one of you take rest while the other watches; sleep you, across this gap. Good ward, you others! God rest us!"

They responded affectionately and respectfully. They did not share the Jew's animosity.

His plodding mule carried him up to the cliff top.

He was too anxious about what might befall him to look behind. Had he done so, and out to sea, he might have seen, under the dense, stormy clouds and above the mist banks, swaying to and fro along shore, clinging at the bottom of the mass to the solitary bowlders, a kind of shooting star with a long trail of fiery sparks. It erratically skirted the shore, now darting outward to round a reef end, now half circling in a little pool, and sometimes held at a point which was with difficulty passed. Finally, by dint of great exertions on the part of those propelling the craft carrying this star at the prow, it could direct its course tolerably straight. It headed for the beach, under the cliff where the three candles feebly gleamed through the alabaster shade.

It was a twelve-oared galley, padded with cork bark on the bow and stern to ride more easily. On the bow sat a man, proof to the spray drenching him as the bow rose and fell. He held a steel wheel, striking against a flinty edge in a tinder box. This sent out its trail of scintillations.

If the Jew had not espied this, it was not so with the servant on guard, who roused his mates, just nodding off, and going to the cave mouth, rapped on the jamb, crying:

"Lady Jacinta! they are coming!"

Leaving his comrade to take his place, he ran down the slope as fast as the clinging mist allowed him, bounding over stones, slipping on the moss and weed, sliding in the sand, but reaching the edge, and even wading into it in eagerness.

The surge came up insiduously and ran back tumultuously, shaking him on his feet.

By this time the transient hostess of the Petrel had come to the door. She tore down the cloth and stood out a little, though having no hood or cloak.

"Thanks be!" cried she. "It is they! I had bad dreams, too! They saw my signal, which was put out in time. They are answering my servant. How timely! how swiftly they have traveled! Emergency must press for such rapidity."

The lackey went in to his mid-thigh. So he and the man at the prow, who had laid aside his fire lighter, clasped hands. This steadied the ponderous boat. Two of the men made a bridge of their ashen oars, which reached the shore, and got a rest on a stone. The bowman and the servant held this firmly.

Up in the stern rose a woman, wrapped in several mantles and boat cloaks. She threw them off, walked along the thwarts, supported reverently by the rowers, and finally went to the land over the two shafts, with a sure foot, however unused to such a precarious means. She still wore a gown and hood like a black penitent's, letting only her eyes be seen, shining gloriously.

Here Sebio, coming out of the water, offered his arm with the utmost respect, and the two climbed the ascent to the place where the new hostess eagerly awaited her.

If there were any awake in the village, it was impossible to perceive it, for the fog thickly enwrapped all.

Having disembarked the passenger, the galley was shoved off briskly, the men laid to the oars, and soon it disappeared in the shadow like a many-legged, creeping thing.

The pilot must have had profound knowledge of the coast to steer among the beetling crags and those sticking up in the seething surge.

"Thank Heaven, it is your highness!" ejaculated Donna Jacinta, clasing her hands.

"It is what is left of me. I am frozen up into a ball, though the seamen took great care of me," was the reply, in a rich voice.

"But, my lord?"

"Let us indoors!" there coming no direct reply. "I feel giddy with the whistling of the wind and the screaming of the sea birds."

As soon as they were within the cavern, the younger lady made the other sit at the high and splendid fire. Then, returning, she hung up the screen carefully, and took down the three lights with which she decked the table, sticking them in a stand of that plate which seemed stolen from a sanctuary.

The newcomer gave a look of intense disgust and unqualified disapproval to Pedro's interior, and, sighing, let the gown and hood glide down behind her.

"Dear duchess! but any port in a storm! Alack! what an *antre* to entice a Braganza and a Guzman-Gonzales into!"

"My sweet Jacinta, we must take things as they come!"

"That seems to have been the war cry here—a mass of pillage! But the duke?"

"I thought the Duke of Braganza would be here awaiting me!"

"And I, that he would be accompanying you!"

They looked at each other in anxiety, trepidation, and then stupor.

The presentiment of evil permeated both, though not easily dejected, as if the low brow of this shelter weighed upon them.

CHAPTER IX.

THE STORM.

If Soleiman, who had pronounced Donna Jacinta haughty, had stayed to see her visitor, he would have withdrawn that commendium and given it to the latter.

For Luisa de Guzman, Duchess of Juan of Braganza, was a Gonzago—that is to say, a pride of the proudest.

She had that matronly beauty which can be massive without being masculine. The ages preceding hers abounded with them—women who could wear those ponderous German panoplies in which a Life Guardsman would stifle. All was superabundance in her: her eyes were large as Juno's, but, unlike the Queen of Heaven's, not at all meek; her complexion was a golden cream, concording with the deepest vermillion of the lips, full and perfect as those of Albani's nymphs; her chin was square, though plumply rounded; it would be double in time, unless the vicissitudes which she courted—although a life of luxurious ease were hers if she chose it—forbade her any repose.

Above the medium, statuesque, but capable of indefinite movement as long as her spirit were fired, she was a Fleming in bearing but a Spaniard in vehemence of action and gesticulation. Her hands should have been short and plump, but they seemed trimmed by a Vandyke, they had the Italian vivacity, and she could have managed a reti-household of Turkish mutes by dumbshow alone.

At this moment she was not attired, as became her, in the heaviest of brocades, beaten gold jewelry and those enormous cameos which we cherish in museums and no lady thinks of wearing—they would seem burlesque. Her traveling dress was of strong stuff, bound with chamois, and without a thread of color; her belt, a *châtelaine*, was of fine Cordovan leather, with stiletto, scissors, fan and other appendages of the lady of a household and court; from a scent bottle with a perforated silver cap oozed the perfume known as *zizethum,* vulgarized as "civet" in a later age.

Luisa de Guzman-Braganza was fairly versed in the arts and graces of the retrograde Spanish and Portuguese courts, the latter a dull reflection. She was agreeable; liked by her dependents; it was said that "she is hard to offend, but hard when offended." If her wicked godmother, who with the good one bestows all one's mental powers, had been content with giving her Satanic beauty, all were well, but she had added his rebellious spirit—she wanted not to rank with the highest, but outrank them! Her husband would have been the most enviable of men, but for this incessant inciter. She left him no peace until her aim was attained.

At present the goal was obscured and distant.

His absence temporarily deepened her distress and impatience.

She wished to be queen.

She had the profound subtlety to gull the priests—they believed they would lose nothing, and she promised that they should be neutral; Braganza made friends easily, though secretive, slow and too tardy in generosity; he guaranteed that he would have the people of Portugal and her leading men. But they lacked what had become, in that era, the backbone of all conspiracies —gold. The great captains had degenerated; few of them would have refrained from striking a blow on the eve of a certain victory if a golden buckler were thrust between.

The precious metals had become invisible in that land where her navigators had brought them almost as ballast; the merchants hid them in their coffers; the princes stripped the gold lace off their coats not to have the Spanish tax collectors forestall them; the common people, from long since, were hoarding, and wearing rags not to betray their well-to-do condition. As for the Jews, recognized negotiators, they were persecuted almost out of existence.

"Your highness must have received my letter, or you would have found me?" asked Donna Jacinta.

The Storm.

"Yes; impossible to find Las Salinas without a clew. It is not on the map! I got it at your country place."

"Is all well at Floriador?"

"Perhaps you should say, 'Are all well?' Your brother has taken away nearly all the men to form a regiment for the king."

"Oh, that Jorge——"

"Who is the dragon to you?"

"He is the dragon, also, devouring our best blood and muscle! So he has gone down to our country place? Was my letter intact?"

"A gentleman—fie!"

"Gentlemen do odd things in these days when ladies have to play the amazon!"

The duchess smiled dubiously.

"I warrant nothing. Seals are so neatly sliced off and imitated. Dear lady of Floriador, who is safe?"

"I am not sorry you are out of it. My brother is one of those faithful who would arrest a queen-regnant if the king ordered so."

"Then, if the duke——"

"Faith! he would not shrink from laying hands on a duke's sword! So, I ask to know if the duke——"

"Returning to our Castle of Braganza, with the key to your new domicile, the duke showed me a formal invitation, very prettily worded, but a command all the same——"

"To go to the Escurial? Woe! they will broil him on that gridiron palace!"

"Not at all! Broils and brawls are forgotten! War between Spain and other powers over, the court gives itself up to *festas*—but for roasting a heretic now and anon there is positively nothing doing that would cause that angel-overseer, who looks at us through a peephole in the skies, to blush and avert the face. The duke went by that desire to attend a ceremony, the launching of a new vessel, the initial one of a fleet. They are going to transform the navy. No more bluff-bowed tubs, but snaky, fleet, sinuous craft which will travel like that serpent who shot out of the surge to devour Andromeda. It is a new fleet called 'The Holy Hope' by his majesty himself."

"Where did they build the novelty—San Sebastian?"

"My dear, they could not have gotten her out of that narrow-mouthed harbor. No; at San Andero del Mar, where, another novelty, they launch her sidewise."

"Oh, if the duke is in good hand; and, for your content, I agree that peace may be lulling suspicion to slumber, I will pester you no more on that head."

"What are your tidings?"

"Excellent! As you know, since Oviedo is thronged with foreigners studying at the university, no one tampers with the royal mail. So our letters thither do not meet with delay or interception. I received there missives from all points. The native party has become national—it augments daily—all enthusiasm, but not the kind which dispenses with keeping the knife sharp and the powder flask full. Revolution is a cannon ball, not a bubble!"

"I wish I had your flame!" though the duchess had nothing to envy in her confidante on that score.

"Was there intelligence out of the North? Will England help Spain in case of the internal disseverance?"

"I doubt it, though the block is a personal one: Prime Minister Olivarez hates the English in the form of its minister, the Duke of Buckingham, favorite of the King Charles—he thinks that the extravagant and fascinating courter of queens made eyes at his wife——"

"Ha, ha, ha!"

"I learned from Don Miguel d'Almeira——"

"Hush!" said the duchess.

"What for? None can hear. Beyond that firm rock, my true lackeys——"

"It is not that! Hark! the wind, the wind——"

"It will soon blow over," replied Donna Jacinta de Floriador, carelessly.

"Do you know that one of the oarsmen in my boar, on the way here, said that a storm was coming, in which we should hear the blunderbuss of the angel Gabriel a-roaring——"

"Droll expression! But why should not the superior spirits profit by improvements—you would not tie the archangel to his sword all these days?"

"Oh, what a wind! Do not blaspheme, prithee, child!"

Like the gun fired to commence a combat, a prodigious thundercloud burst overhead. The cliffs shook so as to precipitate masses into the waters at the foot, which, forced up innumerable channels, heaved the ground and ran out again, hissing, groaning, gurgling like so many half-drowned animals.

The canvas at the opening bellied in, floated off the hooks, and followed by the three serving men, bewildered, gyrating, groping, all were driven into the cavern, up-setting the table and benches, heavy though they were, putting out the lights, and sprinkling the end of the hollow with the embers. Then came a second gust, luckily laden with spray and rain, for it extinguished the sparks, though wetting the women and men.

"The earth will blow inside out," said one.

The other, on his knees, without daring to get up, began reciting the calendar of saints, without omitting one.

The lightning shimmered over the impenetrable clouds and died away, vainly trying to leak out of a split. The water which had been flung upon the beach rolled back and met a flurry of rain with an indescribable hissing. Through this head-high wall, vague and shifting, forms were seen mingling as if the sea had yielded up drowned seamen. But it was the women of the village, swamped out, huddling up their screaming children in anything handy, and racing up the slope. The waters chased them and then another gust propelled them hugger-mugger into the cavern; this time M. d'Artagnan's horse, more intelligent than the mules, accompanied the mass and blocked up the entrance. Had there been any more fugitives, they would have had to stay without.

The two ladies, shielded by the overturned table, had not been injured in the least, but were stupefied. The younger was the first to recover her wits, literally, for she said, in a voice meant to be in bravado to cheer her whimpering hearers:

"That is the heavenly blunderbuss, but it missed fire!"

This time the duchess did not chide. She, too, sat up and forced a laugh at their ludicrous situation.

"Mercy on us! It is the world's end at last, as he

prophesied in the 'Almanac of the Good Farmer!' " said a voice.

Since the eruption of Vesuvius, only ten years previously, those evil prophets who abound to the correction of the unduly mirthful, delighted in drawing ink from its soot to write "murkiness to man" in the pamphlets cherished by the populace, and which they had read to them by the less illiterate.

"Mother of Mercy, forfend that my husband should be on the sea!"

This wish was at the heart of all the fishers' wives, and they set up a wail which would have dispirited a bachelor without a heart. But Donna Jacinta was unaffected.

"Lady," said she to her mistress, "let us pray that he may not be exposed to the malice of men; it is even more to be dreaded than this wrath of the skies!"

"A young sprite!" muttered Sebio to his fellows; "but she is right.

CHAPTER X.

THE CUNNING OF A SEA DOG.

Some men are so gifted that they easily become friends
even with the most uncongenial. One of these was Louis
of Artagnan.

Hard drinking was a defect of soldiers then, so much
so that it was said that all that was gained by the cannon
went into the cup. But he remained sober, perhaps because a southern brain is hot enough already. But while
sober, this did not, for a wonder, offend boon companions.
He drew cards and he threw dice seldom, but lost as no
amateur has the fortitude to do, which made gamesters
comprehend that he was the player for higher stakes than
theirs.

He paid for a fan of price, a jewel, or a yard of lace,
here and there, but never was he cited as a Hector
dragged at any Aspasia's chariot wheel. Come of a
loquacious people, his prudence made him taciturn; still,
he was so capital a listener that the talkative unbosomed
to him sooner than to one of their numerous fraternity.

He had not been out twice with the fishers before he
became a messmate as indispensable as the paper box.
When, at whiles, the wind blew strong and the tiny shell
threatened to burst like a roast egg, he had distinguished
himself by little deeds of timeliness, recklessness, and
steadiness, which are prime qualities on shipboard.

Then he was a rough, but prompt surgeon; a physician
who could cure with a limited drug cabinet; and this endeared him in an age when science was mostly in the
hands of empirics.

Through all this novel experience, one thing puzzled
him: he was among Brothers of the Coast, undoubtedly a
secret fraternity, comprising all the wanderers who had
command of the ocean, from the Cape to the Skager
Rack; but it seemed without a leader. But, like the
bladder-wrack, the crushing of one bulb did not affect the
rest; all were inflated alike; one prominence was not

more prominent than the next or the farthest. What could a community be without governor, elder, dean?

"Head man?" said his mentor, the modest Pedro, "no! but we have a headsman, as you would see if you could see a traitor among us."

So D'Artagnan enlarged his field, each time he resumed his investigations, after the return to the Petrel, where the negress placidly reigned alone over her fire, like a seeker after potable gold over his *athanor* or perpetual furnace.

As the little smack was rarely three days off soundings, he shipped on larger ones, always with Pedro, his "blood brother." They carried cured fish to exchange for native produce along the Algerian coast, making mock of the corsairs, and "passed" closely-packed goods ashore in Spain under the noses of the coast guards, conveniently going blind.

"I could swear that they were ammunition cases," thought the musketeer. "Ho, ho! those whom I heard in the interior declare in a bated breath that with arms they would stir up a fire the king could not put down— they will have their boast put to the test!"

One time, homeward bound, D'Artagnan suddenly slapped his pilot on the shoulder, and said, heartily:

"*Peccavi!* I am a fool to go a-sea for what lay under my hand! Why, it is you who are steward, if not commander-general, of the Brothers of the Coast!"

The ex-host laughed as heartily.

"I thought you knew it all along, and were playing with your fish!"

"I see the cunning of you sea dogs. Would ever your government spy suspect, in a happy-go-lucky, devil-may-care slush-tub like you, the admiral of so imposing a navy! No more than that in your head, seeming to confine no more sense than is in a doornail, the faculties operate in perfection which would mar a prince or make a peasant. Pedro, thou art a stone for the temple! thou art read by the sermon in you, as the English poet says whose play I saw in a visit to London."

"At the same time, think you I would give all my leisure to trim, shape, and mellow a raw, inapt, intractable 'prentice like you! By the holy thumb-and-finger marks on the mackerel! you are a gentleman of the sword from 'heel to head, and I strongly suspect that you aim, not at a sackful of crowns, but at one alone—the golden! and consecrated by the great Papa at Rome!"

"The only imperishable golden crown that a man may attain, if he goes the right way about, is that too far on high to be my portion, unless I am altered more thoroughly than by your lessons. Dear Pedro, there was once a man who made himself wings and flew up, up, up, until the sunbeams singed his wings just as he was peering through a crack in the ether—he fell down as the deuce did."

"That luckless wight fell on the land! Now, had he fallen into the sea, a deep cushion, the sea!"—he blew a kiss over the dancing waves—"he had been living to this day. Ah, *messire*, it is to the hasty climber that comes sudden falls.

"Now, we seafarers hold the head steady to be independent, and no man can be greater than the independent."

"You are the wild dog talking to the one who has worn the collar," remarked the king's officer.

"You look on us draining the pannikin of water squeezed out of the leach of the mainsail when we cannot get Schiedam; eating oat cake when we have no bolled flour bread; dining on a slice of lard and a broiled hake when we cannot do better! All this time we quaff the *elixir vitae*—content!"

D'Artagnan fixed his eye on the suddenly eloquent speaker, without interrupting or mutely criticising by a frown or a smile.

"You are right to keep the hatches battered down; but, if you have not made my acquaintance on a long journey, you have in a small inn, and this coffin of a cabin of the *Xiphias*. Why do I confide in you, a stranger? I will out with it!

"Never since that warlock-priest, in France, Urbain Grandier, captivated a whole convent, was a crew of the lawless so besotted by a mortal as by your lordship! You have heard the priest tell of another world than the land— it is the sea! We who toil on it, and are buried in it, are as remote from the landsmen as the people in those golden galleons which sail above! But the heart is a kind of *cistus* that rock-rose, you know, which clings by one thread if all the rest are broken!

"We came from the land from which the possessors shove us if we linger, after having lightened our pouches! So we love the land, in our dreams, anyway! and we want to live on the land, once in a while, and die there, though we pass too long on the restless billows.

"I myself, look you, captain! tended sheep on the Odriano Mountains over there, where all are shepherds, but the whitecaps drew me out seaward from my flock's white heads. But it comes to me out here that those lambs will not grow if the wolves do. The tyrant in Madrid wears fleece dyed in our lambs' blood!"

"Friend, brother," replied the chevalier, "the colors of a flag are like that dye of old which could not be effaced or diluted. The flag we are swaddled in should be our winding-cloth. Spain has her castles on the deep! the lion's roar is heard in the beating of the sea on her hundred shores—may we not have a faithful follower of King Philip here, where we are of all nations?"

"Hark!" said Pedro, after a pause, lifting his eyes and his hands to point. "That is an Arragonese. I will let him answer!"

Up on the stumpy mast of the *Swordfish*, three-master xebec, more often seen between Africa and Italy than off San Sebastian, a seaman, suspended, spread out like a spider in its web, mending the rigging, was singing:

> "If the Dutch or the Spaniard
>   Come but to oppose us,
>   We will thrust them up at the mainyard
>   If they venture to nose us!"

"But that's English!"

"That is his patriotism! of no country, but of all—it was all one world when Mother Earth was first heaved head up out of the salt water! A man's country is anywhere he is not fleeced. *Deus Protector Nestor!* that is our *Kapitan-pasha*, as the Arabs say!"

"Why should the sea rush upon shore?"

"To wash away the worthless!"

"With what particular aim?"

"A sure end! The people have risen against their

lieges, but ever their blood has enriched the ground of which their enemies took the crop."

"Very true! they rose too soon or too late. You cannot sever the bull neck unless you cleave in the very nick!"

"That's what I say—as well never as to no purpose! This time we attempt not, unless we can accomplish!"

"I suppose these things will be done, and done again, as long as there are aspiring men lusting for lording it!"

"You mistake, brother! me, a king? Nay, nay; I believe in taking down tall things, but not in setting up small things. Do you know, neighbor, what we Iberians are? capable of managing ourselves on the level. Have you not heard the jingle:

"A noble's but air, and proud flesh but dust is!
It's we commons make the lord, as the clerk makes the justice!"

CHAPTER XI.

WIND AND WAVE WAIT NOT.

"Plainly, captain, you propose a popular uprising," said the Frenchman. "What after the troubled sea goes down?—a dead level, with only wrecks, and no head above the calm?"

"No, let there be a king, as always. But bound in hemp of our twining, not silken fetters, which courtiers contrive."

"This is a business which, like your stock fish, requires a long soaking!"

"It's early and late we have been wishing. We are the grandsons of those who saw Portugal its own master. The time has come for Fate, as the Moslems say, to suffer us to succeed."

"What have you thought out?"

"Well, my lord, on the sea we fear nobody, since we are everybody. At any port where any warship touches, I can call half the company to desert. On land whom should we fear? What is a noble now? no longer a man of brawn who lived cased in brass—'lobsters' feathers,' as the boys say! a dancing-master! it is put in the ballads that your great minister danced a saraband to amuse your queen! They eat their estates at a lick, and haste to the court for a perpetual bribe, a fat office! They lock free, I grant ye! but the wildest and highest of their flings is a dog's in a string! Do they even live? They cringe, they flaunt, and they caper—so does an Italian puppet! and they die like a beast, though on velvet—not having done any good!"

"Have a care!"

"That's it! we have all the cares!"

"I heard in the south provinces—'the king's arm is long!'"

"Longer is the arm of the needy! Before the year be out, there will be a deed done betwixt Cadiz and Oporto

which will not be painted on the wall of the Hall of
Spanish Victories at Madrid."

"My brother, it is no common danger you are courting!"

"Without danger one cannot overcome it!"

D'Artagnan shook his head; this peasant had an answer for everything he said.

"We lack the leader who will answer for everything.
A general, a chief who can command men——"

"And money?"

"Men to begin with, as that we have the most of. One
who can divert nature and natures to his will—for we
Portuguese are a stubborn, hidebound folk, who would
take poison from a brother-hand and not the counter-
bane from a foreigner. Above all, we want a man who
will see that the conquerors have the conquest, share for
share, as the Brothers of the Coast divide."

"Have you the forces for such a one to employ?"

"Portugal is heaving with impatience, like that sea.
Half Spain, on the border, through intermarriages and
intercourse—if only through the smugglers—goods are
so dear! intervolutions of petty trades, blighted by large
merchants' transactions, killing the market for the season
—now, these are friendly, at the least. If only, if only,"
went on the innkeeper-statesman, gravely, and fastening
his eyes in his turn on the musketeer, "Spain were
threatened on her hither frontier! But her direst enemy
is a broken serpent——"

"Cardinal Richelieu a broken man? You may break a
serpent, but it will not die until sunset!" retorted D'Artagnan, animatedly and with pride. "And not yet is his
sun gone down!"

This abrupt, self-betraying enthusiasm confirmed the
rebel's conjectures, no doubt; but he beat his broad
breast, as though pummeling a last doubt into senseless-
ness, and in a lighter tone went on:

"I think we may hope."

"My comrade, if it were not for hope, the heart would
break!" cheeringly, but enigmatically, replied the Gascon
adventurer.

"You understand," insisted Pedro as if he wanted his

hearer to harbor no doubt on his side, "we have the force."

"Force without forecast is of little use. Hark ye, the old Spain, which made the Moors walk the plank into Gibraltar Bay, is not so sick that it will not survive a bleeding and the cauterization of the inquisition—ah, you have a tough bone to exercise your square jaw upon."

"Tough becomes tender by pounding," returned the sailor, sententiously.

"The pounding will not be all on one side."

"We catchers of fish do not mind a slap or two of the sturgeon's tail!"

"Well said; but to the immediate prospect! Is not that what you call a dirty sky? It occurs to me that the only fishing for several days will be the fishing for man, and that by Davy Jones, to line his locker!"

"Brother, none could be more right—there will be a flagellation of Neptune!"

"Like that a Persian king gave him for wrecking his flotilla? Remember that the lashing did not restore the lost ships?"

"It is on us will fall the lashes!" said Pedro, solemnly.

Standing up on the verge of the midships, after blowing a shrill whistle, he shouted so as to be heard from the *Swordfish's* snout to the farther end:

"All men on deck! The king storm of the year is upon us!"

Being a volunteer, the Frenchman had no station. But, in spite of the increasing agitation, he kept his seat on the rail, murmuring:

"This tarry sage is right as to Portugal boiling up to the brim, like this ocean—he may be right as to controlling more spirits than I reckoned on conjuring up; but will it suit our premier to have Portugal rip itself from Spain, just to be a larger republic than Venice? I must chance all! There is no time to consult France. For what would this messenger know of politics? Meantime, if we ride out of this turbulence—it is enough! and then—— 'Oh, to-morrow!' as these fellows say!"

Suddenly to the northeast, whither no one was staring, a low boom was heard, and a rumble. Yet the sky there was unclouded.

"What is that, Pedro? A thunderstorm on the Adrianos that you spoke of?"

"That," replied the master, studying by listening for the reverberation, "that is made thunder—man's great guns, sir!"

"Why, there is a truce! Spain and France think of court balls!"

"It is cannon, and at sea. I, too, thought the eternal foes were pausing, but who can tell the duration of truces when treaties last so little long? But we shall hear no more out of that quarter. Because why? the wind is already tossing the white scud over there, as we look, and they must secure the guns or have them dash through the side! We shall be in their midst before long, swept before the blast like lamb's wool over the furze. Look at the *Swordfish*, well-named—ill-omened thing! how she bends two ways at once in her foolish elongation! A pipe-stem, absurd, as the nautilus in these restless waters. They had better have kept her in the soft, inland-locked sea, than let her poke her slender snout into the choleric Atlantic!"

The mariner must have been in a bad way to blame the deck on which he stood.

There came up and there sped over in an incredibly brief time for so much power to be manifested, a gale which should be memorable, but a logbook is written in the lull and the calm. Pedro, like them all, soaked from head to foot, while his men clung to ropes and were twisted in them as the pliant staffs whipped, roared in D'Artagnan's ear, though touching:

"Still afoot, eh? I thought you might have stepped off and walked ashore! Well, that was a lasher, eh? but it's a lady's fan tap to what is coming! Take advantage of the pause to make your peace tighter than those between kings! It is all one now with our schemes and connivings! To think that King Philip will sleep the sounder because the poor *Xiphias* foundered under his guns at San Sebastian!"

The long, narrow, rounded xebec wallowed in the trough, when she did not bend between two waves as if to break in two; half the time one-half of her was smothered if the other end hooked itself upward. Nothing but her elasticity saved her. She was so sinuous that she seemed a water snake. The men breathed only at intervals, when they emerged from the weight of water, like so many grampuses, rising mid-high to snap at flying-fish.

"It was a big bait," thought the musketeer. "To try to secure the Brotherhood of the Sea for my master; but I am a luckless angler, who will be dragged to the bottom with my willing catch! It's a poor lookout for the courtier waiting me at the Petrel! He will not set the seal or my old meed as a model of punctuality! A fine representative of Cardinal Richelieu, who is wont to say: 'Non-punctuality is a kind of falsehood!' This time I shall be an eternity behindhand! Ah, can ghosts redeem debts?"

Suddenly his very mind, entangled in this sarcastic mood characteristic of him, leaped out of it all, and spurred his body to action.

To a man of thoughts, any violent movement was a relief.

By the twisting and wriggling, the seams had opened in a score of places, though the timbers kept unsplit. The low waist was long since full of water, but at each cant some spilt out. But now, as in digging a well, the spade strikes a hidden fount, it welled up in the middle like a water volcano.

"A leak! She has sprung a leak!" was the low wail from the quivering mouths in those white countenances.

Pedro stood knee-deep there, unable to retain footing on the rounded hatch-wale, but erecting the few but imperative operations as if on dry ground.

Three or four lightly-built fellows, knife in teeth or hatchet swinging from a lanyard at the wrist, were furling up flaps of sail or cutting away ropes jammed in the blocks and apt to work mischief.

With buckets and salt shovels the rest were bailing out the ever-flowing well, indefatigable as the Danaïdes, but as useless. They unfortunately believed in their skipper, and his prophecy that this stroke was not the lightest of them dashed their ardor. There was only one boat, and that was dragging by a rope at the stern.

The French cavalier had no bucket to seize up. Beside him, however, was a water-breaker, lashed on two

rests. With a gigantic effort he wrenched it loose and
then extricated it from the wet and yielding ropes. Some
of these remained on it, forming a kind of handle, one
a side. With this enormous vase he leaped into the pool
and, calling to a huge seaman, he said, in his loudest
voice, as if cheering his men in a charge:

"To it, boys! Is the good *Xiphias* to go down under
a shower of brine like the ass of the fable, whose bags
were sopped in crossing the ford? Nay, never believe it
—not when we have yet a work to do! Cease to call out
for compassion and Our Lady of Good Succor! and keep
your breath for the 'scouse yet to come! As for this
wasted pickle, even throw it back whence, it, uninvited,
came! Don't take it heavily, because the West Indies
have breathed us a zephyr! It will not be as lasting as
the Grand Seignior's siege of Cansia, which has lasted
twenty year without the gallant Venetians talking of giving it up!"

He sang to the thrumming of the taut ropes as to a
guitar:

> "Blow the wind never so fast,
> It will lower at the last!"

"Beat on, you blusterer! Never yet did you bully the
true tar into moaning with the Prophet Job: *'Misereatur
me!'* Only to adorn a weeping friar's grace, but not cut
into the mainmast foot with a mariner's hacker!"

In a flurry hail hurtled on the hard-as-iron waterproof
caps like a fusillade.

"Aha!" said the French captain, no less merrily, "are
we in Pope-town now, with the dames showering candy
balls upon us? Faith, the donna who pelted me had her
hand lately to the suds—that tasted salty! Oh, it is the
spice-box holder up above that Don Aquarius, who forgot
to boil the water in his can! But bail away, my hearties!
bail for your hopes to travel into the nether world without a pocket of ice! How it would sizzle down there
and bespatter Abaddon and Company! Bail away what
is our *bale!*"

Here the rain fell in a spout, which depressed the heads
and bowed the backs.

"Heads up! though the captain himself ducks! Ah,

the *chafarize* (Moorish fountain) of fresh water has its turn now—the Moor asserts such a sweet-water pump stands in the exact center of the Eden—so that we now know that we have been swept round to the other side from that spot; and it disproves the philosopher who maintained that the world is immovable! I call it a bark which now is sailing round the moon! More sweet water—thanks, it will unsour the brine!"

Three men had replaced one another on the other part of the cask which he had used as a dipper, but he was as animated as at the first.

"Come, come; is Jack's spirit to fall low, as never was his trade! Soul of Admiral Noah, older you see, that seaman, than your kings and grandees! If Jack dies, he dies. Did not Queen Juno declare that death is the greatest boon the gods can give? Nevertheless, I am in no hurry to be beholden to the goddess, bless her—and save us! Well, we die, chirruping—gay as a gypsy, dressed up for an archangel on Corpus Christi day!

"You may fill me with salt water, but never with the belief that we were fondly brought into this world to be foolishly spirited out of it! Yet, if we die here, out here, look at the fine last laugh we have at them—the doctor can get no fee, and Old Hairy, who hugs his oven a night like this, no soul! So sing—in the name of the Muses, sing—to clear your throats to the rattle of the pails coming up—so, so! full, and coming—whoop! empty!

> "When we are dead,
> We'll take no heed
> Of what they say behind us!"

"So, the congregation will join in the chant:

> "So, pitch it out!
> Now, in! now, out!
> And out, and out, and out again!"

Impossible to resist this man—this force of nature, and good-nature at that.

"Hark to him, lads!" said Pedro, beaming with satisfaction and reinspired like his crew, to say nothing of his being delighted at his judgment being confirmed. In his sea-going tub he had found a Man! "This is not one born to drown! Stick to him, and we shall be saved even as one man at the end of a line may save nine! Keep on and baste the ocean with its own sauce!"

Suddenly the darkness lifted.

"I spy!" said the Frenchman, "there softly slides the sun out again!"

CHAPTER XII.

THE MESSENGER.

By one of those meteorological freaks, born to tantalize man made a football to the elements in strife, there was a long break in the vaporous screen above.

The clouds were in more than one layer, even crossing in one case—the two trying to outrace. What had passed a point, piled up as if a sudden check had come. The broken masses took shapes and the accumulation had the air of contending columns of gigantic phantoms.

The sunlight was of an unnatural tint, like flame seen through smoke. In the chasm, dazzling by the contrast all around it, Sol appeared, a dull-polished disc, flashing down separated shafts to the foaming, spray-plumed waters. In this aureole, a myriad birds, like gulls whose nests had been disturbed, not all of the sea, flew and circled, now low, now high, confused, jostling, falling over on their backs to use their claws, falling, and pursued by ravenous things which the storm had not weakened in ferocity. They screamed as to the monstrous clavichord to which the vessel and its tight rigging might be likened, as she ceased to roll so deeply.

To the northeast, once again, the mock thunder was heard.

There were broad flashes, like sheet lightning.

All looked in that direction, against that evanescent golden screen, forgetting that, to the west, the enemy advanced with reinforcements.

There was sympathy for man above all other sentiments.

Two or more ships were seen there, all of clumsy fashion, low down, as if also water-logged like the *Xiphias*. These had banks of oars, which caught the light like drops of quicksilver. One or two more, whose masts showed like threads, had their sails almost all reefed into nothingness.

They had flags, but, though these were flat as boards, nothing could be discerned at this distance.

"Dutch!" said a graybeard.

"Spanish!" said another, as old, but as keen of sight.

"The galleys are Spanish," said Pedro, "and so the *galiot*—look at the peculiar square-sail forward, which makes her a brigantine. It helps her, too, now! All are Spanish."

"Strange, then," said D'Artagnan, straining his eyes; "the bow-chasers of the galleys are firing on their own!"

"It does look so—but, no! they are firing past her, over her, too, which means good marksmen——"

"See, see—two vessels interlocked——"

"Oh, ho!" cried Pedro, after a pause, "I know what that is—a Frenchman!"

"French?"

"What does it look like? A brig and a schooner lashed together, stem and stern. But it is one ship, that!"

To the murmur of incredulity, he went on confidently: "She was built at Croisic, and they intended her to cruise in the Mediterranean; but they feared the Spanish would stop her at the Straits. She would have given them a run, though! Look at her—fit for a head wind, as you see her now. And on a side wind, she went a wonder. They called her *Le Messier,* that is 'The Watcher'—for she is a spy and a dispatch boat above all! With those four masts, for that jigger is a mast, though they can strike it down——"

"The three others are not firing on her," interrupted D'Artagnan.

"So, they are not! Oh, they have driven another target between them and the shore, and spite of the storm, or rather with its aid, they will wreck her on the rocks! Oh, we are pretty Christians to be so bent on destroying a ship exposed to ruin anyway!"

"At all events," said the Frenchman, seeing nothing in the fog and gloom over the land, "it is not a battle between these!"

"Though we cannot see the flying one," resumed Pedro, "she returns the fire, for there are oars without holders in the hold. But what do they care for the con-

victs? They crack on. I never saw such set effort to
rack and ruin in my born days!"

"There is something also wrong with the Frenchman,"
remarked the musketeer, anxiously. "You understand
these matters—what is ailing her?"

"Strain! too long and narrow—she lays over us by
thirty feet and has scarcely as broad a beam! She has
broken her back, I fear! But all is one if she is sinking——"

"Master, we are sinking!" whispered to his captain a
slim, frail man, almost a boy, who, from a smattering
of learning and writing, was the supercargo, purser and
clerk on board the *Xiphias*.

This was enough to draw attention from the chase and
the French craft on the outer edge of the attacked and
attackers.

D'Artagnan sighed as he wrenched away his eyes.

The hold was sounded.

"Solid water to the false keel," grimly remarked
Pedro to the musketeer, whom he regarded as his lieutenant. "Cease bailing! If we are water-logged, and
we show no rag aloft, the gale may overblow us, since
we lay so low—for these winds glance upward."

Perforcedly idle, drifting with bare poles, the helm
little obeyed, the doomed crew resumed peering toward
the scene of the strange conflict.

Reconciled to their fate, their curiosity was irrepressible about their neighbors in similar or worse jeopardy.

All at once, having probably estimated their own state
correctly, but unable to contemplate with serenity the
cruel attack on the vessel invisible to the *Xiphias*, but
seen by the *Messier,* the latter fired a gun and ran up
a flag of great size on the last of its four masts. This
was clear, as a mass of rain, like a curtain, fell between
her and the land and caused her outlines to stand out.
This same cloud entirely veiled the disappeared vessel.

As if maddened by the first prey balking them, the
three Spanish trimmed sail and ceased rowing on one
side, to bring a broadside to bear on this challenger.

The galleys had long pivot-guns, which were now
brought to bear on the same point.

"The flag of France—it looks novel—a kind of special

ensign which has no meaning to me. They are at war again—for this is an act of war!"

"Or of gallantry! If that is a crippled ship, to intervene on behalf of the stranger is fine!" declared the officer of fortune.

The *Messier* passed between the galleys, but fired in passing, and continued to fire from stern-guns in the cabin after drawing off. The Spanish brigantine came into range thereby, and the two exchanged shots, ineffectual on account of the heaving sea.

The galleys showed a confused, struggling mass in the midships, like a knot of snakes. The oarsmen had been hit hard. They fell off; the banks of oars were shortened, bodies were thrown over, and they headed round as for San Sebastian.

Short of oars, the chance of reaching that port was slight.

Not to share the fate of the unknown enemy, their bows were turned seaward, but the wind and the wash kept them southeastward.

The Spanish brigantine found the shooting wild, hauled in the guns, closed the ports, secured the long guns, and, keeping more out to the sea than the galleys, sped along; but returned from time to time, as if to make sure that the disappeared vessel should not be joined by the Frenchman.

This last had other work to do.

Strained, as Pedro had perceived, the shock of the guns had further injured her. In a kind of despair, which induces human beings to try to die together, she steered for the poor *Xiphias,* now a-wash.

Perhaps, though, it was to assist her with its boats, which, it could be seen, were being got ready for launching.

The *Xiphias* showed hardly any freeboard by this.

"She is buoyed up by what comes in below," commented Pedro, grimly. "I am as likely to sit in that cabin again as in St. Peter's chair."

"Our boat, I think, is gone," observed the amateur seaman, timidly.

"Long ago, my gentleman! If those spars will not make a catamaran, it will be because they shall have been carried away by the next gust, or splintered to splints for broken grasshoppers' legs!"

"Are they coming to take us off? Even if we are not Spanish, in their eyes, humanity dictates that course. Moreover, I will appeal to them in their tongue, and I might use a powerful charm."

"Who knows but that, in half an hour, they may prefer the *Swordfish's* to their own decks? We are down to the edge, but we will float; our cypress planks repel water like the devil's coat holy *ditto,* whereas they have pine under them, and that pine of Old Gascony sops you up the water like a toper's tongue the wine! But, ship, boat, or catamaran, we must pull through the second stroke of the whip! Manuel, the skipper's last act of duty!"

The ship-carpenter had long since made ready. He had brought up from below a large, strong, well-oiled and copper-banded puncheon. It was about two-barrel capacity. It was lengthened strangely by a conical cap at each end, like a pocket, one completely sewed and tarred, the other with a slit prepared for drawing tightly by a cord. The caps were of stout leather, saturated with oil and toughened to resist jagged joints and cutting edges.

The passenger regarded this combination of rounded case and flexible pouch with curiosity.

"The tub ends both ways in a purse fit for a giant spendthrift," commented he. "Are you going to stow your silver in it, as the Turk packs up his in saddlebags, and confide it to the waves?"

"I shall confide our treasure to it!" was Pedro's calm reply.

"What do you call this thingamy?"

"A kedge—the North fishers say *kaggi*—a barrel used as a buoy. The Mediterranean fishermen say, 'Regulus' cask'!"

"Oh, Regulus, the Roman general whom the Carthagenians rolled down the mountain side in such a keg?"

"Save that they drove a few spikes into it and forgot to clinch them, so that his descent must have made him laugh, if he were ticklish!"

Nobody laughed. It was not a jesting place or scene.

The Messenger. 95

"But what mountains, save of water, and what Regulus have you at hand for the roll down hill?"

"Manuel!" called the skipper, without direct reply.

His supercargo saluted. He was a dreamy, studious clerk, resolved for his fate, perhaps, but his sallow complexion was greenish and unpleasant; his eyes kept flitting, and watered.

"Boy," said the master, solemnly, "you have been under my eye and hand, both tender to you, so long that it would take an age to even up. But you can repay me in a few hours. You are young, lasting, patient. You may survive tossing in that tierce, and be hurled upon the shore better than your elders."

"Oh, this is our Regulus?" muttered the French envoy, studying the student.

The latter did not relish this narrow means of escape. But one could guess that he was glad to escape the all-comprising doom.

"It is but a coffin, but even a coffin may buoy up a man —fit, too, the coffin, since it will contain the secret for which we were all prepared for the grave."

The young man twitched his ears and his dull eyes blazed. He seemed to be nearer an end weighing upon him. He gave D'Artagnan a brief and not benevolent glance.

"This is a good day," said he, unctuously, "for an act of faith," wringing his hands; "the day of the Commemoration of the Winding Sheet!"

"It is?" queried Pedro, scoffingly. "We have hit to a dot, lads! We shall be shrouded in the greatest pall ever woven by the Three Grim Spinsters! Behold the warp!"

His finger indicated the West. For three parts of the vault there was impenetrability. No worlds beyond. Incessant rolling of thunder was not once preceded by a glint of lightning, and yet such a din perpetually threatened the flash. It was this ceaseless expectancy which snapped the nerves.

Near the horizon, but undulating so as to mislead the observer, a grey line was now and again phosphorescent. It was the ridge of surge running before the hollow where the hurricane scooped up the waters thirty feet under. All was churned, seethed, compacted, and yet diffused, rushing before the wind at sixty miles the hour. Occasionally the gusts outstripped this movable wall and smote the turbulence so heavily that it smoothed it into oily circles, iridescent as molten metal. Then up-bubbled the beaten-under surge, and all became a creamy white.

Before the great mass of risen waters in the crest of mist, like lumps studded with feathers awry, flocks of seabirds and schools of fish, interspersed, were tossed about and forward, caught as they fell, flung ever onward and onward; hurried to sea, eagles and dogfish ceased to catch prey which they could not bear away, and fought one another like desperate souls, doing all the hurt they could in the sea eddies of Malice; below them in the yeast which flecked their glossy sides, porpoises disported in the unstable playground.

The stoutest and ablest seaman quailed, but, imperturbable, Pedro went on:

"In this casing you may reach land."

So deep a murmur of incredulity from the old sea dogs hailed this attempt to cheer that Manuel turned white under the chin.

"If you are cast well upon land," continued the skipper, "slit the hide and recreate yourself with the provender herein!"

The cook had fastened within the cask by lashings a loaf of bread, instead of the crumb, of which a hunk of cooked beef had been substituted, and a bottle of genuine Colares, fortified with Guinea pepper and ginger.

"Thereupon hasten to the Petrel Inn and deliver this message to the representative there of Braganza's lord."

The plotter spoke so clearly that it was plain that he did not expect any of his hearers but this one would survive to disperse the information.

"What message, master?" inquired the supercargo, holding out eagerly a trembling hand as for a writing.

"That the Brotherhood of the Coast are pledged to place Braganza on the redeemed throne of their country!"

"Long live the country!" exclaimed the seamen, with bated breath.

"Amen!" muttered Manuel, with forced emphasis.

"Ha, ha!" uttered the Frenchman, nipping his mus-

"That knowledge must not go with that dog."   See page 97.

tache between his teeth as if surprised, yet expecting this announcement.

"And that France assists, in the person of His Majesty of France's captain of the bodyguard!"

All started at D'Artagnan, who almost blushed like a scholar at this unexpected exposure of his standing. He twirled and pulled at his luckless mustache, which was often the sole victim of his vexation.

The publicity pained him.

But then he shook his head; after all, this news would not travel far. But he liked less than ever that the sole porter should be the young and pious clerk.

"Good!" was the word struggling on Manuel's quivering lips. "Thrust me into the cask and sew it up!"

"Stay!" interrupted D'Artagnan, authoritatively. "A boy like you would only go under with the weight of that tidings. Let me still carry the secret which I have supported for long!"

All started. Surprised and disappointed in his heroic devotion, Manuel wavered. Then recovering and forming his purpose quickly, he leaped over the "carcase" of wood and skin, as if disdaining its protection, and stood by the side rail, yelling above the screaming of the gale through the shrouds:

"I commend myself and the traitorous message to the deep! God 'a' mercy!"

"Seize him!" shouted the French officer as if he had commanded this quaking deck all his life.

"Hold him!" echoed Pedro, dashing forward.

Both were too slow. The supercargo had leaped as the rollers swelled up to his feet and the scud seethed over his head.

With the quickness of a madman D'Artagnan flung off all that might encumber him, kicked off the loose sea-boots, shook off the sou'wester, and only pausing briefly to see where the swimmer came up, he bounded out as the waves receded from him, as if shrinking at so much headlong intrepidity. In the air his trumpet voice outrode the furious blast!

"That knowledge must not go with that dog!"

CHAPTER XIII.

THE THIRD LASH.

In a trice after his plunge out of sight the last diver's head and shoulders appeared in the surge not far from the other's. The latter shot up and toward him as if impelled by a spring or by the desire for self-preservation.

"Arouse!" said Pedro, angrily. "Why not hand the captain a rope? God knows we have plenty of trailing lines!"

In a few minutes the musketeer was drawn to the side and helped inward. He had caught the cord with one hand and with the other retained Manuel with a close grip at the nape. He dropped the youth on the slippery planks like a caught fish. His fingers were entangled by a cord round the man's neck; it was a blessed string to which was attached a scapulary or similar devout charm. Manuel was sick with the swallowed brine—he made but a feeble motion to recover his talisman.

But the glance of venom was not feeble with which he visited his deliverer. He shifted the glance upon his captain, but the latter's countenance could not be more forbidding.

"Body and bones!" exclaimed the captain. "He is a traitor! A boy who has drunk from my pocket flask! who was nursed out of the black measles in my own bunk! Who has been kept, when with a broken arm, in my own inn! whom I saved from the press-gang of the *Santa Catarina!* Where will faith be found now?"

"The storm! the storm!" screamed out a man at the tiller, hanging on it for a hold, since it had been abandoned after being lashed firm by the steersmen. His face was pale as the luckless Manuel's.

"Justice above all, above life and mercy!" returned Pedro. "On my hope of salvation we must make an example of this runagate! Maybe heaven will let one survive to be living witness that the Brothers, in the teeth

of being washed out, did their duty! Run a line through
the sheaf at the gaff and let's have the slip-noose at the
end tossed hither. I hang him with my own fist, though
the rope I pulled let loose the very sluicegates for another
deluge!"

A thunderous peal responded, without correcting the
blasphemer.

Meanwhile, D'Artagnan had shaken himself and
donned a shirt and overjacket not much drier than his
discarded garments.

"Dear friend, a little more wet will not hurt one who
will never more be dry again—or be too dry! Look at
this!"

He had profanely turned the scapulary inside out. It
contained a stamped leather cross of St. James, bearing
the letters "S. H."

Meanwhile the noose had been fitted to the clerk's
neck, following the red weal made by D'Artagnan's tugging at the necklace when seizing his prey.

"Expound!" cried the musketeer, knitting his brow.

Manuel replied only with the insulting silence of despair.

"S. H. is the *Santa Hermandad*," interpreted Pedro,
hastily. "The Holy Brotherhood——"

"The Inquisition?" said the passenger, twirling the
token in his fingers as if it scorched them. "Oh, this is
a brother, is it—holy!"

"Yes, they are brothers, as Cain was a brother,"
sneered the captain of the vessel. "Ready to bowse
him up!"

A gunshot was heard to leeward.

In spite of the wind the Frenchman had made progress
toward them.

"She signals," said a seaman, laughing, "for a pilot!"

"Very well," said Pedro, dryly, "hoist away! Here is
the pilot to Perdition port, whither we are all bound!"

Whereupon twenty pairs of hands drew up the body.
Whatever the wild seamen's unanimity in thought, it is
the rule, on a free cruiser, to put all hands into every deed
so that none may turn king's evidence as less concerned.

Throttled by a sailor hanging to the feet to prevent

their convulsions also, consciousness was immediately lost and the figure swung violently, but limp.

The spasm might be merely the vibration of the twisting strands.

Angered at this apparent contempt to its demands, the stranger fired a gun which was shotted; yet not to strike, one may suppose; but it ricochetted on a heaving wave just as the *Xiphias* gave a plunge and recovered slowly, and the bullet, cutting a piece of iron firming the shrouds, sent it flying. It cut the rope like a bar-shot and the body fell into the waves. The sailor who had clung to the feet, fell on the rail by a clever jerk of the body and drew himself inboard.

As if that shot had burst the reservoirs overhead the volume of rain descending was incalculable, allaying the turbulence; but close on its detonation was heard a more powerful roar—the winds were hurling all before them as they made the final charge in this battle, and the two other onsets were skirmishes.

The Frenchman had seemed about to run down the three-master, but this blow separated them like two puff-balls. The water-logged one was lifted so high that torrents gushed out of unsuspected gaps and fissures, and she spilt half her deck-wash. The terrible friction engendered electricity in superabundance.

"The Candles of St. Elmo" topped the broken mast-stumps and wandered, like corpse-lights in a cemetery, over the ship, again submerged.

Once more she rose, like a swimmer trying to cast off the water mantle; it was the last effort of inherent buoyancy.

It seemed as if she would sink with her masts held up by the wind in the sails, torn loose and half unfurled; but the attempt only broke them a second time—near the deck, which was covered with the long splinters and the snapped rigging in inextricable confusion.

As if that weight were too unbearable, the sheer hull rolled and sank slowly, severing some ropes and tearing all free from the spars. Over this network and rude raft clambered, in and out of the next to impenetrability, several stripped and desperate figures. Others had caught blindly at trailing ropes and were caught by them, like serpents, and were dragged under.

The giant of storms, which the first Portuguese navigators saw off the Cape of Good Hope, had struck again with his cat-of-a-thousand lashes, and the *Xiphias* was no more.

One would have thought the supercargo's death was avenged.

"Is it possible it is you?" gasped D'Artagnan, nearly nude, and lacerated and stripped as if really from under a flagellating friar's whip. "That was a buffeting!"

In a creature, stripped likewise, but for the struggle of one against the elements, coated with green slime from the bottom of the *Xiphias,* which, in rolling, had given him a keelhauling, D'Artagnan recognized Pedro; but his voice was just a voice, expressing nothing of the joy he should have felt at mere existence.

"Never did I hear of the like since Hercules split the mountains between Spain and Africa and made those pillars bearing his name!"

"It is nothing," replied the impassable sea rover. "Wait for the third stripe!"

"I prefer not. But I am afraid we cannot change our seats as easily as the members of the Parliament of Paris."

"I feel as if I had gone round a water wheel of Segovia Aqueduct," groaned Pedro.

"I have ceased to ache! I could not feel a whip of scorpions! I shall never need body armor! I am proof! The worthy court doctor to His Majesty, King Louis XIII. once told me that in every man is the 'witch's spot' —you may stick a bodkin in it and the victim is insensible to pricks—well, I am one whole spot like that! Pinch me, brother, that you may test the story!"

In this instant he made no secret that he enjoyed the intimacy of court functionaries.

Pedro did not heed his complaint or request, he was looking, with the good captain's fatherly eye, upon the three masts clinging together and bearing only these two corpse-resembling men.

"Not a man left!" moaned he, looking further as well as the spray would allow, floating thickly in the agitated air. "I doubt that those galleys ever made port, crippled as they were——"

"But our Frenchman? I wonder why I have a particular weakness for that Frenchman, though she fired on us!" said the musketeer.

"The beach from the port to little Salinas will be embroidered with the wreckage, like fretwork, and the dead, like pearls!"

"And the Frenchman?" repeated the other, staring about in the mist.

"She wanted a pilot, did she not? Hence, the coast is new to her! What chance has she, then, when, down there at Oporto, I can see the forlorn craft trying to beat out seaward, unable to attempt the bar? I would not navigate the constellation of the ship into a celestial haven on a night like this!"

"Can we do nothing to make head against this third attack, that you unerringly foretell?" asked the soldier, quickly, fearing that they could converse little longer by the ominous whistling and soughing of a coming wind.

"Nothing that I know of, but what I am doing—lashing myself to a pole and trusting to the saint having care of her own. Louis or Pedro, I doubt if one has a better chance than the other. We may be trundled ashore with some of our limbs unshattered. Oh, for a toothful of that good liquor which that double-faced purser sucked out of the bottle to put in that treacherous message! What a master of divination are you to perceive his falseness! I would have trusted Manuel with my life!"

"At present, that is little to trust any with! If the Inquisition had ten thousand familiars of that type, which I doubt not, your scheme to detach Portugal from its clutch would be a harder task than from Spain."

"If, my young friend," returned the Portuguese, paternally, "you should learn that, to conquer, politics must only act when religion is asleep or glutted. Now, the Inquisition does not sleep; and as Portugal has been totally rinsed of the Moors, the Jews and the infidel generally, I consider it is digesting its spoil."

D'Artagnan did not carry on the debate or stop to

praise his congener for his profundity of statecraft, for
the sea horses were once more galloping down.

Again that bellow on high, which was the more terrible as the lightning did not show through the mass of
clouds; the wave advanced like a tidal one; the line was
not perfect this time, for each crested billow seemed in-
tent on outstripping its fellow by tumbling over it.

Columns of rain gyrated twenty feet high and resembled Scythians standing on their horses in a mad charge.

"Brother," said the skipper, with humor, "my poor,
pickle-herring brother, it is none too soon to be packed
up in your cask!"

Spite of all, the curious puncheon had remained by
their side, secured, though the fastenings could be relieved instanter, with seaman's accuracy.

"Not me—you!" expostulated the Frenchman.

"No, you have the wit—the power to redeem poor
Portugal! Save yourself to save her!"

"We should draw for it, then!"

Pedro picked up two ropes' ends, severed by the storm
as by shears. He held them in his closed hand, the ends
protruding. D'Artagnan drew, with emotion.

'You have won, my French gallant!" cried the other,
merrily. "And you will win, as I should not! Into the
cask of salvation!"

"Inasmuch as there are no spikes," stammered the
musketeer. "For, as the clothes I scantily retain, are
riddled and frayed, a few more rips and I should appear
indecently before Queen Amphitrite!"

He plunged feet foremost into the odd buoy, like an
Eskimo entering his night *pajamas,* whereupon Pedro
closed the slit with the *knittle,* or drawing-string. He
clapped the sonorous bulge merrily, and rolled it into
the side where the careening made it a-wash. As he
launched it, or rather had but to let go for it to tumble
off, he vociferated.

"Bon voyage, monsieur!"

D'Artagnan did not reply, for he would not have been
heard. Besides, he was beaten down into the wallow
as if Niagara had descended on his singular life-pre-
serving case.

Pedro could not wait for its reappearance. At that

instant the tornado gathered all its ferocity to make the
last stroke. Lightning blast, and rising sea all united.
In the triple shock the stumps flew out of the sockets.
The disrupted deck split into separate boards. Pedro
slid on the last one parting, blinded, deafened, stunned,
into the boiling caldron, and the vortex sucked him
down, down!

CHAPTER XIV.

THE LODESTONE OF FRIENDSHIP.

Storms are sometimes proportioned in their duration by their violence. Those which cross the Atlantic are tropical in this respect.

Hours after the last three blasts, as foretold by the experienced Pedro, over the sea a calmness reigned. The clouds condensed and fell in sheets.

This fall appeased the waves and spread an oily film which grew more even each moment.

The crescent moon sailed serenely in larger and larger lakes of azure, and caused the drip from the inundated cliffs to resemble silvery cascades. When the undermined rocks dropped from the edges, they sent up jets of spray, glittering as if diamonds had been unearthed and were sprinkled about by the Naiads' hands. In other places, great masses of seaweed, dredged out of depths, trailed down from where they had been loftily flung and burst their grape-like bulbs with crackling, like twigs burning.

Between rocks, fragments of timber stuck up as if a dying warrior had planted his standard there before giving up the ghost. Rags of sailcloth seemed to envelop dead bodies, while the really dead were wantonly chasing each other in little whirlpools.

Ropes wound round pinnacle rocks, iron bolts were stuck in honeycombed piles like pins on a paper; deck guns were mounted in inaccessible points half way up the bluffs.

It was like a Titanic battlefield, along the shore, where a facetious giant had amused himself by fantastically arranging the ruins.

San Sebastian had been badly damaged. One of the towers on the Mole was headless. Under the truncated mass, the least of the two galleys had been wrecked in trying to steer through the narrow entrance. The other had slipped in previously, but was aground under the

Fiscal Office; its prow was run into the wall, and out of the windows the clerks could peer into the splintered hold, where the broken chains of the slaves crossed the seats in confusion.

The ship which conveyed them, in despair of entering after the galley closed the gorge, had stood out to sea. It might be weeks before she brought in news of herself.

The long and snaky Frenchman had gone to pieces on the Moor's head, a black rock conspicuous at the time but worn later to a fragment, little recalling the shape which won the title. It was two miles east of Salinas. Being armed for war, its magazine had caught fire, perhaps from lightning, and the half out of water was burned to the edge.

Before she ran among the reefs, the commander had carefully confided to his own gig a passenger of special charge, with a picked crew under his next officer.

Indeed, the latter passenger was the cause of the *Messier* (for Pedro was correct) being dispatched on this fatal expedition.

Even on a warship, at the dread interval which a boat is singled out to try to save one from the impending doom, a murmur may be heard at a choice being given when the spectators, though of a time and country where aristocracy ruled in everything, are equalized before death.

But they gladly let the passenger depart, believing him the Jonah.

The "send-off" was an ironical cheer.

It could not be said that he and the officer, who occupied the stern-sheets with the four oarsmen, felt any superiority in being detached from the ship. The cockle-shell had little more chance of salvation unless the hurricane should scorn its insignificance.

"The Jonah" did not look his part. He was a man of fortitude. When under the Spanish fire he had borne himself like an old soldier, always a philosopher. He had kept on deck, in spite of the captain's remonstrance. His very tall and broad form, well above the bulwarks, kept erect even when a ball whistled among the rigging. Yet with his brown and ruddy complexion, contented eye, frequent smile and springy step, he had more the mien of a rural squire than a martial leader.

When the storm struck its successive and increasingly severe strokes, he had borne himself as one whose life had created none of the terrors presented by death to him who has a troubled course.

Bluff, broadly merry, drinking twice to others' once, eating like the fabled gormandizers, he was the cabin jest—but not in his hearing.

"He is deported for fear he will breed a famine in France!" declared the table wit.

However, a personage of no importance would hardly have had the dispatch-boat set aside for landing him secretly in Spain.

He was entitled, in a special passport, which placed all the readers, loyal Frenchmen, at his orders, "the Knight of du Vallon de Bracieux et de Pierrefonde;" but the captain, a noble cadet, assured his brother officers that this triple title must be of late creation, as he had never heard of it at court.

When the third outburst of elementary wrath smote the *Xiphias* and the *Messier,* and reduced the former to a hull and three bare poles dissevered from their roots, the latter was driven ashore and converted into portions which an able-bodied wrecker might convey severally away on his back, the Knight of the Vallon had simply fallen asleep in the open boat, as if his large cloak were waterproof and his feet, in the water at the bottom, were turned to the chimney fire. He snored, while the officer vapored.

"This is a numbskull or a sage," observed the lieutenant. "Bail her out, boys—she would ride heavily enough without this man-mountain, for she has shipped a hogshead of brine!"

Ignorant of the country, as Pedro had guessed from the *Messier* seeking a pilot, the officer could only search for a suitable place to land. For a long time, particularly in the darkness following the sinking of the moon and preceding the sunrise, the shore was unapproachable. The water continued to be thrown up and returned, accompanied by the torrents from the rain; the cliffs were furrowed; stones pelted down, and landing would have been more at the hazard of a broken head than of drowning.

Finally, day breaking and a comparative calm succeeding, they saw the headland guarding Las Salinas.

In this cove the accumulation of wreckage was appalling. In one part it assumed the appearance of a breakwater, made not by man, but amphibious animals, such as a sea beaver, if possible. Elsewhere planks and beams supported the dead. Fish were warring for them. Ashore there were human remains tossed so high that they could not be reached without a man were lowered by a rope from the edge.

All were beyond hope of revival.

The distance was short, but currents and swirls made their best efforts, tired and famished, often a mockery; they advanced tediously, only to lose swiftly the stretch they had gained.

Had they been bereft of human pangs, and had they no plaguing thoughts about their shipmates, they might have gazed fascinated at the beauty of the scene in the rosy light.

Everything had its iridescent halo as the mists rolled away, and suddenly it disappeared under the solar heat. The water was blue, flecked by white where the sand and froth clustered; the scales of tiny fish in shoals glistened near the surface; the bubbles broke on the algae; small and large crabs gleamed green in clumps of seaweed. Ropes had been reeved through the pierced rocks; they streamed down from tall peaks.

A battered ship's figurehead was perched in a pulpit-like rock, seeming to address the floating objects.

Now and then, in gaps, the landscape could be seen on the high land, but it was lonely, though gladdened with the recent rains.

"Not an honest windmill to be seen!" sneered the officer.

Alarming noises sounded along the strand; water seeking exit by innumerable holes, choking, gurgling, hissing and roaring.

A poet would have said a young Triton was practicing on his conch-horn.

Our lieutenant was not poetical.

"Give way, lads! let us get to land."

But, beside the natural breakwater composed of fallen rocks, and trees, and rubbish, formidable jetsam and flotsam arose. The worst was the stuff half-submerged, which might smash, perforate, and rend the boat's bottom, before seen.

"Cease rowing! Back-water for your lives! It is a grampus!"

Close under the prow, as if they had indeed started up a marine monster, a glistening, greasy, scratched, and lumpy round object surged up. It was like a basking shark or porpoise, stranded, and wallowing out to sea by instinct. It seemed to have been impaled, but was only hooked on to a long spar, draggled with seaweed, which had weighed it down under the surface. The boat's motion having altered the balance, this mast shook off some of the weed, and all of the mysterious burden, which, as stated, swam nearer the surface.

"It is a hogshead of rum!" said a sailor, smacking his brine-blistered lips.

"It is no whale—it has no eyes, and the body is cedar staves," said the officer, ashamed of his error.

"Rum?" echoed the man at the bow, who had exchanged his oar for a boathook, "it is a barrel, but no liquor is in it——"

By a fortuitous dab, he had entangled his gaff in the draw-line uniting the slit in the leather hood at one end of the cask. His tugging loosened the opening flaps, chafed during a vicious tossing and thumping, and, to the astonishment of all, a human face appeared at the orifice.

The Great Kraken would not have more appalled them.

Some crossed themselves; some drew in their oars, as if contamination were in the touch.

The rare buoy slewed round and came beside the boat just when the passenger, awakened by the stoppage, opened his eyes. He faced the face of the apparently dead form.

He sat up straight, hushed and paralyzed by more than the others' wonderment.

"That—that is alive!" said he, like one who sees in reality what had been in his dreams.

"To be sure it is alive—*pardy!*" ejaculated the lieutenant, these natural words breaking the uncanny spell. "In with the poor devil, though I expect he is a galley slave who has adopted the old device of a beer cask to make his escape from the chains!"

"Slave?" echoed the personage; "a slave, with a sword girdled on!"

"Why, no—not a slave! A slave would not be armed, and, besides, this is a good Christian—the blade has a cross-hilt!"

Two of the men, climbing out on the spar, and two, leaning over the boat's gunwale, had tried to lift the singular life-preserver, but, more sensibly, two more in the boat had grasped the man by the armpits and lugged him clean out and into the French boat.

Their keen eyes perceived the bottle in its lashings, and they dosed him, after prying open his set teeth, with a generous portion of the fiery contents.

They bathed his temples and moistened his lips. Froth appeared on the latter; breathing, which had been intermittent, became regular. The eyes were unsealed, as if they had been incrusted.

The passenger, who had watched all this resuscitation with quietude, convinced that the work was in competent and experienced hands, began to assume a glad wonder, deeper than the mere restoration of a fellow-Christian might justify. He drew a long breath, held in suspense, with final relief, and lifted his sonorous voice into a kind of roar, like a lion perceiving its mate scrambling out of a trap.

"By St. Hubert's horn, it is D'Art——"

Prudence checked him.

As if this recognition were all the almost-conquering death had lacked to relax his chilly grip, the musketeer captain moved in every muscle; as if electrified, he sat up among the administering arms, and glared straight at the speaker, ignoring all the others. His voice pealed, almost as lusty:

"The saints are good to us! Yes, it is I, Porthos, who live! to see the best treasure of God, a true friend!"

And, rising both, the younger helped by the strength of the other, the two embraced, like heroes in Homer.

CHAPTER XV.

UNDER THE DUCAL CROWN.

"I think the salt water has made my eyes weak," apologetically said the lieutenant, blinking.

In the circle of friendship one forgets statecraft, ministerial imbroglios, cabals and even, though warriors, common prudence. Fortunately, there were none but Frenchmen about.

The *Messier's* survivors looked guardedly at the pair so marvelously united, divining that the newcomer was at least as important as the one charged to them by the highest authority of their country.

But the two, on conversing—since D'Artagnan rapidly recovered—did so in a low tone; steering clear of the spar and its dead passengers the boat was directed to the shore by the resuscitated, who was the faultless pilot.

Once they stopped; a corpse blocked their path. The musketeer eyed it curiously. It was none of his acquaintance; it was a galley slave, in fact. How came it so far, to float cheek-by-jowl with him? Who can tell? Storms have these grotesque surprises.

They touched shore under the bluff, where the smoothed sand was soft as down, yet had abraded adamantine rocks over night.

"Orders, sir?" asked the coxswain, ruefully, after all were out of the boat and stamping to supple their limbs.

"Finish the food and spirits, but be sparing of the latter till you have eaten. We must find out the fate of our ship, first thing. Haul up the boat out of reach of the back-wash, and, as soon as we can, we will make a search along shore."

D'Artagnan was greatly restored, but it was thankfully that he leaned on his friend's arm.

"Stay, lieutenant," said he, quietly but firmly, "this is a hostile shore, truces and treaties to the contrary! Any castaways from your warship become prisoners of war by the fact of their being within the royal bounds. And with them, you all will be lodged in the *calaboose!*"

"That is a fact," said the Lord of the Vallon, "but, anyway, I order you to obey my friend, the captain——"

The musketeer came to his friend's help.

"Yes, I am captain in the royal army; but I am the Caballero de Gannarta here, all the same!"

Like most men, the lieutenant, made chief, wanted to enjoy his timely promotion. He was a slave to routine and discipline.

"M. du Vallon," returned he, "I know you only as a state passenger on the *Messier,* accredited from the Minister of State. The directions were precise that you were to be landed at a place called Las Salinas, which it appears we have reached. Good! my task is completed as regards your lordship. Pray let me go on with my own task, imperatively imposed, to save my shipmates. It is the holiest duty. Besides," he arrogantly added, "as I stand, I am the first officer of the *Messier's* complement. Consequently, these men take orders from no one but me! I am the king's officer——"

"Did you not hear that this officer is the king's captain!"

"Sir, a ship captain of the navy ranks with a colonel," persisted the obstinate man.

Du Vallon looked confounded.

"Attention!" said D'Artagnan, without irritation. He had been investigating his rags of clothing and had found what he sought. Next his skin was a waterproof case, slung round his neck by a porpoise hide lace. "You will please look at this, after which obedience to me follows!"

Within the inclosure was a sheet of fine linen paper, for which the paper mill of Angoulême had fame, decorated with two seals, caught between folds for the better protection. Apart from the close body of the writing were several scrawls—the signatures. The naval lieutenant fastened his eyes on the potent lines while the bearer read:

Know, all subjects and allies by these writings, that the bearer does thus for the weal of the realm and under our order.
  (Countersigned) RICHELIEU.   (Signed) LOUIS.

The guarded seals were those of the Crown and the

Minister's office. Utterly submissive, the officer bowed to the arms of the duke, three golden chevrons on an azure field, more reverently than to the lily flower.

"Stay! there is a *post-scriptum*," proceeded the musketeer, hurriedly, being a superior man who wished not to enjoy a petty triumph.

Pointing to a line farther, he let the lieutenant read for himself:

Approved, for the Clergy and the Faithful
                    ✠ ARMAND JEAN (Cardinal).

The lieutenant, who was devout, made the sign of the cross, hardly preceptibly, from long practice. D'Artagnan smiled: the second barrel had brought down the game. But he was not yet done, and Porthos opened his eyes more immoderately than the officer's on hearing his friend read from a vellum fly leaf this *Omnibus* warrant:

To all Officers of France, support the Bearer as he bids, in all Ways, and for acquittance, apply to   DUPLESSIS DE RICHELIEU

Under the ducal crown appeared a monogram or hieroglyphic, which the naval officer might not have known save by hearsay; but he had not required this to obey implicitly.

"Your orders, Caballero de Gannarta," said he, saluting as if the issuer of the comprehensive mandate stood before him.

"You are brave. You are a thorough seaman or never would you have brought your eggshell to a solid land in a storm like that. I owe my life to you. I make you captain as far as my power goes and I will have the promotion confirmed in time. I shall forget myself badly when I forget you."

"And I likewise," said Du Vallon, laying his huge hand over his heart.

"Beyond a doubt the *Messier* is lost. For I know this coast. If any poor fellows are saved they will be in San Sebastian fort by this. Beach your boat as you intended, turn it upside down and take repose underneath it. When you are rested you will be found by some charitable women, fisher-wives, who will bring you comfort. Come you on, Porthos," continued he, glad to get the robust arm to assist his climbing the cliff.

But on going only a few feet his head swam. Even that iron frame had been strained to the utmost.

"Provoking! I cannot go up the highland," grumbled he. "And there is nothing like a path along the beach."

"How unfortunate! Those brave lads will want all you promise them from the village. And, I own, I could resume the nap I snatched in that pinnace last night!"

"A nap of four or five hours' duration! But, it is true, some one must get to Las Salinas quickly!"

"Are you at home there?"

"As much as one can be at home where it is not his country!"

"Ha, ha! D'Artagnan has his castle in Spain!"

"If it is not a castle I own, it is an inn!"

"Verily, at this pinch, an inn is more to my taste than a castle, for I hear that proud Spain has many a lord indifferently housed."

With knitted brow D'Artagnan drew the lieutenant aside to confer with him. As the result two of the stoutest marines converted two oars into litter poles and slung a strip of canvas between them. It was a sort of portable tenter-bed. In this couch the musketeer laid himself, and, with Du Vallon to relieve one porter at need, they deviously edged the strand.

But the sailors did not stumble where the most experienced chairman might have done, and no Landes shepherd on his stilts could have meandered so dexterously among the pools. Though slowly, progress was made surely.

Their slight refreshment had alleviated the men's sufferings, and they carried their burden like a porcelain idol, impressed with the belief that the triple power of premier, duke, and cardinal was lodged in no common individual.

Finally the little party came out on the strand of Salinas proper, where D'Artagnan alighted; cramps tormenting him on the carriage, had vanished by this time. He breathed in relief and gratitude.

"I am worth ten dead men yet," said he, in reply to his companion's mute and pathetic appeal. "Look, that is the signboard of my inn, the Kuril, that is, the Black Petrel."

"I see the sign," returned the other, with moistening lip; "but as for the inn, my sight is altogether out. I am afraid that the gale blew it away, with the last flitch of bacon and cask of red wine!"

"That could not happen, as my inn is all cellar—dug in the firm ground, in that cliff side."

"There! that? a hole! Oh, are those your hostlers? I congratulate you on such strapping fellows! what must your butler be?"

"Strapping fellows!" repeated the musketeer, amazed. But immediately spying Donna Jacinta's servitors, he added: "Spanish! Back under cover! they are soldiers!"

CHAPTER XVI.

THE MUSKETEER'S WARRANT.

"Now, may all the fiends!" broke out Porthos, looking black at this hindrance to his dining at his friend's inn.

"Do not waste breath in oaths, but let us deliberate."

"Agreeable, but it would be more so in your cellar!"

Once ensconced in the rocks, they continued their observation while discussing.

"What the pest are sentries posted at my tavern for?" grumbled Pedro Bitts' successor. "I left nothing but a fat negress to guard the pots and pans."

"Spain is a kind of enchantment," Porthos remarked, chewing his drooping mustache, in default of more substantial nourishment, as a horse champs the bit. "Only, it is not two or three strapping varlets who are going to keep a hungry and a tired traveler from an inn, particularly when it is a friend's——"

So saying, he drew his long and heavy sword, a little glued in the scabbard by the salt water, which, through all, he had kept with that tenacity distinguishing soldiers when hand-to-hand encounters were common. "I and Balizarde will have a word to say on that head—I mean, on those pikemen's heads!" He tapped the hilt familiarly.

"Stop, stop, friend Porthos! Your precipitancy always ruins things!" Du Vallon turned to stone at being blamed for headlong ardor. "Even matrimony has not tamed your impetuosity, Hotspur that you are!"

"Oh, I am a Hotspur, now!"

"If only my black stewardess would come out for a stroll, or to gossip with the fishwives, or some of them—what do I see!"

"The enchantment continues," murmured the other; "the cave becomes a grotto, and the negress a necromancer—at least, that is a fair and young princess!"

"My patron, king, and St. Louis!" ejaculated D'Artagnan, his gaze riveted on the figure enframed in the inn-cave's entrance; "what is she doing here?"

"Do you know the princess? but is my vision double? I see two of them, and both beauteous!"

"My friend, I cannot think that both those dames were wafted hither by the storm, as they would not come from seaward—but, certainly you see, incredible as it be, her highness, Luisa, Duchess of Braganza!"

"It's a queenlike form!"

"And that other, her *alter ego*——"

"An altar angel! I understand your Latin now!"

"Her confidante, her *camerista,* as they say here! the Lady of Floriador!"

"But the Princess of Braganza is a leading lady at the Spanish Court—at the Escurial—her husband is a kind of vice-king to the shadowy Philip!"

"Precisely so. But what brings her to my inn, in this out-of-way place?—it must be Providence!" Thinking of what Richelieu had said about Providence, a new idea struck him. "Is this the envoy I was to meet? Pooh! she cannot bring money! poor as proud! Rather, the plotting duke needs more than they scrape together if he schemes to—Porthos, I begin to believe that when one is plucked from the deep, it is to be firmly placed on the highland! Fortune goes by——"

"Fever! you are in for a fit! how flushed you are, and you tremble!"

"Goes by extremes, I was going to say."

The seamen stood aloof, ashamed and puzzled at two swordsmen letting a couple of footmen daunt them and stay them from a reveling-house.

"My lads, compose yourselves for a space. I promise you a skinful of wine, and bread and meat to ballast it. So, for your comrades! In the meantime, as I want to know the ground for operation, tell me your story, Porthos."

"Luckily, it is a brief one," said the other Frenchman, buckling his belt a hole or two tighter and heaving a cavernous sigh, while fixing his eyes on the inn-mouth, "for I can never tell a long one without wetting the whistle. To begin with, I was in tedium, on one of my estates——"

"One of them? Happy dog!"

"Being Du Vallon, De Bracieux——"

"Pierrefonds, I remember.   Blessed Edens!"

"But in them is——"

"Not the serpent?"

"No, no, the Eva——"

"Your wife——"

"My wife," continued M. du Vallon, lowering his voice, as if by telepathy it could be heard in France, "was widow of one M. Coquenard, a pettifogger of the lowest degree. This proctor found that playing jackal to briefless barristers was most unremunerative.   He established himself as one of those legal advisers on the borderland of the Palace of Justice, who, with the pretense to save clients from the collective fraternity, pluck them entirely for their own mattresses.   He appeared as Hope, in a black gown, to those desperates, with embarrassed estates, who wanted immediate silver at the cost of impoverishing their future generations to the seventh.   Coquenard and the second mortgage were inseparable.

"You do not see in me an authority on money matters, but it seems to me that these lenders on such security are in the position of a man who holds a bull by the horns, one who holds the same by the girth, and one by the tail. The first may be tossed before he gets his steak; the second rolled upon, and the third flung over the pasture hedge.   This picture M. Coquenard showed to the pledger, who in most instances sold out his feeble chance, and Coquenard obtained possession of the property.   At the settlement, the settling always set toward his strong box. Thus he retired rich.   It was his wealth with which Madame Coquenard gratified her second mate when he retired from the Musketeers."

"In short, her wealth outbid her charms and disposition——"

"Well, her disposition—of the property—entirely upon me—that was faultless.   I have not had her horoscope cast, but I expected in a few years——"

"Naturally, but you forget that there really is a phœnix ——"

"That fable! do you tell me that there is a phœnix?"

"Undoubtedly there is a phœnix.   Its name in our tongue is Expectations—from a rich lady in her own right. It still lives a hundred years before it mounts its own pile to revive for another——"

"Hundred years?"

"Or another expectant!"

"Dear friend, I feel that I shall never inherit the pile!"

"That is why you came out here to throw away your life, or find peace of mind!"

"Heigho!"

"Your happiness!"

"Woe is me!"

"Your noble heart, in a scuffle for a prize which will fall to one alone, while the contestants and their adherents will be forgotten——"

"Are the Spanish and Portuguese forgetful——"

"Monstrously, to foreigners!"

"Then, what are you doing here, you who have always been blighted by forgetfulness?"

"My friend," returned the Gascon, with his fine smile, "I have already fulfilled my ambition—I have my inn!"

"Bah! how are you master when you dare not enter it and pour out one poor glass for a friend?"

"Oh, I am in no hurry—I wish the ladies to be at their ease. That is the time when a wise innkeeper presents his bill. But let that pass—to your tale!"

"Now, however rich a wife is, the province where we reside is primitive. They care nothing for louis, though they do for lords. They are all gentlemen or yeomen with pedigrees as long as a tilting lance, and family trees like that Indian one under which the Great Khan stables a regiment of horse. Even stretching a point, my wife cannot do more than claim the nobility of the Black Robe. The consequence is that we have nobody to visit us and nobody to visit. So I maunder in my groves, for Mouston is no company, now he is growing fat——"

"Your old valet—a stuffed dried eel, fat?"

"He is swelled with good living and importance. But I wander in solitary glumness like—the—the——"

"The phœnix again!"

"Burn your phœnix! Like the fellow who retired from the world in a washtub——"

"But even Diogenes had the king come into his shadow——"

"Oh, a visitor did come—not the king, but from his minister——"

"That would tickle your dame! From Richelieu?"

"The duke sent me young De Varech, whom you, who never forgets a soldier of yours, must recall as a Gray Musketeer?"

"De Varech, a young Breton?"

"With enormous knees!"

"Like knots in a hawser? Certainly, I recall him," laughing. "I made him a fugleman, that he might let the others close up. It spoilt the formation to have it looking where he rode as if there were a missing cavalier to either side. I suppose he would not be so young——"

"He is unaltered about the knees, but he wears full-bottomed trunks, so that the folds fall over. He is wiser, too. He left the service to enter the civil one. He courts the cardinal, not the king or queen, as he would court the little prince, but he is too much of a baby, still. He is a secretary, in token of which he brought me a letter in his own hand, but signed by his master."

"Another stab at your besotted neighbors. The prince of the church and premier of the realm writes to you!"

"Oh, my lady would tell them, if she had their ear."

"Well," said the other, emphatically, "they may not care to know all about the Lord of the Vallon, but wait till they hear he is a grandee of Portugal!"

"Has it come to that?"

"If not now, it shall be; those ladies are bringing me the prospect nearer."

"Do you mean that that Duchess of Braganza——"

As he pointed, D'Artagnan smiled in that engaging manner which would be a fortune to a trader.

"I believe she comes to insure my power to dispose of a peerage or two!"

Porthos looked at his brother in the musketeers, whose promises might be far-fetched, but he generally brought them to hand.

"My letter ran: 'My dear chevalier and companion-in-arms——' "

"The duke wrote that——"

"Varech wrote it, but the duke fathered it."

"Then we have here a great man who does not forget that we served with him—if we did not directly serve him—at the siege of La Rochelle. Great men's memories are improving since my father's time, for he shed his blood under King Henry IV., and is but a simple country gentleman, with our domain of Artagnan in the hands of the Coquenards."

" 'As you must know the whereabouts of your friend, the Chevalier d'Artagnan, who has left the king's service since the Peace of Cazal, I pray you to forward the inclosed to him.' "

D'Artagnan frowned, puzzled. Why this roundabout method when his principal knew how to reach him directly, as far as the Petrel was a fixture?

"But you did not know where I was!" said he.

"Not I, but Varech did. It was he who said, in a friendly way, 'If I were you, knowing how the cardinal values straightforwardness, I would go straight to our friend.' "

"Ha!"

"So I told my dame that I was ordered abroad on the king's service."

D'Artagnan burst out a-laughing, to hide a tender feeling. Richelieu wanted to send him reinforcement, and believed that the valiant Porthos would be as welcome to him as a hundred men.

"Well, the inclosed?" asked he, sharply, to disguise that emotion.

"Plague on the tailors! They never give me room in my clothing," growled the other, rummaging his raiment, pockets and lining. "I stifle."

"But, my dear chevalier, your clothes have been soaked."

"But they warranted the Ypres cloth well shrunk."

"The fact is, Biscay water makes everything shrink—a ship is reduced to a faggot of broken wood in no time."

"Oh, I forgot—Madame du Vallon with her own hand sewed it up in my vest! I have it! Alackaday!" bemoaned he, ruefully rubbing his nose with a kind of wad of paper; "it has got a little—damp, I fear. It was an advice to you, of no consequence, believe me. His eminence merely hoped that you were in good health and ready to return to your post as soon as needs arose. Then came the usual flourishes, for which Varech was guilty, written with his tongue in his cheek—the great man's fal-lals about his subordinate future—for even he may desire the humblest retainer one day! My lord is forming a splendid library, Varech tells me, and in it is, I'll be bound, the fable of the 'Lion and the Mou——'"

"Balderdash! The inclosure for me——"

"There! my letter was sopped—I hope yours is not spoiled. What are you grimacing about?"

"Not spoiled! Why, look! Not a word on it of that fliff-fluff, which may be Varech's but is not Richelieu's."

"Upon this hand of mine," interjected Porthos, aghast, "it is blank! It must be the salt water—it has driven off the ink!"

At this, suggesting an idea, D'Artagnan more narrowly examined the paper; then wishing to dry it or at least to warm, he thrust it within his doublet, under the armpit.

The other stared.

Presently the captain withdrew his hand and began to laugh over the paper.

"Ah! I have it."

"What have you—a fit of lunacy?"

If one set of words had been effaced, another replaced it; by the action of iodine and the warmth, letters stood out in blue; faint but legible:

D'A.—This, your warrant to any Soleiman to draw one and one-half million livres, or Spanish equivalent, being first installment. Fire the match!   R.

CHAPTER XVII.

DARBY AND JOAN.

"A million and a half!" gasped Porthos, dazed. "Is there any such a sum in bullion?"

"If anybody has it, it is the Jews. Would they be so harassed if they did not have it all? And from my knowledge of Portugal and Spain, where I have been delving, these Soleimans, by becoming converts—for it is not probing into consciences I was, so I do not guarantee their sincerity—the members of that tribe possess the needful. Yes, they have my cash—that is, what I have the spending of——"

"Then you are the treasurer!" and Porthos clapped his hands, making a sound like two waves slapping. "A million and——"

"Many millions! but I was always sparing! I could not be lavish like our lofty-handed Athos! Only, I wish that up in that cave were my monetary agent instead even of those ladies! And yet I do not want him there under the Duchess of Braganza's piercing eyes. If she bespelled my Soleiman, she is the Queen of Sheba who would make him disgorge!"

"Saints forbid!" groaned Du Vallon, sincerely. "Now, I would trust Madame du Vallon—she loosens the purse-strings so warily! but a princess! she would order the coronation robes and the jewels to bespangle them before the crown was assured."

"Oh, you think we shall take the kingdom, do you?"

"It is positive! When we had only steel and no gold we used pretty fairly to manage matters. With both we can do anything!"

The compliment made his brother musketeer smile.

"I won't flatter you, old comrade of my heart," said he. "But do you know, I would as lief have you by my side as the bag of gold? Happy the captain who has a master mind over him to divine that two of us are better than

one, and that to suggest you should send off a message
to me would expedite you yourself on my track."

"Between you and the great duke nothing is secret!   I
believe your cave up there is that from which the winds
blew in oracles!   But what are you going to do?"

D'Artagnan stamped like a duelist to feel that his step
was sure.

"The French Minister's envoy-in-chief will at once go
to parley with Braganza, who is, in my eye, among several pretenders, the one with the strongest bid for the
Portuguese throne.   He is the heir, look you, Porthos!
and the people want one of the old stock!   If he is with
her, good; if she be alone, also good!   I can come to an
understanding with her first.   Moreover, without her he
is the compass card without the needle.   Ho, you others,
you shall shortly have the good cheer for yourselves and
mates!   Wait, Porthos, till you hear me whistle the air
of 'Should Henry Give to Me Paris,' whereupon come
as if that wind which we outlived were speeding you!"

So, farewelling, he strode up the slope with an alert
step, and proudly, too, although his clothes were discol-
ored, shrunk and ludicrously awry, his cheek pale and a
tremor from exhaustion ran all over his tired frame.   As
he advanced he sang jauntily the ballad of King Henry
IV.'s time, which was to be the cue to his companion:

"Should Henry give to me Paris, his great city,
   For me to quit my love forever, 'twere a pity
   If I did not reply· 'Take back your town! Oh, sire,
   My love is more than towns—I love my darling higher!' "

Spite of all, so distinguished was his bearing that, under this worst of aspects, the two ladies in front of the
grotto mouth no sooner descried him than they waved
their hands to cause the lackeys no longer to stand on the
defensive.   On the other hand, impressed like their mis-
tresses by the martial carriage, they saluted him with
their staves on his nearing them, as soldiers do a captain.

"Alas, sir," said the younger lady, sweetly, with instant
sympathy, which she did not always so spontaneously
express, "have you been castaway?   What a dreadful
storm!   Do you come to ask relief?"

"Clearly, I was coming for relief; but," humorously, "I
was going to help myself!"

"Sir!" exclaimed the duchess, offended.

"Considering that this Black Petrel is mine inn, if buying and paying for it is any test, I see nothing preternatural in that! Aih, here is our ingenious cook, the delectable Quaqua! Tell us, Queen of Ethiopia, am I not the legitimate successor of your lord, master and host?"

The negress, called to the inlet by curiosity, and retained by the well-known voice, grinned a broad welcome. Then, her chops falling, she clasped her hands and with real feeling, inquired:

"Is Pedro lost?"

"Lost! a jewel like that get lost! Out upon you! He is simply blown out of his course! He will return, like all good ships, to his old moorings in time—in good time! He was last seen headed for—for Brest!" He spoke loudly, with that fervent mock sincerity which marks the capital liar, who almost believes what he says. "A wide-mouthed harbor, Brest! But, Lord love you, mammoth of fidelity, albeit he is stout, thanks to your good table, he will squeeze in, as he should, at St. Peter's gate—more likely to be his path-end," he concluded, unheard by the others.

Thus consoled, the black again grinned and mingled with the inner shades.

The two other hearers exchanged glances. They reasoned that there was no immediate occasion for succor in this gentleman, who spoke so jestingly.

The one who had been spokeswoman said:

"There is an error here, sir! Without impugning your statement of purchasing this house—shall we call it a house?—I beg to declare that I am its purchaser, if only for a time, since I bought the use of it of the then tenant for ten moidores, Portuguese."

"Of its tenant?" repeated the musketeer, whose turn it was to evince astonishment. "Eh? what! have the ghosts returned of Pedro Bitts, the fisher, and host of the first instance?"

"He answered to that name! but he was a Jew, looking more like one who sold fish than went out to catch it."

"A Jew! Now, this is getting nearer the mark! Is he in there?" asked D'Artagnan.

Both ladies bridled and drew away.

"No, no, of course you would not hire the house to entertain even that Jew! Did he mention no other name —say, Soleiman?"

"I think," returned Donna Jacinta, trying to give comfort, "before he went out into the stormburst he called upon Father Soleiman!"

"It is my man!" cried the Frenchman, only momentarily glad, however, as he looked around. "It was no weather to drive even a dog—of a Jew—so very far!"

Jacinta blushed. It was probably the first time that she had been rebuked by any man, and surely for what in her prejudice she esteemed insufficient cause—for a wastrel!

To the duchess' surprise she replied not at all tartly but subduedly, if anything:

"As I had purchased the houseroom and I did not desire to take in guests but of my own selection, he rode away on his mule, as I have heard."

"The dolt! We twain are then playing the parts of those figures in the Dutch toyhouses, the Darby who comes out when the wind blows and the Joan who comes out when the sun shines! He will have been blown over the cliffs or drowned in a sudden torrent—that is what has become of him. Oh, indeed, we know not whom we turn from our doors! Why, I would as lief that waif were captured by the Spaniards! Yet, judging by my late experience, it is harder to pluck a man out of the jaws of a Biscayan nor'wester than from the Spanish!"

He ground his teeth, thinking of the untowardness of it, that they should thrust out the bearer of the funds on which hung all they prayed to be benefited with.

"You seem moved. Did you know this one?" asked Jacinta, still astonishing her mistress by a sympathy with this stranger, quite unaccountable.

D'Artagnan was verifying his expectation that his writing on the doorpost was still attached.

"Oh," went on the young lady, following his glance, "have we the honor to address the Caballero de Gannarta?"

"Exactly!" said he, proudly. "At your service, Lady of Floriador, and of yours, Duchess of Braganza."

"Oh, do you know my lady?"

"Every gentleman knows the Gonzagos, memorable for their valor! and the dames for their attractions and their queenlike majesty." The last words were pronounced with studied emphasis.

The princess started, and though meaning to nod slightly, found herself favoring with an elaborate courtesy. This was a man who had addressed queens.

"I do not see that I have any more business here," resumed the cavalier, "since this tenant, who let his house, but should have stayed to receive me, has gone away. Still, though I want no room, will you allow me to send some food and stimulants to friends of mine, who are likewise cast upon this inhospitable shore?"

The ladies had been searching well, but they had perceived no one.

"They are hardly better fitted for a court pageant than your servant speaking," went on the muksteer, amusingly. "The coats of their stomachs are also out of repair, so pranked upon were we by the typhoon—in a word, they are naked and starving. If you would let me send them by your lackeys the wherewithals to revive them and revest them, you will have their prayers to add to those of the thousands who hold your cause in their hearts!"

There was no doubt that this glib speaker knew them very well.

Jacinta stepped aside to let her mistress explain to the footmen.

"Besides," said he, still more significantly, "revived, they will form no worthless reinforcement to your guard, in case the fugitive Jew is caught by the Spaniards and they follow up his track—granting that he will not betray all—to his ignoble retreat!"

La Braganza guessed that this confident and deeply-advised speaker wished to confer with her alone. Another might have been apprehensive, but Luisa de Gonzago y Guzman y Braganza knew nothing of ordinary feminine fears.

The musketeer plunged into the cave, whence he shortly issued to beckon two of the servants. With the negress' help, he had stuffed into two seaman's bags enough victuals to supply the naval officer's crew and M.

Porthos also, with perhaps an overplus, if survivors had been found.

Shouldering their burdens with an effort, but smiling with the hope of doing a kindness to others, who would share their loneliness and watch here, the varlets hastened down the declivity.

CHAPTER XVIII.

THE PHANTOM BELL.

"Now, chevalier, what have you to say to me?" inquired the princess.

"I would I could say that all is well for Portugal and the hopes of those who love her; but since that Jew was dismissed, our fiduciary—alas! I wish we could guess that we may turn away golden angels from our door!"

"What are you saying, sir?"

"That, as far as my searches tell, poor Portugal can furnish nothing but men toward her becoming an independent state. For money she has to turn to other quarters."

"Yes; and always in vain!"

"Not always! not vainly!"

"Then God be praised!"

Proud though she was, she began to weep; those full, noiseless tears, seeing which, in Eve, Adam took her hand and went out with her into the world. Through them, she said:

"You are French—then, your king——"

"My noble monarch," went on the Royal Musketeer, with lofty firmness, "through his first minister, sends his representative, not to be recognized yet—since the court he is accredited to exists not—to meet a banker in Portugal, or thereabouts—who will supply him with the means—the fuel to keep up the fire of revolution——"

"Revolution?"

"And not revolt, mark you! The first portion of the funds is a million-and-a-half livres, being so many pesetas of silver!"

"A million!" gasped the duchess, as deeply shaken as a common person by a windfall in proportion.

"And-a-half," added the Frenchman, emphatically; "don't forget the half-million—it will buy over a citadel governor or two!"

She looked upward with joy, while her attendant looked

at the war eagle, who was their dove of good tidings, with even more gratitude.

The main hindrance was removed in their progress to the throne coveted.

"We shall be delighted to receive this disburser of the boon," observed the duchess, with quivering lip.

"Unfortunately, the Caballero de Gannarta is nothing unless in close communion with the head of the Soleimans, upon whom he draws——"

"But, meanwhile, I suppose we may know——" began the lady, who would rather have received the money than the disburser or the banker.

"Your grace, in so delicate a negotiation, and for such vast assistance, secrecy must be used. A hint as to the existence of such an agent, and to his person, living in a country which he aims to sever from the crown, and—well, his life would be at stake—and his body, too. Egad! they might invent a charge of heresy, and send his ashes, after burning, to my Lord Cardinal; and even he would not strive to clear the wretch's memory by declaring that under guise of paganism he committed high treason! Now, this agent may jeer at even this fate, but if he were done to death, along with the banker, I do not see how the money would be used in your grace's behalf."

"But it is agreed that Mother Church shall lose nothing by the redemption of Portugal!"

"You? yes! but France! She is not party to any such agreement. A Frenchman, an officer in the king's military—intimate service! trying to tear the finest jewel out of the Spanish crown! and failing! that is the point! France would be forced to deny complicity. I should have to say, 'Alone I did it! and I would be sacrificed!'"

"It is true! no, no!" said Donna Jacinta.

"For the present, say—which is quite true—that you have not handled a sou of foreign loans!"

"But the banker's appointment still holds good with his gracious majesty's agent?"

"That agent, madam, has too well examined the ground here. Spain presents the sight of a decaying power—masterless servants, disbanded, unpaid soldiers, officers reduced, jackanapes promoted; the only thrivers, the collectors-in-chief of the revenue. The rest of the community looks upon chance as the paymaster—that is, they rob any next comer! The truce has shut up the warships in the docks to rot—their crews are idling or joining the armed beggars who impede the road. I vow to your highness that a bishop sets out from one town to another with a small army to clear the way! They would stop a saint, and if he kept a carriage, like the present-day saints, they would not only hamstring his horses, but make a fire of the coach and eat the horses roasted by it!

"If that chief Soleiman had all his tribe around him, the news that he had a million or so of pieces in his sack would let loose the locusts, bitterer than Africa's! What will be left of a million-and-a-half if he has to be sifted through the beggars, 'the gentlemen of the night,' the governors, the Holy Inquisition, the corregidors, the al-caldes and their alguazils—not a milrei! Look you, I have been on the deep—a prey to the sharks; well, I would sooner leap in among them than ride from here to Bayonne with that sum at my saddle-bow!"

"What have I done?" wailed Donna Jacinta, wringing her hands and looking so pitiful that D'Artagnan was sorry that he had spoken so truthfully.

"What have you undone?" responded he, with sever-ity, only pretended this time. "As pretty a piece of work as has been schemed in our times. But I may overtake the bearer of the precious bag! Oh, I am forgetting an-other important matter! The duke, your lord, where is the duke, my lady?"

Both the women looked dismayed again.

"I suppose you are awaiting him here? A capital, out-of-the-way nook, is it not?"

"No!"

"Yes!"

"Yes and no! Between two contradictions, the truth-seeker falls to the ground. I have not been long here and in the sister kingdom, but it is a truism that I heard, to wit: the Duke and the Duchess of Braganza were in-separable!"

"If love had not counseled that union, sir," returned the duchess, sternly, "self-preservation would have done so. Together, the hirelings would hardly have dared assassinate us; such a double tragedy would elicit too much comment wherever there was court and sovereign through Christendom!"

"Do they go as far as assassination?" The speaker gripped his sword quickly, as if it had given a leap to leave the scabbard.

"So it was with grief and dread that I consented to part with my lord. He received a royal invitation—mandate, you understand—to attend a ceremony—launching of a new kind of warship—at San Andero. He said that if there were evil brewing, he could not flee —he was fettered, bound to Spain, while depending on news from over the mountains on which hung the fate of his lifelong project—to regain his ancestral throne."

"Madame, I have not been deficient in diligence; but I was timed to harmonize with others in my striking."

"I blame no one! My lord, I continue, said that, if the invitation concealed a deathtrap, he must not drag me into it. Besides, I was, in event of his not joining me at a week's interval, to retire into Portugal. I was, in case he disappeared, to act as I deemed meet."

"Revenge him?"

"One of his forefathers is known as 'the Avenger;' acting for him, I might imitate that monarch!"

"Suppose you did raise the South for that end, there would still be the severed kingdom on your hands. Who would be offered the vacant throne?"

"What other? Never mind! I would not bring on that dreadful war unless I were sure of success!"

"Let me see! Assist at a launching at San Andero—the Spanish fleet would be there to do the royal substitute honor—a new type of warship?" muttered the French private envoy, thinking of the unseen ship at which the three Spanish vessels were firing. "Was my lord to preside—christen the vessel?"

"The duke is generalissimo of the army of Portugal—derisive title! As such he was a royal delegate to the ceremony, but he was merely a guest. Above him in activity ranked Admiral Don Lopez Ozario, whom all the navy officers would obey. My lord promised me, for security's sake, that he would stay aboard a certain fleet vessel, of which the commander and others were true to him, if anybody remains true at these times—such as the Duke of Villa-real, Lord Mendoza, the brothers Mello, the brave De Saa—some remained, some he compelled to go into Portugal, since it was madness to have all sacrificed. Spite of lures, then, he would be on the *Amor de Dois,* a swift corvette. The captain was his *protégé,* the subalterns, his pensioners. Moreover, thinking of everything, the crews were paid to obey their captain in the teeth of his superiors, or die under the fire of all the fleet concentrated."

"Well arranged," said the Frenchman, studiously. "But the trainer is still rash who thrusts his head into the lion's mouth!"

"The wolf's, sir! That feeble Philip a lion?" scoffed the duchess. "He is not another Second Philip!"

"He is Philip fourth-rate!" added Donna Jacinta, as sneeringly.

Darkness had come on, while Richelieu's envoy was cogitating over the duke's separation from his wife, which boded no good to the great undertaking. Everything seemed so cruelly contrary in this affair.

The servants had returned from their errand, not having hurried, divining that their mistress wished her discourse with the strange gentleman not overheard. They reported, when questioned by Donna Jacinta, that the sailors, leaving the French gentleman to accompany them to the inn, had hastened along the beach, as they had come, to succor their companions. They were sure to meet them before complete nightfall. Besides, the undercliff caught and held the sunset light and would longer remain undarkened.

Behind them, leisurely, M. du Vallon strode up the slope.

Alas! who could have recognized the magnificent Porthos, glory of the Three Companies of King's Musketeers, black, red and gray? Absent the gloss—truly, in a pickle! The brine had taken all the curl out of his hat plumes; all the twirl out of his mustaches, of which the points drooped instead of bristling upward, as Philip's in the Velasquez portraits; he trembled with slow fire at not having been able to repair his toilet before introduction to the eminent lady.

"Madame," said his comrade, when the giant life-guardsman was at hand, "I have the favor to present to you, and to the Lady of Floriador, the Chevalier-Lord of the Vallon, of Bracieux and of Pierrefonds, the special messenger of the King Louis XIII., and of his first minister, who begs to proffer his respects and his sword to your grace. The sea, in its impartial severity, has taken the color out of his vest, but not out of his blood, 'the bluest' in France, or his temper and spirit, the highest, or his blade, the best there!"

Porthos made a becoming, stately bow and held out the handle of his sword in its sheath toward the Duchess of Braganza. She tendered her hand to be kissed, and she was not without feeling a thrill as it rested for a moment on the huge back-hand of Porthos, while his mustache brushed it. Madame du Vallon would have been jealous if she had seen the proud Gonzago's pleasure at the ponderous knight's offering.

D'Artagnan, rapping his own rapier hilt, turned toward her attendant, implying that he personally dedicated it to her service. She bit her lip, but a smile of pleasure illumined her averted face.

"I do not believe she is a doit offended," thought the Gascon.

It was by this time darkness complete. There was no twilight in this latitude.

The Frenchman sighed.

"A plaguey, breakneck journey lies before me," grumbled he, meaning to be heard. "To chase a Jewish Frier Rush, without his lantern lit, over a seacliff sham of a road, in a pitch-black night. If he but had the treasure in ingots, I might trust to catch up with him."

"M. du Vallon will be our guard," said the duchess, evidently haughtily unconcerned about one person's safety more or less, and surely not intending to detain the adventurer from a service of such possible gain to her coffers.

Over a million for their military chest, at the price of a stranger's barking his shins.

"Hark!" interposed her maid-of-honor, looking off seaward. "What did I hear?"

"A bell!" said the duchess, negligently.

"It's a bell." coincided Porthos. with his back that

way, for he was sniffing the odor of Quaqua's fleshpots, despite his recent repast.

"Vespers," said Jacinta.

"Vespers, without a church—a bell without a belfry?" said D'Artagnan, who took nothing for granted. "Where is there a bell about here? There is no large ship, carrying a priest! These fishing craft use horns, like huntsmen, or wooden clappers, like the Moorish priests. There is no——"

"But it is a bell, and dolefully tolling, too," persisted the duchess, shivering as the breeze came off the sea.

"Get the ladies indoors, please, you, master," said the oldest footman. "It is a bad sign when a bell rings off on the ocean without being struck by human hands!" and he crossed himself.

"Idiot! there is no bell!"

"Then a phantom bell is still worse omen!"

"I know the cove better than my inn itself!"

Nevertheless, the metallic stroke sounded again, and yet again, regular enough to suggest human impetus or human set mechanism.

"That," said Porthos, to obtain recognition of his science from the ladies, "that is a bell buoy. I have heard of them!"

"A bell mule!" returned his friend, tartly. "I reiterate to you that there is no bell for leagues around."

"Stay," said Jacinta, with unusual desire to prevent a difference, "why may not some portions of a wreck be wafted ashore to which a bell was attached, and some poor wretch, much as was the case with your lordship, be appealing for help by striking those mournful notes?"

"There is something in that," quickly said the duchess.

"There's much in that!" agreed Porthos, wishing the suggestion had entered his mind.

There could not be a doubt now that the sound was continuous and from one fixed spot.

"It is where a rock juts out of the water. The Turban, or Moor's head," said D'Artagnan, yielding. "It is not a man, I guess. Just a spar caught at one end and swinging about at random so as to beat that devil's tattoo on a cresset, stuck by a pole in the rocky pile."

"Would you go and make sure?" said the duchess, wrought up by the fears about her husband.

"As for me," said Jacinta, addressing no one in particular, but the musketeer took it all to himself, "I could not rest this night if I thought that a poor seaman were there, clinging to a sea-washed rock, or a mast, much as the Sire de Gannarta was, beating with dying hand that lantern tipped post—all through the livelong night!"

"I am going." Then, as the thought of Pedro and his shipmates obtruded on his political speculations, he exclaimed with vigor, "I go!"

He saw Pedro, so wise, brave, profound, indefatigable, noble spirit, in a vulgar shape, battling as he had done with old ocean.

He had forgotten the Jew, perhaps in equal peril!

Bracing up his belt tightly and snatching the kerchief off the negress' head as she stood, staring; he bound it round his own brow like a bull fighter's scarf cap. He dashed down the declivity, shouting to his companion:

"Watch and ward over the ladies!"

CHAPTER XIX.

THE DUKE OF BRAGANZA.

All the locality came back to the Gascon, so that he ran in the obscurity as in broad day. He reached the fishing hamlet without a stumble. With his fist he struck at the first door and said, briefly, to the woman outcoming:

"A wrecked man may be on the Moor's Head!"

She was one of those sturdy creatures, fearless of no weather, and as able to help man a boat as a man himself.

"Help me get out something that will float and throw in an oar or a pair——"

"Shall I get another hand, sir? The cable is heavy for one to scull and for a pair to pull!"

"No, we two—to save time!"

The woman drew an oar out of the cabin, being a precious tool not to be idly lost, spoke sternly to her little ones who had begun to whimper, but who hushed like wolf cubs when the hunter is nigh, and rapidly preceded her caller. She was more familiar with the shore than he. Besides, she alone knew where the spare boat was hidden.

Warmth had succeeded a cold spell and fog arose. This lifted a little off the surface, and it had a phosphorescent scum. The woman soon found the boat, raked off a screen of eel grass and helped the Frenchman in.

She waded out as if she had sea boots on, pushed the boat till it was fairly in the water, and leaped in at the stern, where she stood up, easily poised, ready to use the single oar "Portugal fashion," that is to say, in sculling.

"Where to, master?" said she, unconcernedly as a ferryman making a regular trip.

"To the cresset rock, I said. Somebody may be there!"

"The Lord forbid! but there do be some'at making a click-clack!"

She lustily plied the bar, holding its edge against the

boatside while executing the half revolving motion and return which is a marvel of propulsion.

In twenty minutes they were alongside the rock. It was worn from its original rounded shape to a narrow but flat-topped cone; but though from shore looking inaccessible, its platform was sufficient to hold two or three men standing, while it amply accommodated a man coiled up at the base of the wooden and iron upright, sustaining the beacon fire. This man was so huddled up that he might have been flung from a height and broken in every bone. His left arm was, however, sound enough to be twined round the mast, as if he had attempted to clamber up out of reach of the cruel tide and its ruin-laden waves. With his right, armed with the rest of a broken sword, he must have struck more by habit than by knowledge of his act, on the ironwork. It was its vibration, which resembled the knelling over the dead.

"It is a man!" muttered D'Artagnan, heart-pricked at his obstinacy and disbelief. "All but a dead one. That was his last beat! It is not our Pedro——"

"None of our sort," mumbled the woman, with eyes out of which the last tear for the drowned had long since flowed.

He was sumptuously clad! Fine linen, a gold chain—a gentleman.

He seized the armed hand, which relaxed at the touch, utterly spent, and let him extricate the blade as if cognizant that friends had arrived. He ran his fingers over the handle.

"Fine metal—and finely chiseled—a crown on it! This is no common ship's officer! What gilded ball have the sea dogs been playing pellmell with!"

Tenderly he lowered the body into the skiff and returned carefully himself, as if fearful of oversetting it with a precious cargo.

"Turn, and land us! Every moment is valuable!"

Remembering his similar strait and how he had been cared for, he pressed the unconscious figure to his bosom, trying to electrify it if not much to warm. since he was chilled; thaw him, share with the deadlike his own vitality.

The woman skillfully ran the boat on the sands, perfectly piercing the gloom.

"Let the boat go hang!" cried the musketeer, ungratefully. "Out! Take his heels, while I his head! So, so! Steady, for we must carry him up to the Petrel for fire and soup!"

The fishwoman was stronger than he at the time. They quickly ascended. Half-way up, D'Artagnan, with overbearing impatience, and counter to prudence, shouted:

"Lights, lights! Blow up the fire! Get out wine and heat the soup! I bring a drowned man!"

Humanity levels classes. In the case of the duchess, on sharp points as regarded her husband, she felt attracted to this unknown castaway. She and the other lady bustled like Quaqua and the fisherwoman in making the preparations which converted the cave into a hospital.

The lackeys had sprung to relieve the captain and the woman, so that the insensible man was promptly brought within cover.

Already a kind of bed was spread by the corner warmed best by the roaring fire. The fisherwoman returned to her children.

Hardly had the burden been laid on the couch, and D'Artagnan begun to comb back the hair, worn long, plastered over the face by slime from weeds, clotted blood and hardened salt, than he uttered a deep cry, as from his heart, making Porthos quake:

"Don Juan! the hero of the trenches of Susa Pass!"

At the name of Juan, although common enough, the duchess and her tiring-woman bent forward, and from their quivering lips arose simultaneously this ejaculation:

"The Duke of Braganza!"—"My husband!"

The duchess fell upon the body, bedewed its pale, cold features with tears, and repeated the name between sobs. One could not define whether it was in pain or gratitude.

"Juan! oh, my own Juan! my beloved Juan!"

"I am ashamed to be here," muttered Porthos, coughing.

" 'Sdeath!" said his friend, in a hushed voice, "this is the finest fish ever caught in Las Salinas Cove!"

After the first paroxysm of love and thankfulness, the Lady of Braganza allowed the negress, acquainted with the means of resuscitating shipwrecked mariners, to take the patient in hand. Then she and Jacinta continued the proper cares under her direction.

D'Artagnan touched his comrade on the arm, and the two crept out.

At the doorway the servants were on their knees, praying.

"Good varlets! they love their master!" remarked the musketeer. 'This is a good sign for the future kingdom! The love of the subjects is the king's best safeguard!"

"King, eh?"

"Presently! Since I am going to make that man one!"

"You speak warmly!"

"I am hot in his cause."

"Well, Braganza is a duke, and a sort of viceroy already."

"He is much more! He is a hero!"

"So you know him? You hailed him pretty well on the level as plain Don Juan!"

"I knew him as such only. Wait, wait! Did you ever see a ship launched?"

"Not often; and I want to see it less than ever, if, as in the case of this duke, one comes to his fate!"

"The ship will stick to the stocks——"

"Unless they grease the ways——"

"Porthos, your library at your three estates must be well garnished, and, what is more, well thumbed! You know all things. Yes, the ways should be well greased. Well, in case of our launch, that ship of state, whose figurehead is the king, the proper ointment is a golden one. While they are telling that traveler, who has returned over the Styx by way of little Salinas, how he was served with the same sauce as the Knight of Artagnan and scores of finer fellows, let us, being reposed——"

"I like the repose! You reposed, after venturing out again to sea on the heels of your own narrow squeak!"

"Let us," went on the musketeer, not noticing the correction, "go upon the road to San Sebastian. I much mistake, or we shall discover that Jew——"

"Would he not have hastened away——"

"His mule would have a word or two to say on that course!"

"His mule? I cry you, mercy! do you understand mule-ology now?"

"I know that the mule struck up a friendship for my gallant charger, and when a mule gets a fond fit on for a a horse, it is Castor and Pollux over again——"

"I know! so the mule will cast him, and hurry back to your horse?"

"It is likely. Anyway, if we should come up with him, I wager my Constable's Sword in prospect against our Quaqua's skewer that the Jew will be so disgusted with his hours in the open that he will rush into our arms——"

"He may rush into yours, if you like—as for me, I decline to embrace Jews, though I should his money-bag!"

"Come along."

"In that storm, he and the mule would have been sent over the cliffs——"

"It blew inland! And never was the wind made in Æolus' cave which would blow the man far, weighted down with a million of livres!"

But while they were saddling Clamponnier, Porthos, regretting that the darkness prevented his admiring all his striking points, for they intended to ride and walk by turns, the latter, whose campaigning instincts were sharply returning, laid his hand silently on his companion's arm and pointed over the tableland.

There a light erratically showed, gleaming, vanishing, appearing to one hand, darting to the other, bowing, rising, stopping, receding, flashing forward; but, on the whole, nearing them.

"A dark lantern," commented D'Artagnan, "carried by a tired or drunken man. At least, it is open only on the side toward us."

"It is a surprise, intended! We shall simply be overborne by a detachment out of the nearest garrisoned town." Porthos spoke disappointedly but still calmly. "Well, with those varlets, the fisherwomen, who can load muskets, I reckon so! And calling in those wrecked Frenchmen, the narrow entrance to your inn being defensible, I think we can hold that pass as long as those Romans did the bridge at Thermopylae Pass!"

"Good!" said the captain, not losing time in pedantic correction. "But let us reconnoitre, so as not uselessly to alarm the ladies!"

"Oh, as for the duchess, she is a lioness again since she has found her mate; and as for Donna Jacinta, she is not easily frightened, I will swear!"

Leaving the horse, which showed no eagerness to go in search of the mule, or anywhere else, they rapidly went up to the highland top. They had not made twenty rods before the light gave a plunge and was projected upon them.

"Who goes there?" challenged a harsh voice.

There was a clatter of weapons, too.

CHAPTER XX.

KING OF PORTUGAL.

"How now! Why, this is our lieutenant of the *Messier!*" exclaimed Porthos, sheathing his sword with a bang of the hilt. "Ha, ha! he has stuffed a bunch of grass into a wicker basket, flung it on a pole and attached that pole to a mule. That accounts for the wabbling! Sailors are droll!"

"Who goes there?" was repeated in an irritated tone, as if the laughter, no doubt heard, had been taken in no merry mood.

There was a rattle of clubs and of steel, but as the guarded light sent its ray only one way, little could be distinguished in the deep dark behind the animal thus converted into an ambulatory lighthouse.

"France! friend!" shouted D'Artagnan, not desirous of drawing a shot. "Do you not know your best and only friend in these waters, Lieutenant Constant?"

"The French gentlemen!" was the joyous response.

"But what are they carrying on the mule's back?" demanded M. du Vallon. "The money sacks with the millions, by all that's bright!"

"No, no; it is a man in a bad way—flaccid as a jellyfish. Now, if luck holds good——"

"This thing," replied the lieutenant, coming up with a sailor leading the animal, and pointing to the burden across the back, "this is a peddler or *cagot;* a Jew or the like. We picked him up on the wayside when we mounted to the cliff top. The tide is rising all alongshore as if it would never know a turn! We were fairly driven up aloft as those fellows met us. This mule was grazing contentedly hard by the man—so it may be his."

"Did it have no panniers?" asked D'Artagnan, eagerly.

"None, and no saddlebags. The saddle is a wretched cloth, doubled to hide its holes and dirt!"

"That mule has kicked them off!" said Porthos, in horror. "I should thrash a mule like that!"

"I do not think so," said this friend. "I believe that this terrified knave will turn out to be his own money-bag——"

"I have heard of a spy swallowing a message—but a million——"

"Not exactly that way—but, in any case, we shall make him disgorge. And don't be hard upon one who may be of much service. He may be born a Jew, but there are no Jews left in this land lately who are not converts. Recognize the best part of him, if he be half a Christian."

"You are right, my gentleman," interposed a seaman, pulling his front hair; "this is no heathen! See here, sir, is his prayer book!" holding up a wallet of dark morocco, blackened with thumbing and closed with metal clasps. "That is what the priests call a missal!"

"Draw up your light-bearer," said D'Artagnan, quickly, as he took this pocketbook from the finder, and, opening it, he added:

"You are right, my lad! It is a kind of missal over which too many men spend more time than over their breviary! It is an account book which the Prince of Evil will go over with the owner some day!"

Several folded papers fell out, written on China paper, fine and thin, and yet opaque, with that imperishable ink which, to this day, retains its gloss and intense hue. They were picked up with that awe of the illiterate for writing and handed him.

"Ha!" continued he, attracted enough by the glancing over them to hold them carefully. "Go on with him as you were heading!"

"It is the mule who is the pilot," said the lieutenant; "he was heading for the point where we sighted you two, like he had laid down the course with line and chalk!"

"I believe," said M. du Vallon, walking beside the man on the animal, "he is coming to!"

"I shall return him his papers when he is in his right wits," observed the Musketeer Royal, enigmatically.

As they arrived at the cave, Soleiman, for it was he, became alive to his state and his wants. He ran his hands over his person, but not so much to learn if its

joints were in order as to make sure he had lost nothing.

"Ugh!" said he, lamentably, "have these tarry fingers
in overrunning me stuck to my family papers—of no
earthly use to any one, but still dear to me—or were
there pillagers——"

"Hold, Master Elizor," broke in D'Artagnan. "No
Jeremiads, please! You are running the risk of having
your mouth rinsed of foulness out there in the bay.
These sailors are as honest as humane. I it was who
took care of your pocketbook, as well as they of your
person. Sirrah, let me hear nothing," he subjoined, in
a voice for his ear solely, "of your keeping your bullion
so tied up that you want time to meet all rightful demands instanter! I know your pecuniary position better than the high qualificator of the holy Inquisition—ay,
like that forefinger of yours, which has kept tick on its
accumulations so closely that it is worn to the quick."

Startled by this stern address, Elizor let himself be
taken off the mule, which ran over to Clamponnier gladly,
but was met with dignified snorts and restless kickings.
He was hardly able to stand. It might be as much fright
as stiffness from his wanderings.

"Keep your eye on him, Porthos," said D'Artagnan, as
they stepped within the cave with the Jew between them.

Thanks to an energetic brain and a strong constitu-
tion, Braganza, who had well resisted the luxury of a
court endeavoring to make a *Roi fainéant* of him, had
likewise resisted the attacks of the storm. Much is
achieved in the human frame by the tenacity of purpose
in one who cherishes an exalted design.

He was now in clear possession of his senses.

Though pale, wasted, shaken to the core, he presented
a not unlordly aspect. Yet he was seated on a cask, robed
in a horsecloth, and supported by his wife and her lady-
in-waiting. Juan de Braganza was heavy-looking, stolid,
dull, without a great spur, but his profuse color was
gradually returning, and thinness had robbed his lineaments of too nonchalant an expression.

"The Duke of Braganza," muttered the Jew, shrinking,
as if he dreaded any actual contact with this rival of

Philip IV.—it being no secret to him as a financier on what terms they really stood.

There was surprise, too, as if he had knowledge, not of this particular plot of assassination, but of something of the kind in contemplation.

The duke turned his head, but seemed to distinguish D'Artagnan alone. With deep gladness, too.

"Why, save us! it is my captain in the Savoyard campaign! The Chevalier D'Art——"

"Gannarta," corrected the Frenchman, grasping the hand offered and broadening his face with a smile like Braganza's.

They were soldier and soldier.

"He is not arrogant," remarked he to Porthos, who was in a daze. Then, releasing the ducal hand, he said to the wondering duchess:

"Madame, you know your illustrious husband so well that it is impossible that I should present him in a new and more brilliant light; but I must take this opportunity to excuse myself for having addressed his grace so curtly and offhand. I only knew your lord as a Spanish——"

"Portuguese——"

"Portuguese officer of fortune, who volunteered into my squadron of the King's Black Musketeers in the campaign against the Duke of Savoy, in '34. So came many a foreigner into our camp to learn our art of war, some of them concealing a high rank under their beavers, it appears.

"One day, in the van-foss, when we were countermining, we broke into a tunnel where the Savoyards had stored a very pretty fat 'sausage' stuffed with powder and seasoned with Greek fire! They had fled on hearing our picks, but not before clapping the line stock to the slow match. Faith! it was a quick enough match for us, had not my Don Juan here—your Don Juan—sprung forth from our midst, when, to tell the truth, we recoiled, myself first in the drawing back (we are not always in our bravest moment). Don Juan threw himself upon the fizzing serpent and the sausage! Methought, as the smoke enveloped him, that we were all converted into sausage meat, but, I warrant, he was no more glad than we when he arose. With his body he had extinguished the dire flame. Ah, his highness may modestly keep that deed a secret, but your highness could tell of a scar, over his heart, betokening the flame he smothered!

"Our marshal thanked him in the king's name, and his name was read out in the orders of the day—but who, in Don Juan the volunteer, suspected the Duke of Braganza? One who bore himself like a Maccabee in Josephus!"

"Tally-ho!" shouted Porthos, waving his hat as if his hounds were capturing the beast.

"My hero!" said the duchess, embracing her husband with as little perception of the bystanders. Never had she so high and ennobling an opinion of him.

Over her shoulder the duke gave the French captain a glance for altogether another reason than his recent rescue.

"My lord, for saving my men I have far too long owed you a debt. I trust that before so long I shall repay it."

"You have done so, in saving my life! Think, wife, that the invitation to the launch was, indeed, a decoy! No sooner was my corvette between the broadsides of two men-of-war than, under pretense of firing salutes— with shotted guns—an accident! the poor *Amor de Dios* was all but sent to the bottom. My captain was alone unnerved by the murderous surprise. He gave orders, and his men, restored to courage and coolness by his self-control, managed to manœuvre us out of the trap.

"For such a plot it was necessary that not one aboard should survive to tell the tale. We were closely pursued, but it was not until we were out well at sea that the three or four vessels in chase and trying to intercept us in other ways, opened fire on us, as on a pronounced enemy of Spain. The chief pursuer was fleeter than my ship, a long, narrow craft unfit for rough waters. When we replied with our guns, for this was war, war to the death! the shock almost completed our destruction; we were shattered to the keel. Unable to get clear, unable to keep seaward, we were unfortunately driven back toward two large galleys which resumed the cannonade. A storm came up while I thought of closing with the nearest tormentor, and we were forced toward the most dangerous shore on this coast of dangers. In the mists and in the smoke of our own guns replying to the last we went to pieces on rocks far out from the land, this side of San Sebastian. I was forced into a boat by my devoted officers and friends, but all was of little avail. I found myself mingled with them on fragments of our ship—dead, disabled—a last fury of the storm overwhelmed us and I remembered no more. Yes, it seemed to me that a church bell was ringing for my funeral—what hopes are being buried with me, I deplored—well, this brave soldier saved me! I am his debtor forever!"

Once again he clasped D'Artagnan's hand as if never to let him go from his side.

"We saw your gallant fight," observed the lieutenant of the *Messier,* "and will testify to the outrage! The same fate attended our ship, at which the Spanish fired, I suppose, to destroy us as witness."

"A French ship? This is a doubling of the violence!"

"We were conveying this gentleman to Spain, and this part, too," went on the naval officer, who did not intend that he should be ignored by the duke.

The latter bowed to M. du Vallon, inquiringly.

"The Chevalier du Vallon," said D'Artagnan, "was bearing me a message from the First Minister of King Louis——"

The Jew pricked up his ears.

"Ah, you correspond with Richelieu?"

"I have that honor, among others. But I am on furlough, and M. du Vallon brought me an extension!"

"I was put out in a small boat, and I rescued him——"

"Returning hither to await him."

"A regular appointment, between these French gentlemen," observed the duchess, significantly.

Braganza looked around like one who sees in what he took to be separate links a chain which might bind him. On remarking the Jew, he frowned.

"Wrecks, wrecks, nothing but wrecks," said he, passing his hand across his brow. "Ill omen!"

"Not in the slightest, highness!" briskly and bluntly

said the musketeer. "Out of wrecks one obtains treasures. M. du Vallon not only brought me an extension of leave, but a message intimately concerning——"

"Concerning me! I shall be glad to hear it?"

"I do not say it directly concerns your grace; but it does directly concern this gentleman——" and he clapped his hand on Soleiman's shoulder, which made the latter squirm as if arrested.

"Gentleman?"

"This is Elizor Soleiman, the wealthiest Jew left in Portugal! the bravest of Hebrews in that he stays, the last of his race who are not converts! the most generous of Israelites in that he devotes his fortune and his financial talent, a greater fortune to him who appreciates it, to the future of Portugal!"

The whole assembly in the Petrel's best room were in solemn attention.

"Oh, these landsmen!" muttered the naval lieutenant, "never are they so happy as in cutting the stays before they have the mast stepped firmly! I shall get me out of this before I am involved neck deep! I smell halters and gibbets!"

With that he cautiously withdrew. Soleiman looked as if he would have liked to do the same; but he fastened his eyes on the man who had praised him like a rabbit in a cage with a serpent.

"This in spite of the Inquisition! Oh, it is only a difference of opinion between them!" said the Gascon, with his fine irony. "They both want his wealth for a propaganda! now they seek to spend it in smoothing the way of the benighted to the Throne Celestial; he in smoothing the approaches to the Throne Portuguese. I conjecture that never will he trouble himself about the Holy Brotherhood if it will confine its power to Spain. In the meantime, he is about to start the good work with a blow from a golden mallet! Elizor," continued he, suddenly showing him that paper which Porthos had brought over from France and his companion warrant, "you will pay to his highness the Duke of Braganza the sum of one and a half million pesetas of silver on these and my verbal order now given, and such other sums as are held by you in trust for France, per deposit of its Prime Minister, whose warrant to cover you and me you here see—to the King of Portugal!"

"The K-K-King of Portugal!"

"Be ye all witness that I am the foremost to hail the Duke of Braganza as the King of Portugal," proceeded D'Artagnan, in his inexhaustible vein.

He went down on one knee and held out his sword, hilt first, toward the astonished and overjoyed nobleman.

The latter took it, with his hand tremulous, and went through the performance of knighting the kneeling captain, saying:

"Rise, Louis d'Artagnan, hidalgo, grandee, Knight Commander of the Holy Cross of Portugal! And as for your companion, who brings such good tidings, I make him grandee!"

"A grandee! What will madame say?" gasped Porthos. "Long live the King of Portugal!" shouted he, as if to be heard at San Sebastian at least.

"As for this courageous and talented Soleiman," continued Braganza, who had fallen into this bestowal of gifts, which cost him nothing, with truly royal facility, "I appoint him my private privy pursebearer, with a seat at the Council of State for financial matters. For further honors, let us not anticipate time!"

His wife looked at him admiringly. This was to be a real king! Her pupil was promising!

Jacinta gazed on D'Artagnan. Soleiman might be wealthy and cunning, the duke gracious and generous, the duchess correct in her presage; but, to her, all turned on her hero—D'Artagnan was the hand spinning the ball which, by its course upon the dais of state and its fall into the winning pit, or off the board, was to decide everything.

"Death of my life!" said the musketeer, to Porthos, in a dazzled state, "look at this! Over a million in the strong box, two such swords as ours, this petty nucleus of an army—less than this has conquered a kingdom! But," with a sigh, "I miss that brave, sensible Pedro and his brethren of the coast!"

There could not have been an eavesdropper in those

seamen; but this news had spread. The men of the *Messier* and the Spanish servants were fraternizing over a cask of Hollands broached by the lavish Quaqua. They flourished their staves and their cutlasses, and repeated.

"Long live Juan IV., King of Portugal!"

CHAPTER XXI.

THIN THREADS, BUT STRONG.

As a military organizer, the king's musketeer thoroughly proved his capability. Without showing it superficially, Las Salinas was soon transformed. As the fishers came in, straggling from having stood out to the north to avoid the storm center, or from the south, where they had sought refuge round the headland, they were marshaled into a kind of flying picket. No surprise by sea was possible.

Fortunately, for gaining time, San Sebastian was badly damaged. Squalls continued, alternating with land breezes, so that search along shore from that port was limited. The particular search was for the noble prince on the *Amor de Dios,* who was reported certainly dead, as no survivors were discovered, though portions of her hull were met at every turn. Her dead were identified and not treated any too well, from being classed as would-be traitors. All allusion to the assassination was prohibited. Not one of the searchers came into view of the spies from Las Salinas, and those fishers who were directed by D'Artagnan to go to the harbor for news, returned with useless advices as regarded the first stronghold of the upstart monarch.

He had a long conference with Soleiman and the Frenchman, after which he departed, glad in a measure at having the disbursement of the cash, for the pleasure of some money-lovers is in the spending thereof. Between the duke's special knowledge of the officers of trust whom he was to bribe, and the local knowledge D'Artagnan had acquired in his tour of investigation, he ought to remove many a stumbling block when the pretender advanced with a force.

Juan de Braganza had a sea guard, under the ex-lieutenant of the *Messier,* whom he created knight and naval commander; a land guard under D'Artagnan and Porthos. his second: a treasurer in the Soleiman: and a fine chance of escape to a French port if things turned out adversely. Above all, he had a wife of worth, who valued him as never before. The tribute of the Frenchman to his valor and self-sacrifice clasped her to him so that she resolved to win or die.

But fever visits him on the throne steps as on the truckle bed. After the narrow escape from drowning came the prostration from which he did not so easily extricate himself as the inured soldier.

More than once, by his sick bed, the watchers feared that he would never more take an active step, and that King Philip might well rate him out of the lists.

In the painful interval of his rallying and recovering, a fisher or two, whom D'Artagnan had had Pedro's word that they might be relied upon, went away with advices to Oporto, Lisbon and northern points.

Their returns came by other fishers, smugglers and chapmen, sure hands; D'Artagnan received them, smiling secretly in his mustache; he saw a very far-reaching hand in the composition of these excellent tidings, showing that the guiding spirit in this overturning was a finer one than the Braganzas.

"These are thin threads, but strong," thought he. "My word on it, they will be twisted into a rope which will strangle Spain!"

It was due to the ladies, who pressed the fisherwomen into service, that the interior of the Petrel was altered into comfort, nay, brilliancy. Sailcloth made arras, but over the canvas spread rugs, carpets, tapestry, of the choicest Oriental weaves, which came out of Pedro's lockers, but would have been envied by dwellers at St. Germain's, the Escurial or Whitehall.

The Braganzas, in this hermitage, sometimes did not regret their place at Villaviciosa.

From a stranded whale a profusion of oil had been extracted, so that they baked lamps in clay after the antique pattern, bowl-shaped with protruding beaks; these, with candles, so illuminated the reception-room that one entering, from Italy, for example, would have believed he was in the Chapel of the Child-in-the-Manger, at Naples Cathedral.

"You will be able to mount a horse, or begin a voyage

before long," pleasantly said the duchess to her husband as, with renewed appetite, he finished his hearty meal with a rustic "milkpot," that is a kind of custard without eggs. "Let us come to an understanding in the between-whiles."

"About what?"

"This plot——"

"I thought that all cut-and-dried, though not hung up! We are of accord are we not, to a title? For you conspired for me, ay! and did so before I harbored the intention."

"How could that be when you were born for the Portuguese throne? How be it, I am plotting against myself!"

Braganza shook his head, not seeing the reasoning. In fact, although this woman probably understood him to the uttermost, he never yet had fathomed one to whom he might owe a throne.

"You look forward with rapture to your ascension to the separate throne?"

"Not exactly rapture! It is joy of a kind. It is a thorny seat. Portugal is badly situated for a peaceful monarch—between the deep sea and Spain. I shall be likened to the man on the cliff edge, with Satan walking on his landward side!"

"Dear Juan, when you are seated at the fountain's mouth, disposing of offices, posts, places, honors, ribbons, stars—with this foreign loan trying to fill the sieves of the court Danaides, the favorites, all will absorb your time, business and leisure, save your wife."

"Absurd, my dear!" he replied, reproachfully.

"It is a queen's destiny! they are married for policy and reasons of State! It is glorious for pride, but wearing on the heart! I am proud—the Gonzagas have that weakness—but I have a heart. I accept your fate—you I shall never blame! Not only have I wifely affection——"

Spontaneously he uttered a "Heaven bless you!"

"But above all, devotion of a true friend is mine."

"I know that, and I thank the Giver of Good for it all!"

"Being my duty, I do not want to be thanked too warmly for that, sir!"

"Then, despite this future of jealous fears—chimeras, truly—you conspire for me against yourself?"

"Against my happiness, I believe!"

"Well, there is an old detestation in our race against the distaff—the Braganzas have heretofore relied on the sword, but I fear me, since Christianity emancipated woman from the seraglio, that we must sometimes be grateful to them and receive their gifts. Upon my honor, though humiliating, I would sooner owe my crown to you than to those French swordsmen's blades, and, far more, than to the Soleiman's purse! But come, how about your plots—since however remote they spring and perchance deviously run, they flow into the same channel? You know all about mine, precipitated now by King Philip attacking me in person. I am not 'suppressed'—I am forced to return the blow! They call me 'The Mole,' do they? Well, dragged out of my burrow, I shall fight, open-eyed!"

In his eye was a savage gleam and none would recognize at that instant the supposed model prince content at his sovereign's footstool.

"Well, Juan, while you have been spreading the toils abroad, I have enlisted the ladies throughout Portugal——"

"A crusade of the Eleven Thousand Virgins!"

"All they ask in return for their jewels, their husbands, sons, brothers and sweethearts, is a brilliant court!"

"I see! feasts, galas, regattas, tauric combats, balls! Astute policy! this will gratify and repay the trading and merchant classes. And the vulgar like to look on over the hedge of soldiers!"

"Therefore, throughout the kingdom, I have three parts on my side, that is, your side!"

"Good! My lady, you are, may happen, wiser than I. I am like the sea watch who sees clearer what is farthest off. You have been angling at home, while I have been trawling in distant waters."

"At least, I have played with my own line at my fingers' ends—your grace must needs employ agents?"

"As if I were already consecrated, I sent out ambassadors. They were, to begin with, that lineal descendant
of the Rhymer of Albuterra, the versifier of our first
King of Portugal—Don Joa de Palamo——"

"He is nephew of the Archbishop of Lisbon, no
friend——"

"Because he is the king's deputy for Portugal? One
must be somebody's nephew! Then comes the Caballero
lero Roha, called Rodrigo, the Lord Paramount of the
Marches of Ortalegra——"

"A college companion of Olivarez himself!"

"That cannot be—he is too young—it was Luis de
Haro, the Prime Minister's relative, who went to Evora
University with Joa; a boy could not foresee what his
playmates would arrive to!"

"Any other?" inquired the lady, evidently convinced
that her inveterate husband would not readily renounce
his selections.

"Fra Benito, of Segovia, who was the Caballero de
Mariagalante before he took orders—somewhat loosely,
they say—not a sackcloth, but a net through which he
can slip at intervals. Is he a religious brother or a lay
one? I myself believe that, when he entered the mon-
astery from the cavalry barracks he thought he could
walk through the cloisters and out into the palace gateway! Never was dashing dragoon more pious when
he was in the horse company—never is priest so war-
like since he put on the hood! But he is useful, this
man who can pray with the priests and prey with the
free-lances!"

"I suppose chameleons are useful! What powers
have these versatile ambassadors been accredited to?"

"Don Joa, who speaks French, of Paris, went to
Louis, with a view of securing support of the old nobility whom Cardinal Richelieu has estranged——"

"Estranged is a mild term for the enmity at being
decimated by the sanguinary prelate!"

"Hush! speak well of the bridge which carries us over!
The intestinal differences there matters not, now! We
have the great premier on our side, bound to us with
golden bonds. A fig for the boar-sticking king, whose
wife is our Philip's sister—never would France have

couched her lance upon Spain had it not been for the cardinal-duke, who leveled it, for he hates Anna of Austria!"

"A fine prince of the Church to hate a wife for re-
jecting his addresses!"

"Mere chatter of the boudoirs, and musty! Every
coin he tells out to relieve Portugal of her bugbear tells
me he is a great man! She is an aging coquette!"

"The older she grows, the better some like her! I
wish she, too, was our friend! Being our enemy—'let
her trot by!' What have these ambassadors been
doing?"

"Ortalegra's Lord saw the Duke of Savoy, but he is
a sorely beaten man; he passed through Holland. but
the wary Dutch, hearing that their hereditary foes, the
Spanish, are reconstructing their fleet after their own
models, want to see the result before they engage them
again or engage themselves with others. If these imi-
tations swim—well, they will fight them, not in our
waters, but in the East Indies. As for England——"

"Pardon me, these envoys, who have drawn blanks,
do you fully trust them?"

"Madame, I trust nobody, outside my family!" and
Braganza smiled like an Oriental, rather than a Vandal.

"Those gentlemen betray you! You have lost your
money!"

"I paid them in promises!"

"That makes it the more likely you are deceived;
where the master's wage is air, the servants get their
sustenance from the guests. What did you really hope
from the French Court?"

"Little! The king might send me a boar's head, of
his own killing, mounted in silver, on a Palissy platter!
In France the king must not kill higher game than
boars—here, in Spain, the king tries to kill—princes!"

The woman shuddered.

"Never heed! Thanks to Richelieu—an anchor! we
can ride the storm through, at that!"

"What did you expect from England, Luis, from a
king besotted and wedded to a bigot?"

"Not money! Yet a force of those subjects whom
he is so discontenting that they fade away like mists!

Instead, he lets them slip away to the colonies, or ships them there! a pity for us, as the sons of those who beat off the Grand Armada might give a good account of the Spanish off San Sebastian! Ah, to have twenty sail of them under my banner! It cannot be helped—the Stuart will not help Braganza! Heaven help him, then! I doubt not, see you, darling! that when I wear the crown, he will be lacking his—or his head!"

"What do you mean?" she said, in horror.

"Only that Roha sent me, by the smuggler's post, a pasquin in which it was advised, as a certain exalted person had a 'stiff neck,' that a sharp ax would be needed, with a tough stock! The allusion is clear! particularly so to me, from having seen Charles depicted in an Amsterdam-printed lampoon as St. Denis, with his decollated head under his arm—a caricature of a Velasquez portrait."

"The world will come to an end when sovereigns are beheaded like mere saints and martyrs! Incredible! But how did your cavalier-priest fare?"

"Mariagalante went straight to Rome. The Pope wishes to reign twenty-five years without too many wars. He will, I reckon, try to keep Spain passive, if I raise the standard of revolt."

"Keep Spain passive? All the States of the Church, all the riches of the prince-cardinals, all the bulls and epistles, these would not keep Spain from replying blow to blow with an assailant! Oh, these churchmen who live in libraries and do not know yet Spain's three-worded vocabulary——"

"I do not know it myself—what is it?"

"Blood, fire and war! The Spaniard is cradled, swaddled, exercised and buried to that tribrach!"

"True! After all, I did know that! and shall know still more before we have done this business!" said Braganza, frowning and drawing a deep breath, as if preparing for no mean struggle.

Jacinta appeared at the hanging, cutting across the hall, so as to make a retiring-room beyond.

"Please your grace, two strangers have found their way here. When I say strangers, I think I know them a little. They come from inland on poor mountain ponies—but they are not vulgar—they answered the password correctly."

"They must be our envoys," said Braganza; "they have received the intelligence to direct them to our refuge. Let in the one who answered 'Whitehall and The Hague.' It is Ortalegra," he went on to his consort. "Do not you go away. You have already pronounced on them—but stay——"

"To give out my sentence?"

"Oh, a woman is always too merciful!"

The duchess went and took seat where the light did not fall too glaringly. She narrowly scanned the person ushered in.

CHAPTER XXII.

REBELLION BEGETS REBELS.

The Lord of Ortalegra was of medium stature, heavily built; it would seem that an ancestor had brought home from Flanders a wife of another type than his own. He had folds in his jowl and neck; his eyes were blue, with the edge of the iris defined in darker shade; they were good; his nose was not noble; his hair and trim beard were flaxen, a remarkable thing, perhaps, but some of the Portuguese show tokens of the Gothic and Vandal invasions.

His horseman's cloak covered a suit of yellow; this was Spanish livery, no doubt, but, on the other hand, it is Apollo's color; and Ortalegra was a poetaster—but by no means an aster of poesy.

"I expected you, Rodrigo! I knew you would come on the Winged Steed, if possible, so tractable to you singers! This is the duchess, of whom you have sweetly sung, and before whom you can discourse, I hope, as sweetly!"

"For such an audience, my lord and my lady, I should have been more fleet—if I had good tidings!" He looked round, but he must have had a hint that the reception-rooms were not in a palace; he made no allusion to the duke's escape from the licensed sea bravos, but yet he might not have met the news, certainly not published by herald's mouth to cry of trumpet.

"What, nothing to be had out of the cold north?"

"Cold comfort! Charles I. is at daggers-drawn with his perverse subjects: soldiers unpaid, merchants who will not pay up, courtiers snarling because coin falls into the churchwarden's bag and not on the basset-board, faithless emigrants carrying trade secrets into that New England——"

"No prospect of a few ships and able seamen? for England abounds in both, good, sound, ready!"

Ortalegra shrugged his shoulders, between which his head disappeared by half.

"Not a plank, not a toy for my poor lord!"

"I can only hope," took up Braganza, wiping his brow with his sleeve as if to hide discontent, "that things will be brighter in that sunny France of brother Louis?"

"I doubt any good outcome there, my lord!"

"Why should you doubt it?" the duke snapped him up.

"Only because, on my return, my packet out of Dover being driven into The Hague, there happed to be Don Joa of Palama waiting for a ship southward bound."

"What was Don Joa doing there?"

"He was informed that the road through Spain to Madrid was lined with 'evil gentry'—and, not to be delayed, knowing your lordship was fretting, he went back into the Netherlands. So we sailed homeward in company, as far as Bordeaux, whence we rode——"

"By the Right Faith! any one who knew not how faithful ye are, might suggest you change your motto, Don Rodrigo, from 'Serve the King!' to 'Be Strong by Concord!' It would look to the suspicious spectator that you and your brother ambassador met by collusion and collated matters!"

"Sire, pure hazard brought us under the Prince of Orange's ensign."

"Where did you leave your *semper fidelis,* Don Joa, then?"

"Your grace," replied the other, slowly, as if he had to pick his words now, "at San Sebastian we found rare agitation. The weather has been terrible. The wrecks are numerous. The orders were out for the utmost diligence to be exercised in seeking the poor wretches drowned. They were hunting for the dead bodies as if each had a pocketful of the treasure from their hapless ships—you may know that in face of total ruin, the word goes: 'Pocket the gold! each is treasurer here!'"

"Oh, they were recovering the dead to plunder! not correct in his majesty's soldiers and sailors, eh?"

"They were seeking——" he paused, not sure how much was known of the outer world in this isolated nook. "They were seeking the officers and passengers of con-

sequence—because there had been a *festa* at a neighboring port—a new vessel was put on the water."

"I have heard about that! Go on!"

"Large galleys had been cracked on the Mole in trying to enter, like nuts in a baboon's claw! We concluded that, even with our servants united, we could not
make much way against the wreckers, who hovered
around the regular searchers, sparing no one who raised
his voice against their pilfering, and so, came on. At a
little village we left our varlets and hurried here."

"It was well not to publish this retreat as yet. Would
you kindly call Don Joa?" Braganza rose to cause the
other to draw back. "I am deficient in ushers."

"A fig; the court comes where the king is!" said the
envoy pleasantly, and, smiling, he obeyed.

During his fleeting disappearance under the hanging,
the duke stepped up beside his wife and whispered to
her:

"Flattery so soon! where the flatterers are, a fool is
near!"

"Don't you be the fool, Luis! Now, do you doubt
the game they are playing?"

"Madame, usually only the mighty are betrayed—why
gull the fondly believing?"

"Because it is doubly base, and the traitor cannot
stoop too low!"

When Don Roha was seen next he was accompanied
by his fellow noble.

Don Joa de Palama was an elderly man; one of those
who dry up at a certain age, and never after show the
progress of time; their hair grizzles but does not bleach;
their eyes sink, but do not dull; their teeth wear down
but do not fall out. In eighty years they do more harm,
if double-dealing and vicious, than a worthy good man
does good in a century; perhaps, that is why these evil-
doers rarely live to be a hundred.

"Come in boldly, Don Joa," said the duke, affably.
"For I have been fortified as to the bad tidings tarnish-
ing your usually golden smile!"

It was a sickly smile Palama wore.

"Welladay! yea, good my lord, bad!" sighed he.

"You met no obstacles to your seeing the King of France?"

"I saw him several times, truly. There were no difficulties, but the site of the interviews was not agreeable to a quiet man like me."

"Really, ill-chosen, you say?"

"King Louis was always out hunting!"

The duke exchanged a glance signifying "I told you so!" with his lady.

"And, somehow, I have an antipathy to dogs and hawks—they will snap at me!"

"They know a good thing when they see it! But he listened to you in spite of that distraction?"

"As well as he could, between firing of a gun on a rest, and fleshing, in bucks, the knife to which he seldom gave a rest!"

"Since you bandy words, I foretell that he refused my offer, if I mounted the Portuguese throne, to so worry my neighbor that he would not worry his next to the north, for a lifetime—at least, for my lifetime!"

"Well, he neither refused nor accepted. He said that, as a wedded man, you would understand that he would not offend his queen by rending her brother's and his brother's (by court etiquette) kingdom asunder! He added that he could not see the event—he positively would not see it—but he would wink if your grace successfully attempted it! The gracious king would wink!"

"Mere words—anything more, if not better?"

"He said that he had killed a stag 'of ten,' and would ——"

"Have it mounted in silver and sent me on a platter of Palissy pottery——"

"How did your grace know that?" cried Palama, opening his eyes widely.

The duke laughed toward his lady grimly.

"I have an astrologist-soothsayer," said he, "who looks into the To-Come deeper than that!"

"Further, he referred me to his First Minister."

"Ah, not like master, like man! Did the Duke of Richelieu hear you with as much courtesy as his king?"

"There was courtesy enough! Here was no longer a shredded conversation between antlers, tusks and fangs!

but we conversed over treaties of peace, truces, protocols, proposals for a congress of European pacification, a fitting field on which to broach a plot to disrupt a sister-kingdom! *Ay de mi!* a great change has come over the cardinal-minister, whom I saw at the Passage of the Doire, on foot, like the meanest servant-of-the-guns, under the hail and freezing rain, whizzing down from the mountains, when the French army, after giving the Italians a drubbing, shouted:

" 'Long live the bellicose prelate !' "

"My lord, the Cardinal Duke of Richelieu is a dying tree. He whined to me that France was a-weary of broils, that her captains fought only with wine-pots in hand, that their swords hung in the second-hand iron-dealers' stalls because they had no pay and had to dispose of them for misthrows of the dice; that he was overcome by the Pope's chiding him for turbulence, for stirring up of strife. He showed me the Holy Father's autograph—he pointed with a trembling finger, scarce able to hold up the ring, to a line where he was characterized as a firebrand! He protested that he would have to walk barefoot to Rome in penance if again he lent a troop of horse or a file of musketeers, to say nothing of a trifle of fifty thousand livres to support the most just of rebellions!"

The duchess held her great fan to her face to hide her discomfiture—or her merriment.

The duke showed only impatience.

"But as concerns me!"

"Oh, he said, 'Ah, me! would your Duke of Braganza become a king let him take an old statesman's warning, one who speaks out of that hollow veil, the grave: "Do not set a sail too large for your ship!" ' "

"I am indebted to his eminence—for nothing!" responded the ambitious one, with palpable jeering. "There is always some gain in learning an aged politician's advice—if one runs counter to it! It may chance that the ship can bear more than the critics surmise! It will suffice, by Heaven's will, if it carry the honor of Braganza into the haven!"

"What! does your grace persist in his monstrous intention!" ejaculated Palama, surprised, but nudged by his companion to express their feelings.

Braganza lifted his hand as though it held a sword.

"Braganza will quarter the Five Moors' Heads of Portugal again on its coat, or—lose its own single one!"

"If you fail——"

"Another trial will be made. The second of an endless series of essays! He conquers who endures!"

"What, persist, after our intelligence?" said Roha, as if affronted.

"On my estates there is a peasant's phrase—plain talk, plain folk, you know—'He who squints abroad, will not see straight at home.' If you have misinformed me, it is because you let yourselves be misinformed!"

The two counterplotters looked at him, but dropped their eyes. Never had the moody prince seemed so glorified. They ventured to consult one the other visually. Here stood a man, and a woman was, alone, by— they were two swordsmen—and the King of Spain would reward as well for the head of this arch-rebel on its body as off!

They were checked in putting any plan into action by the hanging being withdrawn behind them. Not wanting to be taken in the rear, they turned.

CHAPTER XXIII.

FIRST SWORD, THEN SCEPTRE.

It was only Donna Jacinta who tripped in, a step or two, saying archly:

"It is the visitors' day at Petrel Palace! Your grace, Father Benito begs the favor of a hearing——"

"Fra Benito?"

"From St. Peter's Patrimony direct——"

"Glad to receive the reverend father! He speaks sparingly, but he does not spare the rod of chastening wisdom."

Between themselves, the two hidalgoes smiled, for they best knew whether this was an ally or a disputant who came so timely.

Jacinta had instantly ushered in a man in a monk's frock and cowl; his bare feet had been tanned by dye—or long exposure, so as to defy mud to color them; some treatment—or severe journeys, had made the soles hardy against gravel, and his ankles impervious to brambles.

On the breast of the cape attached to his ample cowl was a white cross, probably to indicate he was a Dominican, but, on closer view, there could be made out, in its centre, embroidered with a fine needle, a naked sword in a laurel wreath, looking like a cross again. This was the insignia of the Holy Inquisition.

Fra Benito, of Segovia, was one of those ambiguous persons of the times; it was always in doubt whether they were high church dignitaries having a dispensation from certain vows—if they took any in putting on the garb; or, lay brothers allowed to wear the robe and ecclesiastical marks in order better to execute mysterious services. It was asserted that he was deeply learned; while, on the other part, he was accused of letting his more reverend name cover pamphlets of controversy which, from their variety, it is said, could not have flowed from a single pen. Fortunately—we say, fortunately—the uncultivated herd who light fires and lamps with any paper "spoilt" by ink marks, have left not a line to parade his or his inspirator's work.

His was a long-drawn face, with straight nose which farther lengthened it; his eyes were fine, but too close together; his brows met in a bar across; his chin was pointed. One would have said that an impudent nurse had left him to sleep too long on one side and had put a folio on the other to keep him quiet. His skin was leatherlike, and had the oil oozing at the pores, which suggested that he bathed in one of those unctuous extracts which, at the time, were supposed to give long life.

A man with a set purpose, this Benito.

When he was a soldier, he was poor in purse; though rich in projects, which his superiors did not adopt.

If he was still poor, perhaps, he had taken the vow of poverty.

It was on his tongue that he carried his silver; he preached eloquently.

Impenetrable, indomitable, indefatigable—these were his points.

He pretended that he had footed it all the way to and from Rome; then, he must have been assisted by angel wings—considering his fleetness; but he had not a jot of the pride illuminating the usual pilgrim to the Sacred City.

His glance was quick but comprehensive in surveying the paltry reception-room. He recognized the duchess without even a nod; he eyed her attendant with repulsion, of which she had not a clew to the cause—it might be another vow of hate to the sex; for the courtiers he scarcely began a bow, although they had bent lowly to him.

His head did not bend to the duke, but he opened his hands and twiddled the fingers in a kind of salaam.

Maybe it was a mythical sign only mutual, but the duchess turned red, and her maid of honor bit her lip at the slight and let the screen fall behind her to blot out the sight.

"I have been showered with unwelcome intelligence," said Braganza. "Are you bringing cheer, *per contra*, reverend father?"

"I have returned from his Holiness and your other

friends," was the evasive reply of the Dominican, folding his lean hands within his flowing sleeves so that now nothing was seen of his upper person but the nose and eyes of the acute physiognomy.

"Do you mean that is all? that you were in danger of leaving your skin, as a foe to Spain?"

The thin hands came out like a knot of snakes, but it was to haul up a rosary of fragrant sandal wood, dependent at his side, as a trained blackbird pulls up its seed bucket, and they set to running the beads through them. He might be murmuring a prayer of thanks for an escape.

"Your highness has enemies who have resolved his death and his friends'."

"There is evidence of it! Yet all men who walk on high have death on the other side to that of the guardian-angel—dukes and rope-dancers! Go on! About my friends? God helping, we shall know how to deal with our enemies the more easily when they are avowed!"

The tone was so emphatic that the three passed a but feebly encouraging glance among them.

"Friends?—your highness stands alone."

"I hear that no help comes out of the north, true! But as a scholar—you know: *Non solus*—— He stands not alone whom God stands beside.'"

"You are as wise as your foregoer, *El Sabio*, but more than wisdom is required to pluck the beard of the lion!"

"Though the lion (Leon, the province of Spain) is housed in a triple Castle (Castile) I am going to pluck the beard, and as much flesh as comes with it in my grasp! Be the finish limned with water in dust, or written with a pen of gold on a silver leaf, the record will stand. If the plow goes, I will hold the handles or drive the reins! Woe to those who fall under driver, horse or plow!"

The hearers shivered; but the monk gave one of those irritating cackles, part laugh, part cough, which come from judges tickled with jail fever.

"My lord, your friends doubt your ability. There, the sharp word is out!"

"When men speak ill, one must live so as to belie them. But what friends—the false ones?"

"The Cardinal Banuccio. for one!"

"I do believe in him! What does he think—not of me—a straw! but of my project?"

"The answer he sent is a jewel—*an icterias*——"

"The stone to cure jaundice! Then, he——"

"Believes you a sick prince, and blessed with visions!"

"Pardy; to see a crown—celestial—is to be a Cardinal! To see one earthly, is to be a sick-brain! I thank the sage in scarlet! As for Giustinanio?"

"He is besotted with fatty degeneration, I lament to say! It was very throatily that he gurgled: (imitating) that he had a horoscopist in his secretary, who had forecast your grace's fate by Catoptromancy, which is done by dipping a mirror in water——"

"I think, I know—I saw two professors of it burnt at Madrid for the practice—one tells by the figures traced on the glass by the water remaining——"

"No doubt. Your highness' figure stood alone among circles—ciphers——"

"By the sword which smote the Five Emirs!" cried Braganza, warmly, losing his great patience at being badgered before his wife, "I shall prove that when the figure is followed by ciphers enough, it is a million strong!"

Up rose the duchess with a flaming cheek.

"What nonsense, father!" she said, in the monk's face. "Every old woman knows that it is a trick; you draw the figure desired on the glass with a candle-end so that the water clouds the surface where there is no grease! Pshaw! these are fool-traps beneath a primate's heed."

Caught between two fires, the monk mumbled, in his cowl, within which he had receded like a tortoise.

"What did the Prince Farnese say?"

"He said that he would have the Trigintals said for your highness in his private chapel!"

"Thirty masses! as if I were dead and gone! By the Inexhaustible Grace! there will be newly-dead, dying deploring that I did not follow some false beacon into the Pit! But the Pope, our Holy Urban, what he sends may not be gold, but it will be worth it!"

"The Holy Father said—said——" he stammered, as if he were rolling a hot but toothsome morsel over his tongue, he said, urbanely enough: "Cups have two handles, in order that two men may make a choice——"

"Of the contents?"

"Of the handles."

"Propound!"

"That Christians should agree. 'Let Philip and Juan reign over Spain and Portugal, turn by turn!'"

"Imbecile!" burst forth the prince, for once losing self-command at so much straining of his patience and self-respect.

Fra Benito crossed himself and rattled his beads like bones in a dance of death; the nobles made similar signs; even the duchess looked demure, like a maid which had overheard a naughty word.

Singularly, a low, smothered laugh was vaguely heard; not Donna Jacinta, surely, if she had overheard the libel; but, plainly, no one in this region laughed at the general Abbo—no, this was some menial, and the sound merely accidentally coinciding.

"Yes, my lord," went on the monk, recovering and burning to resent the slur by a bitter retort, "he said that he believed you were true descendant of Queen Joanna——"

"Of 'Crazy Jane!' I thank him, for the knowledge of my line! Fortunately, a little wit will serve a fortunate man!"

"Your highness fortunate?" sneered the rash monk, who was rapidly becoming a soldier again.

The others seemed to repeat the doubt to themselves.

"Certainly, Juan of Braganza is a fortunate prince— has he not a commendable spouse, and faithful adherents——"

The nobles force a smile, but dubiously. They were a little inattentive. That faint laugh out of the other had puzzled them. They seemed listening to some other sounds, of more meaning, as one guessing an appointed hour wishes the assurance of the clock stroke.

"From the excellent opinion which the Holy Father and my Romish friends entertain of me, I see that it will not be his lips to entone the *Te Deum* for my victories! It will be the cannon's mouth!"

"Blessed Chains of St. Peter! do you still consider

war with Spain! you, with no friend in Christendom!"
cried the astonished monk. "Beware of the Heavenly
wrath! Reject the word of the Lord through his Servant, and you will be rejected from being King over
Israel! Think of the Papal ire. Oh, remember——" and
he chanted with no more reverence than if he were reciting a barrack-room lilt, on an air of Palestrina's:

> "Where wrath of God is,
> The heavy rod is
> That ruins our bodies!"

"Peace!" thundered the duke. "Enough with such
supremacy!" that even the reformed Mariagalante was
hushed.

In the silence, at the distance, a trumpet blast was to
be heard, on land; while, at sea, the detonation of a
heavy gun resounded.

All lifted their heads, and while a cloud darkened the
duke and duchess, the light which their countenance lost
seemed reflected upon the monk's and the two envoys.
They felt satisfaction in some degree.

"Gentlemen, nothing that you had to say dissuades me
from my resolve. My colors are stitched to my cap!
King Philip wished me to be his pensioner; but one may
buy his ease too dear! King Philip wished to rock me
to my death in the cradle of a bombarded man-of-war!
Yea, out at sea there!—that shot too clearly reminds me!
for these deeds shun the eye of man! He tried to hoist
me with his petards higher than my ambition soars! Or
send me to the bottomless whirl where the perfidious
angels fell! It is a duel to the death between us, mark
that well!"

"A duel!"

"If you will not be my seconds, you must stand off the
field; for I shall strike down all that buckler him! this
crowned Nightmare on Humanity's breast!

"I have not solely relied on such as you and those
false friends with whom you colleagued much too closely!
Summer will disclose what winter hid! Never will he
wound who fears to strike! I know it is a coffin or a
crown! but I will pierce this Leviathan whose flounder-
ing carcase burdens the ocean; after the stricken whale
has sunk, in the wake ruddied with his gore, a myriad

happy fish will sport, and feed, and thrive! So do the subjects of a despot enjoy their halcyon hour when he is swept away! Yes, the harpooner may be carried down by the fatal lance, but his memory lives and inspires another, who may better taste the fruit of victory. Crown me not King, if I shall not be the Liberator, too!

"Do you follow? the king's favor is no inheritance—it must be earned. Please me, and prosper! It is hard to live at Court with the king at variance! Men reward with pasture in its old age the steed that carried, not the one that threw!"

He was interrupted by the cannon seaward and the trumpet inland, strong though his exhortation had been.

The two nobles advanced as though to offer him the homage solicited.

"Sirs, the ship is ready. I am going to Oporto with those dear to me!"

The duchess had risen. At the opening, her maid appeared.

"What is that, my lord?" asked Don Joa, of any one who could enlighten.

"I say," continued the prince, "that my friends in Portugal await me, and that I shall sit on the throne in Lisbon Palace, or I shall have joined my ancestors in the tombs therein!"

"Will not your grace," urged Roha. "permit a humble servitor to show the rashness of this step——"

"Gentlemen, I am decided. Follow or fall——"

"Sure," persisted Joa in a bolder tone, having the monk ranged conspicuously by his side as the noble supported him on the other; "we do not believe it is our duty, as your grace s well-desiring lieges, to let you rush upon a certain doom! In such a case our devotion compels——"

"Do you mean you would compel me?" began Braganza, indignantly.

"Our duty—hear us! compels us to oppose such departure!"

The duke laughed in their faces while his lady, standing only a pace back, exposed to the same strokes, for it was in deference, not lack of courage, reflected his laugh—if a smile is the reflection of a laugh.

"By force?" queried he in the bitterest gibing tone.

"By all means!" returned Raho.

"Good sooth! what means have you?"

"My lord," said Fra Benito, at last disclosing himself, as here the others failed to maintain the initiative; "King Philip, on hearing that you had escaped the just penalty for your continual plotting and high treason, and believing that you might also elude the fate Heaven sent others than you, ordered Admiral Ozario to take up the search for your body—living or dead! On finding that your ship had been pounded to atoms, but that you had been snatched from the calamity——"

"I guess! one or the other of you, to make terms for the double duplicity—sent word where you had an appointment with your lord! using my own letters! Out on ye!"

"Exactly!" returned Roha, unabashed. "The cruisers have therefore been sent along this coast, even to this paltry den of fish-fags and wreckers, to cut off your flight by water!"

"While," continued the second noble traitor, "the Captain-general sends a force overland to prevent a flight through the country."

The position looked hopeless; and the duchess herself lost her florid hue. On the other hand, fired by this first opportunity which the Chained Tiger of Philip IV. had enjoyed to show his mettle, her lord glowed with long-penned up rage. In a voice of thunder again he rejoiced:

"Sa, ha! sirs! your treachery is manifest at last! Under a mask of fidelity, you have been fawning upon me these years!"

"My lord!" and they audaciously clapped their hands to their swords.

As for the ex-captain turned monk, he fumbled for his beads, no doubt to pray for a heavenly interposition in this impending fight.

"Do you draw on your highness, and not in his defence?" exclaimed the duchess, dashing down her fan, which, as she drew it, showed it was a sheath for a long, slender stiletto of Italian device—a not unique precaution when princesses, as we see, were not absolutely safe.

"This is a man's affair, Luisa," remarked Don Juan, with cold composure. "Sirs, before being a king, I was a duke; before a duke, gentleman born! Before bearing sceptre, I carry sword! My last order is: 'Way for Braganza!' or, by Him that made me, I will make a way through ye!"

"It is against the king's decree!" cried Rodrigo, drawing.

"Impossible!" added Joa, imitating him.

"In Heaven's name, no useless bloodshed!" said the monk, fumbling with his rosary, but as a prisoner does with his chains when intending to club them to brain his warden.

"Ah, madame, you truthfully declared that these were recreants and traitors!"

The three swords were now out, and beginning to fence, like steel serpents seeking to dart in with a sting. To the amazement of all, Donna Jacinta sprang between the court-sword and the poniard and the two long war-swords.

"Your grace, let me most respectfully say, do not use your unsullied sword on traitors! For them the axe!"

"What am I to do?" asked Braganza, who knew that she did not ill-advise.

"A king would arrest them!" replied she, in the same undertone.

Surprise turned to inquiry on the duke's countenance.

"Call your captain of the lifeguards," the young lady explained.

"Oh, have I a capt——"

"It is beyond a doubt! and he is beyond that door! a thorough one, who has testimonials from a former employer that he has served his apprenticeship——"

"Oh, that French musketeer!"

"Splendid!" exclaimed the duchess. "I would call him!" rewarding the prompter with a smile which promised adequate realization. "Halloa there!" cried Don Juan, authoritatively raising his voice, "my Captain of the Lifeguards!"

CHAPTER XXIV.

THE GRIP OF PORTHOS.

At the clank of a spurred heel, steady and regular as a pump-beat, the two traitorous nobles, and the monk as well, shrank back; but the last, being the more courageous, formed the bulwark to the others. All three stared with consternation at the stranger, who advanced three paces, as if timed, brought his heels together and saluted Don Juan with exactness, speaking of ten or twelve years' daily discipline.

"Your orders, Majesty?" said he, fixing his eyes on the trio, as if in anticipation of their being the offenders.

"As my Captain of Lifeguards, arrest those two worthies for revolt against their liege." In his gesture he conspicuously excluded the holy brother.

D'Artagnan's sword was drawn, but hung by its sword-knot from his wrist, so as to leave his hands free. They had their own out, but their grasp trembled with awe, if not with terror. Nevertheless, he took another forward step, which thrust him between them, and, clapping a hand on their shoulders, where they closed like a vise, he said, in a clear voice, without any emotion whatever:

"By order of the King of Portugal, you are my prisoners!"

The canvas had been furled up at the doorway. There appeared, with naked cutlasses, the *Messier's* boat's-crew, with Lieutenant Constant next the opening. On seeing this formidable array, in regular uniform, Dons Joa and Rodrigo were depressed into hopelessness, and silently handed their weapons to the captain.

"Hang it all!" muttered the latter, "where is friend Porthos? I could wish him here to relieve me of this extra captive. Two birds in the hand are embarrassing!"

Transferring the pair to the sailors, he found that he had not come out of the cavern any too soon.

Rounding the headland, but fairly in the offing, so

much dreaded was the coast, still studded with wreckage, loomed up a tolerably large vessel, the one which had fired the guns. It was the more ponderous in appearance as it was of the old type, retaining in more than name the forecastle and the monstrous poop. It bore the royal standard of Spain. Farther off, nearing gradually, was another of like dimensions.

But confronting them, on D'Artagnan's left hand, each wave-top seemed transformed into an embarkation of some sort; the heaving sea was teeming with flashing oar and bellying sail. Vessels innumerable thronged the expanse to the very horizon, where still more sails dotted the verge.

"Peril of my soul!" cried the startled officer, "all the navies have made Salinas their rendezvous!"

The mere enumeration of their local names would fill pages of an archaic dictionary.

But if dissimilar in build, size and rig, they were alike in their ensigns—on a white field of the universal flag, five black heads showed plainly.

"The Moorish Chiefs killed by King Alfonso the Deliverer," thought the Frenchman, delighted after having been stupefied. "That is the old Portuguese flag, not displayed these fifty years! Come on! come on!" shouted he, as if he could be heard a mile off; "you cannot overdo it!"

With admirable manœuvring in so diverse a fleet, the larger vessels were seen to steer out free of the smaller ones, and take up position to form a barrier against the Spanish.

The soldier criticized the operation with an unerring eye.

"Surpassing fine!" ejaculated he, clapping his hands. "Is there a Richelieu of the ocean, then, who provides a million-and-a-half of floats for Don Juan, as ours did the same number in silver pieces?"

"If there is, his name is Pedro!" uttered a voice, softly, in his ear.

The new royal life guardsman spun round swiftly and with delight—and no awe—gripped the brown hand offered him.

"If my heart jumps like that again, it will be out of

my service altogether," observed he. "Why, my master,
I thought that you had Father Neptune for your host,
in his under-sea tavern of the Cod-on-the-Trent!"

"And I deplored the same of you! As you see, while
the sea does not always give up its dead, it grants the
living a respite. I must be one of the reprobates to be
spewed up after sinking so deep in the swirl!"

"I was picked up next to lifeless," resumed the other,
in a tremulous voice. "What are those countless sail?"

"A few I called together! Where the carrion is, the
vultures gather! We have old grudges, all of us, against
this Spain, a 'blasted' whale, and we have come to cut
her up and 'try' her sorely!"

"But look there, landward!" added D'Artagnan, "those
are soldiers!"

"More Spanish! but never fret! See, my men are
landing, jumping out and wading up the sand. Those are
Dutch, and they have their knives whetted for their old-
time foe. They want to be at them the first! I have
enough of them to spare off the decks to take San Sebastian, if that was logged to do. See them swarm up
the cliffs like rats abandoning an eaten-out grainship for
a full one!"

Indeed, the landed seamen rushed up the height and
streamed out along the edge of the highland so menac-
ingly that the Spanish bugles called a halt, and the on-
comers mustered in a mass.

A battle array had not been expected in this lonely
spot.

"Hold them in check," said Pedro, as if he had been a
military general all his life, to several officers who came
for instructions. "No bloodshed, unless it is forced upon
you. There are friends pressed into service against their
country in those ranks. You will lose nothing in the
long run, as I promised you. Fishes shall feed way up
the inland rivers, and there will be a blush on Portugal
soil as if all the vermillion of the Almaden mines painted
it!"

"What are they? What are they?" demanded D'Artagnan, seeing, but unable to realize the fortuity.

"Our Brothers of the Coast, of course, burning to
singe the Lion's muzzle a little!"

Simultaneously with this land movement, the free-sailors' fleet made a hostile demonstration against the Spanish. Outnumbered, surprised by this overwhelming force, where a few fishing boats had been expected, at the most, the two or three sailing barges and ships turned smartly and made good speed toward the point whence they came.

All at once, while D'Artagnan was still clenching his restored shipmate's hand, they heard commotion inside the Petrel—a woman's scream, a man's guttural outcry, and then a terrifying silence.

" 'Sdeath! What is going on there, when all seemed smooth?" inquired the French knight. "In your inn, comrade, we have the Duke and Duchess of Braganza. We must have no mishap to one whom we are going to seat on the Portuguese throne."

"I thought he was your man," returned Pedro, coolly.

The two hastened up to the cave mouth.

The expeditious manner in which, upon Donna Jacinto's hint, the Duke of Braganza had been served by his Captain of Guards lifted him into the serene heavens. But he had to return to the earth at a touch on his arm. It was the duchess, who indicated that they were not left alone by the removal of only two of the false messengers.

Don Juan looked coldly at the statuesque monk.

"What are you waiting for? to be arrested in your turn?"

The monk shrugged his shoulders, as if defying the lash.

"Pah! your robe saves you! Go, and lie no more!"

"His robe need not save him!" broke in the duchess, having taken a dislike to this person. "We may not have to look far to find one who would use his cord upon his back more honestly than, I guess, he ever corrected himself!"

"You may go," repeated the prince, with bitter scorn, somehow sharing his wife's disgust.

"But," spoke the brother of St. Dominic, "before you go on the way to rive Portugal from Spain, let me know for those whom it most concerns how you intend to deal with Mother Church. As you had those gentlemen re-

moved in the king's name, remove my doubts in that of
the Pope, whose officer I am."

"Oh, the wind blows from the Seven Hills, eh?" muttered the duke, hesitating. "I thought all was allayed in
that cardinal point."

"My lord is the Mother's devout son," interpolated the
lady, regretting her hasty threat. "This is a political
matter, and only the sword and the sceptre are involved.
Do not try to puzzle the bull," continued she, trying to
blot out her misstep with verbiage, "by flourishing the
surplice before his eyes, or you may be trampled un-
awares. We go to pull down nothing—only to replace—
to revive rights. Let the people, if they like, rectify
their wrongs."

This was still half a menace; perhaps as far as the
woman cared to go again; it was sufficient to infuriate
the priest. He drew himself up to his full height, becoming quite another and more redoubtable figure than
the typical cringing friar.

"My lord, I have the papal plenary absolution for
what I do. I am the direct representative and the envoy
of Bishop Remoro, Grand Inquisitor, and, as such, I
must stay your departure until you pledge, by something
too solemn to be broken, not to interfere with the work
of the Church!"

He held up an ornament of his rosary, probably a fragment of the True Cross.

"Orders to me?"

"Your repugnance to answer is a fault, your promises
of treasure to your followers a crime, when you well
know that all the powers have closed their coffers to you,
as when a thief creeps up!"

"Thief? You shall pay for that!"

"Aspirer in vain to an earthly crown, you shall pay for
your presumption! Die!"

Instead of the rosary, it was a dagger that he held as
he darted at the duke. The latter was contemptuously
and yet indignantly turning away to call some one to
deal with the insolent monk.

The blade shone over his head, so that the duchess,
usually strong, was petrified and turned pale. Her eyes
shut in spite of her will. Her arms were extended, but

that was only at random, as if she were blinded and groping.

Jacinta, at the door, was engrossed in contemplating the cordial greeting of D'Artagnan and Pedro.

"I am a dead man!" thought the prince, with the fleetness of the mind at its point of extinction. "Jesus! Maria! have mercy!"

On the threshold of so much!

He wanted to resist, to throw out his hands—anything to repel this descending death—but he was paralyzed. Not by the fear of doom, but because he saw what seemed the hand of Heaven which he was praying for. Overhead, indeed, the canvas ceiling was rent, and a large hand and muscular arm, not at all aerial, darted downward.

This immense hand closed on the monk's head like an ape's on a cocoanut. Not only was the skull crushed, but the neck was twisted. The dagger was released from the grasp and rang at the duke's foot, but not long before the dying man writhed his last beside it.

When the duchess looked, it was a dead man, and the duke, blanched but re-nerved, was picking up the dagger. It was meant to inflict a sure and agonizing death, for, with a subtle Florentine's ingenuity, its blade was one that, after the stroke, divided in two, and, opening, must have made an incurable wound, to say nothing of the impossibility of withdrawing it.

"Horror!" breathed she.

The duke examined it with more than horror. It was very plain; one forging of iron, a cross, of which the long arm became the piercing instrument; usually, such had this point merely to stick in the ground for a hermit's orisons; but this cunning doubling of the blade betrayed its fitness for other ends.

"The Inquisition!" exclaimed Braganza. "He spoke truly. But whom have I to thank for this miraculous interposition? Holy to me, but to how many will it be pronounced sacrilegious?"

"To whom, indeed?" said the duchess, leaning on Jacinta's arm.

The stepladder in the angle creaked, and a huge form sedately descended. They saw this over the top of the

"The step-ladder in the angle creaked and a huge form sedately descended."   See page 180.

canvas screen, which was drawn aside, and, stooping, though an ordinary man could easily have passed under, Porthos smilingly entered the reserved compartment.

"Have no care, my lord," said he, mistaking the horror as a doubt that his intervention had succeeded. "I warrant his neck is broken! It is an old wrestling trick of the lads of the Morbinan."

"The Chevalier du Vallon?"

"Odzookers!" went on he, "I had to do some act to prove I was not unworthy of being made a grandee!"

The duchess bent over and would have taken his hand, but the duke grasped it. Porthos saw a tear drop, and he did not believe the man lost it.

"No, thanks, my lady, or I shall be indebted to you, and will have to throttle the first boor who looks at your ladyship askew, to vent my regret at causing you a stir!"

"The duke! the duke!" was the clamor at the door.

They rushed thither over the corpse.

"There were Spanish vessels, but they have fled; there were Spanish troops, but they are in full retreat!" said D'Artagnan.

Braganza stared like a clown at a market fair at the prodigious naval display. Never had he seen so many sail together; the concourse at San Andero was ridiculous beside this. What banner was this, too? Never had he seen, so numerously flaunting in the broad day, the ancient emblem of his forefathers.

Ecstasy was tempered with perplexity.

"What is this I see?" stammered he.

"A fleet of honor to escort your grace to Oporto, where the authorities will have been notified that the king is due," said Pedro, in a clear, deep voice.

Braganza looked inquiringly at the musketeer.

"This is Captain Pedro, commanding the Brothers of the Coast, and the sail you behold are but a portion of the forces he has at his whistle-call."

"All at your service to free Portugal," went on the free-sailor. "They of the long and African voyages will meet us at Oporto or Lisbon, later."

"You mistake, chevalier," said the enraptured prince. "This is not a captain of rovers, without a flag, but my

Admiral of the Fleet! It is not plain Pedro, but Don Pedro, and Knight of the Red Cross of San Jago!"

Pedro bowed; he turned red; recovering, he blew his silver whistle peculiarly. This call was repeated among the landed seamen and from boat to boat of the fleet. A weighty silence fell.

"Brothers," said he, lifting his voice, "hail the King of Portugal! Hail, Juan IV.!"

"Long live the King of Portugal!" was the stunning acclamation.

A thousand pieces of ordnance rang out—each vessel was enveloped in a white plume, following the fiery ray.

Juan de Braganza never had a finer moment in his life. The enthusiasm irradiated him. He waved his sword, and cried:

"Officers, gentlemen, brothers, friends, to Oporto!"

CHAPTER XXV.

A cynic asserts that the "City of Ulysses," that is, Lisbon, requires an earthquake to animate its inhabitants. Another critic says that they are so indolent that they hire peasants to do their work and gipsies to "amuse themselves" for them.

Be this as it may, in the year 1640, at its opening, this beautifully-located capital was furnished with over-much excitement.

That forerunner of "the Forty Thieves," who goes before the band of War, Pestilence, Sack-and-Pillage to chalk in red on the doors, seemed to have set his awful mark on nearly every house on the rambling streets, even far out into the suburbs, outside the walls.

Stores and shops were sealed up, particularly in the goldsmiths' street, so that the usual gaudy display in the unglazed show windows was eclipsed. Still the general effect was not sober or dull, since nothing covered the fronts, frescoed and stuccoed, the Moorish-tiled archways and the Dutch-tiled roofs. After taking in curtains and tapestry, commonly airing out of the casements, no one thought of taking in Nature's garlands and rosettes; the hanging-gardens, for which the chief city of Portugal is noted, offered their rare attractions in endless loops of wisteria, white and purple oleanders, hollyhocks, pepper-plants, grown for their hue, and camellias perfect trees.

Ever since the Pretender landed at Oporto without opposition to mention, so that the cry of "We are betrayed!" resounded and echoed even to Madrid, the wealthy and timorous classes had been transporting their portable valuables, after the Turkish manner, in coffers and trunks, all ready, into the country, much going into Spain, where the owners, if of the official kind, belonged. Those remaining after this exodus had either too much property or too little to lose. They hoped that their sig-

nificance or their insignificance would similarly make
friends with the invaders. After all, with a change of
crown comes no change in the taxes; the citzens have
to pay the bugler in war, as the piper in peace.

But curiosity brought many out into the streets, spite
of the dull housefronts, and, the day being fine for the
first month, the ways became as crowded as on a feast
day.

Most of the faces were wrinkled and down-drawn. It
was easily to be seen that body and purse were at stake,
the anvil and hammer between which the poor soul very
often comes out flat.

The Church of Carmel (disappeared in the 1754 earthquake) then occupied a space, with its plaza, denoting its
importance. In early times it had been an earthen fort,
where citizens stood a siege of the Spaniards. Many
glanced now at its massive stone walls with calculations
how they might jump up to the windows and enter by
them in spite of having to obliterate the stained-glass
saints. The substantial doors were not to be forced without a battering-ram, and the small door in the large one
was fastened within. For once, the Psalm, "The Lord
is my strong castle," was interpreted literally by the
quaking priests within, who had retired to the belfry to
watch for the coming of the enemy.

The publicans, knowing that a wine vault is a sore
temptation to the soldiers who capture a town, had sold
all they could and shut up their cellars; all these places
were barricaded within. It was not the warm season,
but the dust made the promenaders thirsty, and many an
eye looked disappointedly at the signs dangling tantaliz-
ingly overhead, for these signs bore tokens, such as
Silenus on his ass, Bacchus with a ponderous bunch of
grapes, nymphs at fountains, and the like, poignant in
mockery.

To respond to the demand for refreshment, those volunteer *viviandieres,* whose irrepressible spirit causes
them to set up stalls with dubious drinks and as mysterious eatables wherever there is a popular gathering,
as on the edge of battlefields, the brink of craters, the
margin of overflowed rivers, and the verge of a burnt-out
city, they abounded.

They were supplemented, on this occasion, by swarthy men and women, taking up the trade at once as their own occupations were suspended. These, who had a seafaring and waterside look, carried casks; if small, on the shoulder or hip, or, if large, between two of them. They set them up at corners and in nooks, sure that the watch would not interfere with them.

The only remarkable thing about their goods was the singular effect they had upon those customers who wore the varied uniform of the garrison of the towers and the citadel.

These soldiers were specially welcome, the women not scrupling to beckon and to call in the *patois* of their provinces. When they drank, there was a first cup thrown in because of "the fellow-countrymanship." When the soldier received his change, although he had tendered the smallest coin current, he would look at it with the air of the beggar who has a gold piece fall where he expected a farthing. Then, falling into abstraction, like an ecstatic, he would so blunder that, instead of proceeding to quarters, he would stray toward the walls. At the first breach or practicable spot to scale he would mount and cross and jump down on the farther side. Then, still under the odd influence of this cheap but magical vintage, he marched off farther and farther from the city. In keeping this course, he could not fail to arrive at the hostile lines.

In this way, it was a simple calculation to figure how long or brief a period must pass to place the whole garrison in the command of Don Juan.

But, while there were slaves of thirst, the greater demand was for news.

Decided events were grave. The rumors were portentous, but they clashed. Every now and then a group would form around a person bursting with his intelligence—as likely invented for a purpose as for no gain whatever. All centered on the fact that the Duke of Braganza, long suspected of wishing to kick over the platter held out to him by King Philip, had thrown off all dissimulation, and launched himself as a thunderbolt at his sovereign's head. One thunderbolt is more or less to be dreaded, but when it is accompanied by a whole flight of meteors, one puts his cloak over his head.

"The duke has run the gantlet of the Spanish fleet and landed at Oporto. It surrendered to him as if awaiting him for weeks. He is fortifying there to stand a siege. The other way he defies the fleet, as he is assisted by the most enormous gathering of Barbary corsairs, Mediterranean fishers, Norman wreckers and Catalonian smugglers ever leagued!" said one pair of leather lungs.

"This is a partisan of the Independent Portugal," commented the conservatives.

"Don Fernando de Contreras, Governor of Castile, has refused, politely, but he has refused, to call out the reserves to let the Madrid garrison come to the rescue of that here. And the Master of the Royal Arsenal has refused the wall-pieces. So, the royalist cause looks glum!" said another vociferator.

"A Philipist spy!" commented the liberals.

Public gazettes had been known almost fifty years in Italy, and in France about ten; but Lisbon boasted nothing of the sort.

The nearest approach to newspapers were broadsides, having the blank available for a correspondent to write his views, or illustrate the reverse. These were brief, eked out with portraits and scenes of the incidents chronicled. Unfortunately, as the engraving was executed with the draw-knife and wood-carver's gouge, the likeness lacked that beauty of work which often redeems a poor design. Men with a memory, after inducing a neighbor to buy these "Novelties of the Day," pointed out that the pictures had seen service in previous sheets, then labeled, "Victims of the Auto-da-fe at Salamanca," "Heroes of the Spanish-Netherlandish War," and "Capture of Cities During the Long War." The interspersing of these hoary cuts with the so-called pronunciamento of the Pretender on invading Spain and Portugal, and the reply-pronunciamento of King Philip, offering a reward for his rival's head, did not enhance the value.

At times, a military officer, a public functionary, or a priest was mobbed for tidings. Their replies were fluent, but not reconciliable.

"The cloud enwrapping the Country of Camoëns is

about to break—whether for sunshine or storm, the future will disclose!" "Never was the political horizon more clear! Spain and Portugal are at peace with each other and all the world, including our Colonies!" "That mushroom, the Prince of *Braggadocia*, abandoned by his clique of tatterdemalians, was forced out of France, and is in full flight into Piedmont!" "Our beloved Don Juan has 15,000 armed men at Oporto. Five Ships from England bring him several regiments of horse and foot!" "El Rey is scattering silver on all sides. The Jews are pressing money upon him, in revenge against their persecutors. Look out for reprisals when they come into Lisbon!"

Through this tumult, the masses swaying diversely, a man moved with the easy strength and suppleness of one who had mingled with greater multitudes in his career.

He had ridden up to the gates, but the guard, whose officer was preternaturally civil, on account of his isolated post being surrounded by a crowd of no pleasant looks, had assured him that all horses were taken over for his Majesty's cavalry. He would give him an order, however, on the Master of the Mint, who was also Royal Treasurer, for the amount settled by himself on the steed. The cavalier, accustomed to discipline, acquiesced, and, with his warrant in his pocket and a roll from the crupper slung on his back, as an officer suspends his cloak, walked through.

He progressed nicely, as, like fire and water, an old soldier makes his way.

At times, when it was civil to speak—for here even the gruff by nature practice courtesy—he would speak blandly, though briefly, in that old Cantabrian tongue which most of the people comprehended, just as one could pass fairly with Elizabethan English in rural England.

"Way, please! Aside, man!" And his hand, open, but the fingers touching, like a hatchet, cleft, and his somewhat sharp shoulder advanced, and his knee, hardened by riding between other cavaliers, drove on like a mangonel-ball; he obtained his desire.

Still the conflicting chatter did not pacify or enlighten

him. But he listened to it like an officer on the retired list, who relishes gossip.

"Ha!" interjected he, finally, "now we shall have something official—I will not say trustworthy," he subjoined, like one who had lost many illusions of youth.

Two trumpets preceded a herald or town-crier, in a surcoat emblazoned with arms of the kingdom and the city. They were all on the way to a wooden block, for mounting a horse in ordinary times, for attaching a thief for whipping, or for the neighboring butcher to flay a calf upon.

The crier stood upon it as a stage.

The trumpets flourished which thickened the crowd.

"Hear ye all! this is the Bill of the Archbishop of Lisbon, appointed Ruler by the King of Spain: All good citizens are to deposit at the Royal Mint their jewels and plate, to be melted and applied to the defence of the Realm! *Nota Bene*: The Master of the Mint will give receipts as Treasurer. *Secundos*. Excepted from this order are the heirlooms of the nobles, the articles in wear of the notables, and the property of the Church."

The cheering for "I, the King," the tail of the proclamation, was feeble, and the trumpet fanfare, rising noisily, died in a tremor, like a novice in singing, whose voice went *diminuendo* in spite of himself.

It was the matter, not the singer, which was demurred at.

"I wonder," said the officer, in the silence, "would the receipt for my sword defend me if the rebels came over the wall?"

"Humph!" exclaimed a townsman, encouraged by this sarcastic *trope*. "Catch me turning over the fruit of my exertions to any mint before I am coaxed over—by main force! That would make me out to be a very poor witling, and of very limited faculties!"

But this spark of disorder was not fanned by any other breath, and the gathering, shocked, fell away to collect in another place.

Apparently disgusted by this placidity, the military officer went up to the church wall, and, setting his back against it, reviewed the passengers.

"A scrubby pack, these townfolk!" grumbled he.

"The peasants are hardy, honest and laborious. It was they who made the rank and file and the crews which possessed half the world of the East for Portugal. But that was a hundred years ago. The gentry are more *cabal-heroes* than caballeroes, plotting and counter-plotting, but doing nothing—waiting for to-morrow. When it knocks down the 'sun-eggs,' as they prettily call apricots, they will be agile in the scramble. As for these cits., slow at a coming, fickle at a stand, a score of my friend Pedro's tars would make the whole city turn itself inside out. I shall have to advise my other friend, Don Juan, to advance—not to wait for a rising here. He should be the ferment to cause the wished-for rising, and may be crowned King here in three days!"

Then, studying the action of the wine being dispensed by the perambulating dispensers, he frowned, puzzled it out, and muttered, amusedly:

"Why, these are Pedro's fellows at work! Look at the soldiers made tipsy and given the traveling money under guise of change to desert! Whew! Soleiman's cash is melting away like snow on the mountain when the dry gorse catches fire, and the defenders of Lisbon are melting therewith!"

He was interrupted in his soliloquy unspoken as all sensible persons soliloquize—by a member of the crowd, on its far edge, in an angle of the great blocks of stone at the portico, violently gesticulating. This was nothing in itself, where the people overflowed in pantomime. But on catching the eye he could but conclude that he was the object of the beckoning. She—for it was a woman—seemed offering all she paraded before the public of her wares to M. D'Artagnan. For the reader will have already guessed who was the stirrer up of dissension among the apathetic Lisbonese.

The captain left his side and proceeded deviously, as the strayers were dense, to the point.

On a post to which church notices were affixed was hung a well-known object; it was the signboard of the *Kueil*.

"The Black Petrel!" exclaimed the Frenchman with some pleasure; "my little inn! I am haunted by this bird."

He recalled the figure of the seller under this memento, although it was bedecked barbarously with finery, tinsel, jewelry, in even a less chaste taste than the Portuguese. But, if the figure were not recognizable, there was no forgetting the visage of Quaqua.

"The cook! Pedro has sent on his establishment with a goodly crew into Lisbon to prepare to feast for his coming. Ah, now there will be a good fire!"

Quaqua had put a board at the end of the church pediment at right angles, so that she enclosed a square space between board, the cornerstone, and the church side. In this compartment she put two Moorish stools. On the board was a broached keg; under it empty or full ones. Several drinking vessels, noted for variety, shone on the plank. Room was left for a heap of small coin, diverse as one would reckon on in this port. It was a bait, since money attracts money, and if she had no faith in the honesty of the bystanders, she had reliance on her own hand, while two or three sailors lounged about, attentive to her nod and sign.

"Sit and try my wine, master," said she to the musketeer. "I do not like to see a gentleman jostled by these scarecrows."

She meant scared crows.

As this was still a good post for observation, and D'Artagnan was not sorry to be among friends, he acknowledged the civility with a smile and applauded silently the protection at back and flank. All this in dumb show, for that "caution kept the castle" seemed the guiding rule among these seamen, masquerading as fishermen and venders of popular beverages.

At the first sip of the wine offered him he broke the silence.

"Marvelous!" smacking his lips. "It is a muscadine of which I have not tasted the like since we warred under the Alps. How do you come by Bergamasco here?"

"The cask was floating—and the lads gaffed it and drew it ashore," she returned, laughing.

Seeing an officer drinking with relish, several passers returned and kept Quaqua busy supplying them.

A tradesman coming out of a closed and shuttered

house, with a bundle in his arms, was stopped by one of these bibbers.

"You look hot and breathed, Marco," said he. "Where are you off to, with your valuables? Into the country, I make bold, like the most of your fellows?"

"What, Tomas! I steal off to the country!" He took the cup tendered him. "Do you not know what order has gone out from the king's deputy? The royal procla- mation——"

"Define! There have been so many proclamations lately."

"The one requiring all loyal subjects and faithful citi- zens to leave their plate and trinkets at the mint——"

"For the mint master to eat off the one and deck his wife in the other?"

"You jester! To be coined to pay the brave warriors who defend our houses and bodies! That malicious turnspit of a Braganza—he has kicked over the roast and the fat is frizzing! We shall all get burnt!"

"The fat may be all in the fire, but I am not a tallow candler, and I see no good reason why our gold and silver should be dumped there, too!" This Marco was a prosaic, selfish being, who had, after D'Artagnan's cue, protested his disagreement with the royal request. "If you are going to trust the king of to-day with what the king of to-morrow may demand of you, you are a greater ass than I have thought you these fifteen years!"

"You anger me, Tomas! What do you mean?" But his anger did not stay him from presenting the negress with the pay for two other cups in return for his friend's offering. Ought not a good citizen and a taxpayer, who pays at the first call, set a fine example of a good patriot?"

"A fine example of a hare-brain!"

"Are you not going to carry your precious metal to the king's mint?"

"Not my precious brass fire-irons, even! Not until all in our street have emptied their strong boxes, and then——"

"Then?"

"I should reflect."

"You are a miser, and Satan chooses the miser's chest for his bed."

"Is that so? Then I hope so to fill it that he will be unable to squeeze in!"

"All the neighbors told me they were going."

"Where? To Satan's bed?"

"To the mint, noodle!"

"The hour hand waits for the minute hand to thick sixty before it strikes."

"If I were to imitate you in dawdling, Tomas, I should be at the end of the tail, like the tuft on the cow's, and all would have obliged the king before me."

"The tail? The mint will have no end of a tail—like the little pig called the cavy, out in Guinea! His majesty will get as much Guinea gold out of us as out of so many cavies! on the faith of a draper, whose far-famed sign is the Colchian Ram!"

"'Mas, you have a poor spirit, for a true Lisbonite! after fifteen years having the honor to dwell in this city of the Leal! I tell you, shortcoming fellow-townsman, that our friends will carry all their meltable valuables to the mint."

"Suppose they do not?" broke in a third party, who had stopped to taste the Quaqua wine.

"Why, they will be compelled, neighbor Quintino."

"If the compeller prove sufficiently strong!" replied the new wrangler to the man with the parcel.

"Why, who is stronger than the King of Spain? Not this new-fledged King of Portugal!"

"Well, the King of Portugal may not be as strong as the King of Spain," returned the fresh logician, to the entertainment of D'Artagnan, "but the King of Spain is less strong than him of Portugal and all Portugal together!"

"By Bacchus!" hiccoughed a fourth shopkeeper, who had been drinking silently while listening to the debate, and who had come in for the dregs of the wine; "there is one thing stronger than the Kings of Spain and Portugal—that is this juice! It has cut my mouth from ear to ear; but fill me up again, worthy priestess of the bottle, thou Ariadne, who art comely, though coal black! I could wish my gullet were long as Segovia aqueduct, to thoroughly enjoy it three thousand paces, though! It is strong!"

"But," added still another toper, clacking his tongue, "but it is sweet, like Samson's Lion's Beehive in the mouth, for which see my sign, under which I vend the cheapest honey——"

These praises increased the customers tenfold. Quaqua disappeared behind the hedge and the heap of pence.

"Then we may consider that you are convinced and are going back home with the budget, eh, Marco?" said the incorrigible Tomas.

"Not a step, disloyal one!"

"Well, I am going to the mint," said another.

"There, you see!" cried Marco, triumphantly.

"What for? To take your——"

"To take back my goods for the receipt——"

"How, Annibal, did you give in your jewels, ninny?"

"Not so; but I induced my wife and her mother to be patriotic and loyal—it is inscribed in my name, so that the king will be grateful to me if——"

"Goose! if they will not hand them back, though you presented a hundred receipts, what will you do?" said the human interrogation point.

"I will summons the master of the mint before the alcalde."

"And if the alcalde hangs fire?"

"Oh, you be hanged!" returned the man, exhausted of patience.

"And if I am hanged, what comes then?"

"The crows! They would have soft pickings!"

With that they left the man with the pack, inde-cisive.

"How come you into Lisbon alone?" asked the muske-teer. "I found the roads none too safe—and you are a woman and carrying spirits."

"I was never alone. There was a caravan of us. Only we entered the town by all the gates, each alone, not to draw suspicion."

"Your entrance was well-contrived, I dare say!"

"We had no need to draw knives——"

"No, only to draw wine!"

"Yes; the Lisbonese being timid, they shut up their

shops; when a crowd kicks up the dust, a dealer in refreshment profits."

"I see that the Petrel never forgets her inn business, if she does presage a storm! Did you see——"

"I know you mean your gentleman companion. Well, he was on the road with us, but, being mounted, advanced us. I knew how eager he was to join you, for he kept asking about you and his pace all along the road."

"Porthos! on horse, of course, he will distance you. Then he should be here?"

"Without his horse, though, for they take all horses over to the king's service at the gates."

"And Porthos would resist, for he is a cavalier who loves his steeds."

"Señor Porthos would not resist giving up his mount, sir!"

"No, for it was the one you left at the Petrel."

"The Clamponnier! Ho, ho!" and he laughed as no one in that distressed assemblage thought of doing. "Oh, I wish the gatewards well out of their task of conveying the Clamponnier to the mint! But, Porthos—a stranger in this ragged rout! He lost! Hang the Crown Debatable on a mast for the first climber to get it down! I would none of it! Why, nor, Porthos—no sun! The world would be one vast grave!"

CHAPTER XXVI.

A WAIVE.

Quaqua was right as to Porthos passing into Lisbon shortly before her own entry.

On seeing the puissant Lord of the Vallon ride up, the guard presented arms to him, concluding that he was a rural potentate preceding his tenants to be offered on the altar of the kingdom. They expected some opposition on the part of so magnificent a sire to giving up his charger, according to the prescrite, but, on the contrary, he resigned possession of the famous "Plegon" without much concern for the receipt.

He swaggered through the archway and plunged into the maze.

At first the animation engrossed his attention, but the sense of being a foreigner was too frequently upcoming, and he began to be oppressed with the dread that, Lisbon being a larger city than he anticipated, his meeting with D'Artagnan was unlikely.

"That musketeer!" muttered he. "A needle in the haystack of politics is never manifested until it pierces the rash seeker's hand. Fool that I was, to quit the company of that adroit negro cook, for where she is, good cheer presides. She is cleverer than she looks, but these gross people are often deceptive. Fat jowls and fat wits are not always companions. She must be bright, or Captain Pedro would never trust her with such commissions. Who would believe me?—he sent off five hundred of his bravest sailors under her command! What a crew they are! They will rush you to this city when the whistle pipes, as if it were built of cheese and they were rats! Now, she would get me in touch with my captain, or devil grid me! Talking of grids, this town without a siege is suffering from short fare, I judge! All the cookshops are shut, if it had them in long lines, as Paris does; and the taverns (for there are taverns) are

sealed up as if they had been passing false coin and the
mint master had come down upon them and put up the
shutters! Apropos of mints, what the mischief do they
give me the equivalent for my—that is, D'Artagnan's—
Bucephalus in an order on the mint for? There must be
precious little of hard money where the high officials
snap at the bribes the Prince buys them with through
that wily Soleiman. Everything locked up! Here will
be the nice fare of the mouse starver's table!"

The church bells rang, for it was high noon; but it
was not an alarm—only for the Angelus, set at that hour
by Pope Calixtus.

The thirsty and sharp-set Porthos did not recite the
aves prescribed while the bells reverberated. What he
grumbled sounded more like imprecations on this churlish
capital.

"Confound a rebellion, if it makes shopkeepers squir-
rels of our kind, sneaking nuts into their hollows-and
munching their hoards, when better creatures prowl the
woods gnashing their teeth. Never since the first hermit
brooded by himself have I felt such a yearning for a
joint and a loaf, saying nothing of a flagon of sack, and
this the country of origin for sack! Ah, if the new
king reforms the price of canary to six *sous* the quart
he will win his crown more likely than offering reforms
of other matters, for all the topers will be on his side.
Don't tell me—these are topers who have not had their
usual potations, these who are loitering, hanging the
head, with their tongues a yard out of their mouths! I
know the signs of a drouth!

"Folderol!" snarled he, as a flock of women fluttered
by, wrapped up to the nose like the Algerians, and
mumbling in the woolen muzzles: *"Domine, salva med!"*
"A sliice of dumpling would be the best *salve*, you are
right, ladies!" He sniffed like a beagle tracing a scent.
"My senses fail me, or I smell that Bergamasco wine, of
which I have two puncheons in Pierrefonds cellars—pray
Heaven, my stout Mouston does not tap them and let
the spigot leak when he goes to sleep between them!

"What are those beggars doing yonder? They must
have a keg of something enthralling amidst them to take

things so quietly while the better-to-do are making such
a to-do, like rats in a pit! Oh, happy the beggar who
recks not whether Philip or Juan reigns! He is not
afraid that either can extract gold out of his rags!"

But the beggars on the Carmel Church steps were not
regaling themselves, except intellectually—they, too, were
discussing the flying news.

A very fat cripple, intertwined with his crutch like the
serpents of Mercury with his rod, observed complacently:

"They say that the freebooters whom Don Juan of
Braganza hires to help him put down the loyal have
sworn to put to *Vige simatinn* all the good folk they
capture, and they are sailing up the river even now!"

"If that is anything like vegetarianism, which the
anchorites practiced and King Nabucho went down on all
fours to test," said another, who had the cropped top of a
priest expelled, "I hold they are barbarians in troth. As
long as there are sheep and goats, I preach: 'Eat what
will make good bone and flesh.'"

"Long may you preach, then!" commented Porthos.
"This is the land of Alfonso the Wise, D'Artagnan tells
me."

"You dolt!" interposed another, who looked like a
Moorish sophy who had discarded his creed but not enormous scraped horn goggles, "Vi-ges-i-mation is just to
put every twentieth man to death!"

"Then, judging by the bulk of that Lame Man there,
he will count as two, and I will place myself next to him
if he is partly nineteen!"

Poor M. du Vallon turned away; what hope where
beggars dined in the Barmecide kitchen? He circled
round the church ruefully, scanning its grimed and battered facade. In a window a sundial indicated an hour
after noon. Two or three heretical books, fastened by
great spikes to the walls, between stones, said to be
brought from the Holy Land, fluttered the loosened part
of their leaves like wings of pinned-up owls. A ragged
rogue, with his back exquisitely pressed against one of
those petrean wonders called "warming stones," was
droning a seditious song to the thrumming of an Arabian
atabal:

"Must aye we commoners be made
A galled, a tame, a hackneyed jade,
    That all by turns may ride us?
Till we are tired; and, then, at last,
We kick, and far our riders cast,
    'Cause they won't feed or guide us?"

"There is nothing *solaceious* in this!" murmured the French wanderer; "I looked forward to entering this town at the head of a storming party! It would not be a supper party, to be sure! Oh, to hear twenty thousand intoxicated devils shouting hoarsely: 'Town taken! Sack and slay!'" He stamped his foot and the shock silenced the *atabal*. "But the cannon have a stopper of gold cloth! and—zookers!"

"Out on the choleric bawler!" cried a voice at his side in French, "choler is a good common soldier, but a bad commander! whom have we here, under a church wall, brought from Palestine, too, bellowing like a Papal Bull of Excommunication! It can only be that pagan Don Porthos, who expects to blow walls down!"

"D'Artagnan!" gasped the Lord of the Vallon, relieved by the sight in more than one way, although stupor-stricken.

He had worked round to Quaqua's *al fresco* café. "How come you here, and why sip that muscadine wine I smelt around the corner, instead of assaulting the Citadel, as I was bound you were bound to do?"

"*Tace et face!*" said the musketeer, cautiously.

"What are you saying now? I did understand your last address, but, you know, I am not familiar with Portuguese."

"Be familiar with this cup, and as for assaults, assault this sausage! What I said means: 'Hush and Act!' Now, I require you to sit down on this stool, if it will bear a budding grandee and his fortunes, and share my snack."

The giant musketeer tried the Moorish stool hesitatingly, but it kept on its legs after a groan or two. He nodded to the negress, who grinned cordially.

"You have acquaintances everywhere!" He took up the cask by the ends and held it up above his head, with the bunghole down over his watering mouth; but only a few drops trickled out and stuck to the wood. "Confusion! have you finished an *anker* of ten gallons to your own palate?"

"I had excellent assistants! But I am ignorant of the worth of the cook of the Petrel if she has not other resources!"

Indeed, foreseeing that a demand would arise with the coming of the French colossus, Quaqua had blown a whistle, suspended by one of her coils of shells. Two or three of the loitering fishermen understood, and, without waiting to hear her clap her hands twice to signify with how many barrels they should renew her stock, dived into one of those caves under a shop window, let off to cobblers and tailor renovators. They backed out, dragging the one, a cask, and the other a canvas bag containing, as turned out afterwards, bread in long loaves and sausages of large dimensions, so old as to be blued like ancient cheese.

In a short time the little table held a plain but substantial course of food, over the demolition of which by the valiant Frenchman—for D'Artagnan ate and drank for company's sake—there would have been spectators ten deep but that they were more seriously occupied.

As it was, the two chatted and feasted without regards from the seekers of tranquility where all was perturbation.

"I hope you have taken the edge off," remarked the Musketeer Captain, delighted as ever at the robust appetite, for the reason that he had found the quick eater a quick worker, "lean back against the wall, avoiding that carving about a sinner, who, it appears, was buried in the very masonry to cheat Old Nick, who would have had his soul were it either in or out of the church—and, narrate! But have you grown a hump, or is it a haversack on your back, like Samson carrying off the gates? Have you been plundering along the road, you veteran marauder? That was forbid! Wait till we carry the war into Spain!"

"You are wrong," returned his friend, blushing not altogether from his drafts; "it is a suit of new clothes!"

"With which to be present at the coronation?" and the

questioner, knowing his friend's innocent vanity, smiled invitingly for more revelations.

"It will serve; but I got it to show Madame du Vallon, when I return, how the Portuguese dress."

"All this to please the Lady of the Vallon? Then you will be keeping it packed up in lavender until you return?"

"No; clothes smoulder in disuse. I counted upon giving it an airing after the battle that was to come off here! I am too old a campaigner to fight in good clothes."

The captain nodded in approval.

"I see you agree, for, no offense! you seem to have had the bottom of the ragman's bag!"

"I will own it," replied the Gascon, "a threadbare doublet is the best breastplate against the free rovers of the king's way, since all sorts are without fear of the constables and archers."

"Are you afraid of your money, then? Has the new monarch already rewarded you for captaining his guards, if he has guards?"

"Juan is as bad a paymaster as Louis, so far! but I am looking forward to a finer pay."

"But why dress shabbily, if you have nothing to lose?"

"Only my skin, Friend Porthos, only that; but I take it the inclosure is worth the envelope. A steed is none the better for its trappings. But, tell me, after you replenish your cup and dip that crust in it—pshaw! you have eaten nothing!"

Porthos sighed, ogling the sausage, certainly a moiety gone.

"I confess that, used to the saddle, a long walk destroys my appetite. That horse of yours has an extraordinary gait; only knowing camels by reading of them, I judge he is an excellent imitation of that jolting quadruped. But he was up to my weight, which is rare in anything I have seen here as yet."

"Did he not kick?"

"He tried, but I just settled down with all my weight, and he checked the impulse. I wish the watch who relieved me of him and gave me an order on the Treasurer of the Mint for forty pistoles—it is here for you—well, quit of him!"

"Keep the receipt! you may collect some day! I have the like for the creature I rode! Those steeds will be useful for the deserters to get home to Madrid!"

"Oh, you think the garrison will desert?"

"I think that Pedro has able agents in the city. But tell me——"

"What?"

"Where you found a tailor to make you a costume so quickly. I will give him my custom for a court suit and my captain's coat of Portuguese Musketeers when I am champion at Don Juan's coronation."

"Oh, I could not find an expeditious tailor," said Porthos, in a burst of shame-faced confidence.

"Then one of those circumnavigators who discovered Patagonia, land of Anak, brought home the big chief's costume——"

"No," returned the Lord of du Vallon, humiliated at the idea of wearing second-hand clothes, "it was this way: At Braga, which is——"

"A suburb of Oporto——"

"A cathedral town of itself, I commanded a detachment to bring in some church bells which had fallen and were useless from cracks, except to recast, so I proposed their being made into cannon for the siege of Lisbon. The prince said that I should go after the metal, since the devout would not handle church property. While there I hobnobbed with a man of my inches, who was the beadle of the church. On holidays the beadle wears a uniform which——"

"Which is thinly trimmed with gold lace and scantily supplied with bright buttons," said D'Artagnan.

"Quite the other way, for you are joking. It is profusely adorned with lace and braid," said the other simply. "But I did not regard the trimmings. Coat and undercoat, they fitted me to a charm, though they were brand-new and had never been tried on him. Now, this tall fellow was a man from Murcia, and he vowed that he would never officiate where the rulers were Portuguese, so he gladly transferred the attire to me."

"I shall be delighted to see you as a cathedral porter! With the gold-knobbed cane you will plainly be taken for a drum-major. Madame du Vallon will be enchanted with you, and your neighbors, though they come from a Bourbon, will be impressed. And the duke and duchess——"

"And Donna Jacinta de Floriador," added Porthos, "they——"

"Why do you bring that young lady in to admire you in a new coat?"

"Only because one may seek the approbation of the friend of one's dearest friend, may he not?"

"Porthos, you are a deep dog! What causes you to think that the señorita deigns me a second glance?" twirling his mustache. "What have you remarked in her my way?"

"Nothing in her. I am no judge of woman. But what I see in you decides me. Ah, the crown will not cure the headache of our prince, or the guards-captain's baldrick the heartache."

The musketeer stared at the speaker like a magician who learns that his apprentice knows the charms as well as he.

"The truth is, and among friends the truth should be spoken, if only to prevent the tongue becoming rusty, the cream and crown of life is to love!"

"You are getting on, young captain! There was a time when you declared you burned your heart with the first love."

The young but indurated soldier passed his hand over his moistened eyes; but his voice was as steady as ever when he spoke again:

"It is out! Love and a cough cannot be hid."

"So there was a void in the breast?"

"After that loss you filled it, dear, my friend!"

"Aha!" and Porthos humorously surveyed his huge limbs and girth, "now I should have thought I could do that alone! Well, I guess rightly! you stay in this dry land—not that the wine is not good, when one gets it——"

"That is not home-grown, but Montefiascone, which Brother Pedro fished up the Lord knows where."

"Well, I conclude that you stay here, not so much to make Donna Luisa de Guzman y Gonzago a queen as to make Donna Jacinta de Floriador, her Abigail, queen over Artagnan?"

"Feel right, and you will never judge wrong! Ah, Friend Porthos, we have seen court balls in our time; but, confess; never have you seen the like of this breeder of pleasant pangs—one who eclipses even Anna of Austria, that glory of her kind!"

"Why, the young donna is well-looking, for a Portuguese," rejoined the referee, with that calmness in one who is heart-free.

"You are an enemy to beauty!" cried the younger man, indignantly, "a foe to nature not to be thawed out by a glance from Donna Jacinta! To her, Diana, up above, is a burnt-out coal! Look at her eyes, diamonds dyed jet to cast the stronger lustre! kisses dangle on her lips, so that the lower one pouts like an overladen fruit tree bough! in silken sails, that nymph skims the ground like Venus from the surge skimming the waves! she is my general, Porthos, and where love commands, angels are all the army!"

"Dream aloud like that, Louis, and she, coming along, will reward your mouthings as the princess did Clement Marot!"

"Do you chide me?"

"Not I! no herb will cure love!"

"I want to die unhealed!"

"Oh, sympathy will cure you—her hand will appease the pain. And since the lady's tresses are interwoven with the Gordian knot of this imbroglio of the thrones, I do not fear that your weakness will make you less useful to the crown-seeker. She rises and falls with the royal mercury, just as the column does in that weather meter invented in Italy."

"Assuredly, she is wedded to the fortunes of her mistress——"

"The 'man' of the Braganzas——"

"So I make my court by making theirs!"

"Better than that," said the other seriously. If we fail, they will shut the duchess up in a nunnery and strike her husband's head off so far that it will never find a crown; but the camerista will not even have a dark camera to languish in——"

D'Artagnan frowned; never had his happy-go-lucky comrade spoken in this vein.

"What is your meaning?"

"Then, I bring you news? On hearing that Don Juan had escaped the death-trap at that launching, King Philip assembled his notables, and they decided to put the duke out of the pale as a prince—any one may cut him down as a refugee from justice; the duchess is threatened with life imprisonment, and—and——"

"Go on."

"Named by name as an arch-priestess of sedition, Donna Jacinta is declared by Church and State a *waive*—"

"A waif?"

"A *waive*," said the pronunciamento. "Much the same thing. Don Pinto de Ribiera, first secretary of the duke, who was at Oporto to welcome his master and assure him that the fox Soleiman had bought off all opposition, he explained it to me. A waive, which poor Lady Jacinta has become in Spanish eyes, is a pariah, lower yet than the leper, the witch—oh, worse, my poor swain! for these are doomed to be killed at sight like vermin in a preserve; but a waive, Lord help us! she is to be let live, so that her punishment will come in this world, if it is life to be spurned when she seeks for bread, or a truss of straw, or a drink of water! When freezing, the church disdains to warm the heretic!"

D'Artagnan listened with such indignation that he was about to interrupt more than once; du Vallon's fluency astonished him and his warmth endeared him.

"What cruelty!" he exclaimed, looking terrible. "Look you! I went into this quarrel as a soldier obeying my superior! Now, I will not take my hold off the lever until I shall have overheaved this heartless King Philip's throne. On the ruins of bigot Spain I will set up my altar to love and insulted womankind!"

"Not so loud! they are turning to listen to us! and this is not yet town-taken! *Tassy ate fassy,* as you said! Though, after all, where is the treason if we speak French?"

"To war thus with women," went on the musketeer; "savages in their snowy cloth and gold and purple!

women to whom we owe birth and nursing! alone to
them we trust our fame and name, and if we strive, it is
to share the honor!"

If Porthos 'had surprised his comrade by his enthusiasm, it was his turn to be surprised by the vehemence of
his friend.

CHAPTER XXVII.

TO THE RESCUE.

"Then, you are more resolved than ever to carry out this high project?" asked the Frenchman.

D'Artagnan tapped his sword-hilt, as if it had in it the sprite famed to inhabit such receptacles of favored fighting men.

"As I live and love, I would tear down twenty thrones to uprear Don Juan one."

"I am with you. But Juan is reserved. Do you think he is generous? Serve a great man and you will know what sorrow is!"

"The old grandfather's story! I serve Richelieu, a great man, and though this heart of mine has often dangled on the tenterhooks, I can take it off to give it away to this witching woman, none the worse for any repining. Besides, what is gallantry good for when a woman, a great one, calls for it?"

"Donna Luisa? yes, she is grand! But these princesses! There was a queen——"

"The Queen of France——"

"We did Anna of Austria a service or two, but she is a princess among ingrates!"

"Anna has had all her troubles fended off by the Pre— she has not wanted for a friend of our mettle—unfortunately for us! Gratitude is not like friendship, which increases with age!"

"Well, I judge we cancel the debt by ousting her brother from his seat!"

"We pluck away his Portuguese footstool," said D'Artagnan, grimly. "In order that he shall come down on the vulgar earth with such violence that he will drink standing toasts, only, for a while to come!"

"Very well! I would drink standing if all wine were as good as this; but I regret the battlefield; it might be nearer home; so that I could run indoors for a good dinner before supping in Paradise."

"Bah!" said the musketeer, with his philosophy, "it is the breakfast next morning which discomposes one——"

"I see you prepare for the morrow——"

"Like all the wise, and the foolish! see up at these windows——"

"They are blinded and shuttered. I see no one, alack!"

"Depend upon it, the women are there. They are trying on the Braganza colors to look their best when Don Juan makes the triumphal entry!"

"You notice the women a good deal now! To think of a D'Artagnan exchanging a single thraldom for a double strife!"

"Speak from your experience with Madame du Vallon!" retorted the captain, gayly. "Still," surveying the glutted and rosy gallant with pleasure, "you do not look henpecked!"

"Well, for my part, I am looking for something more solid than a flower of Portugal on my return from making a king! When a wolf goes so far from home to steal, he should not hark back without a fat bird!"

"Well, it would not do for you to take home to Madame du Vallon a duck of your choosing! Beware, she may not believe you bought that gorgeous costume for her delight!"

Thus, merry over Pedro's good cheer, the pair presented a highly contrasting sight to the terror-stricken groups on the plaza.

"What were your orders?" said the elder musketeer, stretching as if rest were the best thing.

"'To take time and do the business well.' There must be no failure, to uselessly compromise our King."

"To take time is poor advice for feverish France, but——"

"This is the idlers' pleasure ground; we shall not be surprised by the Spanish! In fact——"

Trumpets were heard, and drum beats, as though to object to him.

"There's your rebuke!"

"Thunder! it is the garrison sallying out of the citadel!" said the Gascon, rising.

"We shall be massacred in the ruck of these goosecaps, unless they scuttle into their cellars!"

"Stay! my friend, Don Juan has not lived so long in the Spanish Court to learn nothing. The garrison is simply vacating the fort and the gate towers!"

"But I heard no sound of battle!" objected Porthos, lazily rising, and looking down the Vintners'-Ward street, which commanded a view of the wall by the river side. "Clarions, but not a shot, not a petard!"

"You have forgotten. We are fighting the Spaniards, not so much with Captain Pedro's thousands as with Richelieu's millions!"

"Oh, you think——"

"I know that the Lisbon garrison ought to retire, not before leaden bullets but with those of gold in their knapsacks!"

"But I hear marching—not very regular, but it is marching, and of a numerous troop!"

"It is coming this way! I do not know what they are; but I stick to my opinion: there will be no fighting for the fortress; you know how it occurred at Oporto."

"Surely, it is a column coming," went on Du Vallon, standing up so as to look over all heads.

"I can tell you, masters," Quaqua said, grinning, as she stowed away in her apron the proceeds of her illicit trade, and rolled it up into a girdle which she suspended around her vast waist; "it is just the trainband going on guard-mounting as the regulars come off."

"She is correct, this model hostess," cried the officer, standing upon the stool to rise to a level with his friend's head. "See, the citizens are relieving the archers at the gates, not only of their duty, but of their partisans and *arquebuses!*"

"If this be their way of conquering towns, I do not see why men of the sword are sent to take the place of your only victors, these money-grubbing Soleimans," grumbled the other.

"Oh, I daresay, we shall nick our blades yet!" amended the swordsman, who respected others in their lines; "the sons of Cortez and Pizarro inherit brave souls and will do all honor dares."

"Do you know what they are cheering about now, you who seem to follow all tongues? Is it whooping over this purchased victory?"

"No; the soldiers are mingling with the crowd and excusing their retirement on the ground that visions appeared on the battlement during the night."

"Visions of the paymaster with bags of coin?"

"No, a dread apparition."

"Just my fortune," moaned Porthos, in burlesque. "I would I had arrived over night. Never yet have I seen a ghost, and a Portuguese one must be uncommon."

"It was a decidedly native one—none less than the spirit of an ancient king, Don Sebastian, a monarch when little Portugal was a nursery of memorable rulers."

"I never heard of the gentleman," said the other, airily, as if his royal acquaintances were all reigning.

"He was a Crusader, and went off into the Holy Land, where he was killed."

"Then I consider him an extraordinary spirit to come all the way across seas and Sahara to persuade a sentinel into yielding what it takes a quarter-million to induce a governor to give up."

"Ah, but the story goes that he was not slain in Africa, but came back here, to be put in durance by the King of Spain."

"This Philip seems a nice imprisoning sort of sovereign——"

"Not this Philip, but the one of his times."

"But if he was only imprisoned, why should his spirit leave the rest of him to promenade Libson walls?"

"That Philip was the Second one, reigning fifty years ago."

"Oh!" said Porthos, with the air of one profoundly stored with demonology, "it could be his spirit, then."

"They knew it was."

"Hem!" said the doubter, "how was any to recognize the ghostly-returning king?"

"Certainly, no one was a living witness, but—what do you say, Quaqua? for this gentleman puts more questions to me than I can answer."

"The apparition bore the likeness, all a-shining, of Don Juan de Braganza, who resembles his ancestor, and the celestial light proved it was unearthly, while the arms of Braganza proved the identity."

So could Quaqua be interpreted.

"You see," took up the Gascon, triumphantly, "not only does the cardinal's gold raise men for the cause, but spirits. Time will come when these grateful creatures will erect an arch to Armand Duplessis like Aurelian's——"

"I have seen it, at Besançon," said Porthos, convinced that a great plotter was at the working-springs of this movement; "but I still regret there is no fight."

"If you want to see fighters and not intriguers, pray go out of the Oporto gate and reconnoitre for the approach of our vanguard."

"Will Pedro be with them? So you think that, though the advent is so peaceful, the adventure will yet turn out stormy?"

"My friend, it is a soft nut of which the flinders do not fly when the shell is cracked. But we want the kernel. Go—take time, and do your business well."

"As the cardinal-duke said that, count on my not distressing myself with haste. Besides, nothing so impairs digestion."

Porthos let out a buckle-hole or two, finished his cup, wiped his mustache and curled it with a sugary mixture. He turned his bundle round so that it hung like a hussar's jacket, and sang, at odds with his sobriety, as he pushed aside the throng like a porpoise among little fishes:

> "Here comes an old soldier with slashes and scars,
> Who never used drinking in no times of wars!"

"It is astonishing," soliloquized he. "I used to long for that honest fellow's company—but now it lacks something to round out life which men cannot supply! Oh! that fair Jacinta, most precious of precious jades:

> "The seed that Love's hand scattered
> Sedition now has watered,
> And in Rebellion now 'twill bloom!"

"Poor girl! put under the most comprehensive of bans for clinging to her ambitious mistress! 'Fore Heaven! no prelate can stay me from being her protector!"

Idly he let his eyes, filled with a vision more material than that of Sebastian the Regretted, which had terrified the nightwatches, loiter over the throng, a little less troubled because of the garrison's evacuation. All at once they kindled.

"Death of my life!" exclaimed he. "She would not leave the mistress for whom she had forfeited everything! But who then is this alone over there? That figure is peerless!" He sprang over the stool vacated by his guest. "That turn of the neck—spite of the peasant dress and that all-hiding mantle—it is she! that is Jacinta, or all the sex is one Jacinta!"

In ten paces he confirmed his impression. At the same time he failed to attract the gaze which had enflamed his without being in contact. This woman in rustic apparel was walking rapidly as the gatherings permitted, and looking over her shoulder in affright.

"'Sdeath!" ejaculated the musketeer, his left hand carrying his rapier round to be handy for drawing, "it is a knave following her. Well, this Revolution moves so lazily that I believe I shall have time to give a lesson to this malapert without delaying anything."

At the same period, the fugitive, having quickened her pace on seeing her pursuer as clearly as D'Artagnan did, threw herself upon the latter's arm, crying:

"In Heaven's name, sir! that pesterer is chasing me! Tell him I am your sister, cousin, kinswoman——"

Then stopping, she recognized her protector, with a suppressed scream.

"Let us say 'sweetheart,'" said the gallant. "Madame, you are under protection of my sword!"

"Nay, you must not kill him!" cried Jacinta, quickly, and with a fervor he thought wasted on a ruffian, and could not comprehend.

CHAPTER XXVIII.

PORTHOS FARES BADLY.

The Chevalier du Vallon, enlivened by the rest, the sup-and-bite, and above all by its being partaken in good company, started on his military observation with the nimbleness of a newly-oiled wheel.

He had thought it the easiest thing for even a stranger to return to a starting point. But the Lisbon of the seventeenth century was many decades behind cities of its size in the more enterprising North.

Apart from the main thoroughfare, whether called Royal, Grand or High, it resembled them in being a maze, and of short and sinuous streets, blind alleys, ways over which houses had been built, and open spaces which were depositaries for refuse, masterless dogs, haggard cats, and vagrants, who indifferently slept between pillars of palaces and sacred edifices.

The streets went deviously between walls of monasteries, which were also palaces, as at Belem or Mafra, with convents, mysterious habitations and storehouses.

The absence of shops of which the signs would be some clew, made the side streets blanks to the wanderer.

The unavoidable result was that, in a few minutes, the Frenchman was lost. He knew not which way to turn, having turned so often. He knew not how to extricate himself from the labyrinth. Usually, in a fog, one can listen and by the greater hubbub in a crowded way, make for that spot where some help might be afforded. But with business at a standstill, all was silence, except the muffled din of the thousands of foot passengers who might as well be traveling in the air.

He therefore came to a stop, chafing, shifting his steps, like one trying the ordeal of fiery plowshares.

Then, seeing people stream past the end of the kind of tunnel in which he was bewildered, he proceeded thither. It was a small square, encumbered with empty stalls for a flower market on some other day. A number of persons bustled about, but they were very base-looking indeed. They were the dwellers in the ghetto of Lisbon, outcasts, seething with a dull hope that their condition might be changed. Or, at the worst, during the conflict expected, in spite of the defection of the garrison, they might plunder and revenge.

"This is the beggars' quarter," thought Porthos; "varlets out of collar, menials who have turned their coats, ship-kennels, whose musty courtier-masters have returned to Madrid. If only I could espy a gentleman's valet who might have crossed the mountains with his lord and picked up a few phrases of Christian talk! a fine thing! a gentleman of landed value of a hundred thousand a year, astray in a dirty suburb, for want of knowing Portuguese! a mongrel jargon with which I would not address my pack of hounds! D'Artagnan might as well vouch for my learning Arabic off yonder titles which, he assures me, have the text of the Mahound Bible!"

All was useless; the smooth walls were only pierced with airholes through which no curious eye glittered; the windows above were grated and too high to reach, unless one within let down a friendly rope-ladder; the roofs, in red clay, had not a cat straying on them.

Decidedly, he was lost.

The thought of Madame du Vallon probably prevented his praying for an Ariadne. But it seemed to be Theseus who came to his relief.

A young gentleman appeared, more material than foppish, although he was elegant. He was bronzed; had a short chin beard and black hair, cropped and chafed as by a helmet lining. His boots were very fine, with golden spurs with rowels like barbers' basins; in his broad, flapping beaver were costly black and yellow plumes, clasped with a brooch chiseled so as to outvalue gold, flashing a Brazilian diamond of size. The length of his rapier forebade envy looking too long on this gem, for the wearer looked capable of defending it.

He glided out of a small door in the thick wall around large gardens; old trees towered over, and the parapet was spiked and liberally strewn with potsherds.

On this site, though the alien was ignorant, King Alfonso I. had defeated the Moors. If the walls and the buildings it enclosed had been removed, Porthos could have seen not only the Tagus but the sea at its mouth.

"This cavalier wears Spanish colors," remarked Porthos. "He must speak the tongue."

Convinced by this straightforward logic, he nipped his hatbrim between his finger and thumb, and, with a bow, accosted the Lisbonese landlord, for he had emerged from the door like a master.

"Excuse me," he began, "but I am a stranger to Lisbon——"

The gentleman seemed annoyed at being stopped, but as politeness should be met with the same, he halted and showed that he understood the Spanish used, by responding in the same tongue:

"You will also excuse me, sir, but I am almost a stranger here, too, as the Northern Wars kept me away from my home. There are great changes here, yet——"

Porthos was not in the mood to appreciate Lisbon's recent embellishments, nor had he the opportunity, so he replied, a trifle jocularly:

"There is room for improvement. But, surely, your city wall has not been altered in your absence. My way to the Oporto Gate, if you please?"

"To the right, sir," replied the native, testily.

"And then?"

"Still turn to the right."

"But, then?"

"You will always do well by keeping to the right."

"Whereupon I shall be——"

"There."

"Sir, I am delighted to meet with one so courteous where most of my encounters have been with boors."

"Sir," returned the other, beginning to depart, with a bow as deep as the Frenchman's, "I felicitate myself on our too brief acquaintance."

And, trying to make up for the lost time, the Lisbonese opened his legs in wide strides and plunged into a cutthroat-looking alley, as if fearless. He disappeared.

"A little blunt," criticised Porthos, relieved at bottom, "but doubtless the young man is speeding to a love-tryst. In the lulls of war trumpets, the lute peals out. But I wish I had that beadle's costume on my back, in another

sense. I must have appeared shabby to one spruced up
for meeting a *bella donna*. They don't dress badly in
Lisbon after all—the feathers were superb, and that diamond in his hat must be worth three hundred *piasters* if a
maravedi. Perhaps, when we are done kingmaking, I
may wear the like, to thunderstrike Madame du Vallon
and all Pierrefonds."

But, although he fully followed the instructions in
"keeping to the right," they did not profit him. He remained a straggler in the circuitous streets, unable to
reach any part of the walls, although he thought they appeared in vistas.

It began to darken in the narrow streets, particularly
where the houses were built overhanging.

For the hundredth time, he stopped, perplexed.

He was fatigued by his march in riding boots, and
almost regretted the uncomfortable haste of the Clamponnier. Here he stumbled over the dirt road, where
broken earthenware stuck up; the channel wavered from
the middle to either side, as if to be convenient to the
houses.

Moreover, his bundle became oppressive, never fitting,
wherever he shifted it.

To double his misadventure, the street here, behind the
Martyrs' Church, was deserted. In gaps, at the dips of
the wall line, he saw phantoms flitting—citizens hurrying
to man the ramparts, or going indoors to pass another
night in trepidation as to what the morrow would bring
forth.

At last, as in desperation, the wanderer would have
kicked in one of the doors, small, thick-set and firm,
just to see a human face, though it might be angered, a
man staggered along, seeming to mimic him, since he was
burdened with a parcel. There would hardly be room
for them to pass in this narrow issue.

"Good, a porter," thought he; "he ought to know his
city; may he also know a talk common to Christians as
well. Let me see! the porters are Gallegoes, and know
Spanish better than Portuguese. In that case, I am encouraged again, and I may get out upon the country to
receive Captain Pedro and the duke before nightfall, if
they are ever coming."

The other lumbered along. It was that conscientious and loyal citizen, with his household treasures, whom his like had derided for laying his offerings on the shrine of the country.

"Neighbor," commenced the Frenchman, dexterously steering between "sir," which might seem sarcastic, and "fellow," contemptuous, to a unique guide, "I am strange and seeking the Oporto Gate——"

"To the left," said the man, only thinking of getting this obstacle out of the way, as his load was irritating.

"Oh, to the left now? I was thinking that gentleman was a little wrong. Well, turn and turn about ought to bring me out somewhere. Tell me, since you are so civil," he went on, though the other danced with ire, "may I ask you, are you not a light porter that you struggle with that load when mules and asses abound?"

"I am not a porter. I am a citizen transporting to the mint what should not be entrusted to a second hand."

"Oh, the mint?" repeated Porthos, delighted that the conversation was easy-going, "you have sold your horse, then. After having disposed of the animal there, are you carrying its harness to boot?"

"It is baggage which the king will guard with his soldiers' muskets better than we can with our 'prentices' clubs."

He had put down his burden, and found the rest agreeable. Besides, he was a true gossip, and thought Porthos' stumbling parlance to his taste.

"Hum!" coughed Porthos, "after the way his garrison guard his citadel, I doubt the excellence of his ward."

"All is safe in the mint, because they give receipts," said this profound believer in black-and-white and forms.

"You are right—all goes well when the king gives receipts. Yes, I have heard from a child, 'Safe as the mint!' Still, obliging citizen, though I am a stranger, I should advise your depositing your valise in your own chimney corner, unless, like myself, you can carry it in a sling."

"Sir, will you kindly let me go my way while you go yours?"

"I have been asking nothing better these ten minutes, albeit your chat is engaging; but—which is my way——"

"Oh, go to the left!"

"To the gate?"

"While I go mine, to the mint——"

"Oh, if you persist in going to the mint, have your way. I will go to—you are sure there is no mistake—by turning——"

"To the left!" bawled the man, having passed.

"I keep to the left, eh! that will bring me to the gate of——"

"Gate of the deuce!" halloaed the man, thinking he was well away!

"Insolent lout!" cried Porthos. "I will chastise you for that!"

As his burden was light and the man's heavy, he must have easily overtaken him, but at that moment he heard the clash of steel. A good soldier should march to the sound of . cannon. Porthos turned, renouncing his course of vengeance on the caitiff, and, feeling that Balizarde played easily, hurried toward the sound.

In his excitement, and from old association, he uttered the Royal Bodyguard's war cry:

"If a friend, stand! the Musketeers to the rescue!"

Turning a corner of the wall, defended by a watchtower at the angle, he uttered an exclamation of unadulterated surprise.

He had issued out upon Carmel Church Square, where his friend, the Musketeer Captain, was crossing swords with the first Lisbonite who had told him to keep to the right. Behind the contestants was a young woman in peasant attire, whom it was impossible for him, having well studied her, to mistake.

"Donna Jacinta? you cannot keep lovers apart, I warrant ye, though that caballero seems trying!"

CHAPTER XXIX.

A TALK OVER SWORD BLADES.

Whatever the gentleman's intention in quitting his residence under Porthos' eyes, whether an amorous or a sterner one, all was changed in him on coming out by a short cut, into Carmel Church Plaza. For he singled out, by her form, carriage and distinguished manner, the woman in the peasant's frock and mantle whom D'Artagnan had most surely recognized as the bosom friend of the Duchess of Braganza.

"It is Jacinta," muttered the Lisbonese, in as much surprise as anger. "She has returned to disgrace her family. It is her step! her grace! and her features as far as I could catch a glimpse of them. The unhappy girl! for her disloyalty and active stirring up of turbulence, she has been shut out by Church and State! She is the rowel of that spur, Braganza! It is well her poor mother is no more, or this stigma would kill her! It is well that our sire is no more, or he would kill her. I am heir to his sword, yet I cannot slay my own sister. The good nuns of Carmel shall take her into keeping, spite of the outlawry!"

Meanwhile, Jacinta had wrapped her head in the *reboza,* like a sultana taking the air at the Sweet Waters of the Bosphorus.

"Chevalier," whispered she to her champion, "it is of the highest importance that he should not know who I am!"

"Rest easy! he will not learn anything through me," was D'Artagnan's reply, whose sword traced a circle for the inquiring gentleman to check his advance.

The latter thereupon drew his long sword, evidently sharpened and pointed for war, and his conduct denoted that he was a military officer, with a previous appointment rather with Bellona than the Goddess of Love.

"Pardon me, Sir of Lisbon, but is it the custom of the city to quiz strangers as you take the liberty of doing?"

"I ask your pardon, sir, but I have no regards for you. I am looking at the person whom I should see all the more plainly if you were not very much in the way!"

"In that case, you had better change to a better point of view—at a distance—don't stint yourself in the matter of distance!"

Slowly retreating, as the woman on his arm suggested by a gentle tugging, the musketeer covered her with his weapon.

The two at sword's point saw nothing, but she noticed that a door in the house front was opening warily.

"I am exceedingly sorry," rejoined the Portuguese, "but it is not in my power to fulfill your desires."

Executing a flourish which threw the other blade out of the line, the Frenchman responded:

"How is that?"

"Because, when a lady is concerned, I am near-sighted, and I never yet knew any reason why—though the Reasoner carries a sword—to keep my distance!"

"For what reasons should you scrutinize a lady?"

"I am dying of curiosity!"

"I have heard of persons who thought they would die of curiosity," the musketeer dryly answered, "but, really, they died of something else! Say, an injection of cold iron!"

Upon which he parried a dextrous lunge of the Spanish school and eclectically returned it with a thrust in the Italian school, which forced the other to leap back with celerity or he would have had his sleeve pinned to his arm.

"Like the monarch who saturated himself with poisons," said the native, in the same tone of banter, "I may believe myself ironproof, for I have not gone un-scathed through your wars."

"Oh, to a soldier, a soldier's frankness! Well, brother of the blade, this is my kinswoman!" said the Frenchman.

"Eh! are you sure?"

"Quite!"

"Any nearer than by our grandmother Eve!"

"Much nearer and dearer than any other of her daughters! Now, sir, that you know as much as you are entitled to know, you must not be offended if——" changing his accent from jesting to severity, "I bid you go your way!"

"I am not offended; and you should not be so, if I answer: I shall do nothing of the sort unless that lady's way is also mine!"

"Offended? I, offended!" repeated D'Artagnan, coldly. "At a gentleman asserting his privilege? Only, it is my habit—perchance because my tutor, my own father, was a gentleman of the old school—my habit, when I am followed too closely, to use an expedient with which I have always freed myself of a burr——"

"May I inquire, that I may use it at another time?"

"Certainly; only there has so far been no other time for the practice of the secret. I merely walk to the house fronts, gently thrust the person on my arm into the first open door——"

The man with the parcel, who had been so unceremonious with M. Porthos, had skirted the house walls. On arriving at a door behind the disputants on etiquette, whom he did not heed in his own abstraction and desire for privacy, he drew a key from his girdle and with it opened a heavy oaken panel. To his amazement, while he was stooping to pick up his inseparable parcel, Donna Jacinta, releasing her defender's arm, glided past the citizen; and, as she turned and stopped in the passage, blocked his entrance.

Over his astonished face, she smiled her thanks on D'Artagnan, who thought those teeth were rows of pearls, finer than those which his Queen Anna prized above all princesses.

"And," continued he, sharply turning round after this fleeting glance, "barring the way she went, I say to the pest—a little chapfallen, no doubt:

"'Sir, if you have need of information or instruction upon deportment as regards ladies and their warders, dispose of me since I am ready to give either.'"

"Sooth, sir, I am wistful to plunge into this well of knowledge!"

"Oh, you choose the lesson! Well, stand where you are five seconds and the lesson will have made its mark!"

The next instant the swords were anew intergliding

" He might well be vexed, for he had never met a fencer of this finesse and prowess."   See page 221.

with that clicketting which the wandering Frenchman
had heard.

But, after his immediate recognition of both the combatants, and also of the witness and cause, now in the
doorway, he still farther recognized the citizen who had
played the cicerone so badly. He had just dragged his
bundle within his portals. As the musketeer did not feel
sufficient apprehension regarding his captain to interfere impertinently, and his gall was as much overflowing
toward the second of his misinformants as the first, he
directed his ire upon the last.

"Sirrah," said he, completely blocking all sight of
Donna Jacinta from her pursuer, if the latter had had
any leisure to look after another than himself, "is this the
mint? and is yonder church door the Oporto Gate?
Wait till I see my friend out of his encounter and we will
nail your ears up against your doorpost, with a neat little scrip detailing your mode of directing visitors! I will
teach you what 'Turn to the Left' really means, rogue!"

And seizing him by his jerkin sleeve, he held him despite his wriggling, while coolly looking on at the fencing bout. He showed more calmness than Jacinta.

"He won't be long killing him," he remarked, as a
connoisseur in duelling.

"Do you think so?" stammered she, making no secret
of her identity with the Frenchman, so piteously that he
started.

"I mean, disarming him!" amended Porthos, who
perceived that the sinner might be disciplined, but ought
not to be slain.

"By San Jago! the means is ingenious to let the person escape!" said the Lisbonese, vexed.

He might well be vexed, for he had never met a fencer
of this finesse and prowess, whose front was impregna-
ble.

"I thought you would admit it. I am glad all is served
up to your taste," said D'Artagnan, who in extreme action became garrulous as a Gascon. This chatter over
the sword blades might not be in dainty taste, but it often
threw an antagonist off his guard.

"But I can overtake her!"

"She is too far!"

Bang went a door, slammed.

Wrenching himself free from the strong hand, which had crushed the Dominican monk and held the citizen like a fly in a web, the latter slipped out of his waistcoat, dashed fully within his doorway and fell over his parcel. This entry caused Donna Jacinta to recede, but seized with panic, she grasped at the door and shoved it to with all her weight. It not only closed, but some kind of a spring bolt shot, and Porthos, returning to the charge, had his ear boxed by the massive boards.

There was a cry in the street; the door closing so loudly had given a sound like a cannon shot.

"The war is at our doors!" cried the citizens, and there was a general flight.

"By speeding," said the Lisbonese, parrying a deadly stab, and thrusting twice in succession without touching, so nimbly had the other bowed himself backwards, "I might yet overtake——"

"I doubt!" fencing up so closely that the hilts met and the points menaced the balconies. "In my turn, I must give you the lesson. Be honored, sir, for the thrust, *in quarte,* after a false foin, thus, was invented by his Most Catholic Majesty, Louis the Thirteenth of France! the thirteenth, mark you, so that it must be unlucky for somebody! he was practicing with his captain of musketeers."

"Oh, he is going to kill him or he would not reveal the secret," thought Porthos, giving up his attempts to break in the door and wholly engrossed in the duel.

The Spaniard drew back and saluted.

It was his last effort. His arm sank. He caught the sword in his other hand or it would have fallen.

"I have the lesson, graven on my arm," said he, wincing and biting his lip.

He was losing blood, but not from the jesting vein.

"You may think yourself blessed that it was there, and not in your heart," interposed Porthos, stepping forward. "Let me hope you will shortly recover, that I may have the honor to give you another lesson out of my own book!"

"Porthos, be quiet! What has this gentleman to do with you?"

"He wrongly directed me to go to the right——"

"That is little——"

"And told me to keep to the right!"

"A fig!"

"No; I have the right to right the insult by sending him to the right-about at the first chance!"

"Sir, I can use my left hand," said the stranger, proudly, and to show he was two-handed he began binding up the wound with his left hand.

But D'Artagnan intervened, and finished the dressing with tenderness and much surgical skill. He did not forget that Jacinta had urged him to be merciful toward the provoking stranger.

"Really, your courtesy is not out of a common jar!"

"Now, put your hand in your doublet where I have undone a lace! so, so! There it is like in a sling. If possible, make no movement of the disabled arm, and hie you home. Give me your address and I will send you a leech, if I have to knock at all the doors in the town."

"My own household will content me. You will find nothing surprising in my wish to know the gallant whom I encountered. I am not a stranger to any citizen, having town house and manor without the walls. There is some merit in having dealt a sword stroke to the colonel of the King's Light Horse Regiment of Loyal Portuguese. I am Don Jorge de Marianda, Count, and Lord of Floriador."

"Floriador! the mischief!" muttered D'Artagnan, the scales falling. "Her brother, by all that is red!"

"Her brother!" echoed Porthos, too deeply astonished to speak above his breath.

"Colonel Jorge, the Count of Marianda," repeated D'Artagnan. "Well, is not this the most singular event since Orson recognized Valentine at court? It is needless to say that I am the bear, while your lordship is the knight," went on the Gascon with that honeyed loquacity which made him at times the bond between good fellows.

All this to the stupor of our good Porthos, who had known duelists to be reconciled, but not so heartily as on this occasion.

"What is singular?" faltered he.

"That I should meet the very person in all Portugal for whom I bear a kind of letter of introduction."

"A recommendatory letter to me?" cried the count, sharing Porthos' amaze.

"Would you have expected the like, Porthos?"

"Never," said the one appealed to, not knowing which ear to listen with. "What the deuce and all is this fertile Gascon going to invent next?"

"You see here," continued the musketeer, bowing to his companion, "a gentleman of arms like myself, of France—he of the North, I of Gascony—officer of fortune, I! He, man of fortune! weary of the long peace promised between France and your country, our brows are wrinkled like an old boot! so are our purses, at least, mine, wrinkled with emptiness. We come to offer our swords to Spain to quell this little rising on her frontier."

"Faith of the knight, if your friend's sword is of the same metal as yours, sir, the king himself might accept them both without any other recommendation than mine."

This new turn to the dialogue so interested him that he forgot his wound, beginning to sting.

"We came with nothing but our swords, to Bilbao, wishing we had at least a line to pass us on to Madrid; when the road was infested with malefactors, who prided themselves on being disbanded soldiers, but whom I suspect to be of the Brigade of Waylayers and Regiment of Tainted Sheep. The company of them with whom we fell into contact were amusing themselves with stripping a Jew, previous to flaying him, I daresay. This was because he had not rewarded them for stopping him, with more than a roll of writings and a bag hung around his neck. Now, at the last inn he stopped at, from the care he took of the bag, the landlord, in collusion with the highwaymen, had judged it was full of gems. So he informed his friends, 'the Moonshiny Knights.' But as we arrived, they had discovered that the sack contained merely earth."

"Earth?" repeated Porthos as well as the colonel, to both of whom this story was new.

"Dust, absolutely worthless—ask Porthos."

"It was," said the other Frenchman portentously, "without doubt, dust of the earth."

"It appears," proceeded the musketeer, "that pious Jews, inasmuch as none can be sure of dying just where he likes, carry with them a little earth scraped up in the neighborhood of Jerusalem. It follows that, when they are dying, outlandishly, they place this bag under the nape and pass away literally on the soil of Judea."

"I never before heard that those people vied with our Loyolaists in casuistry," observed Jorge, chafing to get away. "Does this lead to your recommendation?"

"Right up to it. My friend and I remonstrated with the freehanded caballeros and saved the merchant's hide. As he had little but his thanks, and we were above recompense, he presented me with a skin of parchment, did he not, Porthos——"

"For saving his skin he gave us a sheeepskin, to be sure."

"A parchment——"

"It was a mortgage on a property called Floriador, near Lisbon——"

"I see, my estate, pledged by my father in 1632; there is a dozen years for it yet to run.

"There would be, but I conclude that I have stopped its running."

"Then this Jew who owes his life to your lordship, was Elizor Soleiman of Algarve——"

"That is the name—it would be on the document, eh, Porthos?"

"I never knew him under any other name," replied the obliging friend, who would back up his comrade still farther.

He began to understand the artifice.

"Giving it to me, he said that the party of the first part would be my banker and host on presentation. Colonel and count, allow me to hand over the mortgage. Cancel it forthwith, for, in these ticklish times, one knows not into whose hands such papers may fall."

"Cancel it, and gladly! My father pledged Floriador to procure means to equip a regiment of our tenants for the war against France. Now, I will pledge it again for this war against the rebel Portuguese. Never shall sword of mine or pike of my peasants be borne against France, whose true knights I can appreciate."

He turned away, smoothing his wounded arm to lull the pangs.

"Gracious! you have done a pretty thing, D'Artagnan," whispered the other musketeer, "you are arming him against our side."

"Wait! this war dog may not snap at the cake."

"True, he may not accept us. You gave him an ugly stab—blood rarely cements friendship."

"My gentlemen," said Don Jorge, holding the mortgage with his sound hand, "you appear embarrassed. Ho, I have it, you believe that your favor will be the less well received now than a day ago, had you met me then?"

"Frankly, I have a little doubt that way," replied D'Artagnan, "on account of the *post scriptum* I added to it——" indicating the bandaged arm.

"You mistake a Portuguese gentleman," said the count, proudly. "This afterpart does not alter the main play. Not as a codicil a will. Here, as in Madrid, in town or out on my own manor, I am your obliged servant. Since you are strangers here, you and your amiable friend, allow me to exercise my rights and select your lodgings——"

"The garrison have evacuated the fort; perhaps we shall have quarters in the casemates," muttered Porthos, dubiously.

"Hush! Whereabouts?" asked the captain of the colonel.

"My mansion; that stands to reason."

"Never!" said the Frenchman too warmly not to be pretended.

"Never, on my life!" echoed Porthos, still in a daze.

"Hold! do you think I am to rank lower than you in civility?"

"Oh, since it is a contest of civility now, and I owe you your revenge," said the Gascon melting, with that gayety always animating him when he had played his game to the winning point, "I surrender."

"I surrender with my friend," added the other.

"Luckily, I do not live far from here," said the count.

"I know. It is to the right," said Porthos, for a wonder, with sarcasm.

Don Jorge smiled, but the pain of his wound marred the smile.

"Lean on my arm, dear host," said D'Artagnan, affectionately, "for the brother of the woman we love is not undear to us." Then, to himself, as they walked out of the church square like host and guests of long standing, with Porthos stalking behind, wondering at his comrade's pilotage, he said:

"I hope, if Donna Jacinta saw us now, she would think I was taking care of him. Her brother! Oh, these intestine wars. Still, it was lucky that I went out to pick up Soleiman on the cliff—those rude mariners would have lit their fire with that excellent letter of introduction."

Porthos looked moody, for hard thinking depressed him .

"D'Artagnan seems to think the lady can take care of herself," he mused. "Well, while I am no expert, I believe I can find that house which sheltered her, and I shall, although I am not so much interested in finding her as that curmudgeon who bade me keep to the left. Who knows, as quarrels turn out in this crisscross city, but, after I shall have pulled his nose and trimmed his ears a little, he will offer me the pick of his goods. Lucky she, if that rogue plays the host to her as finely as I foresee this Count of Marianda will to us! Oh, that D'Artagnan! never should he be rich, for it is only in a needy captain's wallet that one finds such schemes."

The count-colonel did not re-enter his dwelling by the private way, but by the grand one. Great gates of splendid ironwork opened by a steward's order to two stalwart varlets, and others bowed their way in between statues to a marble portico. The building was in the shape of a letter L, the missing wing having been torn down or never completed. In the spacious gardens, partly as the Moors left it, were fountains and pretty summerhouses. One of these, for permanent living, occupied a space by itself nearer the river. The cream-colored stone blocks were massive, to resist the overflowing of the Tagus and the convulsions of the earth.

Numerous servants, in livery which would serve as uniform, were marshalled in the lobby like soldiers. It was plain that Colonel Jorge's establishment was as much military as domestic.

These saluted the strangers as though they were everyday guests, guided by their master's conduct.

"I see," thought Porthos, drinking in these evidences of their lines having dropped into sweet waters, "anything will do for an introduction, if properly presented——"

"True, oh sage of Pierrefonds, but," subjoined D'Artagnan, "but it is rare to present it winsomely on a sword's point."

CHAPTER XXX.

FOR THE KING.

It was a cycle when the greatest generals carried out the ductile doctrine that all was allowable in war. The same men, often knights of the boudoir, justified themselves in shady transactions, before Cupid's court, with the same axiom.

The outcome was, in our heroes' minds, that, when a case involved both love and war, their course was perfectly warranted in becoming friends of Colonel Jorge and his guests under false pretences.

Without any qualms they would sleep under his roof and eat at his board. It must be admitted that had the beds been less soft and the fare less praiseworthy, Porthos for one would have felt compunction. It was war time, but such great establishments as Count de Marianda's were provisioned to hold out a siege.

Many a time, in these residential forts, a lord offered long resistance—to the rabble, frequently, the king sometimes, but seldom to the Church, when represented by the Holy Inquisition. The line of independence must, in Spain and Portugal, be drawn somewhere.

The dining-room in Marianda Mansion was superb. The musketeers, knowing of Vincennes, St. Germains, and the Louvre, were dashed. The conquerers had modified the Saracenic glories without altogether spoiling them. Walls and ceilings were covered with openwork in scented woods, gilt and tinseled, and with old glass, set in interstices, of hues difficult for our subtlest chemists to imitate. They seemed rooms plastered with jewels. Here and there, squares had been cut out and panel paintings inserted, a happy medley of sacred subjects treated with simplicity, which was grotesque, and homely ones heightened into fantasy by artistic revelry.

Porthos admired the table more than the surroundings. D'Artagnan was as usual sobriety itself, having still a hard game to play.

While they were making themselves at home, Don Juan had the same task as regarded all Portugal. He seemed to be "laying on his oars" at the great seaport. If his naval scouts had penetrated the capital, as we know, their presence was not published.

Daily, the Spanish officials flocked into town, reporting monotonously that the provinces were gone over to the Pretender, and that resistance was a farce since the soldiers had been bought. If the garrison had vacated the citadel, it was to remove any fear of the citizens that its cannon would be used to demolish the place in case of a rising. But the loyalty of the Lisbonese was not doubted; at least, to let the inhabitants guard their own walls was in witness. This liberation of the troops allowed the generals to march out and give battle to the revolutionists in event of their showing a menacing front. In the meantime, the guards of the public buildings and the vice-regal palace were doubled, and the monasteries fortified, it was said.

With the soldiers, then, outside the wall or confined to the palaces used as barracks, never was the town more quiet, save for the everlasting babbling over the news and rumors.

The two Frenchmen had had a sumptuous breakfast, which was really an early dinner—beef soup thickened with rice and vegetables, a saddle of mutton roasted before the fire, lean but desirable game which Porthos could not have bettered out of his own warrens.

"My father," explained the count, "was high game-keeper to the old king."

He had preferred the camp to the court and passed most of his years in the campaigns.

"So, my dear Gannarta," said the host to the musketeer captain, as the steward filled the rock-crystal cups with a wine equal to Quaqua's, "you come to Lisbon to uphold the old royalty and, like us, oppose any attempt to overthrow fixed order in favor of this self-constituted king?"

"I am always for order, dear Knight Hospitaller, and I am hoping that you will furnish the chance to display my zeal."

Porthos had on his fork a redolent teal, fed before its

doom on the most fragrant wild herbs. He nodded at intervals of pulling it to shreds, instead of speaking.

"Plainly, are you not better here than sleeping out on the church steps? for I must acknowledge that our publicans show much anxiety about the result of the approaching conflict by shutting up their hostels to even their friends——"

"Probably it is to arrange their wares attractively to the foes——"

"The foes will be inside the works as prisoners, then! Do you imagine, because the garrison withdrew, it was to fall back on the Madrid road? My dear sir, the old fort is untenable. The soldiers have been in all the strong points, in house forts of the church, nobility and officials here; they control the town better than cooped up in the citadel. Depend on it, the rebels refrain from intruding on hearing of this fine disposition of the forces. Besides, it leaves a flying column to which my command belongs, to harass the enemy's advances. I suppose you have seen the Italian old cities?"

"I was a prisoner 'cantoned' in Sienna once," returned D'Artagnan, drinking avidly as if a reminiscence of the dungeon fare enhanced the relish.

"Well, Sienna is typical. Our nobles' houses also were constructed for a house-and-house fight. The Moors were not easily driven out after the army had been beaten. Until we had this castle painted and repaired there were marks of Greek fire and bullets over the walls. Don Juan may take the ramparts with his rustics and pirates, but he would be so long occupying the town that reinforcements from Spain would arrive to turn the tables."

"I am sorry we put you out, as the Don-Juanists seem to intend," laughed the guest of honor.

"Not at all! I owe you so much that I feel ashamed at my slight return so far. You must know that this portion of the unshapely building—for the part to complete the plan fell down in a quake, I heard, was the former harem, where the emir installed his favorites. You are my favorites, and I bestow it on you. My father, a tassel in the court cap, rarely inhabited it. When the king became devout, and longed to see an *auto-da-fé* rather than a battle, sham or actual, my father was displeased. He contemplated passing time on his estate or here, but Heaven disposed. He died out there, in our country seat of Floriador, which you have so gallantly restored to me, free of liability. This house has three ways out into the thoroughfares."

"How convenient for sallying out—to love appointments," said Porthos.

"To rush upon the enemy," corrected the other musketeer. "There is a detached house in the grounds," added he, without apparent meaning, "which would do admirably as an outwork."

"Oh, that is a summerhouse. It is remote both from the fish market and the church plaza—which are noisy on certain days. It was my mother's *buen retiro*—you know, who speak Spanish with a talent scarce in the French, I think. It was originally the Moorish owner's sultana's, I conjecture; such a fairylike court with a marble fountain and stained glass making it always sunshine inside. My tutor, the chaplain, used to read me the Chronicles of the Cid, and Arabian fairy tales there, with my sister by, when we were young and were free." He sighed. "She always loved the resort."

"We have not the honor of seeing the lady," said D'Artagnan with an emotion he was vexed that he could not subdue. But he rubbed his hands under the table, like a chess-player who had decoyed his antagonist into a series of moves by which he would gain.

"Yes, Donna Jacinta," sadly continued Don Jorge. "She never liked the convent—she always longed to be at the court—her father's taste, while her mother tired not of dissuading her from the vain glitter of that world. Jacinta took that pavilion to herself until, evil was the day, she went into the honorary service of the Duchess of Braganza—that intermeddler and plotter who will never rest until she has a queen's coronet, or the fool's cap, with which she should do penance on the horseblock."

"Pillory a lady, a duchess," protested Porthos, with his mouth full, which deteriorated from his indignation.

"Why not? A traitor has no sex," and Jorge de Marianda was surprised at his insensibility exciting criticism.

"The pillory is a mild substitute for the gibbet, which she and her spouse deserve."

"Of course," said D'Artagnan, nodding sagely, "a traitor has no sex."

"I shall never forgive her for deluding my poor sister into her mad projects. Will you believe it, gentlemen, that subtle creature leads the world to suppose that my poor sister, fresh from the convent, originates all her plots and perfects them—for they have given King Philip and his council many a heartache. King, Court and Church fear her—hate her, and in their abhorrence have collectively executed such a decree as proclaims her a waive, in other words, a prescribed one, exempted from all claims to consideration. Shall I be lenient to Jacinta's tempter and perverter? No, by my—— Never mind. Let us talk of ourselves, now that we are friends."

"Of the best kind," said D'Artagnan, smiling. "Being friends, then, I am wanting to know for whom you took that fugitive?"

"The person I pursued?"

"The rustic——"

"Why ask me? Rustic or lady, you ought to know all about your kinswoman—a Frenchwoman, of course?"

"King's-woman," said Porthos. "She is loyal, I warrant."

"Her distinguished trait," went on the other musketeer, "is loyalty, though she is a Frenchwoman, as you surmise. But she is a milliner—she has a room in the house where you may have seen the porter open to her knocking——"

"I saw the porter," said Porthos.

"I did not hear the knocking, but——"

"She is the niece of the worthy oilman, who is the porter."

"Oilman?" said the other Frenchman, into whose head the wine fumes had penetrated. "Tobacconist, you mean! Did you not see the jar over the doorway?"

"Certainly, I saw the jar—but with bottom pointed and two ears for handles—that is an oil jar all the world over! from the time when the Romans overran Iberia!"

"My dear comrade, I do not know when the Romans overran Siberia, but I do know that the jar was flat at the bottom or it would not have stood on the ledge—a snuff-jar!"

"Peace, gentlemen, peace! let us have no jars here!" laughed the host. "We will put it that the milliner took shelter with her uncle, who sells both oil and tobacco. In this case, I was in error. To be sure, the girl was dressed like a country kin of a town tradesman—and, oh! I am a fool! my sister would be leagues off, with that embroiling duchess!"

"Ha, ha, ha! did you take that hoyden for an illustrious lady, your sister?"

And D'Artagnan's laugh was only outdone in heartiness and volume by his brother musketeers.

"She had the air! but my sister would never quit the fool-fire which will burn her at the last! She is welded to that proud Gonzago!"

"I do not suppose she would leave her—particularly since she has no one else to turn to, now that she is outlawed!"

"Not a soul," sadly observed the count. "Not even this roof can be hers now."

"I should think not," said the captain, broadly, "not with two captains of fortune under it! Ha! ha!"

"I mean that I am going to draw out the servants to enter my regiment—I will defend the town as long as we can hold out. You have full range of this portion, with a street outlet. The domestics will obey you as the master!"

"If we were prisoners, we should have the most admirable jailer," said the captain. "Oh, have you the latest news?"

"It is reported that the insurgents have united, the force more or less maritime out of Oporto, with the rural rebels. This army of rabble would be close to us. Vasconcellos, our governor, representing the king, is stubborn, and will not coincide with the military chief, who withdrew the garrison on his own responsibility The civil lieutenant is vacillating. The townsfolk are not to be relied on; citizens who will throw down the keys when the first siege gun is trained upon the gate. But we have strengthened the strongholds in the city, and it will cost dear to dislodge us."

"You think that this Don Juan would dare——"

"Madmen will dare anything—which is why they often succeed. Then, his wife ever brandishes the whip. But we can rely on many—such as you."

"For the king!" said D'Artagnan, draining his glass. Porthos drank like a duplicate D'Artagnan.

"As your desire is for active service, I will speak of you to the commander of the Horse, and have you finely mounted——"

"Our steeds are at the mint, or, at least, our receipts for them emanated there. I would not have lost my charger for——" And the musketeer almost wept over the ungainly Clamponnier, tears of the crocodile in which Porthos joined.

"You shall have the pick."

"Let mine be of generous dimensions," added the ponderous Frenchman, "a little larger than your mountain ponies and not so much bigger than a Mecklenberger."

"Right!"

"I thank you a thousand times," said the young soldier.

"And I two thousand," said the other, not to be outdone.

The host explained the topography of the mansion. They could enter his part by a secret passage.

"That way leads to the church square of the Martyrs, whence you can see the tower of the Carmel. You see you are prisoners who have 'the key of the streets.'"

When he had gone, followed by the servants, Porthos looked with admiration at his leader.

"My chaplain used to read me into an after-dinner nap with Roman history," said he; "but never did I think there was reason in the adventure of Caius Marius, who walked in among the Volscians, his foes. But I realize it now, or rather you do. We have a charming Volscian in this host, with open doors and open arms, maugre your having disabled one of said arms. But how long are we to keep up this diversion?"

"Did you not hear? Don Jorge is going to clear his house to reinforce the Spanish. Then this place will be empty. Now, who will so well know how to get into that pavilion as the young lady who lived there? I do not mistake by a line that it is there she will guide her inseparable duchess——"

"It is likely."

"And the lord will follow the lady close. It is here that the duke will have his headquarters—who would suspect that, where the ultra-Spanish colonel, Count de Marianda, dwells?"

"Bats, bats!" cried Porthos.

"Are you alluding to us, or the Spanish?"

"To our king in France, to his minister, to all their court; bats not to have made you a marshal long ago."

"Bah! honors are ephemeral; the only solid thing is the love of a beautiful, virtuous woman!"

"I never know when you are joking—until the joke is ended. Is this joke lasting?"

"We stay here until Don Juan enters Lisbon. Then the farce will be a tragedy. The lion is not going to give up its prey without a blow of the paw and a snap of the jaws, believe me. In the interval let us go forth, since we have an open outlet."

"Go out?" said the *bon-vivant*, in terror. "Go out immediately upon so hearty a repast, and the dessert untouched? Those Arab *bonne-bouchées* look delicious."

"Why, my friend, do you think I am gulled with that story—that our gentle Amphytrim is going out to a council of war and to engage his two recruits?"

"That noble lie!"

"Well, we are noble, and we lie—that is, dissimulate, do we not? On my side, I am going out to see if Donna Jacinta is safe at that oil dealer's——"

"Tobacco——"

"At that shopkeeper's," politely returned D'Artagnan, with evasion; "and if I do not make haste, Colonel Jorge will have outsped me."

"I foresee," sighed the gigantic musketeer, "that his other arm will suffer, and he pours out good wine so gracefully, too."

"Do you not also see that he must not meet his sister? She is here to prepare the dwelling for her mistress, if not the prince. He is one of those antique Romans whose antics are detestable—he is capable of denouncing his

sister as a spy and a leading spirit of the rebellion, so
that they may applaud his sacrifice of brothery feelings
on the shrine of loyalty."

"I heard once of an executioner who struck off his
own son's head because it fell in the way of his duty—
but his own sister! Come, come, come, I never heard
of a man arresting his own sister!"

"At all hazard, I must go and warn her."

"When D'Artagnan says 'Must!' I leave him alone.
Now, do not you run into danger."

"No, I shall 'keep to the right.'"

"You must return, D'Artagnan, for I shall go mad all
alone in this hateful city."

"Oh! I will return, and no doubt in good company—
a company of Pedro's navy would not be amiss."

"Good fortune, dearest friend! It is astonishing, but I
feel like St. Jerome's lion when the saint is not by."

"Faith, you are far more the lion than I the saint. A
man who enters the enemy's lines as a volunteer."

He buckled his sword up short, that it should neither
beat his calves nor get between his knees, pulled his
cloak round him, drew his hat down, and departed street-
ward, with a stealthy step.

"How wonderful!" exclaimed Porthos, insensibly returning to the table and leisurely encircling it, like a
voyager circumnavigating a delightful isle before landing, "how much a lover looks like a footpad." He skir-
mished among the pastry and confections, semi-oriental
sweetmeats. "I should be afraid to meet that rogue—I
should give him the wall."

CHAPTER XXXI.

HIS OWN HOST.

The lone knight sat for a time in a drowsy state.

"Shall I call the servants to remove these breakfast things? No, they would miss my friend, and, without questioning me, they might tell too much to their master. Why did D'Artagnan persist in going to seek his beloved, alone? Can he be jealous because I sounded the praises of this avowedly beautiful Jacinta? Absurd, to be jealous of a married man! a long, long married man! Heigho! Madame du Vallon imagines me camping out in the mountains, little dreaming that I am in a veritable palace, with an inexhaustible larder and surpassing cellar!"

He took up a bottle, and, sad to say, for a gentleman of a hundred thousand livres a year, drained it from the mouth.

"Really, Portugal was not robbed of her fame in being called a wine-producer! She ought to be fostered. I will import some of these brands and be 'memorated like those who introduce nicotina and other weeds! Let but this count and colonel continue friends and I will exchange vines with him. But new beds and new acquaintances are dangerous! At any nick, our false play may be made palpable! Then, I must draw on my host, as D'Artagnan did, and recall his having misguided me! It is duplicity which takes the fine edge off honor——" and to console his fastidious conscience, he sang lustily:

> "Honor is like an isle with rocks about,
> No getting back when once without!"

Hazily he reviewed the pictures on the wall, nailed on over the arabesques; they were Canos, and Riberas, with some Dutch masters; trophies, not art purchases, by the elder Marianda. A pink and sky-blue Guercino, depicted Luxury as a dancer with provoking eyes, tossing locks and tempting smile; the lifelike figure was about to leap out of the scroll frame, and, flinging her lapful of flowers on the beholder, finish the caper on the floor.

Soon the art critic yawned.

Getting up, with an effort, he strolled to a window, deep in a recess, for it was cut in the wall and went out into a balcony; but it was all a wooden box, perforated but annoying the eye; the women who peeped out must have had little view for their pains.

"Impossible to get a sight," grumbled Porthos, seeing double, although he complained. "And what to see at the best: that river running, running to make one giddy! The wall where the citizen-soldiers are playing at soldier! the shops closed as in a great pest, frightened grocers fleeing from the wrath, thieves marking the houses they plan to plunder, all to cast the ignominy on the poor soldier! Bah! Would that the witches' dance would begin!"

Although bored, he stood there a long while, too indolent to move. He looked at the detached pavilion in the gardens.

"Oho! Not at all a bad nest for a hornet to sally out of to make things hum! There are two or three cavaliers, whose horses were not taken from them, at the gates, halting at the garden wall. Can that Gascon be always right, and is that the rendezvous for the timorous duke? What skulkers! I shall always picture the Portuguese as cloaked and doing all deeds at midnight!"

Returning into the room, he placed nearby a splendid Moorish panoply, on its frame and stand, and drawing his sword, tried to rouse himself by fencing at it. He pinked the joints so that the original tenant, after this bout, would have resembled a patient under acu-puncture.

"There," said he, ceasing, and rubbing the slightly upturned point, to straighten it, on the carving knife, "if that had been even their Don Manuel the Lucky, he had been wounded so that all Beyra's oil would not appease the aches."

He straddled a chair, as if in the saddle again.

"As the colonel said, it is finer here than on that

church square. I wonder if that negress cook is still carrying on her trade as a war device? To drug a whole city! No, her lord, Don Pedro, is too high for that low trick. How drowsy I feel, since I partook of her Italian wine!

"I trust my brother musketeer does not again come to crossing swords with our host! He is less delicate than I am, if he could continue his court to the fair Jacinta over a fraternal corpse. They might use strong language to each other—real brothers will abuse at times—some are so jealous of their sisters—but words! bubbles on the breaker! a fig for them!

> " 'Words are but wind—
> Swords are unkind!'

"Well-a-way! a smooth life flattens out wrinkles! And still nobody comes to town—Don Pedro or Don Juan! D'Artagnan or the count! Not a shot, not a shout! a fine thing if this revolution, lovely in its bud, comes to no blow! That Braganza will leave us to roast in the fire! Zounds, I am not a pagan, but I fear that my memory is so bad that if the Inquisition should put me to the test, I should gabble a camp ballad for a canticle, and not so much piety could be sweated out of me as to save me from the San Benito cap!

"A finer thing yet, to leave my verdant Vallon, my blooming Bracieux, and my peaceful Pierrefonds, all to be toasted at a stake in the Madrid Plaza Real—that cold burlesque of the Place Royale! Ah, life, life, we like you the better the older we grow!"

At noon the streets were very bright for the season; only on the sheltered side a few passengers wandered, muffled up to the eyes, and carrying weapons under the folds if they intended to defend the city, or valuables if they sought flight.

"I believe I shall be left alone here to await the Pretender," groaned the lonely one. "I will have it made into a carving to set over my mantelpiece: 'The Lord of du Vallon, as grandee of Portugal, opening, single-handed, the Lisbon Gates to King Juan IV.' "

Happily, just when he had determined, at all risks, and in the teeth of the injunction to stay still, to quit

Marianda House and venture out in search of the musketeer, he heard soft steps.

Under orders of the major domo, four or five servants
cleared the table and replaced the first meal with a
lighter but still more varied banquet. It was the mun-
cheon of our forefathers—debased into "luncheon"—a
meal between meals.

There was more than enough for three, so that the
master and D'Artagnan would not fare badly unless
Porthos devoured all. The steward was discreet, or
doubted the solitary guest's lingual powers from what
he had heard of them. He courted no conversation, and
passed no remark about the other's absence.

The Lord of Du Vallon had not yet succumbed to
the climate. Under the Equator he would have eaten
as unsparingly as here. When the menials had withdrawn, he gently sauntered up to the board, surveying
it with a growing welcome.

"They seem to know me here," he said, chuckling and
taking the head. "The appetite grows in eating, I believe. But I will wait an hour, as the sun tells it off,
and then, to it! at a feast like this, ill fares the hind-
most!"

The hour over, punctually he began.

"I cannot find a fault except that I must be my own
varlet. But I shall not be the gallant who told the
King Harry that he was his own servant, and the king
answered that he was ill-served! I must have been
hungry to think the count's cook was a slow-coach!
Prime! I can see, as D'Artagnan told me, the Portuguese are heirs to both Roman and Saracen. For
here"—he laid the large knifeblade on a chine, pat-
ting it so that the unctuous jelly oozed out and glazed
its brown, "here we have a bit of boar, baked, worthy
of a Roman cardinal's buffet, and here a mess of boiled
rice, each grain a pearl! studded with sun-dried grapes
of Almeria, and stuck with cloves a little more thickly
than milestones in France or crosses to the victims of
robbers in Spain!"

He ate as if he had to look back a week to the last
treat.

"Halloa!" he exclaimed, replete, leaning back, as a

scent of unknown source titillated his nostrils, "this is
—is what? A Turk water-pipe, inseparable from all re-
spectable siestas. That poor D'Artagnan, setting up
as a philosopher and tripping after lovelight on those
scorching streets! with this dessert neglected! That
pipe smells good, and the amber cools the mouth! This
is the way a warrior is chastened into a sybarite! I
shall return to my lady, asking for only a stuffed-back
chair and a footstool, to munch roast chestnuts and
crab-apples swum in hot sherry! St. Pantaloon the
Shuffling will be my patron."

Then he looked up with pretended horror. He had
forgot to say grace!

"The sharp stomach makes short grace!" sighed he,
apologetically. "I was wishing D'Artagnan here—I
withdraw the desire! he would have blighted all. Don't
tell me! He would have soured the junkets by crying
at each glass: 'To the bride that I shall have!' And
he would have prayed to have his Jacinta, over there!
As if I pray to have Madame du Vallon play the spoil-
sport here! Still, were she here, I know how a fond
husband should behave—luxuriously—the Lord forgive
me, uxoriously, is what I mean!

"Madame," continued he, filling up two glasses with
some unsteadiness, "allow me to offer you some pome-
granite-ade—infallible for dispelling the megrims!"

He drank off his, and he drank "hers."

"But why these little trifling glasses for cordials? best
of the set-out! What blockhead was he who had the
whim at the first to offer the thin wine in goblets and
the syrups in thimbles? When I am a high official at
the new Court, I will, by this flask, alter it."

He shoved his chair back, but had not the force to
rise.

"Faith, I have fairly broken my fast—I can wait till
dinner!"

After a pause, during which the lighted pipe continued
to exhale its aroma, curiosity lent him the strength to
make the effort to get up.

He did so, and, trailing the pipe stem, found in the
recess, a pile of cushions on which he sank like a pasha.

"Never have I smoked a boa-constrictor of a pipe like

this," mumbled he, "with an alchemist's furnace at the tail, and a bubbling like a watchpot! Yet the Orientals know a thing or two about the table—since they have tables, though low ones—but they are a people who squat on their heels—yet they can fight like gladiators. Natheless, this Indian weed has cheered many a poor wet, chilled mortal in the trenches; many a poor comrade laid by the heels in the guardhouse, to my knowledge!"

Several times, the mouthpiece had eluded him as if the head of a serpent in fact, but, inhaling from it, he finally dozed off. They might have rung the changes on the chimes of the cathedral and he would still have slumbered—our good Porthos, who never did things by halves.

In the middle of the afternoon the attendants came in like a sultan's mutes, and noiselessly removed the things. They listened to the deep breathing without a smile, contemplated the devastation due to one man, and departed without any heed farther than for one to linger. He looked to see that the hookah was in good order and that the mouthpiece was handy to the smoker, so that he could put it in his lips when awaking.

Dark came on quickly, and the snoring diminished like a passing thunderstorm. The town showed no lights, distressed by reports that the rebel scouts had been seen in the vicinity, and that the Spanish, who had marched outside, had made common cause with them instead of defending the road to Madrid.

All of a sudden, a scene on the wall (a Jordaens, "Skaters on the Great Canal, Saardam") opened on hinges like a panel painting, and after a little hesitation, a black woman, low in stature, peered in. She could not see any one, since Porthos was in the recess, curtained over.

The panel opened at the foot along the floor line. She stepped forward with a lightness not to be suspected of her build, and made the circuit of the room as if she saw in the dark. It was like an African warrior who had entered an Arab marque, and judged everything by touch.

"They have gone, lady," said she.

CHAPTER XXXII.

A FAIR EXCHANGE.

"You may come in," continued the woman, speaking very low.

"Are you quite certain, Quaqua?" inquired Donna Jacinta, appearing in her turn, but having to stoop to enter by the picture door.

Reassured, the maid of honor tripped into the apartment. All the light was the glimmer through the windows, set with large Venetian panes where the blown glass of the Moors had not been retained, but this evening there was that after-glow which astronomers attribute to the stars. "Lady Jacinta," went on the negress, "I saw the French gentleman who hired our inn, who is to the stout one as the pestle to the mortar, go out into Carmel Church Square!"

"He was seeking me, at my timely and temporary refuge?"

"Not a doubt of it."

"How was he to know that an old servant of ours kept that Indian store?"

"How, indeed?"

"But what are you snuffing at?"

"There is something burning—no, it is tobacco! Oh, they have been smoking!"

"It was a good idea of mine not to linger there, where my brother would put questions of Marco, but to proceed instantly to the summerhouse in our own gardens."

"Very good! But you had a better one to press me into your train."

"Indeed, I do not know what I should do without you."

"That is what my Lord of Braganza says to my Lord Pedro. We are neither of us beauties, but we do handsome deeds."

"You tell me my brother was hurt in that encounter?"

"The French gentleman ran him through the sword-arm as if gaffing a halibut. Clish, clash, zip! and the battle was over."

"And yet my brother is accounted one of the best blades in Spain."

"There never was a smith forged a blade but he might make a better."

"I suspect it was not so much the blade on the sword handle as the one holding the handle!"

"The colonel also came back to the square, but he was in haste, and a mounted soldier riding up, they went off together. Great events are overhanging."

"You tell me we may expect——"

"The duchess will demand your hospitality——"

"What a happy thing that the summerhouse is detached, as far as my brother knows, from this house."

"He does not know. I do not know how Pedro found it out, but, you see, he told me of the secret passage under the ground and into here."

"They have been eating here!"

"Drinking, certainly—there are empty bottles under the table! They are lodged here, I suppose. Your brother has taken them to his bosom!"

"Impossible, Quaqua. He does not swerve in his duty. Embrace a man who wounded him, on the eve of battle—men who are against Spain!"

"Perhaps they have coaxed him over!"

"Coaxed with a sword thrust!"

"Marry! There are odd somersets in politics!" said the cook, with her notions and language above her condition. "When Don Juan crosses the threshold, you will see the citizens, not in uniform, wearing turncoats," and she laughed in a low key. "Besides, the Caballero de Gannarta can talk the leg off a table!"

"This is awkward," mused the young lady. "This room is in the route continuing this passage by which we would have had an egress to the streets. In case of a repulse, Don Juan and the duchess should have means of flight."

"I don't think we can be beaten. We have a great force secretly in the town. Our sailors are lodging with the fishermen in their quarters, and they enter freely. As for the king, I thought he would enter with flying colors, on a white horse, and stop at the gates to receive the keys from the Alcalde?"

"Oh, the day has gone by for pageants, I fear! tourneys, open-air fighting on open ground. Now we undermine, storm in the dawn, and open city gates with golden keys."

"All this will not please Captain Pedro and his crews—they want close quarters, only room to swing a handspike—that is Jack's play!" and the negress' eyes blazed in the dark.

"Heaven forbid that my brother should find that the Caballero of Gannarta is endeared to the native cause!"

"There is a worse thing—to find out that the Caballero is in love with a Portuguese maiden endeared to him, Don Jorge."

"What do you mean?"

A little more warmly and the sleeper must have overheard.

"He is more concerned in whom you love than whom the Caballero loves!"

"What, do I wear my flame emblazoned on my bodice?" hissed Jacinta, almost angered.

"Madame, it is something which I saw!"

"Are you a witch?"

"No, a cook! Our eyes are Cupid's fortune-books—any one can read the leaves."

"My eyes betray me now! But as a cook——"

"Why, the cook noticed that your appetite fell off. When a young woman eats no more than a lovebird, she must have a mate to feed her, or she pines!"

"Hem! here is a valise," said Jacinto, to turn the talk, as she paused by a window, illuminated by the reflection of a bonfire on the plaza.

On a settee was Porthos' purchase at Oporto.

"A bundle of clothes, anyway," said Quaqua, feeling the find.

"It is laced up."

"My knife laughs at ties," observed Quaqua, drawing a knife from her hose-top band.

"What, would you open——"

"Snick! It is open!"

"You have slit it——"

"As I would a man, if he had a state secret in his chest!" responded the negress, calmly.

"Why commit such a rudeness?"

"My volunteer fiscal officer," said Captain Pedro's housekeeper, "we must see if they have gone over to the enemy! If King Philip has bought them, the Caballero of Gannarta at your valuation and the Knight of the Stupendous Appetite at Don Juan's, this ought to contain a huge order on the mint, which it would stagger the Soleiman tribe to cash, or an amount in gold to crack a mule's back!"

"There is nothing but new clothes!"

"They have found them uniforms, then! What is this?"

"A piece of vellum!"

"What did I say! the order on the High Treasurer of Madrid!"

"Nothing of that sort!" holding it up against the pane.

"Would it be a love letter?"

"Pish! stranger than that! the law script is entangled, but I know enough by the names—this is the mortgage of Floriador to Soleiman, by my father."

"Oh, I know something about that!"

Is there anything you do not know?"

"When the Jew Elizor came to his wits, after having been picked up on the cliff, instead of thanking his savers, he accused the French sailors of robbing him of a packet of valuable papers. The Caballero de Gannarta hushed him with that keen voice of his which would silence a tattling termagant, and showed the wallet, of which he had relieved him, no doubt. In a little, the usurer, seeing what we all saw, that the gallant had fallen in love with the princess' lady attendant——"

"Oh, all saw that?" biting her lip.

"A ship need not fly her flag to declare her home port and her cargo!"

"But you do more, soothsayer! you declare the port she is doomed to! But go on! I am as transparent as crystal! I am a condemned creature, alas!"

"The king's order holds you out as a waive, indeed,

but, love you! wild horses should not drag us apart!
I do not shrink from you!"

"No, I have not noticed you shrink!"

"As soon as the money-spinner saw that the chevalier loved your ladyship, and your ladyship the chevalier—in short, as Hymen came forward to relieve Cupid of his watch, he gallantly gave the paper to the
Frenchman as his wedding present!"

"Incredible! a Jew, and we old Christians! so much
gallantry in a Jew, so much generosity in an usurer!"

"I guess he did not give it as a money-lender or a
Jew, but as a man who loved excellence in man and
woman!"

"I shall admire those people all my life!"

"Well, lady, where I come from they eat folks. When
our king objected to a follower who devoured an
albino, he said: 'They are all one, under the skin!' Man
pretty much the same, lady!"

"Ugh! But you are a dear woman! and that Elizor
prince of Israelites! All this is plausible, but how
comes the document here, at my brother's!"

"In the Frenchman's valise? He handed it to your
brother to plaster the stab he made!"

"Upon my faith, you may be right again!"

"What are you going to do about it?"

"Take it into safer keeping—my family paper—my
mother always wanted Floriador to be mine! But I
will leave, instead, a writing of my hand."

So saying, Jacinta took down from its long cord attached to the wall a hand looking-glass. She scrib-
bled upon its face with a finger ring. This little mirror,
scratched with the diamond, she thrust back among
Porthos' habiliments.

"Quick! I hear!"

"Steps!"

With great activity, the corpulent black shot the bolt
in the door and furthermore lowered a strong bar across
it into an iron socket.

Donna Jacinta had already darted into the aperture.
Quaqua followed her closely, and drew the picture-
panel shut, hermetically.

At the same instant, a hasty hand tried the fastened door, and then began pounding on it with a hard fist.

Porthos sprang up, awake, like a good soldier who sleeps on his arms, and, sword in hand, hastened to the point attacked while his eyes were opening.

"Porthos, Porthos!" was the call.

"All's well! D'Artagnan! Why not come right in?"

"Come in? Are you drunk? How can I come in, when you have barred and bolted the door!"

"So I have," replied Du Vallon, feeling, without ability to see that it was so. "I do not remember; but you could not have done that from the outside!"

He undid the door gropingly. A dazzling light blinded him. The musketeer appeared, illumined by a two-light candlestick held by a servant.

Porthos drew further back, and his friend followed him well into the room. The footman placed the light on the console, and seeing that Porthos had overturned the hookah, took it out with him.

"What a time you were opening?" grumbled the newcomer, falling into the first chair.

"He did not find the prize," thought the amiable knight, sympathetically, "that is why he is cross, for once! Oh, these lovers!"

Without being a wiseacre, he had discovered that the best way to counteract disagreeableness is to redouble one's good-humor; his broad face instantly beamed and his smile widened.

"I was killing time in your long absence," began he.

"For which, to have no witnesses, you locked yourself in! But with what? All 'the dead men' I see are under the table."

"Oh, the voided bottles; you are right. I was drinking, eating and smoking!"

"I can smell smoke, but I see no crumbs——"

"That is because I ate all up! It was a light collation. If there were any scraps they fell off——"

"With the dishes?"

Porthos stared; he was unaware of the table having been cleared.

"Never heed! but you were in the dark, like you are leaving me."

"So am I still, about what is going on. What is the town doing? I could not question the servants, and I believe they are the tongueless ones of the Grand Mogul!"

"Why, the town is a cave of the winds, and crossing ones, too," said the musketeer, undoing his belt and rubbing his compressed sides. "From opposite parts came cries of 'Long live' some one or other. 'Death' to this or that—the loudest shouters being indoors. Half the houses on the Palace Place are illuminated, the other in mourning. The boys are making bonfires and burning effigies—the stock of effigies running short, they are burning tradesmen's signs and saints in wood from the corner shrines. The citizens who carry water on both shoulders hang out banners with Philip on one side and Juan on the other!"

"Poor crown!" said Porthos, pretending interest in this worn topic.

"Yes, a bone for which the foolish dogs tear one another; then a third cur, perhaps, rushes in and runs off with it!"

"If it is Pedro, he would make a good king!" said the giant guardsman, without prejudice.

"Porthos, those are not empty bottles under the table, but trunks——"

"Trunks—we had no traveling trunks."

"Very baggy trunks; large as a bombard! true 'cannon' breeches!"

Porthos looked along the floor—it was strewn with his new garments.

"Who the plague carpeted the floor with my suit?" he growled, cross as his friend when he was kept at the door.

"It seems to me that, in spite of Marianda House being guarded by janissaries, more or less mute, they are probably more or less deaf and blind, since they have let cloak-snatchers run all over you while you slept!"

"Well, I grant that I must have winked. But, thieves—how could there be thieves when the door was barred and bolted?"

"That is the puzzle!"

"My dear comrade, there is magic! enchant——"

"Enchanted fiddlesticks!"

"It is magic! Lisbon is haunted! If, when Rome was in a pinch, ghosts caracoled up and down before her temples, why should not Lisbon have its spectre or two? Besides, you yourself have said it—the ghostly Don Sebastian appears on the wall walks! and in my dream—now it comes to me—I saw phantoms glide about this room!"

"Phantoms caused by your puffing at that *nargilye* which you do not understand!"

"I had it on my tongue-tip, though! I did see something!"

"Porthos, you have no originality! You saw something white in a sheet?"

"Not a bit! It was black, and in gay colors!"

"Don Sebastian burnt to a crisp by the African sun! ha, ha! Did this black ghost take any money out of your pockets?"

"No; I have my purse here, under my hand."

D'Artagnan kicked the fallen clothes together.

"There is something shining on the heap on the chair," continued the musketeer, taking up the hand reflector. "Curled darling that you are, do you carry a mirror to inspect your toilet before you go out on parade?"

"A mirror!" said the other, certainly little like a Narcissus. "I never carried a mirror! unkind D'Artagnan!"

"It is not merely a mirror, but a book!"

"A book?"

"At least, it is a leaf with writing——"

He was not much astonished at this vehicle of communication. Ever since the invention of glass windows, say a hundred years before, crystallography—writing on glass, not writing about crystals—had been popular with those who wished to show not only their calligraphy, but their possession of a diamond. As proficients in the art, Queen Elizabeth of England and King Francis I. of France may be cited.

"What are you reading that causes a red face?" queried the stout cavalier.

He was handed the mirror to read, as the scrawl was in his own language:

> "Kin may have bound me,
> Foes deep may wound me!
> They pain the heart, but all they do's restrain!
> Oh, would you know me,
> Love you must show me!
> And find the noblest, surest way to reign!"

"Faith, this poet, I think, has drunk full from Parnassus' pump," commented Porthos. "I take back any accusation that there were thieves here, or the Don Sebastian spirit—it was just a sapper who——"

"Bless us and preserve us! A sapper for a Sappho! Porthos, a sapper is one who carries on his boring with pick and spade, while a Sappho——"

"Bores with pen, or in this case with diamond! But I am half right—this mansion is tunneled and mined! Hark! here comes the poet for his meed!"

"His? hers! If this be Sappho, her feet are not poetic—but in horseman's boots and she is armed for war! Let swords rest—it is only our host."

It was the count, armed with back and breastplate and gorget; his morion had a steel bar to protect the nose. Each side of this his eyes glittered with liveliness. In his belt was a pair of very fine pistols such as princes carried against assassins, and balancing them, on the other flank, was thrust a folded paper, ostensibly a warrant or order.

"Sorry to disturb you, sirs," said he, quickly, "but a most grave circumstance hurries me home!"

"At all hours your lordship's servant!"

Porthos bowed.

"The double kingdom's safety is at stake. A terrible plot is winding among the loyal. We are trying to seize the coils before they strangle loyalty!"

"Let it coil, as long as it does not strike," returned the French captain, tranquilly.

"But it has struck—a stroke of unparalleled audacity!"

"Indeed!"

"Only some fifty strong, the fishermen of the Varinha Ward, who have free access into the town, came to the Corregidor's house, with their panniers, as if bringing deep-sea food as usual to the soldiers there. When I say fifty, half the number were concealed in the baskets, carried between two or four men. Once in the yard, these leaped out, handing their comrades weapons, and the fifty invaded the castle!"

"Capital!" and D'Artagnan's eyes sparkled.

"The baskets also contained grenades and port-fire; so that the Casa del Corregidor cannot be approached under penalty of that part being laid in ashes!"

"Bravo!" cried Porthos.

"Bravo! to the insurgents?" said Jorge de Marianda, frowning.

"My friend means that so little will not cool the Spanish ardor! How did the Corregidor meet the surprise, being a man of war?"

"He was made prisoner, this poor Balteazor de Zumaya! But that is not the sting! The successful villains, headed by a seaman called Captain Pedro, kept so quiet over their taking, that Colonels Carinha and Potargo walked into the house, with their escorts, thinking to attend a council as usual! This makes me senior colonel but one!"

"A Captain Pedro? It seems to me that this usurper of a Don Juan must be short of soldiers to employ fishermen for a stroke of war."

"Very short!" added Porthos, frowning.

"Soldiers or fishers, he gains that position in our midst," said the colonel, sulkily. "The one thing is to assemble all the stray soldiers and the able citizens, and deliver our friends at the Corregidor's!"

"At the risk of the smelt catchers blowing up the whole?"

"Trash!"

"I can see," muttered Porthos, "that our friend owns no houses in that part!"

"In a word, we must turn out these rebels, since we meet them face to face at last?"

"I am asking nothing better! For one, I should like to have that Captain Pedro within grasp of this my hand!"

"I have gathered two hundred men, and they are in the Clothworkers' close——"

"Against fifty netters and gaffers, ample!"

"Then, come! the invitation to the dance includes your friend."

Through all his haste and martial ardor, a thought sent a pang through him; he could be seen to wrestle with emotions, the better of which conquered, for his features became composed and a smile, pale but lofty, filmed over them. He strode to a table with writing materials, and wrote an address on an envelope hastily made, which he sealed. This he covered over with blank paper, also sealed. Returning to the musketeer captain, he said, in a voice not very steady.

"I go smiling forth, but may come home with death's grin on my lips. If that befalls me, I charge you with delivering this to the person named within. You can touch hands with her without contamination!"

Afraid that he should, in saying more, add too much, he sprang away, calling "Come!" as he left the room.

"Porthos," said the musketeer, peremptorily, "go with my lord!"

"And you? But, if I am under fire?"

"Fire back! only I know you are too good a marks-man to hit one of Pedro's girth!"

"And you?—you back out of a chance medley?"

"My friend, I am going into the heat of this medley!"

Having no doubt that the new recruits would follow him, Don Jorge had run out to give instructions to his servants to arm and reinforce his company.

"*Adios!* as they say—meaning that we shall meet again!"

"If it means that—*adios*, with all my heart! But what mean you by going into the heat of it, in that direction!"

"Where my heart is! I want to verify this writing!" waving the mirror.

"That won't parry a musketoon ball! Oh, I see! I am to take care of the brother while you——"

"Take care of the sister—and her property!"

"Property?"

"Do you know what packet the colonel gave me?

No; in that blank inclosure was the mortgage of Floriador, directed to Donna Jacinta!"

"On the eve of battle, he remembered the poor lady! Come, he is not so bad at heart after all! He shall not be hurt in this affray—not while Balizarde can be brandished!"

"Helloa, there! are you never coming?" shouted the count from the gardens.

"Have with you!" responded Porthos, in his lusty voice, which was heard through doors and walls.

"Then, what are you hanging back for?" queried D'Artagnan.

"To put on my clothes," said Porthos, hastily stripping in part; "do you think I bought these to equip ghosts!"

And attiring himself in the beadle's suit, he appeared after the other, glorious as a pupa which had become a butterfly.

He descended the stairs five at a jump.

"Now," said his friend, left alone. "I have no time to go for a locksmith, but will make my sword pierce this mysterious entrance, by which a black spectre rummages Porthos' clothes, purloins that packet and hands a companion phantom, of another hue, I guess, this glass on which to discourse in loving metre!"

Having a good idea of the nice cabinetwork of the period, he found the panel picture by the removal of the dust on the floor by its opening, inserted his sword as a chisel, cleft the spring bolt and plunged into the orifice.

CHAPTER XXXIII.

A CORPOREAL SHADE.

Porthos, glorified by his resplendent apparel, found in the *patio* several footmen left by the impatient count-colonel to be his escort and to guide him to their meeting place. With the better-armed he had gone off. He gave them no time to admire his change, but, with his sword out, put himself at their head, the steward by his side, and motioned the start. His lieutenant translated the gesture into words, and they sallied briskly out of the gardens. At the little door in the wall convenient for the pavilion, two or three squires were holding horses, as Porthos had descried from above, but they passed them without being challenged.

The streets were so lonely that it was with amaze that they unexpectedly found their way completely blocked at a turning.

A long wall, with towers at the angles, was that of the Carmelite Sisters' Convent. The square building was visible over the parapet, spiked and studded with shards.

A mob covered the space from the wall to the fronts of the opposite houses, mean and low. Instruments of every trade were flourished as weapons, showing that the men had come out of their shops at a general call.

Porthos could see over his followers, who gathered around him at the halt, like hens around chanticleer. He made a little way into the press by sheer weight, and demanded, through the major domo, his interpreter, the cause of the collection, of a cook's boy, who waved a saucepan like a mace.

"Sirrah, pastry maker, why this obstacle to the highway?"

"Master," returned the culinary artist, flattered by the address of a finely-clad gentleman, "that wretched old monk, the doorward to the Carmelite Convent, on seeing us coming, locked the gate in our faces and threw the key over the wall."

"Why should he not? Surely, even nuns may choose their visitors!"

"Cry you mercy, noble sir! It is a begging sister-hood, and it is written, 'Beggars should not be choosers!'"

"Witty, but it is not charitable. For what do you want to enter the sanctuary? Are there no men to clout and claw?"

"There are plenty of Spanish to fight, certainly, but they have sneaked into the strong-houses, do you see? We have little to force them out with! Taking the pet-ticoats—I mean, the frocks—for protection, the Gov-ernor has stored two tons of powder and three or four cartloads of pig-lead in the cloisters, with seven or eight hundred stand of arms——"

"Humph!" said the honest Porthos, "that makes your disorderly conduct a military precaution——"

"Military necessity! We are not only depriving the enemy of solid comfort, but arming our side, which is lamentably deficient in firearms."

The steward intimated to Porthos that this was a self-confessed rebel, and that parley was out of place.

"You are a fine though incautious speaker," said the Frenchman, "and I am indebted to you. But, since the old man threw the key out of reach, which was his duty, why pull him about?"

"The lads only sought to take the rope girdle off him to try to scale the wall, but he resisted tooth and nail, so that those who were scratched fell on him savagely. He still resists, crying out that the rope is a blessed one, having belonged to a saint of the order——"

"The dotard! Who would not lose a fathom of rope to save an inch of skin?"

"To tell the whole tale," continued the youth, whose eloquence was collecting an audience around them, "the lads, finding the rope too short, were making up the deficiency with his sackcloth robe, whereupon he shrieked out that they were flaying him."

"Yes, they are using their knives to undress him! They will disjoint him!"

"Have no fear! Those with the knives are curriers, trained to shave close without harming the pelt!"

"Zounds! They shall not murder a poor old man for doing his duty!" protested Porthos. "Do you understand this?"

Dispensing with his informant and his interpreter, he drew back a little, only to plunge forward with lowered head, like a bull. Expecting no onslaught from this quarter, the crowd gave way right and left, and his first rush brought him nearly up to the door set in the wall.

In the recess, with his only garment half stripped off, lay the janitor's emaciated body.

"We'll teach you how to lock doors! We'll show you how to scale walls!" cried his tormentors, flagellating him with his own blessed cord.

"And I," roared Porthos, opening his arms over the victim so forcibly that he sent half a dozen of the foremost sprawling at their friend's feet, "I will teach you not to disgrace humanity!"

The shout in the unknown tongue startled everybody, but when they saw, flaming with indignation and splendid with gold lace, this superhuman knight, a panic thrilled them all. From several white mouths was uttered the common impression:

"Don Sebastian! The ghost of King Sebastian!"

Whereupon, nearly everybody of susceptible feelings turned and fled.

Porthos thought the field was clear, but he had not counted on another element of the horde; this was the scum of the Lazaretto-Jewry, such as he had been among on his first acquaintance with Lisbon. Outcasts, reveling in the withdrawal of all constitutional repression, they were intoxicated with their sudden freedom and draughts of beverage more potent that Quaqua's. They had a chance to vent their hatred for all controllers, priests, soldiers, watchmen, and they abused the opportunity. They did not seek the ammunition in the convent so much as wreaking their spite. They wanted the blood of this monk, as a representative of his order.

Recovering from any superstitious fears at seeing the supposed ghost in their midst, very corporeal, they mustered to attack him, trampling the janitor under foot as they gathered.

Porthos used his sword reversed as a mace. then smote

with the flat of it, and was beginning to pierce and cut when the Marianda servitors came to his aid. All disappeared under the dense rioters, like bulls under a pack of dogs.

As if to infuriate the rabble still more, some one inside the inclosure, standing on stones, threw boiling water and missiles over, with more violence than discrimination, for the old monk's defenders had their share.

This added oil to the flames. The chorus of threats, imprecations, groans and shrieks of pain and choler increased; pistols and short-cut guns were fired at any risk; one or two shots threatened to spoil Porthos' suit, and flattened on the door. All those improvised weapons which bristle at a popular rising menaced the newcomers; spears made of shears, knives tied to dyers' poles, meat-choppers mounted on clubs, bludgeons of vine-stakes; those who had been in Africa used sticks as *djerids,* and darted them at the knot of defenders around the fallen wretch.

The latter bid fair to be trodden to pulp. Luckily, if it was good luck, the revengeful hands drew him out from the press and finished the last stripping—his robe was converted into ribbons, which waved as triumphant banners over his dilapidated form.

At the same instant that Porthos and the steward tried to disengage themselves—not to retire, but to charge to the deliverance—the mob recoiled and dropped the prize.

One of them had plucked from the body, suspended by a thong, an iron dagger, of which he had attempted to make no use; either he had scruples against blood-spilling, or it was not a weapon, but a token.

While the finder of this instrument held it in doubt, about, perhaps, to settle it by plunging it into the ill-fated janitor, the ruffians made the final attack on the interferers with their pastime.

Front and rear, from all sides, weapons and projectiles rained; blinded, hampered, unable to strike, the servants of Marianda were forced back on their two leaders; Porthos, losing his footing, feeling that the hands on his arm and sword hilt might wrest it away, shouted, in desperation:

"France! France! Brothers of the Coast! Sustain me! The Musketeers!" words of no avail.

At this instant a bystander, whose hair and beard bristled and whose face turned pale, gasped, as he knocked the dagger out of his companion's grasp:

"The Holy Brotherhood! It is the token of the Inquisition!"

One look at the dagger, similar to that which Fra Benito had drawn upon Don Juan de Braganza, sufficed the mob.

As one man, they took to their heels, throwing down what might impede their flight. In a twinkling the street was bare. Relieved of the pressure, the Knight of the Vallon staggered back against the wall. The steward raised the insensible monk. Another took up the dagger, fallen from the frightened rioter's palsied hand.

"This is a superior of the Inquisition," said the steward, awed.

The Frenchman was amused at the retreat.

"Hum! a great fight, if it were a poor monk," criticized he. "A poor one if it were a superior officer of that institution. But your master awaits us. Strike on the door and tell the sisters that the riffraff have fled. Get the poor fellow in to their care, if he is not sped. Let them look to those reckless wretches, too, if they will."

The street was strewn with the disabled.

The inhabitants of the convent must have had their peephole. The flight had been perceived, for the door opened quickly. Several old men, gardeners and porters, issued and took in the sorely-buffeted janitor, if janitor he was. He had revived a little; he looked with deep and glazed eyes on Porthos, whom he had seen in his finery at the onset, and seemed to wave his hand in gratitude. But the soldier was paying him no heed—the whole incident was out of his consideration by this.

"A well-tousled man," muttered the steward, seeing the profound care with which the men treated the cause of the contention. "It is no business of mine, but since when have the Carmelites had a leading spirit of the Inquisition to keep the gate? Those villains guessed rightly enough—there is a treasure in that convent."

"Haste! haste!" cried Porthos, girding his sword on and preening his torn and ruffled feathers. "Let us join your lord!" He rubbed himself here and there, where stones had left a bruise. "Take me for St. Sebastian, did they? For St. Stephen, I would sooner think. Strange that D'Artagnan did not come up while we were so prettily delayed. It's that feminine Robin Goodfellow! They light our path, but it is to perdition! Fall in; forward—march!"

CHAPTER XXXIV.

TAPPING THE VOLCANO.

To Porthos' troop no further resistance arose; they were soon at the Casa del Corregidor. Count Jorge was there, compelled to sit down before it for a siege, since it was shut up close. Here and there, in fresh-cut holes in the floors of the overhanging story and balconies, musket muzzles protruded, with a brass blunderbuss or two.

At the small windows dangled by iron handles those hand-grenades brought by the Coast Brothers. These were not fixed upon or grappled at, for fear they would explode at a touch and rain down inextinguishable fires.

Beyond the small body of Spanish formed another ring, or several circles, augmenting each instant, as if the darkness called the wolves out of their coverts. Among them, Porthos thought he recognized more than one of his assailants; they had bound bandages over their heads as if they had been cracked over the pate by his sword-flat, or pommeled. Marianda was fretting sorely.

"Your delay was bad, but, altogether, our being held at bay is fatal!" grumbled he, after thanking him for the arrival and asking after his companion. "My men hesitate to attack, fearing the prowess of these pirates, as they esteem them, and that this gathering rabble will fall on our rear, if we meet a reverse. Lookers-on may be leapers-on in such in-and-in fighting."

"My lord, they fight like desperadoes, though indifferently armed. And those seamen are indeed to be dreaded, using pike and axe and delighting in hand-to-hand encounters. That crowd does not murmur—I most distrust those long cloaks—they are hiding firedogs, I wager!"

The lookers-'on were too calm; no murmurs, as Porthos said; staring, counting the soldiers and their arms; seeming to wait patiently for a signal, but whether to fall on the Spanish or aid them to assault the Corrector's castle. none could tell.

"If they had a head, I would question him," said the colonel. "A gentleman cannot address a horde!"

At this, a rider made his way, with difficulty, and more by wheedling speech than his horse's shoulders, through the concourse; he could define that Porthos and the other were the commanding officers.

"General," said he, judging the Frenchman by his coat, and, besides, like a clever subaltern, wishing to court favor by promoting him honorably, "the mob is immense around the Viceroy's palace; it has been swelling from five this morning."

"They have taken their time!"

"Oh, they are not pressed. Many came in from the countryside; they ate their dinner off their palm."

"What news? You have not hurried it."

"The people put the night-chains across the streets and dug trenches here and there to mire the artillery. I had to leap my horse, and strained his tendons. The police lieutenant sent out a file of us to bring in all straggling soldiers, but they have got out over the walls. They say the enemy's van is at hand, and gladly receives deserters—every private is made a corporal, and so on. But hasten, if you would save the vice-queen! I hear shots! You may be too late!"

"Well, sir?" asked Jorge, of the Frenchman, politely.

"Well, colonel, I should leave the Corregidor to discuss the price of fish with this Pedro! A vice-queen is worth a couple of corregidors, sex apart! In picking this fish, the bones may prick our fingers. Let us hasten to the great lady's aid, as this worthy cavalier suggests."

Porthos had no desire to charge upon his friend Pedro.

Count Marianda might be obstinate, but his men did not like the prospect of an advance under a rear fire. Those cloaks had unmasked short guns, as Porthos had surmised. They had the impression that the castle was a crater and they did not court tapping the lava.

At his sign the two fifers struck up and the long-barreled drum was thumped. They formed a solid, if thin column, and pierced the crowd, which sullenly opened and closed immediately.

"Mark!" said the musketeer.

He was confining himself to monosyllables.

Jorge looked over his shoulder. The long cloaks were cast back; their wearers plainly shouldered firearms, which, if of obsolete patterns, might riddle his column at close range; they formed a battalion more numerous than his and followed step for step, as if their curiosity about the invested Corregidor's was passed.

Indeed, the firing of musketry at the palace was animated and attracting. The palace had been engirt since morning. Thousands had come from curiosity, but they were unable to wriggle out when other thousands arrived, impelled by a stronger sentiment.

All classes were confounded in this seething pot; the plaza of the royal palace: nobles, traders, merchants, shore toilers, workmen, priests and women, who were agitatedly holding their companions' hands until the moment when they would put the weapons in them.

Well into the day, the front wore its usual aspect.

The gentlemen in attendance, officers and courtiers, inhabiting the residence, pretended not to believe danger menaced them and carried on the ceremony of the vice-queen's morning reception. The guards' officers on service chatted and laughed over-loudly in the central courtyard. The mock Moorish minstrels who had played while the vice-queen took her chocolate, in semi-public state, had chosen the lightest and liveliest airs—and Spanish ones, too.

But the confluence toward this spot became so appalling that even the most stolid were enfevered, and the prudent slipped away on one errand and another. Some young officers spoke of pointing cannon on the gazers who came too near the gateway, but found no echoes. Such action would be rash, and rashness is folly, when a people are in ebullition.

In fact, all Lisbon and all Portugal (only the country loved the cause more fondly and openly) was honeycombed with mutiny. D'Artagnan could have told the chief all about that. For the most part, the older officials, accustomed all their life to merely discontent, had become fossils; they appeared to drink that Rio Tinto water which is fabled to petrify.

Suddenly the square, filled to the edges, flashed over its sombre surface with white points and rays. At least every other man had thrown back his cloak and displayed a "white" weapon—that is, one of burnished steel. As for the others, they had firearms, pistols, *petronels, escopetas,* firedogs. The musketry covered the swords-men, and all marched directly to where posts had been assigned.

There were four main columns. At the head of one, a Portuguese ex-captain of the royal hunt charged the watch house at the main entrance. Not taken by sur-prise, the guards, having only their halberds, retired into the stone roundhouse. Three or four porters began tugging at the iron gratings to swing them shut; they managed this, but the wooden doors, bound with iron, had been imbedded in the mud flirted on them by the coaches. Levers and picks would be required to loosen them. A hail of stones, bullets and sticks drove them away from the useless attempt. Some pierced the open ironwork and splintered the wood.

A warder who tried to lock the gates successfully closed, had the enormous key driven into his breast.

At the next instant the rush broke down one of the gates and bore the other back, crushing those who were struggling with the inner one.

Part of the storming party faced round and poured a volley into the guardhouse by the airhole over the door and the small windows.

Shortly the courtyard became a cockpit. The two marble fountains were dyed with blood, and the basin, one shattered, poured out the ruddy tide over the ground.

Up in the windows gentlemen with fine fowling pieces, servants with the furniture converted into projectiles, and guardsmen showered all that would wound and maim on the intruders, although they were in some cases grappling with defenders whose rage had carried them too far out.

Soon marksmanship was useless, for the *patio* was choking with smoke and dust. The large wads of the blunderbusses, entering the windows, had set the curtains and *arras* in flame. Some hung, smouldering, out of the casements, whence the sashes had been torn, and by these burning ladders the assailants entered the first floor.

The interior began to be shambles.

Ribero, Braganza's secretary and lieutenant, knowing

the palace, guided another column. He was one of the first to acquire a footing in the corridor. In his brigade were Brothers of the Coast with boarding hatchets and boat hooks, which no door or barrier could resist.

"Portugal!" cried the gentlemen rebels.

"For our own hands!" shouted the sailors.

Indeed, the ensign of these strangers in Lisbon was two hands enclasped on a white field waved with blue; enough of the arm was shown to present the bared one as the sailor's, the one in a sleeve was the fisher's.

In the north wing, the governor-general was living. It was Vasconsellos. One of his officers came out on the landing, where the axes had shivered a door, and challenged the infuriates.

"We are driving out our tyrants!" they deigned to explain.

A magistrate who had been closeted with the governor came up beside the officer. It was the police chief, Soarez. His studied speech was rendered inaudible by the clamor.

"Long live the Duke of Braganza! our own king! Death to all tyrants!"

He and the officer madly hurled a "Long live the King of Spain!" but before they could draw back they were pulled down; their coat and robe were ripped off, and they were trampled under foot. As the rioters surged over them, pistol shots were fired at the bodies, but soon all were swept up to the closed inner doors.

Palleria, Vasconsellos' captain of guards, urged his master to escape by the back stairs, but the assaulting party were hammering on the last barricade while they were arguing.

"Fly to the Corregidor's," said the captain; "it is manned and stored to hold out for an age!"

He had no idea that this chosen stronghold for the ultimate stand was already in the hands of Pedro and the fishers.

The governor-general stole out as the mob tore in, spread over the room and, making "an *olla podrida*" of the furniture, books and papers, as record says, probed all nooks, cut open coffers and trunks to make sure the hated one was not hidden, and pierced the walls for secret receptacles.

In a back room they found an old servant, white with terror. Between two pistols to his ears, he pointed to a clothespress; with axes the two doors were split, and, with the gaffs, the oppressor was drawn forth. He had collapsed, though brave on earlier occasions; he had not the voice to implore mercy.

Transfixed on spears and swords, he was flung out of the window.

"The tyrant is no more! So be it with his master!" was the cry. "Hail to our rights again! Liberty forever! Long live our own Don Juan!"

At this juncture, Captain Pedro arrived with his men; he had left the Corregidor's, turned into a prison for his own captivity, and overawing that part of the town, the fishers garrisoned it. At the northeastern corner his men deposited a barrel of powder, setting fire to it with a red fire stick. A portion of the wall was leveled. All entered at the breach, ten times the seamen's number; they were carried on by the accession to their ranks, like corks on a freshet. In the yard they had a glimpse of a red shuttlecock with which madmen were playing; it was the remains of Vasconsellos.

The vice-queen's apartments were invaded by a third column. Its leader had sagely added a number of fisherwomen to his cohort to handle the lady without accusation of ungallantry.

This representative of Philip was the Princess Margarita of Savoy. Her advisor was Don Carlos of Arragon, to whom she had refused to listen since he spoke of submission. He now pleaded that she must retire indoors and not breast the insults of women. But she came forward, with the Archbishop of Lisbon at her side, in spite of her desiring to be alone, and her trembling ladies at her back.

She was haughty, cold and feelingless, like a princess confronting the baseborn.

"Sirs," said she, ignoring the fishfags and addressing the leaders with swords and in spurs, "I confess that Vasconsellos has exceeded orders and humanity. It was justly that popular hate and indignation fell. When the subjects' love weakens, the king's power is no longer strong."

"Vasconsellos is dead! and in as many scraps as the death warrants he signed!" said a voice, grimly. "He said, the last time he was remonstrated with about grinding the people, that his heart was with his king alone. Now, I am going to send his heart on to the Escurial to be with King Philip!"

Margerita turned pale, for this Ben Hamet de Lastries was a Moor and a Portuguese who hated the Spanish and all foreigners, with double cause. But her voice was as steadfast as ever.

"Chevalier, having slain him, your animosity ought to be assuaged. If you do not at once retire you will be held guilty of high treason, and I shall be out of power to absolve you of the crime before our dread sovereign, the king."

"You are out of power already," said one Menezez, who had been a secretary of hers, "so many gentlemen and the highest of the old nobility of Portugal have not risen in a body to take the life of one spoiler, for revenge, but to place on the head rightfully entailed the crown of our dear land! Long live Don Juan IV., our Señor of Portugal!"

The Savoyard understood before this defiance that she had no sway over these lawless ones. But she was not disconcerted. She harbored a belief that her presence and apt speech might control the populace. She proposed going out on the plaza.

Several nobles, not all Spanish, threw themselves across her path. Her maids locked hands to stay her.

"What can the people do to me?" she cried, passionately and without abatement of her insolent contempt.

There was a silence. Plainness was exacted to convince this proud princess who had never heard it, perhaps. Portuguese or Spanish nobles and gentry, all shrank from this step.

"What will they do? They will cut off your head, *ma donna!*" said a voice, in Italian, wholly strange to her, as to all else.

She looked, like the rest, that way. A man in showy attire, impaired by the shocks of combat, towered a head

and shoulders over the others; he was leaning on a sword
which, in another, would have required two hands to
wield it. It was D'Artagnan's brother musketeer.

Outside rang a tremendous burst of triumph; clarions,
bugles, fishermen's horns, whistles commingled. It was
silence called for on all sides.

In this perfect quiet arose a voice, hoarse and strong—
that of Admiral Pedro (at least, the Frenchman knew
it); he had followed Colonel Jorge so closely that he was
at his heels. In his presence the fishers of the Tagus
bowed low.

"Hear ye," said the seaman, "in the name of the nobles,
the gentle folk and the people—the people—the people!
I proclaim the Duke of Braganza Juan IV., king of free
and independent Portugal!"

The cheering was deafening—not for Juan, the nobles
or the gentry, but for "free and independent Portugal!"

Then came a thunderpeal which made all quake. Ten
thousand firearms were discharged in the air; they were
wanted to kill no longer!

"An Italian?" queried the princess, of Porthos, clutch-
ing at a straw.

"No, madame; French!"

"Save me!" After her proud front, the weakness of
her sex came. Besides, her native tongue had softened
her, where all were so alien. The din and fusillade had
daunted her.

"Hark!" said Porthos, in his best Portuguese, "the fort
is firing on the town! This palace will be abolished!"

Poor Porthos! he meant to say "demolished," but, to
the mass, a ponderous word has its effect, despite its
meaning. The gravity of the crisis was not questioned.
A panic seized most, and the building was vacated of the
inquisitive and the coarser grained. Floors and stairs
shook under the countless feet, and out of the windows
poured files of the frightened.

"You have saved me!" said the princess, startled by
the exodus.

Her maids fell at Porthos' feet, sobbing, with southern
extravagance.

Porthos passed his large hand over his eyes; never in
his dreams, when he was vainglorious about his con-

quests, had he pictured himself surrounded by kneeling beauty. He stood, the hub of radiant spokes.

"But the multitude may return!" stammered a chamberlain.

An hour ago, they would have been "that scum."

"They are returning, the misguided people," said another.

"Madame, here is a table," said the musketeer, and he shoved several dead bodies off the overturned board and righted it. "Pen, ink! Write, lady: 'Governor: Capitulate!'"

"Never!" began the princess, her obstinacy returning.

"Wise counsel," whispered an old clerk, whose white head was matted with blood.

"Or every Spaniard in Lisbon will fatten the fishes!" said Pedro, who perceived the Frenchman's aim.

Porthos looked at the vice-queen, twirling his mustache as if he had heretofore been irresistible.

The Savoyard looked at this giant in the gaudy dress which only a Portuguese or a mountebank should have worn, concluded that it covered a great commander who had the will and the wit to move the masses, and, without understanding why she should cause pity, wrote as he dictated. Her signature was perfect with all its flourishes.

The old clerk countersigned and set the seal upon it; he would have finished off a court document though the earth yawned.

"Now, madame," said Porthos, taking the paper, "get out of the barriers as soon as you can!"

Their colloquy in Italian was an enigma to the others.

"Because the citadel will fire in spite of my orders?"

"Sooth, no! We took the citadel long since! the historic mule laden with gold!"

Striding to the nearest window, he and Pedro stood in it, on the sill, and the sailor-general showed the paper.

"Brothers," said he, "of the coast and the country, the vice-queen yields to your wishes! This spikes the citadel guns! A cheer for the Lady of Savoy, returning to her own country!"

A few careless shouts arose; but they might be in relief for the removal of the bugbear of all fortified towns; the dread that the city would be destroyed by its guns.

"On my head, you will be rewarded," said the dethroned lady to Du Vallon, who bowed and kissed her hand before her ladies hurriedly bore her away, like swans surrounding Leda.

"I would rather have a better security, pretty as it is!" he muttered, dubious about royal memories. "But what will D'Artagnan say to this? Bah, he is in love—no woman is strange to him!"

He put the state paper in his doublet, useless though it was and examined the scene at ease.

Out on the square, carpenters were raising a stage, scaffold or dais, for execution or a coronation?

"They are much alike!" mused he.

Here and there, men with swart faces, nervous action and rapid glances, were carrying bags; wayfarers shunned them at a warning whisper going before.

"Are they going to blow up the chief houses? Woe to the land where the nobles are the assessors and the gentry the collectors!"

They were firework-makers, going to set up the frames for parti-colored artifices to celebrate the victory and the entry of the new monarch.

The universal cry was: "Long live Don Juan IV.!"

"This is all very fine. Everything in my country ends with a song and dance—here, with a bonfire! Tastes differ! But what has become of my friends while I have been overturning a rule—or, at least, the king's vice?"

Pedro was collecting his men. As for Don Jorge, Porthos could not be expected to worry about him—a married man, he might not love him for his sister's sake!

"My good angel was my valet to put this coat on!" said Porthos, complacently remembering the bevy of maids of honor.

CHAPTER XXXV.

TO SAVE THE QUEEN.

During this exciting episode, the Royal Musketeer was deep in the labyrinth, boring, like work of the white ant, the foundations of Marianda House. More familiar with it, Donna Jacinta had come out at the lower end with her sable maid; it was in the summerhouse. In its principal room was the Duchess of Braganza. She had ridden from the rebel headquarters on a pillion, to the gates and entered like a humble fugitive. A sailor, awaiting her, had guided her to this refuge.

"I hope your highness has not been uneasy or fatigued in my absence?" said the young lady. "I know this house is very simple. It was here my mother retired for her 'retreat,' and she did away with the pretty vanities of fountains and flowers. It was never destined to receive a queen!"

"Pray, do not use a title before it is consecrated," reproved La Braganza, playfully. "This is a palace to the accommodations along the road, and to the hostel of the Petrel!"

"At least," continued Jacinta, "it can offer what palaces do not always contain—loyal hearts and devoted spirits!"

"What news?"

"The people are having the word passed that their rights will be restored them, the traders that tolls and custom duties will be lightened, the Lisbonese that trade will go no more to Madrid."

"Nothing new of Don Juan?"

"Madame, there are fears that fanatics will try to assassinate him! Those in charge of his precious health are on their guard. They have determined to baffle them; three or four coronation suits have been made, and each has its place of deposit. But it is here where I count upon his coming—the other dressing-rooms are but traps for the bravos!"

"You are a fount of hopefulness, but I doubt more on the sill than on the long journey to the goal!"

"Yes, my heart is full of hope! I doubt nothing now!"

"Is it hope alone that swells it?" Then, seeing a blush, however promptly subdued, she significantly added: "One of the first things we shall do is relieve you of that stigma of being a waive."

"Gnat stings?" sneered Jacinta, haughtily as a duchess, or this duchess. "I have no need of the Church!"

"Nay, the finest entry into society is by the altar aisle!"

"Marriage, do you mean? This is no time to talk of such things!"

"Well, I think of others, no longer about myself. All have your confidence. The valiant Don Lasquez de Peleta accompanied me to the gates, where we were received by the Mellos. With them at the door, I feel tranquil."

"There are more. Menezez, who comes from the palace, where all resistance is terminated—I might say exterminated—brings word that my lord duke must be within the walls, but he does not know how ushered in."

"Well guarded, then; but I could wish those two energetic Frenchmen were with us."

"I cherish half your wish!"

"Ah, I shot close! Your chosen half is not the married one?"

"Does he not, at times, look it? How odd that so valorous a knight could be some woman's meacock!"

"Mystery of matrimony!" said the duchess, sincerely having not the faintest notion that she was called a Xantippe. "Did you find your road to this pleasant refuge as unimpeded as I?"

"I had only one hinderance, but it was serious. In a crowd I nearly ran into my brother's arms——"

"Count Marianda's?"

"He is colonel now! Would be general if his side won, which all disprove!"

"He is with Philip, eh?"

"Dyed ingrain, as we say on the plains."

"Ran into his arms, did you? A very proper place!"

"Sometimes! But I plucked myself from his embrace, as an enemy's."

"But he recognized you?"

"I hope not. I was in this peasant's dress!"

"How dreadful if he had snuffed out this very flame of insurrection!"

"No, no! your highness is the flame! I am the candleholder! I am standing yet! I shook him off and I left him transfixed to the spot!"

"Transfixed with disappointment, or the dagger which the virtuous peasant maiden wears?"

"With disappointment in the first place; but, after, with a swordthrust in the arm!"

"If you had a Brother of the Coast with you——"

"Well, a new brother. Affiliated with them, and a great friend of Captain Pedro. But I will descant later about my deliverer."

"Why not at once? plenty of time! When I ask a boon for him I want him amply to deserve it!"

"While the unknown cavalier disarmed your brother, you ran here to make me welcome! I thank you! Palace or villa, my house is always open to you in return. But if your brother is at hand?"

"This house is quite detached from the mansion. Besides, his military duties must keep him from home. Let me go, sure of that as well as other matters. Mark, your highness is in safety here. Supposing danger came, you could flee by a secret way into the main building, as I will show you. Those nobles are in call. Strike this African gong and at each stroke a defender will appear!"

She took the princess' hand to kiss it, as if it were a queen's, but the other repulsed her, and, drawing her to her, kissed her in a sisterly way.

The adorable fanatic for the new royalty blushed and left the room.

"Most charming of creatures!" ejaculated the duchess. "To think that where calculation and genius fail, the heart finds the way. I am in our capital, thanks to that darling above all. When I have flagged, she has spurred me! But, a waive! they were partly right—she is not of this sordid world! So, she loves? and a marvelous knight! one who makes you shudder with his inexhaustible devices and strength to carry them out! That will

anchor our sprite to the earth. It was easy to guess—this
Gannarta—that is, D'Artagnan! redoubtable chevalier!"

"At your grace's service!"

The voice was at her elbow—the speaker kneeling at
her feet.

"I am delighted I am called! Then, there is danger
nigh!"

"Strange apparition!"

"Lisbon is prolific with apparitions! Don Sebastian
has appeared!"

"On the city walls?"

"And within them—he has saved a whole nunnery
from a mob and eke a visiting prelate, who happened to
be in the way! but there are other goblins! My friend
Porthos, who has never seen a ghost, had his incredulity
shaken last night! He saw one, black as the Africans!"

"And you, who are always with him?"

"I was hunting spirits of another hue! Mine shrinks
from appearing bodily—a spirit can manifest itself bodily!"

"Was it one of those agreeable spirits who communicate with us by music——"

"No, madame, its medium was writing! Not on a vulgar scrap of paper, with liquid soot on the tip of a
skewer—nay, nay! but with a diamond—emblem of light!
on crystal—in a word, my spirit wrote to me on a mirror!"

"Sir, I shall believe I am to be queen, not over Portugal, but the land of the Fata Morgana!"

"Oh, my lady, even fairyland has its counterweights.
To the fays, the elves and the sylphs are opposed the
gnomes, demons and imps. Now, that your grace's rest,
of which she stands in need, may not be disturbed by any
of these, I beseech her to go to a safer resort by this unknown door——"

He opened the secret panel by which he had slipped in.

His tone and text were airy, but his look was solemn.

"I came by it, so that I know, while devious, it is safe.
You need not carry a light. There will be unassailable
solitude until you have the company you desire."

He put a candlestick into her resistless hand. This
man had such a way, even convincing to queens.

"I can depend on your sending the duke?"

"As on my being between you and danger! Lisbon rages! hark! but there may be enemies nearer home!"

She hesitated a little. He was accusing those on whom she relied—old upholders, proven friends!

"In that main building, whence all the menials have been withdrawn, the rooms you will reach are barricaded."

"Do you suspect something?" She pointed to the partition.

"In rebellion I suspect all! But some one comes——"

"It may be the duke——"

"Not with that fox's step! Your lord marches proudly now. Go, your grace, if you would be styled majesty! Next time that is how I shall have the honor to address you! Remember, it is my place to guard your grace, as captain of the Royal Guards."

Respectful and imperious, odd mixture! La Braganza nodded grateful without knowing for what, and dived into the outlet, warmed by a sudden thought. The door glided to behind her, so swiftly that D'Artagnan, who was not listening to her, could not hear her murmur:

"I have no fear that he will play me foul who loves my maid!"

CHAPTER XXXVI.

THE MARPLOT.

"Who the plague has separated her from her lord when never in their linked career ought they have been parted less!" meditated the envoy of Cardinal Richelieu, taking the vacated chair with ease, but listening all the while in the opposite direction to that she had taken. "There is a counterplot in operation."

"I wish that Jacinta were here! If we could lay our heads together, light would sparkle out as when amber is chafed. Peradventure, if there be underplay, they have secured the maid before the mistress!"

Invigorated by this fear, keener than any misgiving on the duchess' head, he left his chair, and, mousing a little in the tapestry, found a chink in the partition. It might have originated naturally in the old warping wood, but he had no doubt that the cranny had been enlarged by a spy. In great houses few hear any good of themselves, and they listen to have warning.

This crevice commanded a view of the other room, where, at a long table, some men sat jauntily upon its edge, some sedately around it.

Two or three of these persons he had seen, at a distance, at Oporto. The others were strangers to him, but he had no doubt that they were high placed at court. There was nothing so ominous in them, but they had thrown off their capes and cloaks so as to be free to move in close *just-au-corps*, narrow trunks and hose; those who wore shoes of soft leather under their riding boots had discarded the latter. It was one of these who had softly approached the door to listen.

They had stacked their long swords against the wall, and carried short hunting knives, daggers and fine pistolets. But everybody has such arms at this crisis.

The watcher was not allowed a prolonged scrutiny.

The one who had singled himself out from the body by common consent, and listened at the door, tapped at it.

and, as D'Artagnan coming out of his hiding-place made no answer, he walked in.

It was one Don Pablo de Riqueza. He was nicknamed "the Count by Surprise." He was a penniless cadet when the loss of all that debarred him from a title and estate perished by a holocaust. An upset log on a monstrous saint's-day fire, enflamed a house where a family reunion took place and all his kin disappeared in the flames. He became count in a trice.

But never had the Count by Surprise experienced the emotion seizing him when, instead of the Duchess of Braganza, he saw a man alone in the chamber.

"A man whom I do not know!" he muttered, drawing back hesitatingly. "Not the Count of Marianda, I think! one of his household? In that case, a royalist like him. A swordsman, surely! a foreigner, on a second look! We are overburdened with these captains of adventure —they scent the battle! Where has the duchess gone? These old houses are perforated with hidden ways! I had mine rebuilt! and I will recommend the count to do the same. This is some hireling! seeking hand money to enlist! He gets no pay under the Spaniard—he will take from ours, or any purse!"

D'Artagnan was whistling a camp song between his teeth.

"Hem, captain!" at a venture.

They bowed stiffly, yet the Frenchman seemed easy, here at home.

"It is a Marianda, I guess—a foster-brother or sidescion. I know no end of cousins claimed me as their own when I took my place as the head of the house! Fortunately, I have the password to touch the stone! 'Braganza, Madrid and Lisbon!'" Then, raising his voice out of his monologue, he inquired:

"Could I learn of your lordship what star we live under?"

"To be truthful, we live under no star at this hour, it is a planet, the Moon!" replied the other as simply as Porthos might have done.

"This is one outside our Cause," thought the Portuguese.

"Politeness for politeness, is there anything more to

learn? Yet, I warn your lordship that I am not overfond of questions!"

"Only two others, of little consequence. I am Don Pablo de Riqueza, and occupy this pavilion in part. May I know your name and how I find you here?"

"You find me here without my having been for a single instant lost! As for my name, I am puzzled, for in these times one changes so many things that a name is not unvarying. Still, I am for the moment the Caballero de Gannarta, of old Cantabrian stock!"

"Oh, old Spanish to the core!"

"That depends on the site. At present, Lisbon is restless under the Spanish blister-fly!"

"That sounds sharp—you ought to be cautions!"

"Yes, I am the most incautious of speakers—frankness and openness are my defects! My friend Count Jorge tells me so."

"Oh, if Don Jorge is a friend of yours you are a true Spaniard——"

"I have the honor to drink with him!"

"Ah!"

"Eat with him!"

"Oh!"

"And fight with him!"

"Good! A man who fights with the Count of Marianda must be true to the king! He is a follower of the Military Governor—you must be for the Government——"

"I am for all established governments!"

"I am surprised, then, that you are not in the company of our dear Don Jorge, who, I saw with these, my eyes, departing with his servitors to reinforce the defenders——"

"He went forth to deliver the Corregidor and his colonels, but they are delivered now."

"Then they would be on the road to take the usurper——"

"Unless they are on that to Madrid——"

"Why to Madrid?"

"For help to recapture Lisbon."

"I did not know that it was captured."

"It is and it is not! The garrison have handed over

the fort and the walls to the train band, while the officials
and the nobles take to the public buildings and mansions
to defend, each in his own guise. Don Jorge, for example, will defend Marianda House. I am his lieutenant
to do so."

"A good idea!"

"I thought you would approve. Only, as one thing
may serve two purposes, I thought that the house, while
a castle, might serve another end."

"That is called killing two birds with one stone!"

"Oh, I do not want to kill the birds. I shall sell them."

"What birds?" thinking this man was an entertaining
but perplexing discourser.

"Crested ones! Did you ever see a cat catch birds?"

"I never noticed."

"Oh, it is worth noticing to apply the system to catching royal game."

The count frowned, puzzled.

"A cat does not rush at a nest and claw at the first
head presented!"

"No?"

"She waits about and catches the little ones as they
fall, ripe! Then comes the turn of the parents. But
she does not snap at them indiscriminately, either."

"No?"

"Certainly not! If she were to catch the male first,
the female would——"

"Pine at the loss!"

"Or fly away for consolation!"

"Ah!"

"So the cat catches the mother bird first, and the mate
hovers round looking for it, and falls into her jaws,
fatigued."

"So!"

"Ergo, having secured the Duchess of Braganza in my
cage—that is, my friend, Count de Marianda's mansion—
I——"

"Oh, it is you who have spirited away the duchess?
That explains all!"

"It explains half!" returned the musketeer, smiling
graciously. "The explanation of the other half is, I
think, in your hands, dear count!"

" He was turning to flee—to call his friends, there was not a moment to be lost."   See page 281.

"Oh, you allude to the male bird?"

"To the duke! The only way for him to enter my trap, since the other door is in the house of an avowed royalist, is here, where you and your friends are on guard—old friends and ancient adherents whom he could not suspect to betray him!"

"No, he would not suspect that," said the traitor, dreamily.

"Then the game is in our hands. That is, I have the duchess. You, the duke. It seems to me that we—that is, I and your league—can make fine terms with either the Madridlenese or the Lisbonese."

"Why with either?"

"It is plain. The latter want a king and queen; the other, these usurpers. I will treat with the Lisbonese for their desires. You, with the Philipists for theirs. The higher price wins. You are count—you can be marquis! I am a captain of fortune—I shall be a fortuned captain! This is saying nothing of our friends. If yours are embarrassing, sell them in the bulk to the Spanish, while I sell my Joseph—that is, Jorge—to the Portuguese——"

"Upon my word, sir, such audacity!"

"*Sapere aude!* Audacity is wise!"

"I—I must consult with my friends," faltered the count.

It is evident that he feared this proposition coming from one whose daring appalled him.

He was turning to flee—to call his friends. There was not a moment to be lost; but before he could be run through, whatever the musketeer's celerity, he would send up an outcry. To the surprise but happy relief of the Frenchman, he suddenly saw the secret door behind the count fly open. In the aperture appeared Donna Jacinta, who was carrying a fine pistol. Appreciating the situation, from having been listening, she clapped this to the head of the Portuguese, and he, hearing the click of the door, slightly revolved his head. In consternation, his opening mouth let out not even a breath.

With the rapidty of lightning, D' Artagnan stuffed his own cravat into his mouth, laid hands on him, disarmed him, bound him with his sword belt and scarf, and rolled him under a divan in the corner.

Taking the pistol from Jacinta and thrusting it into his belt, he said to her, in a low voice:

"We are beset!"

"And Don Juan will be walking right into the thick of them! What are we to do?"

"A great deal; and you can do much of it."

She was so brave, proud and eager that he knew he had a promising acolyte.

"The duchess being safe above stairs, let us save the duke."

"But these traitors will not let me pass!"

"Yes, they will, thinking that you go—not to warn my lord, but to bring up your brother's regiment to take the prize. Say that Count What's-His-Name has arranged all and that you acquiesce in your brother's wishes!"

"But they will still wait for the duke——"

"Say he is here—slipped in by another way!"

"The duke is here?"

"His clothes are; you yourself said it; and the clothes make the man—why not the king?"

"Inventive rogue that you are!"

"Would I look the king?"

"In my eyes you are a demigod! In that closet, all laid out, complete to the shoe buckles! But you won't let the coronation suit overexcite you, will you?"

"At times even Gascons are cool!"

"Oh, Heaven watches over us!"

"I prefer Olympus——"

"Why, you heathen?"

"Because that had Cupid in it!"

"Love be our guard, then!"

"The countersign, and you pass!" and, seizing her hand, he kissed it.

She fluttered away, and, composing herself at the door, entered among the cross-plotters, calm and radiant.

"The count?" queried they, rising hotly, for the conspirator stands on coals.

"It is done! Don Juan is in our hands!"

"The duke?"

"And the duchess. He joined her by the other way—

through our house! Do you not know me? The Lady
of Floriador——"

"But you?"

"I am no more what I was. My brother has persuaded
me of my wrong course; besides, no one could bring as
redemption so good a price as the duke's head! I am
going to fetch my brother from the Corregidor's with his
regiment! Ah, he will be a duke, and you all made
men!"

Joyously she passed through them and left by the outer
door.

They stared at one another as though a comet had
streamed among them.

"The count was in collusion with the Mariandas," said
one.

"Well, gentlemen," said another, an old man, "I owed
my marquisate to Don Juan's interest at Madrid. I
would rather not huddle him away with my own hands!
If my varlets can be of any use——"

"And I, Count d'Exilis, pestered with numerous syco-
phants, I never asked this Braganza for an office but he
found the letters-patent. It would not look well for me
to take him by the sleeve and hand him over to the
butchers——"

"And I," said a third, "when I was in Toledo Castle,
in the Inquisition's grip, for having, unwittingly, heretical tomes in my library—which, thank God! I could not
read!—he obtained my liberation, when, too, the fire was
blazing on the plaza for me! Now, it is not for me to
call the Spanish in to apprehend him!"

"I see," said still another, ironically, but as backward
as any of them, "none of us itch to be the actual giver of
the betraying kiss. Come," looking out of a little window commanding a peep of the garden gateway, open on
the side street, "why not employ that citizen soldier yonder, who accompanied us from the gates to make sure
that our horses would be delivered to the Spanish Commander of Horse? A captain of militia arresting our
sworn liege will not compromise us as would our squires,
lackeys, or, above all, ourselves."

"Viazma is right! but yet, a trainband sergeant to arrest a duke, a prince, all but a king!"

"Tush! The touch will ennoble the villain! But we must dispatch, or," sarcastically, "Don Jorge will be brought up by his sister and we shall be outraced in this contest to sell our prize!"

"The king at Madrid will weigh us down with guerdons. I have news direct from there that he has not slept of nights since Don Juan escaped from his ships! We shall have enough and to spare among us!"

Thus reassured, they let Viazma call in the town soldier to execute their orders.

CHAPTER XXXVII.

AS THE KNIGHT, SO HIS SQUIRE.

Donna Jacinta lingered at the corner to see that she was not pursued; on the contrary, one of the courtiers called in the militiaman. She hastened, then, to communicate with the Brothers of the Coast, interspersed with the citizens, and notify Don Juan to change his destination.

About the same time D'Artagnan dressed himself, with little attention to strictness, in the special suit which he found. Unlike Porthos' purchase from the beadle, his suit was easy, but, on the whole, was a fit. Besides, the trimmings aided the illusion of royalty. It was an Utrecht velvet, lustrous in its black dye, spangled with jet and pointed with crystal drops, tipped with pearls; in the saffron beaver, with one flap looped up with a gem, floated noble ostrich and heron plumes; the gold spurs were large, in the Portuguese fashion; the baldric was white leather mounted on silk ribbon; a sash was of scarlet and gold thread.

He left the ornamental sword in the chased, beaten gold scabbard, content to hang his own under his left armpit. The full cloak of ruby velvet, fringed with gold, concealed this and half his person.

He looked at the pistol of which he had relieved Jacinta, and smiled.

"I saw it was not primed; but it is not loaded! Oh, those women have faith; an empty pistol should kill, in their hands!"

He looked himself over.

"By my fay! Porthos and I have shed our cocoons, and I believe he would envy me!"

As he stepped out of the cabinet, a soldier was entering the larger room. He had his sword drawn.

"Duke, your sword," said this man, bluntly and yet with respect.

The honor thrust upon him made him tremble.

"Are you addressing me, sirrah!" cried D'Artagnan, seeing that he had to do with an amateur apprehender of noble offenders.

"I ought to say 'sire,' " stammered the poor man, thinking he resented his oversight. The splendid dress did its work. As a draper, he knew that only princes could array themselves in velvet at a doubloon the Flemish ell. "All resistance is useless, for I am in force without. Your sword, if you please, my prince!"

"Are you not well enough armed to do without my sword?"

"He jokes," thought the sergeant; "oh, we have an easy catch here!" Then he added, aloud: "Your sword!"

"You do not seem partial to a little parley——"

"Not in these times, sire, when the fluctuations outnumber those of the Tagus in the spring floods. At any time the town, which is nobody's, may be somebody else's! Your sword, or——"

"Oh, well, since you are so set upon it, take it!" and the Gascon tendered him the court blade.

"Kindly wrap your cloak round you, for the smoke will taint your doublet—astonishing how smoke lays the nap in velvet! The mob has fired a house or two, I believe! Then, to the palace!"

"Any particular palace?" asked D'Artagnan, merrily; "for the vice-regal one surrendered to the mob, as you call the patriotic citizens, long ago."

"Has that gone? Then, to the citadel!"

"Are you truly of Lisbon, not to know it was occupied by my friends over night?"

"But the Corregidor's——"

"The House of Correction has been corrected, knocked into a cocked hat by Messrs. Tag, Rag and Bobtail."

"Then to the next watchhouse!"

"Is not that too abrupt a transition from the steps of a throne? But one moment; what is your post?"

"I am sergeant of the town militia, at your majesty's esteemed service!"

"Arrest me by a sergeant? Your employers have no idea of etiquette! I make you a captain! It ill consorts with one like me to yield up sword and liberty to a sub-officer! If you must lodge me, be it befittingly to your present rank—if not to mine!"

He followed the promoted trainband man like a poodle.

In the outer room the Portuguese nobles lingered, but they averted their eyes not to meet the reproachful gaze of him they had abandoned at his altitude. All they saw was the superfine costume, and the magnificent sword, carried triumphantly by the militia sergeant.

"Whither am I to conduct him? All places are in somebody's hands!" said the puzzled man.

"Any stronghold. Hasten!"

"But they won't take us in!" objected he, piteously.

"Fool! the retired garrison is encamped on the Madrid road, just by the gate. Surround him with all your soldiers and lose no time. On the way you should meet Don Jorge de Marianda, to whom you can transfer your charge!"

At the garden outlet the sergeant found his men, restless, timorous. From the uproar around them they were still unable to tell whether the pyrotechnics would celebrate the expected prince's elevation or downfall.

"To the Spanish camp, Madrid Gate!" said the officer, quickly.

He congratulated himself on having the opportunity which comes only once to an ambitious clothworker or others. Not for the world would he have his men guess what captive he was hurrying out of the city; not for twice as much would he have met Don Jorge or any one likely to wrest the palm from him. A captain, already! why, his reward at this rate, would make his fellow-wardsmen green with envy. He saw himself draper to the court—of Juan or Philip—as he should contrive it.

Familiar with the ways, they reached the wall by a short route. The petty gate of the basket weavers' lane was guarded by acquaintances; they passed through, with a joke about the fine tailor's model they had dressed up for a patron to choose his wedding garment by.

Within the hour D'Artagnan was lodged in a marquee in the Spanish encampment. To prevent injudicious excitement, only the principals were informed of the identity of the capture. It caused a deep and varied debate. The Spanish commander, bribed to quit the citadel, thought that his remuneration only covered this with-drawal to without the walls; if he could dispose of his forces in as high a market, he was not loth. With the chief of the party to which he was already indebted within his lines, he could make excellent conditions.

Unlike his hosts, all in stimulation, D'Artagnan called for refreshment, partook of it in solitary state, serene as a mummy of Pharaoh, and slept the whole night through.

"Oh, these monarchs!" said the sergeant, as he looked in at every watch; "now, a common mortal, between lay-ing his head on the pillow and on the block, would not sleep a wink! But he, he just recruits for the long jour-ney. I hope he will be removed to Madrid, if the king is to deal with him, and have time to get my commission signed and sealed. Ah, me! sovereigns' promises are but piecrust; but even the crust of a dream pie is nice eating to a poor fellow whose dreams have always risen no higher than his counter!"

When his prisoner woke up, his jailer had a fine re-past waiting. African maize in cakes, done on an ashen fire, guinea fowls with cream and honey, fruit in pro-fusion, and steaming chocolate, so thick that a finger of bread stood up in it, and, indeed, it was eaten, then, as a kind of butter.

"Poor ruler!" said the warder; "he has no rule over his gullet! That is eating like one who knows not whence comes the succeeding meal!"

"I suppose nobody has asked after me?" inquired the captive, like one who has said good-by to the false, falling-off world.

"Yes, the Spanish officers of the night, they questioned me every change of guard."

"I alluded to the messengers of a lady!"

"Oh, the duchess?"

"She would not be fool enough to venture faithful servants here!"

"Stop! While there were no court ladies, no one with the air of being a princess' go-between, we had one poor, lubberly fellow, blubbering in the early hours. He is a huge lump, with a voice like to blow the tents over! He has only two words of Portuguese and three of Span-

ish, but I am used in my trade to all sorts of outlandish
talk. I could make out that he had been a squire of your
lordship's in the French campaigns———"

"Oh, you have had my squire ask after me———"

"Or your porter; that's what he said———"

"It would not be Porthos, would it?" and the captive
brightened up as a prisoner would at finding that he was
not utterly ignored. "I think I should like to see a familiar face."

"He takes it very cool," muttered the sergeant, a little
set back. "Now, I should jump at the neck of a friend
who sought me out in prison! But these monarchs—
hard as nails! Well, sire, he is in the by-lanes. The
Spanish tried to drive him away with their halberds, but,
being an overgrown moon calf, as I said, he wrenched
two staves away and snapped them, the two together,
over his clump of a knee as I would a rush. So they let
him be, if he would not disturb the sleepers with his
lamentations."

"So this Porthos has been stupidly hanging about out
there all the night?" asked D'Artagnan, coughing, for
something out of his breakfast stuck in his throat.

"All the morning; he just curled up there like one of
those great Pyrenean sheep dogs, big as a ram!"

"At the risk of spoiling his—his livery?"

"His livery—the livery of the court of King Dagobert,
where they go without breeches to save wearing them
out! Why, the man is long out of place, I think! He is
as soberly clad as the clerk in the priest's house, where
the curate licks his spoon!"

"Porthos, in quiet apparel! Only for a great purpose
would Du Vallon shed his gorgeous shell and rejoin his
old comrade," thought D'Artagnan.

"Captain," said this mock Don Juan, "I am used to that
squire, although he is clumsy compared with a dapper-
dandy! He saved my life once in the wars, so I e'en let
him dingle-dangle about me. If he were at hand to dress
me———"

"Ah, I suppose you great dons can do little with your
own hands?"

"Very little," sighed the musketeer, rolling his eyes.

"Well, I wager that he will be as glad as you to meet.

Oons! after five or six hours in the cool morning breeze of the river, I doubt not that he will gladly embrace——"

"A squire embrace his lord!" protested the sham prince, with offended delicacy.

"Embrace the chance to pacify the wolf in his commissariat department!" laughed the trainband officer.

The other laughed with him. It is noted that a jailer rarely laughs without his charge laughing with him.

"You shall have his services!"

"Are there no superior orders, captain?"

"They forbade you having company! Now, a squire is one man, not a company! Friends are not allowed; but a squire, a varlet—Heaven save us! that is not a friend!"

"Rarely!"

"Besides, we are all soldiers here, and we are above clearing away broken victuals, though of a royal hand's breaking."

"Very proper! Captain, you argue like a prefect of the Congregation of Sacred Doubts and Sophisms——"

"I do not know that gentleman!"

"The Pope has such an officer to settle all fallacies."

The sergeant shook his head.

"I prefer to be captain, if your highness wills so, and can obtain confirmation from his brother of Spain."

"I shall suggest a colonelcy! and my lady shall work you the thread-of-gold epaulets, if I have to urge her, at *longo intervallo!*"

"After your majesty swears by that oath, I retain no fears."

With a light and assured step the obliging warden left the tent. With as light a one Porthos entered; he had cast his beadle's uniform and now threw off his mien of a weeping churl.

On seeing that they were alone, they rushed into one another's arms, and their breastbones cracked in the vehemence of their brotherly hug.

CHAPTER XXXVIII.

THE LAST CARD.

"How is this brought about?" cried the elder soldier, snuffling to hide emotion. "You leave me going to the scuffle with Count Don Jorge, intimating that you wanted an interview with his sister first. The next I hear of you is from one of those iniquit—I mean, ubiquitous, is it not?—Brothers of the Coast! He had seen you, caparisoned as a prince, in this same sumptuous silk, satin and velvet, with feathers culled from the birds of Paradise. You were borne away, merrily enough, by a squad of citizen soldiers. The next I heard was that this captured *exaltissimo* was in the power of the Spanish, treated like a king! this king of ours! I do not say that you do not resemble Don Juan, but it will be carrying the likeness too far if you put your dear head under the ax——"

"An ass is always an ass, notwithstanding the harness!" sighed the captive. "I sometimes doubt that I shall ever be wise again while I am in love!"

"Does the donna want a prince? What do you gain by masquerading?"

"I gain what men would pay diamond weight for—time. Thanks to my being in custody—*quod,* as the Arabs say—our lord must have had time to ascend his throne."

"I believe they are crowning him on the grand plaza by this."

"Have they removed the archbishop's scruples——"

"Or Captain Pedro would have removed his head."

"Then you see how right I was to put on his garb—or how right Donna Jacinta was."

"Oh! if it is at her hint, then I have not one word to say. Still, Madame du Vallon will not forgive your pretty plotter if, when the blind worms discover the error and my own cheat, I fall immolated——"

"It looks so, unless my friend in the camp——"

"Oh! the count?—to be sure, if he is at hand——"

"Oh! he is a fanatic—a Brutus who would sacrifice his own table-guest. I speak of a soldier—that civic guardsman who let you in. Your jeremiads softened his heart. There was a squire who disguised himself as a minstrel to reach his lord prisoned in a castle—but, save us! had he caterwauled like you, the sentinels would have stuck him full of quarrels from their cross-bows like my lady's pincushion."

"If I had not bellowed, they would not have let me sleep, on the condition of silence. But since you have revived my courage, I will notify the king—since he is made king by this time—wnere his shadow is. Nails and hammer! we will release you."

"Wait! you are not released yourself."

"Eh?"

"This wears the semblance of our being fellow-prisoners here."

"A prison of canvas."

"Ah! but there are civic guards outside."

"A fig for the townsmen!"

"And Spanish pikemen outside them again. Now, like you, I detest having handsome clothes spoiled in a chance encounter."

"Bought out of the fort they could have held a year, we can bend their pikes of lead, and their muskets are choked with their Judas silver."

"They were bought out, but not to lay down their arms. That is another bargain. Perhaps Soleiman is not present to make it. A bout of two to ten thousand, and we shall not return whole to France, and in glory mundane."

"That is true. The Spanish fight well—foot to foot."

"So I have made up my mind, since I am king for a day, to have all the honors. As we Gascons say: '*A diac andiro*'—let us do all things grandly! I shall enter my royal capital triumphantly!"

"This tinsel crown has turned the man's head, though of copper," said Porthos, sadly.

"That would please my brother, Pedro, who said that I was not rated up to my value."

"You are mad!"

"It is plain that no knight is a hero to his squire. But

cling to my fortunes a little, Squire Porthos, and you will see that nothing so meetly rounded off my assumption of majesty as my laying it off."

"Well, what is a squire's bounden duty but to obey his lord?"

"Porthos, you may remember, some five or six years ago, that a craze overran Paris——"

"There is always a craze running over Paris; define——"

"A cunning knave filled one part of an hourglass with wine and, bidding you take it in your hand, professed to tell by the red fluid mounting into the upper and vacant cup, how prone you were to the tender passion——"

"The heat of the hand——"

"Made the spirit rise. Porthos, I always said that a profound metaphysician was prevented in your taking to arms——"

"That is odd! At the age of sixteen, I was seized with growing pains which threatened my stature would be colossal—otherwise, my mother would have had me study for the medical art at Rheims University——"

"You revivify me by good counsel and good-humor. This love-meter, as the rogue styled it, by which one pretended to tell the loveableness of the holder, was useless. For my part, I study the progress of a passion by the countenance."

"For the most part, man does bear his disposition there—you are right."

"So, studying Master Diego, the trainband sergeant, I foretell that disloyalty rises as this muddle thickens. When he seized me, oh! with all the courtesy of his race, he was lukewarm; this morning, he was melting."

"And to-night?"

"We shall see what he is by noon. By eve he will be a cream curd."

"I should like to witness the churning of Master Diego."

"Hist! he comes, I think."

"Halloa! they have allowed you your sword."

"They took the royal one, but the old one—ah, I like it! Where is your Balizarde, by the same token?"

"To my regret, I had to bury him in the rushes when

I cogitated to rejoin you. Ah, well I know what the valet feels who has lost his master!"

"The Spanish may regret its resuscitation!"

The civic guard was amiably looking in.

"These Spanish," observed he, sharply, "have the reputation of being the best in Europe——"

"Of the two semi-spheres," said D'Artagnan, as affably.

"I do not agree. Half of them have strayed over to the town, and are clambering up the walls to see what is going on."

"Strange, indeed, after they were paid to keep out of it!"

"Curiosity pays with a tempting coin."

"Then, there is something going on?"

"Yes, my city is a great one for something going on, or coming off."

"Yes, when crowns go on and heads come off—it is enthralling!"

Porthos had concealed D'Artagnan's sword.

"That is the fault of my squire here—devouring curiosity. See his ears prick up? That is your doing. I warrant that he will be uneasy and useless until he has also seen what is going on over the city wall."

"I do not blame him. I, myself——"

"You are so obliging that I could trespass still farther on your ceaseless kindness. I suppose you could not let my servant go and quench his curiosity?"

"Oh! he came freely—he may go the same,"

"That is handsome! I—I could almost ask the same favor for myself—I am curious——"

"That is natural, after being brought to the capital, to want to know what happens in it!"

"But your superiors' orders——"

"Know, sire," said the "colonel" of his creation, "that the Lisbon civic guard take no orders——"

"From these aliens? Hem! I comprehend and esteem you. My faithful squire, take advantage of the good colonel's offer, and leaving that old blade, which I suppose you picked up on the field, sally out for tidings."

"You may go," said the sergeant, loftily.

Porthos put the sword within his friend's reach and

left the tent. The guards admired his proportions, but
no one stayed him; besides, as the civic guardsman had
said, most of the regular soldiers, who were Portuguese,
or who had friends in the town, were struggling thither.
So he had considerable company.

"That was obliging of you," said the musketeer, cordially.

"Sire, I am only doing my duty——"

"Toward the King of Spain?"

"Toward the States of Portugal. I hope that, as the
events are cast out of fate's dice box, your majesty will
bear in mind that I conducted myself with all the respect
due your position."

"You assuredly conduct yourself like a true Portuguese!"

"Sire, believe me, if Lisbon had not been cowed into
obeying the foreigners' yoke—our nature, our spirit, our
business, all resent being trodden on by the crowned
viper's hoof!"

"Viper's hoof is good!"

"Look you, I was a leather supply factor before I had to
turn to cloth dealing. Why? because the Spanish held
back the soldier's pay, notably the Portuguese, so that
they went barefoot in summer and bound up their feet,
like peasants, in any old rags, in the wet weather. Such
policy was fatal to the leather trade! So I took up cloth
working. But the insurrection breaking out, no one buys
clothes——"

"I should not have thought that!"

"But, sire, who would buy what they can steal?"

"Who, indeed! Is stealing so easy?"

"In war times, to be sure! It is a warrant to behave
like disorderly soldiers—the beggars stroll the streets and
take down the frippery hung out to attract custom; the
highwaymen strip travelers; the soldiers rob the fallen;
the wretches, who infest the ghetto and dwell outside the
walls, strip the corpses—in a word, no one buys clothes!"

"I see that, if I should reign, it would be over a people
in aprons of fig leaves!"

"So, I owe the Spaniard nothing—or, rather, so keen
and close are they, they will not let me owe them anything! The boot is on the other leg; for I have my books

full of the officers' accounts. Well, my fellow-townmen have treated me more creditably."

"They would."

"They made me a watchman, because I pulled the ears of a boy who tried to run away with my till. They made me a captain of the watch, a civic guard, a sergeant! Your majesty capped all by making me a captain!"

"I said colonel—seeing your merit——"

"Colonel is better—but if you were to raise me to greater eminence——"

"Why not? I fear that modesty is your glaring defect! To be commensurate with your deserts, a commandership of your town militia——"

"Oh, you overload me, sire!"

"I do not see why! what does the alien do? appoint aliens to the chief posts. Now, if I were ruling, I should amend all that! A Lisbonite, respected by his fellows, who have known him from a babe, that is the man to compel order in the wards—he could rule with a simple cane in hand——"

"The fact is, some men by their presence——"

"The only drawback is that, in this tent," moaned D'Artagnan, "I am without the power——"

"Alas! But what is that hubbub?"

"It is for you to learn, or shall I——" and the Frenchman easily moved toward the opening.

The vacillating town guardsman spoke with the sentry at the doorway.

"Why, sire, your squire has been stopped by the Spanish——"

"Provoking!"

"But he produced a paper and they——"

"Let him pass?"

"No; a superior officer runs up and reads it——"

"What can it be that Porthos is supplied with?"

"Oh, it is an order to the citadel governor!"

"My squire, with an order to——"

"From the vice-queen; it bids him 'Capitulate!' Oh, they will abandon the last post of the fort!"

"Porthos is right! this is a land of magic!" muttered the musketeer, not having heard anything of Porthos' adventure, and his saving Margarita of Savoy.

Sergeant Diego had come to a conclusion. He wheeled round, not noticing that his prisoner was holding the bared sword.

"This alters things! Since the Spanish give up the last vestige of their hold, Lisbon belongs alone to the Lisbonese."

"Admirable logic!"

"Then, as chief of the town forces——"

"I repeat it!"

"I command here!"

"Command, then!"

"If only I knew what was happening in the town?"

"The quickest way to ascertain is to go there——"

"That is flat!"

"And, since I am dying with curiosity, and you cannot wish your captive to die on your hands, take me with you!"

"That solves it! Come, come, and lose no time!"

"I precede you!" cried D'Artagnan, leading the way out of the tent.

Without a speech in the tongue he did not feel expert in, Porthos, assisted by some fishers who had added themselves to the civic guards, had stirred up the perplexed soldiers. On seeing the brilliantly-bedizened musketeer emerge from the tent, these set up a welcoming cry.

"To the town!" cried D'Artagnan, waving his sword.

"To the town, fellow wardsmen!" said the sergeant, waving his sword. "It is in the hands of the mob, and they are pillaging your stores!"

At this touching appeal, the citizen soldiery waited no longer; they surrounded their leader, and the immense mass, in front of which was borne Porthos, unable to approach his friend, began to move toward the walls, with a front of two hundred, touching shoulders.

Along this impenetrable line a Spanish officer rushed madly, trying to make himself heard. Annoyed by his efforts, a dozen pikes threatened to pin him down, but Porthos, recognizing Don Jorge, thrust them aside with Balizarde, and said, while covering Count Marianda, sarcastically:

"Keep to the right, my lord; keep to the right!"

So, pushed to the side, and forced to travel along the

whole line, the colonel was left at the end in a cloud of dust.

In the distance he saw the multitude racing for the walls, tossing caps, with the old Moors' cry of, "Yah, ha!" and *"vivas,"* carrying D'Artagnan shoulder high, and shouting, with echoes on those walls and within them:

"Long live Don Juan, our own king!"

CHAPTER XXXIX.

THE TRUE KING.

"A cheat! a strategem!" growled Don Jorge, following the disappearing host; "that Gannarta I always suspected as deep—but that other, bluff and honest—a trickster! I believe in nothing now! Swords are toys when battles are fought with pens and masks and bags of gold!"

The walls and their towers were covered with whooping men, glad faces, tossing arms with weapons sheathed; banners, women's kerchiefs, a kaleidoscopic vision of all colors in all shapes. If cannon and musketry commingled their dread din, it was harmlessly. Spanish and Portuguese hugged frantically, and the publicans, who had been reserved for a time, opened their doors widely and rolled casks into the thoroughfares for everybody to drink the king's health.

Count Marianda drearily moved among the carousers, as if his sword was broken in its case.

Trumpets sounded merrily, drums were beaten lively, and the monks perambulated the streets in long files, with the churches' choicest regalia, vociferating:

"There is a king come to Israel!"

"Why, the church has gone over!" said the one Abdiel in the flood of apostates. "I am descended from the Roman—I will run upon my sword!"

"Hold!" It was Porthos who laid his heavy hand on his sound arm. "Not on that sword, please! it is mine—you are my prisoner, and, as such, your good blade is mine!"

Thus he was conducted upon the palace square. On the partially thrown down walls, converted into a stage, gonfalon poles had been fixed by the Brothers of the Coast, and rigged so that they upheld a vast awning; most of the material was scarlet and gold. With the taste suitable to a bright sun, the decorations turned the plaza into a kind of open-air reception and coronation hall. If there had been any color wanted, it was supplied by the

throng. All the spectators had donned gala attire, and
Heaven knows what wardrobes and lockers had been ran-
sacked to provide old jewelry and variegated weavings to
enliven the scene. There were enough armed men mixed
with the country nobility to show that this spectacle was
the fruit of a civil war.

The uninjured part of the palace had been given up to
Luisa de Braganza, who appeared, with a number of
ladies, her own friends, augmented by wives of local dignitaries, functionaries and officials, pledging them as hostages for their good behavior to the new rule.

The transfer of Lisbon to the substitute for Philip had
been, on the whole, so bloodless, that no mourning flecked
the gay and luxuriously-vested crowd.

"Long live the queen!" was the hailing sound, as the
proud and luminous princess stood out in full glare.

Don Juan had been satiated with greetings. He was
able to look around in a sort of leisure. At last he descried what he was seeking, "his" two Frenchmen; but his
smile was dampened by his spying Don Jorge between
them.

"Who is this?" he demanded of D'Artagnan, as the latter approached, under the inviting glance.

Donna Jacinta, who was near her mistress, pale where
the other blushed happily, shuddered, fearing her brother
would show his unshaken loyalty offensively.

"Count, you can put your case stronger than I," said
the musketeer to Porthos' prisoner; "speak out!—masks
and veils are cast off this day! To-morrow, as the court
will be in swing again, we must hold, with the stoic, that
silence is the one virtue to cherish. Couch your speech
prettily, for at the dawn of a reign all should be courtly."

The Count of Marianda stepped forward, and in a
guarded tone, announced himself.

At the title, which caused some emotion, Jacinta looked
appealingly to the princess, who nodded encouragingly.

"My ancestors accepted a fair defeat by the Spaniards,
and ever since we have been true to the treaty made on the
battlefield, where no shame mingled with our blood. I
am aye faithful to King Philip, and I am opposed, as ever,
to your exercising sway over my country!"

"My prisoner," said Porthos, implying that there was no fear of his actually harming this new rule.

"Pray, sire!" urged Jacinta, clasping her hands.

"My lord count," returned Braganza, full of joy, which tempered his usually stern voice, at this exchange of a ducal for a regal crown, "you are making a mistake—but this is a day of mistakes. Have I not had my similitude" —here he glanced roguishly at D'Artagnan—"as my ancestor, the regretted Sebastian, had his appear on our dear town walls? I see in you, not an officer of the king removed, but the brother of my queen's most near and faithful servitor. To Donna Jacinta I owe, under the King of kings, much of the power to occupy this long-desired throne. But while she sustains her dear mistress, it is meet that you, with your good sword, should stand beside me as a supporter."

"I thank your majesty, but I can only say God save you!" and Jorge de Marianda turned coldly away.

"What, do you reject my favor—my amity—my hand?" cried the king, not easily rebuffed on this day of pride.

"My dread lord, I want no man's favor—only this gentleman's, whose prisoner I am! I want no man's amity but his, since I am his slave! and I want no man's hand but this!"—he grasped that of D'Artagnan—"by means of which I trust to lend my sword to his king. Never more shall it be drawn in Spain or Portugal. The hand which, as head of my line I can bestow, I give back to its owner—my sister can give it, in her own sweet will!"

There was a grumbling murmur. Where all had been honey, the drop of gall was unpalatable.

"God keep your majesty!"

"Nay, gentlemen," said Don Juan, "make way there, and salute that noble man! We shall be right happy if he leaves many of his stamp behind!"

The two musketeers set the example by saluting Don Jorge, so that he left the improvised court, after all, with a tribute to his constancy and respect for his oath of allegiance, signal where recreants abounded.

"He gave me my own hand," muttered Jacinta, "but he did not throw me a look! But," added she, sorrowfully, "these men of the wars, they are wedded to their swords! Oh. fie!"

"Jacinta," interrupted the queen, "are you all alike in your iron-headed family? Are you going to refuse me a boon as your brother has that of the king?"

"Refuse your ladyship anything?"

"Sire," said the beaming Luisa de Guzman, "I wish formally to present to your majesty the Chevalier de Gannarta, to whose skill, devotion and prowess great help has been given to this blessed enthronement!"

"I understand that, upon the sheaf of those services, you gained us valuable time by leading off the road those traitors who might have impeded the ascension!"

"Sire," replied the Gascon, at as much ease as before his own regiment on parade, where he knew every man, "I have no excuse for playing the king but that, they say, your majesty suffered no degradation by the personation, since no one perceived its shortcomings."

"You risked your head!"

"A soldier does that every day of his service!"

"Gentlemen," said the king, addressing a great audience, for already the flock of high nobility was considerable, "I ask you, and notably you, my royal lady, what does such daring and devotion deserve?"

"They are illimitable, sire!" answered Luisa; "it is impossible, even for a monarch, to recompense such deeds——"

"Then we are all in a quandary! The owner of the pearl must price it! Don Luis de Gannarta, fix your price!"

"You will have your castle—in Portugal!" whispered Porthos, red as a rose at his friend being duly appreciated, and forgetting any expectations of his own.

"Illimitable, as the queen says," went on Braganza, letting his eyes stray quizically upon the recalcitrant's sister and then back to D'Artagnan, "yet try!"

"Faith!" and the Gascon looked embarrassed for once, "I am afraid that what I crave is out of the power of king and queen!"

"Ah!" in surprise.

"I see," said the queen, merrily; "it was not only the head that was at risk, but the heart!" The flame spread from Porthos to his friend, and Donna Jacinta caught the glow. "Unfortunately, while we can dispose of hands, we cannot bias hearts!"

"I understand," said the sovereign, with pretended sorrow and regret. "The King of Portugal is not going to be a tyrant. He may dispose of the kingdom's treasure for its weal, its enlightenment and its defense, but never will he utter an order to suggest that he ruled over slaves whose lives and liberty and happiness were at his beck. Don Luis, you are in love. Love has a realm of his own —over his subjects I have no control!"

"Love!" repeated D'Artagnan, with his eyes twinkling, "I am not swayed by love! Sire, since I set foot in the Peninsula, I have been tormented by a demon—one I could never shake off! I wished to be a rigid soldier, a sage statesman in good time, losing no hour in caprices and even tender elegancies that the ladies like.

"This unearthly creature has made me do the contrary! It has glided through walls and fastened doors to bemuse my wits, make me renounce my vows as to celibacy, risk my soul, and blot out my future of an old soldier's cell in the Military Monks' Hospital!"

His mock remorse drew a smile out on every countenance.

"This spirit is the more dangerous as its form is that of a charming, intellectual and adorable woman!"

"Yet you love her?" queried the king and his consort, in the same breath.

"Love her, a demon?" ejaculated D'Artagnan, returning an imploring, but facetious glance upon the prelates interspersed with the courtiers, "I must hate her! and if I would endeavor to chain her with wedlock, it is because I could avenge myself upon her—leisurely, you understand; as the Italians—epicures in the matter, say: 'Revenge is a dish to be eaten cold!'"

"Are you sure it is a demon?" asked the queen.

"It is outlawed by the church—proof positive! It is a waive!"

A shudder ran through the assemblage, and some of the ladies left a wide space around Donna Jacinta. A church dignitary, old and reverend, whispered with the king.

"It is evident," said the latter, solemnly, "that a waive should not be permitted any longer to wander up and down the world to imperil poor humanity, tormented by sufficient frets and worries. Wherefore, we authorize the Señor Don Luis de Gannarta to aprehend, for himself, and as captain-in-chief of our lifeguards, the human form of this said sprite, and by the aid of Holy Mother Church, become its lifelong custodian!"

Those of the audience not in the secret gazed around bewildered.

"You are his prisoner, 'Waive' Jacinta de Floriador," said the royal lady, pushing her blushing ward over toward D'Artagnan; "beware! he is a redoubtable Christian knight!"

"A knight of San Jano, of Portugal!" added the king, significantly.

"Oh, your majesty, I shall try to defend myself. But," sadly added the noble damsel, "who will make the sacred transfer of a waive to a Christian knight?"

"I," said the feeble, but imposing voice of the prelate who had communed with Braganza.

"Don Remiro, chief of the Holy Inquisition," cried the entire gathering, bowing.

"Zookers," muttered Porthos, "this is the old friar-janitor of the convent whom I plucked out of that human carding mill!"

"In the name of the Holy Father, Urban, whose legate I am to the court of Portugal, I absolve thee, child, from all onus and concomitances of the ban, inflicted upon thee by error. And I myself will perform the sacrament of marriage between you and your chosen bridegroom!"

Retiring, he edged toward Porthos, to whom he darted a sly glance with his deep-set, keen, gray eyes, showing that he had as much wit as gratitude.

"That was a good outlay of mine," whispered the knight of Du Vallon to his delighted friend. "Those misguided nuns threw water over on my coat, but I can dry it at Hymen's flambeau!"

Pedro received confirmation of his admiralship, and other honors were conferred upon him. His disposition was not one to accord with courtiers; he perished in an expedition to repel the savages invading a settlement at Cape Delgado. The Brothers of the Coast remained an organization as long as "the laws of *Oleron*" ruled, but

never was their power recorded as making or undoing a
kingdom.

D'Artagnan was given an estate to justify his title of
Gannarta, but he was more heartily pleased by a missive
from Cardinal Richelieu, thanking him, in the king's
name and his own, for his skill and success. For all of
the premier's rule, Spain was checked by independent
Portugal.

EPILOGUE.

When the happy musketeer went into the Royal Arms Hotel, he found his brother kingmaker at a table, writing —unwonted occupation!

The latter looked up, lost his frown in a smile, and, seeing that he had a printed paper in his hand, inquired:

"Court news?—good?"

"It is court news—but from the other court—of the Escurial. Never will Spain forgive us for making two bits of it and Portugal, as the Douro River does of Leon! They cease to throw bullets—the court poet is set to throwing paper pellets—but they are steeped in bitterness."

"You might read it—we are cloyed with sweets!"

> "'Our neighbor now, our pride to balk,
> His idol fells of Spanish chalk;
> How long will last the new one, pray,
> Molded of Portugal's dull clay?'"

"Suppose he tries to overthrow it!" said the grandee, firing up like all new champions.

"Oh, it will stand—its feet are of gold—French gold! But what are you doing?—writing home to announce your speedy return to Madame du Vallon? Well, it was a fine holiday Cardinal Richelieu gave you, all things counted!"

"Oh, I have not finished my holiday," returned the other, biting the feather end of the quill, embarrassed. "I am writing to tell her that I have to do the king the compliment of going to inspect the lands he gave me! They say it well bolsters a grandee! One of those rogues had it, whom you saved from imprisoning this good king!"

"The count by surprise?"

"I am going to surprise his—my tenants! They say that the figs grow as large as my fist, and the oranges as large as my head—as my head was; I suppose it has expanded lately."

"Never will your head be greater," said D'Artagnan; "it is your heart, dear friend, which enlarges perpetually!"

"Oh," added Porthos, checking his writing again, "what droll fellows those seamen are!" and laughed.

"Sometimes! They call it a joke to capture Lisbon! In what way are they funny as regards you?"

"It is that Don Pedro. He came to me to breakfast, and over the *kahve*, a new drink this hotelkeeper brewed in his honor, hearing that he had been landlord of an inn in his time, he said:

"'Brother Porthos, I am eager to do you or your friends at home a good turn, now I have command of the sea. Have you not an institution, useful to heirs tired of awaiting an inheritance, husbands fatigued with their burdens, nobles wearied of parasites—called Blank Sealed Royal Warrants——'

"'*Letters de cachet*,' said I; 'yes, they are useful!'

"'Well,' said the sly dog, 'it is not this tender-hearted king here who will furnish such blanks, but his lord high admiral will do what he dare not. If you know of any such burden to be removed, why, get your overladen friend to bring it to the coast, and notify me. I will send a boat's crew to take it off his shoulders and off shore! I have a little the acquaintance of the Dey of Algiers. Poor dey! The Turks gave him a trouncing, and he is but the sultan's khedive, or deputy, at present. They carried away as tribute his slaves, and he has to grease his own boots and clean his own pipes now, and sing and dance to amuse his harem, reduced to one or two *odalisques*. He wants slaves of all kinds! "The French baggage" will be welcome.'"

"Gracious!" ejaculated the musketeer; "if Madame du Vallon were to come to the seashore to meet you half way, this unregenerate pirate——"

"I thought of that," said Porthos, simply, and sighing, he shook his head. "It would fail. As soon as M. the Dey saw her, and had a bit of her temper, he would send her back to the Vallon! No, I shall prolong my holiday."

"Poor Pedro! it is written that we shall be beholden to him."

"As to all these others! While they are genial, I am not going to hurry myself."

"You need not. The queen has given us an heir to the French throne; but until Richelieu dies, what stirring times can we expect? Nevertheless, while all is quiet, with this clog upon the Spanish chariot going down hill—Portugal, I mean—in the minority of a prince—the workers of wickedness flourish. We shall be called back to France, so keep your sword bright."

"Swords, swords! they may well say, 'Prompt to whip out as a Gascon!'"

"Don't you know our old custom in Gascony? They used to hurl old men and those who could not bear arms over the rocks into the gulf! It was a shame to lead a peaceful life! I am, I fear me, a true Gascon!"

THE END.